MW01129953

★ ★ ★ ★ ★ ★ ★ ★ ★ ★ ★ ★ ★ ★ ★

In my opinion, Elana Freeland is an exceptional researcher and writer. This quite amazing Sub Rosa series is proof of that. The beauty of fiction is that you can speak of things that are real under the guise of the unreal. From my experience, the technologies and capabilities that are described in this book are real - which explains why they must be talked about as fiction. Humans and human values are being challenged on all fronts. This series addresses significant assaults by the State and their psychopathic accomplices on our ultimate desire and goal - to be happy and free - and the coping strategies developed by some exceptional personalities in the contemporary drama we call life.

Harry Blazer, editor, *If I Were King*

★ ★ ★ ★ ★ ★ ★ ★ ★ ★ ★ ★ ★ ★ ★

SUB ROSA AMERICA

AMERICA

A Deep State History

SUB ROSA AMERICA

A Deep State History

Book II:

The Future Arrives By Stealth

By

Elana Freeland

Copyright © 2012 Elana Freeland

Second printing, 2018

All rights reserved.

ISBN-13: 978-1-4700-2669-1
ISBN-10: 1-4700-2669-4

Cover art by Louise Williams,
"The Guardian of the Innermost," 1991

Layout & Cover Design
by Robert Ross of
Last Word Press

This fictional series is based on actual history
and available on Amazon.

Dedicated to the Three Kings

John F. Kennedy
Martin Luther King, Jr.
Robert F. Kennedy

and what might have been, and may still,
far in the future

and for researchers and whistleblowers, living and dead,
who have spent thousands of hours studying
The Man Behind the Curtain...

Sub Rosa America
Major Characters

Seven (Lilya Eliade) Old when the novel opens in 2019 and flashes back to her early twenties in 1970 when she met Hermano and underwent an extrasensory initiation in Santa Barbara. Nexus for all characters. Born in 1947.

Hermano Eastern European Time-traveler known in past ages as St. Germain and Christian Rosenkreutz. Traveling the Americas with Ghost Bear. Ultimately, sets in motion the *geist* of the pilgrimage to Dallas.

Ghost Bear Lakota Sioux Time-traveler medicine man traveling with Hermano.

Thomas Gardner Seven's true love, scientist and recluse on the run from the elite New England Gardner family and Dr. Greenbaum. Half of a Mengele twin experiment with his "dead" identical twin Didymus. Yale graduate, born in 1943.

Didymus (Didy) Hauser Thomas' twin brother taken at birth and reared under Paperclip Nazi MK-ULTRA. Programmed to be a CIA assassin.

Simon Iff Didymus' CIA handler with an FBI cover. Reports to Dr. Greenbaum and keeps a distant tail on the vehicles en route to Dallas. Born in 1927.

Ray Kofi Black disillusioned Marxist graduate student and Seven's friend. Sought as a scapegoat for the April 18, 1970 shooting of student Kevin Moran. Born in 1944.

Mannie Brooklyn Jew who arrives in California after a long bus ride and ends up going to Dallas with the pilgrims. Naïve and good-hearted, Mannie sees into the heart of people and events. Born in 1948.

Baby Rose Beautiful blond girl programmed under MK-ULTRA and found wandering near Ojai; sought by Dr. Greenbaum. Has a variety of "alters" ("Alice") her new friends are unaware of. Programmed with Didymus under Drs. Greenbaum and Gottlieb. Born in 1952.

Vicente Liputzli Timekeeper grandson of a powerful Mayan archaeologist Timekeeper. Sent north with his grandfather's *Book of Days* to guide him to chronicle the demise of *el norte*. Born December 7, 1941, Pearl Harbor Day.

Hiram Gardner Thomas' uncle. Raised between Scotland and America by fascist relatives and placed in key positions for the sake of the Enterprise. Ruthlessly dominates Thomas' family, even to sacrificing Didymus at birth to MK-ULTRA. Elite gopher for Dr. Greenbaum. Born 1918, graduated Yale 1940. Lives in New York.

Laurence Gardner Thomas' father, dominated since childhood by his brother Hiram. Born in 1920, graduated Harvard 1942. Lives in Philadelphia.

Colonel Seven's retired U.S. Air Force neighbor; served in every major 20th century war up to Vietnam. He and his Cadillac join the pilgrimage to Dallas.

Dr. Greenbaum Paperclip Nazi and MK-ULTRA "spychiatrist" under Dr. Sydney Gottlieb. Programmed Didymus and Baby Rose, oversaw Thomas under the Mengele twin program. Member of elite Satanic cult in Mexico. Lives in Washington, DC.

Sibelius/Magician/ Jaguar Priest Works for Dr. Greenbaum. Occult capabilities. By day, a corporate CEO; by night, a Jaguar Priest of elite Satanic cult in Mexico. Lives in Washington, DC.

Qabalist High-end astrologer working for the Magician in Philadelphia.

AUTHOR'S NOTE

The reader may now and then feel confused while reading a history in the guise of fiction like Sub Rosa America, given how we have been educationally conditioned to think of history as facts and fiction as made-up fantasy. But truth and memory interweave with both fact and fiction, particularly in an era of public lies and disinformation. Imagination[1] must always work hand in hand with Memory and Intellect, and in the end only the reader can decide what they take with them as true. A 63-page bibliography is available at elanafreeland.com under "Sub Rosa Bibliography" to give the reader an idea of the general direction my Imagination wended.

[1] "When visualization comes in contact with the outer world through perception, it points to reasoning, but through the inner process we have described it points to what we call inner imagination in the true sense."

– Rudolf Steiner

BOOK II

The Future Arrives
By Stealth

Though this be madness, yet there is method in it.

- *Hamlet*, II, ii, 207

We've unmasked madmen, Watson, wielding scepters, reason run riot, justice howling at the moon.

- Sherlock Holmes in *Murder By Decree*, 1978

In the dark time, the eyes begin to see.

- Theodore Roethke

Table of Contents

The Rockies 2019

26 Scotland

27 Singularity

28 Vicente Liputzli

32 The Trail Heats Up

Augustan Society – CIA – Captain George Hunter White – Operation Midnight Climax – Cryptozoologists – Mustang – Reinhard Gehlen – Wewelsburg Castle – Jesuits – Knights of Malta – Pro Deo – Opus Dei – Mormons – Francis Parker Yockey – James Jesus Angleton – Frank Olson – Technical Services Staff (TSS) – Office of Security – "Wild Bill" Donovan – Sydney Gottlieb – *Vorkommando Moskau* – Noble Order of the Rose – The Fellowship – Shickshinny Knights – Order of St. John of Jerusalem – Woodpecker Grid – Little Mermaid programming

33 The Bagdad Café

U.S. Navy – Strategic Studies Group – "The Electromagnetic Spectrum in Low-Intensity Conflict" – Classified Information Procedures Act (CIPA) – special administrative measures (SAMs) – Strategic Defense Initiative (SDI) – U.S. Air Force Bentwaters Rendlesham Forest base – Harold Dahl – Kenneth Arnold – Lt. Cmdr. William Bruce Pitzer – E-Systems – El Toro airfield – Bobby Ray Inman – PROMIS – 1987 Iran-Contra Hearings – Evergreen Airways

34 The Mars Men

Quetzalcoatl the Plumed Serpent – A.E. Thierens – *Nâǵás* – H.P Blavatsky – Maya Empire (*Nohcan*) – Troano Manuscript – *Amaruca* – *HYGEIA* – *Pharmakia* – *ayahuasqa* – reptilian brain – Dragon Court – "hive mind" – temporal lobe – limbic lobe – Ramón Medina Silva – astral light – *magica sexualis* – Alexander Graham Bell – Jekyll Island – Hunter Thompson – adrenochrome – belly or organ clairvoyance – *Minority Report* – monacle – Artichoke – Candy Jones – Bernard Jensen – Sirhan Sirhan – Mark David Chapman – David Berkowicz – Tammy Wynette – narco-hypnosis – *virotes* – Vitzliputzli – Science

Applications International Corporation (SAIC) – energetics, bioenergetics and psychoenergetics – quantum entanglement – JASON – Saturn continents

35 Fey

Time – Julian calendar – Gregorian calendar – Masonic calendar – tachyons – Huitzilopochtli – ATL – *Naqoyqatsi*

36 Laurence Mulls Over a Pint of Beer and Hiram Dines With His Actuary

Grand Lodge – Scottish Rite – Lyons – Lindow Moss – Watling Street – Mayer Amschel Rothschild – Knights Templar Round Church – Fleet Street and the Temple Bar – Regency of the Sun and Archangel Micha-ël –

37 The Qabalist Seeks Out the Hudson Oracle

Göbekli Tepe temple – Qabala – MK-ULTRA – The Hudson Oracle – Lord of Karma – Satanism – Dragon Court – Illuminism – Saint-Germain – Vitzliputzli – Edgar Cayce – JASONs – Pluto – Christian Rosenkreuz – Warburg Institute – Hebrew lunar calendar – *Amalantrah Working* – *maggids*

38 Crossing the Colorado

Andrija Puharich – EC-130E Commando Solo – *Watchtower* – Operation Garden Plot – Synarchy – Hegelian dialectic – Orwell's *1984* – Pan-European Movement in 1922 – I.G. Farben – Bilderberg Group – Arnheim Bridge – Bretton Woods – Black Eagle Trust – Gehlen's Organization – Golden Lily – Third Reich – Altamont – Weather Underground – Anton La Vey – Werner Erhard – Zodiac – Manson

– Jack the Ripper – *Diagnostic and Statistical Manual of Mental Disorders* (DSM) – Manichæan – *phantasy* – Cristóbal Colón – Albigensian heresy – Lorenzo de Medici – Iroquois League – Cesar Chávez

39 Southwest Sword of Damocles

Extraterrestrial Highway 375 – Little A'Le'Inn – SR-71 Blackbird – Keyhole – Area 51 – National Reconnaissance Office (NRO) – *vimana griha* – LIDAR (laser radar) – Janet 747 – Tonopah Test Range – KLAS-TV – Howard Hughes – Ancient Arrow – Kingman, Arizona – Richard Wayne Snell – Alfred P. Murrah Federal Building – Omnibus Counter-Terrorism Bill – Communications Assistance for Law Enforcement Act

40 LUCIFER and Glastonbury

The Nine – Kontental Ol AG ("Konti") aka ConocoPhillips – Karl Blessing – I.G. Farben – Senator Eugene McCarthy – State Department's Office of Policy Coordination – Nixon – CIA Director Allen Dulles – Heritage Groups Council and Nationalities Council – Third Reich America – AT&T – Watergate – IBM – LUCIFER algorithm – Lucent Technologies – Inferno Operating System – *Limbo* programming – *Dis* virtual machine – Styx – Project OXYGEN – New Atlantis – Declaration of Interdependence – Taranis the Thunderer, Esus the All-Powerful, and Teutates, god of the Celtic tribe – Druids – Bridhe – King of the Elements – Joseph of Arimathea – Arthur and Guinevere – St. Alban's – Glastonbury Hill – Rose Line – Matter of Britain

41 Hi Jolly and the Sheikhs

Omar Abdel Rahman – Defense Language Institute – Emad Salem – World Trade Center bombing, 1993 – Hadji Ali – the Hadj – Kali

Yuga – Satya Yuga – Time – KRMA – Houlihan Report – bad jacketing – Kent State University – Hualapai Indian Reservation – Grand Canyon Caverns – Fabians – Burma Shave signs – Stargazer Drive-in – Navajo code talker – Cuban Missile Crisis – St. Anthony – Essenes and Desert Fathers – Organic Light – *Valis* – Jahve (*Yod-Hey-Vav-Hey*) – Yeshua – *Bajadores* – Heisenberg's uncertainty principle – Veil of the Threshold – *I Ching* – Harmonies of the Spheres – John Worrell Keely – Aleister Crowley – Order of the Golden Dawn – Sonora Aero Club – Jack Parsons' Suicide Club – skull and crossbones – depolar repulsion – *Titanic* – John Jacob Astor – J.P. Morgan – Edison – *Mash-mak* – *etheric force*

42 The Nines

Second Coming – Sun Myung Moon – Alice Bailey's World Goodwill – Pearl Harbor – Etheric Advent – Jerusalem – Tom O'Bedlam – *Flight of Apollo 11: The Eagle Has Landed* – NASA – Don Bolles – Center for the Study of Democratic Institutions – CAPINTERN = COMINTERN – National Security Agency (NSA) – Interpol – NGOs – *Ordo ab chao* – Trotskyites – Socialist Workers Party – Nines – John Lennon – Brian Epstein – *Revolution No. 9* – Church of Satan Council of the Trapezoid or Council of Nine – Order of Nine Angles – Argenteum Astrum – Brotherhood of the Golden Dawn – Nine Gates Mystery School – Ruth Forbes Paine – Egyptair Flight 990 – COINTELPRO – Joint Protection Enterprise Network (JPEN) – men in black – Richard Brautigan – *Deep Space Nine* – Syd Barrett – KMUD – KLAS-TV – *Jane's Defense Weekly*

43 The Threshold Beckons

Manetho – *Hue Hue Tlapalan* – Israeli Prime Minister Yitzhak Rabin – Nicolas Berdyaev – Einstein-Podalsky-Rosen – Van Allen Radiation Belt – *Stargate* – Alexander the Great – UFOs –

Washington, D.C. – *Eye of Horus* – Masonic House of the Temple – *War Room* – Waffen SS – Mithra – 27 Club – Martha and the Vandellas – Robert Johnson – Demonbreun Bridge – Hank Williams – Knights of the Golden Circle – Elvis – Tammy Wynette – GENI (Global Environment for Network Innovations) – MUFONs – LRADs – Kurt Cobain – Radiohead – Brian Jones – Jerry Rubin – Abbie Hoffman – Daniel Ellsberg – *Operation Mind Control* – Walter Reed Institute of Research – National Institutes of Health (NIH) – Personality Assessment System – Human Ecology Fund – A Course in Miracles (ACIM) – Findhorn – Association for Research and Enlightenment (ARE) – RHIC-EDOM – Jonestown – Sun Myung Moon "love-bombing" – Mircea Eliade – *The Mind Possessed* – Pavlov – *interspersal technique* – Mockingbird – BASK dissociation (behavior, affect, sensation, knowledge)

44 No Place Like OM

12-atonal rock music – *Om* – *Do re mi fa so la ti do* – *hyperspace* – Grateful Dead – Augustus "Bear" Owsley Stanley III – resonance – Judas Priest lawsuit – electrical stimulation of the brain (ESB) – Billy Campbell or Shears – Luciferic – Leo Théremin – Jerry Garcia – Timothy Leary – Ken Kesey's Acid Test – Ultrasonic Acoustic Heterodyning – *etherwave* – Loews Cineplex Theatre – S-quad – LRAD – Metallica – 'The Scream' – Operation Desert Storm – Voice of God – *AUM*, Amen – JASON Group – Hubble Space Telescope – EBEs (extraterrestrial biological entities) – *Ramayana* – *Mahabharata* – reptilian brain – *Smithsonian Institute* – Air Force Office of Special Investigations (AFOSI) – Defense Investigative Service (DIS) – Idi Amin – Yellow Lodge – Low-Frequency Active sonar (LFA) – *Anti-matter* – infolded Whittaker wave structures – negentropy – Maxwell's quaternions – Bohm's hidden variables – remote neural monitoring (RNM) – LEDs – Camp David – Mount Weather – Greenbriar Hotel – Mount Pony – Continuity of Government (COG) – Project 908

45 Firewalk With Me

46 First International Dark Sky City

47 The Sorting Hat

Constitutional Convention – St. Andrews Lodge – Junior Warden Paul Revere – Argonauts – Oddfellow handshake – U.S. Senate Select Committee on Intelligence – Freedom of Information Act – MKSEARCH – OFTEN-CHICKWIT – Edgewood Arsenal Research Laboratories – Frank Olson – STS-48 – Phobos II – Soviet Colonel Marina Popovich – National Security Act of 1947 – Senator John Glenn – Charles E. Brady – *Easy Rider* – van Eck phreaking – TEMPEST monitoring – Immanentizing of the Eschaton – Seven Rishi and Seven Sleepers of Ephesus – Pluto – Jupiter pulses – Neptune-Pluto conjunctions, 1400 and 1892 – Grey Brotherhood – Murrah Federal Building – Magic Kingdom – Club 33 – warlock Reverend George Burroughs – Holy Land Experience – *2001: A Space Odyssey* – superconducting quantum interference device (SQUID) – *Sorting Hat* – hexidecimal color code – *Captain EO* –

48 Maharishi and Meteor Crater

The Aviary – Air Force Office of Special Investigation (AFOSI) – *Com-12 Briefing: Mind Control Operations/Aquarius Group Activities* – Swami Vivekananda – *Hail Columbia! Motherland of liberty!* – Theosophical Society – *occult imprisonment* – Jiddu Krishnamurti – Bolshevist Communism – Royal Institute of International Affairs – Lucis Trust – Palladian Brotherhood – General Albert Pike – Tenzin Gyatso – People's Republic of China – Sanat Kumara, Lord of the World – McREL – Cathedral of St. John the Divine – Ascended Tibetan Master Djwhal Khul – UNESCO – Baba Ram Dass – Alan Watts – Jack Kerouac School of Disembodied Poetics – Esalen Institute – Maharishi University of Management – Idries Shah – Club of Rome – Acquired Immunodeficiency Syndrome (AIDS) – Center for Disease Control (CDC) – Age of Maitreya – Mithraism – Robert Strange McNamara – Pelly Amendment – Sputnik – National Reconnaissance Office (NRO) – intercontinental ballistic missile (ICBM) – surface-to-air missile (SAM) – Six-Day War – Keyhole – Sir Halford Mackinder – Telstar – signals intelligence (SIGINT)

2019

The Rockies

Here is a country that, like Venice, has set its heart against its once proud role as a creative producer. It exists today in a state of ever-increasing shopping-hazed indolence, wrapped around with shiny art, its public services flogged off to incompetent pirates, the whole decadent hulk crewed by a sub-working class shipped in from the world's poorest countries and treated little better than galley slaves.

- Jonathan Glancey, "2020,"
The Guardian, September 18, 2004

In the organization of a civilization of the future we anticipate that the individualistically oriented man will become an anachronism. Indeed, he will be viewed as a threat to the group organization as well as to his fellow man. Hence, as stated, he in all likelihood will have few individual expectations. While such a picture may not be pleasant to contemplate, when viewed with our present orientation and value judgment, we would be amiss to deal with unrealistic imageries that would blind us to future reality. The new world of the closed, automatic system will necessitate a radical change in the political, technologic, and social thinking. All too often, however, we remain bound by the conventional tenets and wisdom of past generations. The cyber-culture revolution is changing all this.

- Charles Osgood and Stuart Umpleby,
"A Computer-based Exploration of Alternative Futures for Mankind 2000." Mankind 2000, funded by the Charles F. Kettering Foundation

1

To live in a sacred city was to live close to the borderline between life and death, between the 'middle world' of living humans and the multileveled realms existing above and beneath it.

- Ptolemy Tompkins,
This Tree Grows Out of Hell, 1990

America! The Mayans called America *Hanahuac*, Peruvians the Land of the Plumed Serpent *Amaruca*, the Mandæans in southern Iraq *Merika*, Egyptian for Venus in its western setting, marking a wonderful and distant land. The occult name for America is Columbia. *District of Columbia*. One hundred thousand years ago, the capital was in the Rockies.

In the America of the early 21st century, starlight had been banished from cities and even little mountain towns, thanks to the plasma cloud cover laid by jet and drone chemical trails. Seattle had gone from being a provincial seaport to the future's Emerald City of Techno-Oz, a tip of the hat to Hermes Trismegistos who once engraved alchemical formulae on an emerald table called the Tabula Smaragdina. And emerald is as green as the jade sacred to the Americas—a fact forever tainted for old Seven by the Jaguar High Priest in Veracruz and Baby Rose's MK-ULTRA keeper Dr. Greenbaum, both hopefully rotting in the lowest hell by now.

In western Wyoming, old Seven paused in front of a Radio Shack window of a tiny, all but abandoned town to wonder at the Disney Boy Toy robots with frubber faces miming one human emotion after another and enacting some perverse ritual. Beside them, Albert Hubo the Soothsayer— an Einstein head on top of a lab-coat body—was lip-syncing with Einstein's voice. A blurb said that the PCs hooked up to these ghastly "toys" were running Massive Software, the code that ran the humans and elves versus Mordor Orcs battles in the film version of Lord of the Rings. Seven turned away.

Vince had taught her about the Mayan collapse in the

9th century, when cities and half-finished stone projects had been abandoned overnight. Temples or cathedrals had been great cities' dominant landmarks then; today, it was financial centers. American nuclear supercarriers were now in the business of protecting the fat cats of tiny Dubai and the neighboring Emirate of Abu Dhabi, both built on the backs of South Asian contract laborers who'd worked 12-hour shifts seven days a week in desert heat, and paid for by breakaway money derived from drugs, sex, and child slavery. Aleister Crowley's ethos *Do what thou wilt shall be the whole of the law* was the clarion call of neoliberalism, despite the fact that freehold ownership and the freedom to "do as thou wilt" depended upon keeping populations utterly disenfranchised.

Seven smiled: "neoliberalism" was a Ray word. Thomas had reported that after the pilgrimage, he'd become an ACLU lawyer with ideals intact and anger transformed to resolve. Ray insisted he owed it all to the Dallas pilgrimage.

Globalization was modeled on the good old slave-indentured servant days. At every turn, the elite had blocked, undermined, and co-opted pesky democracy, and until the arrival of directed energy weapons (DEWs) and the technology that could map human brains at a distance (along with every human emotion and gene combination under the Sun), containing the post-Marx masses had kept Army War College thinkers awake at night. Now, they slept like babies.

Cities were going up inside cities like nesting dolls with their own satellite-linked weather systems and factory sealed Hyperion miniature nuclear reactors encased in concrete. The middle class still had its horizontal gated communities, but underground mansions with entryways guarded by retina scanners from Israel had superseded vertical skyhouses for the very rich. Slums were engineered to act as buffer zones minus the old concertina wire, blast walls, watchtowers, and CCTVs, now that the AI-run Space Fence and Internet of Things were fully operational. Ecowarriors in superhero costumes and masks continued to prowl, sabotaging cell towers wherever possible.

The urban population of 2019 was greater than the entire

world population of 1960, with the countryside available only to the 0.1% class. By the end of the 19th century, Frederick Law Olmsted had already recognized that cities were engines of inequality in which the masses were thrust into tenements at the bottom and elites lifted like ruling angels above the bustle and grime to high-rise apartments. His urban parks like Central Park in New York City were meant to be democratic spaces in which all classes could enjoy family, friendship, and the outdoors. But structural adjustment had changed all that. Parks had driven up the land values so much that the landless, unemployed, and undereducated poor couldn't afford to live close to the park and instead were consigned to sprawling concentration camps of mega-slums. By the late 1970s and early 1980s, post-industrial visions of modernization and Marxism for masses had been replaced by a permanent disconnection from the world economy, a fact graduate school leftists like Ray would not notice for decades. Water tables, sewage, shelter, and urban services were collapsing in tandem with the rising sweatshop service economy. Everywhere was coming up China.

Military thinkers had foreseen the problems cities would have once urban industry was outsourced to developing countries and thus added urban planning and architecture, psychology, sociology, and anthropology to their close quarters battle (CQB) and urban operations (UO) under AI-run "Master the Human Domain" agenda. In her dystopic novel Oryx and Crake, Margaret Atwood labeled mongrel city extremes as Compounds and Pleeblands. CQB and UO were designed to handle the maze-like Pleebland streets overflowing with those who had been disenfranchised during the Huntington "clash of civilizations" wars. Class, not race, was the pressure point to which asymmetric warfare was being applied, given that the military worked for global elites and their Egregore-driven corporations. What television, drugs, engineered illness, and debt didn't control, directed energy weapons and programmed super soldiers would, supplemented all the while by ongoing genetic, chemical, and electromagnetic modification.

After the last world Inundation, the first cities to be built in Mesopotamia, Asia, Europe, and North Africa had served as quadripartite realms that mirrored the divine cosmos. Pyramids and obelisks were built to reinstate the free energy of sacred Atlantis for the technology that assured communication with parallel worlds. (Shades of CERN.) Minoans, Persians, Athenians, Macedonians, and Greeks had perfected sewage systems long before the Romans by connecting latrines to vertical chutes that dumped into stone sewers, brick-lined septic tanks, and enclosed drains—systems far superior to the present chemical intermingling of sewage and drinking water loaded with antidepressants, antipsychotics, dioxin, PCBs, pesticides, lead, fluoride, and mercury. Unlike the ancients, corporate power mongers care only for their bottom line, not their cities' citizens.

Since the 1970-2000 Saturn cycle, national identity had been all but replaced by global identity, and the nuclear family once necessary to the Industrial Revolution that had driven young plebes from family land into the cities was no longer needed. Keeping men tethered to a job and locale to support rearing the next generation of workers had served for stability while industrialism and urbanization stripped them of self-sufficiency and made them dependent upon corporate feudalism. Once that phase was consolidated, World War Two had drawn the untapped cheap labor of women from the home with promises of freedom, self-expression, etc., and without the hearth keepers, marriages and families had begun to disintegrate. As in China, children grew accustomed to the loneliness of institutions and impersonal surroundings. School and corporate uniforms had RFID chips sewn into the logo so scanners could record every move, so it was no wonder that as adults citizens fell prey to epidemic depression and hypochondria that spelled massive profits for the pharmaceutical, psychiatric, and medical industries. By 2020, depression would be second to heart disease, and yet women were continually lauded for striking a blow at patriarchy and "liberating" their children, despite the fact that aggressive male values reigned more than ever and male approval was still necessary for the one in five women allowed to earn more than their male counterparts.

Courtship, marriage, and the requisite 2.4 children slid into the Memory Hole, along with the rest of Western civilization. Divorces doubled, cohabitation and single parent households tripled, births outside of marriage quintupled. Stepfamilies and serial monogamy attempted to fill the emotional breach, gay parents co-parented, nannies and daycares raised the children of working mothers watching from office webcams. Legions of clever PhDs wrote about how wonderful and liberating it all was. After all, the elite had been raised by paid others and look at how they had turned out—like 41-year-old Amschel Rothschild found garroted and naked in a Bristol Hotel bathtub in Paris on 7/7/96, dead from either autoerotic asphyxiation or ritual murder. Maternal employment reached 75 percent as America became China. In the name of liberation and "progress," children were being hardened into adults who would unconsciously cling to the corporate nannies of global feudalism.

The word *human* was derived from the same root as humus, the organic material in soil from which the "enhanced" Transhumanist human was to be separated in every way possible. Pleebs were to be born and raised for labor and TV lobotomies, a gnomish biotechnical slave class genetically modified to meet specific corporate needs on- and off-planet, meat machines of flesh and metal conjoined for maximum tensile strength and remote control, thanks to embedded nanobots breathed in during the chemtrail era. Beside them in the mines and oilrigs would be *Blade Runner* clones and robots with glow-in-the-dark bioflesh grown in vats, all programmed to work specific technological jobs from Petri dish to immolation.

At the edge of the Wyoming town was a rundown AEC (Army Experience Center) video arcade where pimply adolescents out of school or jobs were already plugged into PCs via their brainwaves and firing laser guns at enemies lodged somewhere between MindSet and Emotiv signal processing biosensors. Appropriately enough, George Harrison's album *Brainwashed* was playing—

. . . And I've been traveling through the dirt and the grime
From the past to the future through the space and the time
Traveling deep beneath the waves
In watery grottoes and mountainous caves

But oh Lord we've got to fight
With the thoughts in the head with the dark and the light
No use to stop and stare
And if you don't know where you're going
Any road will take you there

A career military man with dead eyes and a ready smile for potential recruits was operating the board. Somewhere behind the two-way mirror winding around the game room, a military behavioral scientist with Luke Binoculars (optics and EEG) was zeroing in on gamesters, tapping into their subconscious for abuse, anger, and intelligence. To him, these boys were already virtual soldiers flying simulated Apache and Black Hawk helicopters, driving Humvees armed with VMADS poised to EM-waste brown, black, and yellow urban terrorists hiding in slum buildings teeming with terrified women and children. Their brainwaves were already skilled at manipulating balls inside clear towers and along obstacle courses. Of course, the boys themselves were oblivious to the thousands of microscopic image sensors lodged between the liquid crystal display cells in the LCD screens imprinting their young brains and feeding images to Fusion Center Intelligence Platforms. The geekier boys (officer material) were silently challenging Deep Blue's offspring, moving chess pieces on the screen with their brainwaves. (Twenty years earlier, Garry Kasparov had been pitted not just against Deep Blue but also against backdoor elite nerds covertly conferring against him somewhere in cyberspace.)

Stepping inside the arcade, Seven quietly activated a tiny device Thomas had developed to measure the presence of low-intensity low-frequency ultrasound (LILFU) often used in video games, broadcast music, concerts, and mind control. LILFU had been publicly tested during live performances of bands like the proto-industrial Throbbing Gristle, and 49 years ago, Seven and the pilgrims had encountered similar technology in Hobbes, New Mexico. Yes, LILFU was present; no surprise. Thomas thought that mass weddings like those at Former Soviet Union Nashi ("Ours") annual camps were subject to LILFU, given that ten thousand uniformed youths sleeping in the heart-shaped Love Oasis all wore transmitter-receiver RFID badges.

For two generations, plebe children had been bombarded with TV golems, clones, homunculi, Wizard of Oz munchkins, Willy Wonka and the Chocolate Factory Oompa Loompas, Happy Meals, Barbies, GI Joes, Transformers, anime, Pokémon, and Yu-gi-oh like Arabian jinn, Jewish Shedeem, and African yumboes. It was all entrainment from beyond the Magickal Threshold disguised as childish TV entertainment, like the Teletubbies popping out of the Earth's morphogenic field, entraining tots to mesh with the entities entering their pliable psyches. "Toys" housed in metal, ceramic, cloth, plastic, electronics, and nanoparticles supported genetic and biotech "enhancement" by conditioning plebes early to identify with technology instead of Nature. Entire generations were being conditioned to welcome quantum entanglement with subnature entities driven by their own nature to suckle at light-filled human souls.

Studying the entranced faces of the boys, Seven recalled the Wonderlic employee intelligence test that separated the chaff from the wheat, dividing the few bright people for management from the obedient drones the rest of the way down. Schools and television had been dumbing them down for decades. Once plebes left school at sixteen, their choice was trade school or the military, college being prohibitively expensive to all but the upper and upwardly mobile classes.

Culture designers knew what the future needed: consumption units below, skyhouses powered by sun and wind above, huge chain stores everywhere, governance and dominance by the right and further right. It was America's turn to be Soviet. The rich few would have restorative plastic surgery, bone marrow and skin in thirty shapes, scar-free healing, face implants, and serial heart implants; well-to-do couples unhappy with their genetics would turn to geneticists for disease-free, superior embryos. Meanwhile, plebe children would continue to be conditioned to yearn for absent mummies and daddies until they grew up to sell their souls to the corporate State and pop statins like vitamins.

Seven sighed and kept trekking, recalling how simple everything had seemed when they had set out on Highway 1 in the spring of 1970 without a clue as to what lay before them.

26

Scotland

Dico tibi verum:
Libertas optima rerum;
Numquam servili sub nexu vivito.

I tell you truly:
Freedom is the best of all things;
Never to live under the bonds of slavery.

–Sir James Fergusson,
William Wallace, Guardian of Scotland, 1948

The secret behind secret societies and cults and hierarchical religions is the artistic creation of a universe which is then frozen for mass consumption. The pressure of major elites in government, war, [and] power struggles involved the slowing down of the imagination so that a central mural about reality can be set in concrete. From it, an agenda can be spun off . . .

–Jon Rappaport,
The Secret Behind Secret Societies, 1998

I have hardly taken a step, yet I feel I have gone far.

- Parsifal on Good Friday

The very morning Thomas was catching forty winks at the Wigwam Motel in San Bernardino before rising to take the wheel again, his father Laurence was bound for London and then on to Scotland, land of his forebears.

It had taken some conniving to escape Hiram's dragnet. Laurence had told all the servants and left a message for his brother saying he was driving his International up to his lodge for a fortnight of fishing and relaxation, having already arranged with an FBI muckety-muck to go in his stead and not answer the phone unless it was the coded ring they agreed upon. The Agent thought he had the picture: a secret tryst far from the wife's eye. Winking, he'd promised Laurence that his lips were sealed and his hook baited. Such was life under Hiram's omnipresent eye—secrets, subterfuge, lies, false trails. Brotherly love in Philadelphia.

Waiting at Heathrow for the night train to ponderous Edinburgh, Laurence caught a glowing headline in what he thought was tomorrow's *New York Times: 403,713 people died in Nazi concentration camps; less than half were Jews*. Remarkable. He bought the paper but before he could read it (or notice that it was dated March 3, 1991), the train was there and he dozed the entire way. By the time he reached Edinburgh, the *Times* was gone.

Caroline's Sinclair cousin and his wife met him. The cousin was an urbane man in his early seventies, knighted years before by the Queen, and his wife the bustling, no-nonsense sort of woman many men in Great Britain seemed to marry. They were appalled that Laurence had come straight from America and insisted on plying him with tea and crumpets in Rosslyn village before going on to the famed chapel. The village was far older than Edinburgh, the cousin said, here since the second century after Christ.

Rosslyn Chapel had been built overlooking the river Esk in 1440 at the very tip-top of the Romans' Great North Road or *Lactodorum*, now known as Rue St. Jacques, stretching south all the way to the Channel coast and even then continuing into Portugal.

Thirteen foundation pillars support the chapel's arcade of twelve arches representing the twelve constellations—*the Apocalypse in stone*, the cousin whispered as they strolled around the interior, marveling at the stars, lilies, and roses carved into the ceiling. Laurence was surprised by how many maize and aloe plants there were; he thought they were indigenous to the Americas. Myriad Green Man heads grimaced down at them.

The Sinclair cousin pointed out the Apprentice pillar Boaz, pillar of strength, saying that the second pillar Jachin was down in Portugal at the other end of the Lactodorum.

"Why Portugal?" Laurence asked.

"Between Scotland and Iberia lie the seven planetary oracles, with the Sun oracle in Carnuntum between the Loire and the Eure, above which is Notre Dame de Chartres. The Moon oracle is where St. James, Jesus' brother, is buried. The Mercury and Venus oracles, Toulouse and Orléans. The Mars oracle, Notre Dame de Paris. The Jupiter oracle, Notre Dame in Amiens. And Rosslyn Chapel, hardly the cathedral once planned, suffices for the Saturn oracle. Our Earth as cosmic Temple along the Atlantic side of Europe. Goddess *Natura's* cathedral Milky Way, perhaps an older version of your Jesuit and Franciscan missions along your Pacific side."

He stole a look at Laurence. *Didn't the American Brotherhood teach its members anything?*

The Sinclair then explained that the lilies carved in the vault over the choir represent sacred Grail family bloodlines, humbly glossing over the fact that his family was one. In fact, the chapel had been founded by Lord William St. Clare, born in 1402, Grand Master and Adept of the highest degree. Curious, Laurence inquired as to what might be the good purpose of losing the right brain's ability to see into less visible realms?

The Sinclair descendant explained an unusual piece of history. "My forebear lived at a pivotal time. The spiritual faculties inherent to the right hemisphere of the brain were in decline as the analytical left brain rose in power so as to be able to grapple with a new kind of science dependent upon observation and thinking. At least this is what the Austrian initiate indicated."

Laurence was about to ask about *the Austrian initiate* when the cousin's wife approached with news about a bed and breakfast for Laurence near a battlefield filled with bones and a cave in which William Wallace had hid from Edward Longshanks in the late 13th century. The cousins again invited him to stay with them, but he begged off, saying he had some tiresome work to do. The truth was otherwise for both parties: Laurence longed for a retreat, and the Sinclairs were relieved that the American cousin by marriage wouldn't be taking up their time. The three were then free to enjoy a picnic lunch together behind the chapel on the Esk, chatting cordially as they ate their pork pies and soda bread with crumbling white slabs of goat cheese and washing it all down with old French wine. Finally, they dropped Laurence at the rustic bed and breakfast run by a young Scottish couple, the wife having inherited not just property but an old mahogany library whose historical treasures she placed entirely at his disposal.

That night, too wired by jet lag, Laurence stayed up reading about William Wallace and Scottish history. His throat grew tight over the Declaration of Arbroath, cut of the same freedom-loving cloth as the Declaration of Independence: *For as long as one hundred of us shall remain alive, we shall never in any wise consent to submit to the rule of the English, for it is not for glory we fight, nor riches, or for honour, but for freedom alone, which no good man loses but with his life.*

After a few hours of delicious rural sleep, Laurence took his Scottish oats, toast, and tea and then set out for Wallace's cave. He climbed the crags along the burn and slowly made his way up to the cliff his host had described, already feeling Scotland and ancient family memories warming his blood. Though he'd never lived in Scotland, he had visited and could feel its geography coursing up his legs, its wild beauty entering his eyes, its rushing water in his ears, the heather in his nostrils. It was as if all his senses had become a sense of touch. It was mysterious. Was this how Indians in America felt on their land and conversely the loss when booted off? His body had not felt so alive, so in touch with the Earth since boyhood. Why could he not feel this way in Philadelphia?

The cave was larger than he'd expected, its several chambers gouged deep in rock. The acoustics were perfect, and his tenor sounded extraordinary. He sang songs while walking through Wallace's "rooms," pondering how many people had hidden or resided in this one cave throughout the ages. Wallace had loved Scotland and fought for it. After the royal Plantagenet witch Longshanks massacred 20,000 Scots in 1296 and Wallace's beloved wife Marion was brutally executed, he had led the Battle of Stirling Bridge with a small ill-trained army against the undefeated 50,000-strong English, including 1,000 armored heavy horse cavalry. *Tell your people that we have not come here to gain peace*, Wallace informed the English envoy, *but are prepared for battle, to avenge and deliver our country*. That was September 11, over 672 years ago, the first time in history, really, that common people had fought on their own account for their land and national identity. Longshanks, his heavy cavalry foundering in the marshy Scottish ground, had lost; Wallace had cut off his forces at Stirling Bridge.

Laurence ran his hands over the cold, rough walls of the cave, in awe that the six-foot-seven hero had once stood where he was standing. At Falkirk, the Scots had been routed by Longshanks' Welsh archers and Wallace had hidden here before being taken in 1305. After a quick trial at Westminster, he was publicly drawn and quartered and his head impaled on London Bridge. But it wasn't over yet. On St. John's Eve nine years later, Knights Templar fleeing the French Inquisition assisted Robert the Bruce and his Scots at Bannockburn. Legend said that the Scots marched into battle behind the Monymusk Reliquary, the Templars' model of the Temple of Solomon, and that when Longshanks saw it and the red cross banners, he and his five hundred knights fled. Once the Declaration of Arbroath crowned Bruce king of the Scots, he founded the first Scottish Rite Freemason lodge to receive Templars now fleeing Pope Clement V.

Laurence paced, inspired by Wallace to at last admit that his brother and men like him were plotting to steal from America the freedom it represented to all the world. Stripped of its fine words, this was what their Enterprise was up to. He could not live with himself another day if he did not take hold of the shred of courage Wallace was now offering him. Laurence had been cowed by his brother his entire life. Like a schoolboy, he had spent years pining for a lost woman and abandoned the lost woman he had married. His son had seen through him and set off to find the courage to struggle with his soul and his times elsewhere. He could not allow these failures of courage to be his only legacy.

In Wallace's cave, he began to find himself again.

27

Singularity

. . . In three days time, the people awakened to a wonderful rainbow bridge stretching from the highest mountain on Limuw to the highest mountain on the land across the water.

"Go forth, my children," said Hutash, blessing those who stepped up onto the sky bridge.

Halfway across, one Chumash after the other made the mistake of looking down and then fell into the sea. The earth goddess heard their cries and as she loved them, with a wave of her hand she swept away the fog and calmed the sea. "As there are people who walk upon the land, so shall there be people who swim in the sea." And with her words, the drowning Chumash turned into dolphins. Above them, those Chumash who had not looked down continued their journey to the new land. When the last one had stepped off the bridge, it disappeared.

–From *"The Rainbow Bridge,"*
retold by Audrey Wood, 1995

Within 30 years, we will have the technological means to create superhuman intelligence. Shortly after, the human era will end.

- Vernor Vinge,
retired professor, San Diego State University;
"The Coming Technological Singularity," 1993

Dr. Greenbaum was landing at the little airport in Weed, California, yet another hop in his MK-ULTRA itinerary, given that centralizing the work at this point would attract too much congressional and public attention. In 1953-54, the first year of MK-ULTRA, he'd flown all over the country ironing out problems in the 429 tests they did that year alone, not including the 220 college student and other clandestine field tests. Oversight of the 149 subprojects was essential—Artichoke, Shade, Often, Marker, Delta, Bluebird, Naomi, Phoenix, Search, etc.— as were his demonstrations to medical, military, and intelligence staff at various bases and hospitals. Chestnut Lodge in Rockville, Maryland was one of his most regular stops, given that he worked on all the politically sensitive cases with Dr. Gibson. Greenbaum smiled. Gibson was the son of the famous magician who'd created The Shadow. *Who knows what evil lurks in the hearts of men? Only the Shadow knows!* Psychiatry, after all, was magic. It was through Gibson that he and Abramson had made the acquaintance of the magician John Mulholland.

The small plane was rolling to a stop and the U.S. Army colonel he knew only as Charlie was waiting with a driver. Charlie had founded the Delta Force Commando unit and was a counterinsurgency expert. He had been an invaluable source for the CIA's Phoenix Program in Vietnam under the COORDS program and a few other black operations disguised as classified programs. Every six months, Charlie and Dr. Greenbaum did a walk-through of the covert field training going on at Mt. Shasta and discussed state of the art programming of Special Forces soldiers mandated to be the CIA's covert military arm, some destined for Vietnam provincial reconnaissance units (PRUs)— murder teams programmed to systematically liquidate more than 40,000 dissidents (village leaders, business people, teachers, artisans, bureaucrats, farmers, unskilled laborers, those unhappy with American presence) in the name of *De Oppresso Liber*. Sometimes, Charlie and Greenbaum would have lunch with actor Clint Eastwood at his ranch.

Over the rainbow from the usual physical requirements of swimming 50 meters in full gear, pressing 42 pushups and 52 sit-ups in two minutes, and running two miles in less than 15 minutes 54 seconds, every man there had an imaginary friend he had had since his abusive childhood who was tougher and meaner than the host personality could ever be made to be. Each man had passed the MAT and Special Forces Suitability Inventory and Critical Decisions test and had been screened for attaching little value to human life. The atrocity studies were looking for men who could torture and kill while maintaining a normal public persona. Commando teams—*Spetsnaz*, the Soviets called them—of Navy Seals, Delta Force, and counterinsurgents had all undergone hours and hours of films and demonstrations (some actual rituals) showing people of all colors and ages and genders being tortured and killed in a variety of ways. Thus acclimatized, they set aside empathy and nagging consciences and were able to kill without remorse or memory of doing so.

Greenbaum had made a careful study of the Kurd *peshmerga* ("facing death") and the ancient *Ashishin* under Allahudin described by Marco Polo in his journals in 1298. Preparation of ruthless soldiers had always entailed drugs and a tortuous initiation of some kind. He had also studied Israeli infantry training tactics, systematic policies and methods of stress, uncertainty, and shock that break down the civilian in soldiers and rebuild them as lethal units. The Gladio *strategy of tension* was coupled with techniques guaranteed to break down one personality and build others: hypnosis, sensory deprivation, forced drugs, electric shots in the stomach and back (probes, electrodes, cattle prods, etc.), cacophonous sound, infrasound, forced immobilization for long periods, 4- and 6-point restraints, reversals (light/dark, pain/pleasure, hot/cold, right/left laterals), isolation in darkness, refrigeration, heated tin rooms, deep wells, graves, cages, caves, hanging from one limb, virtual reality (earphones, flashing lights, surround screen), spinning head-down on a table or chair, anal/oral/vaginal rape while being tortured, serial orgasms forced by terror, high-frequency sensations and sounds (animal and human cries of pain), perforation of eardrums, dislocation of limbs, witnessing or participating in the torture and killing of loved ones, etc. MK-ULTRA was in the business of exploring full spectrum programming, whatever the method.

And the operation was big. Masons, KKK, neo-Nazis, Nazis, doctors, nurses, psychologists, Army and CIA personnel, Mafia and south-of-the-border syndicates, clergy of every denomination (Catholic, Baptist, Dutch-Reform, Missouri Synod Lutheran, Reformed Jewish, Episcopal, etc.) were involved at varying subcontractor levels. Besides CIA and DARPA black budgets, more funding was being squeezed through black fundraisers like drug smuggling, child slave market, pornography, and snuff. Various United Nations NGOs were involved at one international level or another. Oh, it was big, all right. Money was being conduited toward MK-ULTRA by the truckload through the CIA's Human Ecology Foundation, Josiah Macy, Jr. Foundation, and the Geschickter Fund for Medical Research. NASA's bioscience advisory committee was deeply involved, the U.S. Naval Air Development Center, Johns Hopkins University, and on and on. Thanks to the Nazis, it was endless, a cornucopia of funding for an MK-ULTRA future, including but definitely not limited to the super soldier.

During the drive to the high-security base under the mountain, Charlie briefed Greenbaum on the present group, mostly Army 160th air wing Night Stalkers, including the 5th and 101st flown in from Fort Campbell, Fort Bragg, and Hunter Army Airfield. While listening to Charlie with one ear, Greenbaum's sensory apparati were stretching into the northern California geography of Shasta-Trinity National Forest, half of his mind contemplating the thousands of years before the Europeans had finally opened America and Canada from sea to shining sea. Mt. Shasta or Tschastl was a volcanic peak from the Holocene epoch, erupting from the same molten sea that shaped the Cascade Mountain Range within the last 10,000 years, back when the Atlantis catastrophe occurred.

Due to the etheric breach beneath her, Shasta was not just a mountain but an interdimensional gateway. Tribes in Southern California considered it to be the upper *kiva*, with Cougar Meadows being especially sacred. The Bureau of Land Management (BLM) believed itself to be Shasta's guardian, but her true guardians were the Hupa, Karuk, Modoc, Pit River, Shasta, and Wintu Indians who knew that only the dead should go above the tree line while finding their way to the flowery path (the Milky Way) and back to the World's Heart. Wherever Wintus died, their bodies were oriented toward the mountain.

As they approached the Shasta stronghold from the north, Greenbaum noted the lenticular cloud hovering near the majestic peak jutting into the blue.

"Extraordinary," he murmured.

Charlie glanced at him and smiled. "Look closely. Is it a lenticular cloud or something else? Maybe your welcoming committee?" he finished mysteriously.

Greenbaum stared at the saucer-like cloud, musing not on holographic technology but on the guardians of Shasta who demanded that the living be purified before approaching the mountain. Six months ago, in the context of how little the military presence had disturbed the surroundings, Charlie had talked about the medicine people still receiving training at sacred sites on the mountain and collecting medicines like pennyroyal, wild onion, celery, and mountain fir. Dr. Greenbaum was sure they knew what had burrowed beneath their mountain, despite the Age of Aquarius legends the military had disseminated and encouraged in the area—ghost ships slipping in and out over the summit, tunnels through the eastern base to the interdimensional ghost cities Iletheleme and Yaktayvia bounded by frequencies emanating from the crystal pyramid, etc. They'd even spread stories of Saint-Germain visiting.

The chill Dr. Greenbaum associated with geographic prescience shot up his spine. He looked about as the driver maneuvered his way around the mountain toward the hidden entrance. *Saint-Germain?*

Dr. Greenbaum's sixth sense was working well. Saint-Germain had visited Shasta during the previous fall with Ghost Bear and a Karuk medicine man. Setting out from Klamath, the three men had walked and talked their way through the Marble Mountains into Scott Valley, then Dussel Rock and Shasta Valley, approaching the mountain along the tree line on the sacred north side.

"When the Pit River medicine man goes to hear the voice of *Mis Misa*," the Karuk explained, "he is instructed. Visitors who behave disrespectfully and fearfully are driven crazy by dangerous little *Je su chin* that live inside the mountain, which is why young people less than fourteen or fifteen years old are not allowed to attend Wintu ceremonies at the spring above Panther Meadow."

After turning west and arriving at a cave, the three men walked clockwise around the mountain. Only when the circle returned them to the cave could they proceed above the tree line.

"The north gate in the mountainside opens like a doorway, though vents in the cave provide access, too," the Karuk said. "Guardian spirits called *tinihowi* guard these gateways, so one must be cautious. During ceremonies, these spirits from the inner realm gather and speak. The mountain also listens and speaks through its spring, like a telephone line. As the plants draw a higher mineral content from the mountain, so the mountain is a great transmitter. Inside its rock are spiritual forces called *axeki*, or pains. Seismologists call them piezos, from the Greek word for squeeze. Thus for medicine men and women, traveling to the top of the mountain without going there physically is less arduous." He smiled at Ghost Bear.

"Doesn't Southern Pacific Railroad own the slopes?" Ghost Bear asked as they wound their way.

The Karuk nodded. "Sadly, yes, and the American military is pursuing bad magic in the bowels of Tschastl. But the twelve and a half square miles at the summit are protected by *tinihowi* and shaman guardian spirits *tamakomi*. The etheric mountain above the physical mountain is seven times larger. The light rays local people see—not the blue-white lights inside the base of the mountain that belong to Southern Pacific's military guest—emanate from the portal at the etheric mountain's lower edge. The bonding there is particularly elastic, what whites call the Zero Point Field, a perfect laboratory for military stone hearts. Holographic experimentation here is big, due to the etheric quality of light. Spiritual seekers provide cover stories and a constant supply of guinea pigs, like the poor Green Beret CIA who wanders around talking about space brothers."

"Every conquering military," Hermano said, "with its occult-trained priests and magi in tow targets ancient sacred sites in order to exploit them. Tschastl is no exception. Spiritual sites retain piezoelectricity, phantasmal memories, transits, and conduits. As you know, those who die there are often bound to the place, depending on the rituals. These after-effects can be reactivated and are often useful to those pursuing power, not to mention that acquiring indigenous places of power enervates the conquered culture."

The Karuk nodded. "We know something about that, don't we, Ghost Bear?"

Ghost Bear smiled. "One of the many Tschastl legends tells of a visit by an 18th century Ascended Master named Saint-Germain, said to have talked to a *wasichu* named Guy Ballard in 1930." He glanced impishly at Hermano.

The Karuk chuckled. "*And* the Brotherhood of the White Temple and Morris Doreal, who said not Lemurians dwell beneath Tschastl but Atlanteans guarding the Lemurians imprisoned beneath the Caroline Islands."

Ghost Bear shrugged. "A little bit of truth, a lot of *wasichu* hoo. Lemurian Fellowship in Chicago moved to Ramona, California in 1936, the Radiant School, and all the rest to stir the Age of Aquarius soup intelligence *wasichus* are exploiting. *Wasichus* are easy marks because they have no geography to set them straight."

"Mother Earth is old," the Karuk stressed. "Much has transpired since Mu, including continents."

Hermano agreed. "The British naturalist Alfred Russell Wallace studied animal distribution and resemblances of rocks and fossils in Central India and South Africa and pointed to a former land bridge. It was the lemurs present in Madagascar, Africa, India, and the Malay

Archipelago that led to the *wasichu* name Lemuria. The real name is, as you say, Mu."

"*Elam-Mu*, wasn't it?" said the Karuk. "Africa, the Indian Ocean, the East Indies and the South Pacific. When the axis tilted, survivors made for the four cones of light in the east: Mt. Hood, Mt. Adams, Mt. St. Helens, and Mt. Tahoma. Later, Ieka, the natural pyramid Tschastl, appeared."

Hermano nodded. "Then two or so thousand years later, Atlantis sank beneath the Atlantic and migrations from Central America, then called Guatemala, went west and north inland up the Colorado, Mississippi, and Missouri rivers and to the coast as the Cascade Range rose, the vast inland Bonneville Sea from Sierra Nevada to the western base of the Rocky Mountains separating it from the mainland."

Ghost Bear took up the thread. "And what about the underground networks of caves running from Shasta south through the Sierras all the way to the Loltun caves of Yucatan and Silpino caverns in Cayuga of eastern Guatemala? When the Hopi and Zuñi and Pueblos say they came *up* out of Mother Earth through the *sipapu* long ago in another world age, are they referring to those interlocking caverns?"

The Karuk stopped to drink from Tschastl's cold stream. "Maybe you're right, brother. California's ancient Sequoias and redwoods, and the frankincense tree in the Borrego Desert . . ."

". . . and the Painted Desert and Petrified Forest in Arizona, two to seven million years old . . . ," Ghost Bear added, kneeling beside him.

Hermano too kneeled at the stream in which grasses wafted. ". . . and all from under Late Triassic sedimentary deposits two hundred million years old, from northwest Colorado through New Mexico to southern Nevada. Yours is an ancient, extraordinary land, my brothers, filled to overflowing with mysteries—some very old mysteries, some young."

The three men stood and were silent, breathing in deep draughts, looking up to the high regions yet ahead where they would set a few changes in motion according to the old law of two or more gathered in His name.

Now months later, Dr. Greenbaum and Charlie entered the netherworld of military national security under Mt. Shasta. Through windows and open doorways, the two men whose signatures decided life or death looked in on men, women, and children strapped in chairs and on gurneys, electrodes on their heads. Some were being implanted with subcutaneous transceivers powered electromechanically via muscle movement to send and receive data directly through the brain, while those already implanted were being tested for brain-computer interfacing. Still others were wired with biology-based *performance enhancement* technology that DARPA was field-testing, or swallowing biosensor implants that detected biological and chemical agents, tracked DNA, then released the appropriate vaccine or activated the appropriate pharmaceutical skin patch. Knocked-out snipers were getting eye implants. Some were swallowing or being injected with various time-capsule drugs or magnetic resonance patches to fool the body into forgetting that it needed sleep. In cold and hot rooms, doctors and nurses were checking soldiers' chameleon-camouflage exoskeleton armor for climate control and the haptic interface sensors that could read everything about the soldier's body state.

DARPA viewed the human as the military's weakest link and wanted counterinsurgency teams that were smarter, tougher, faster, and stronger, meaning a superhuman, augmented, assisted performance virtual soldier. Having cracked the brain's neural codes, they would soon have remote-controlled weapons run by thought alone. Tactical intelligence would download into soldiers' brains and they would communicate with each other by thought. Pilots would fly high-performance fighter jets from the ground, their brains connected with their jet's computer. Training wouldn't be as expensive or time-consuming as it was now: soldiers would simply upload others' memories of combat, as well as training courses.

Brain-computer interface: the future.

Dr. Greenbaum and Charlie got into a golf cart and headed for the inside battlefield they called the *playroom*—where the kinks of gadgets and brain hardware were ironed out before night exercises along the sides of the mountain. While Charlie rattled on about tests and equipment, Dr. Greenbaum's brain went over the presentation he would make that afternoon.

Where MK-ULTRA truly contributed was in the virtual soldier's ability to kill remorselessly. An officer at the School of the Americas at Fort Benning had explained how they trained Central American counterinsurgents. First, they took poor kids off the street at thirteen and exposed them to Nazi SS rituals and eating and drinking blood and other bodily fluids and feces. Then they were tortured and raped and trained to do the same to women, men, and children, along with sado-masochistic murder, cutting up the body, eating parts of it, and spreading parts around the city or countryside to traumatize the public. Terror would be followed by passivity: *Schrecklichkeit*, the strategic use of terror. The desensitized boys were then sent to SOA to learn regimented, systematized *special warfare*.

Dr. Greenbaum preferred electromagnetic mind control along the lines of Dr. José Delgado's acoustic psycho-correction device. Via bone conduction, it transmitted an infrasound ELF wave of commands, anxiety, euphoria, or any other emotion or "thought" in the target's head under cover of music, static, or white noise. The ingenious device could control, demoralize, disable, or enhance friendly force performance to almost superhuman capability, depending upon how the dial was turned. In world leaders, it could probe and correct the mind's psychic contents by telephone, radio, or television. Greenbaum had had the honor of meeting Delgado once in Mexico.

Greenbaum was fascinated by how cerebral tissue on a cellular level could be transformed with electromagnetic radiation. Destroy the cerebral tissue and then, with the proper electromagnetic pulse, reproduce new cerebral tissue for an entirely *other* personality. Alter the blood-brain barrier and neurotoxins could cross over and create severe neuropathological symptoms so *something other* came forth, like Lazarus from the tomb, a *Doppelgänger* like in the *golem* stories he'd heard as a boy. The brain's true nature was that of a receiving and transmitting device, the wavelengths and frequencies acting as roads or lines of resonance along which beings with exactly that frequency would then travel. Send out the call letters and the being would have to respond. Magickal rituals and electromagnetic rituals were not all that different.

The Nazis had discovered the low frequency that could awaken a person's *Doppelgänger* and produce paranormal abilities. Greenbaum had witnessed just such a demonstration at Los Alamos, when an 18 KHz oscillator modulated with various types of stochastic noise was placed near a subject's head. That the natural personality could be taken captive or even erased by the more elemental personality of the *Doppelgänger* was remarkable. Soviet chronal emitters and guns could literally tear the human aura to pieces and destroy all vestiges of biological defense. Aimed at the head, they could shatter the nimbus and permanently impair the target's mental capabilities. Where would the *Doppelgänger* stand in that case?

He leafed through the latest U.S Patents Office weapons catalogue Charlie had handed him. How quickly the technology was coming now! A 7-11 Hertz signal stopped hearts by synchronizing a pulsed ultra-high-frequency microwave signal of low power density with the depolarization of the myocardium and beaming the signal at the thoracic area. Clever, very clever. Ah, and the audio tooth implant, the molar mobile phone.

> *Media Lab Europe, working in partnership with MIT Media Lab, is finally going public with the wireless, low frequency receivers that turn audio signals into mechanical vibrations that pass from the tooth to the inner ear as words.*

And the 3-minute hysterectomy.

> *The National Institute of Clinical Excellence (NICE) has approved MEA (microwave endometrial ablation) for hysterectomies that will*

save taxpayers $60 million per year. A hand-held "wand" emits low-powered microwaves that heat up the tissue on the uterine wall to 60-85°C and destroy it.

For nervous system pathways, pulsed fields were much more effective than continuous radiation. Radio-frequency signals, ultrasound signals piggybacked on radio or television signals or just transmitted through the air—all could work.

The Soviets were clever about using atmospheric electricity to suppress the mental activity of large populations and tuning sonic generators to infrasound to create feelings of depression, fear, panic, terror, and despair. Jam thinking the same way signals from a radio transmitter could be jammed to stimulate fear and confusion. No one, not even the Germans, could match the Soviets for their psychotronic weapons research.

He wanted to read the patents on the FBI Division 5's ultrasonic intracerebral control (USIC) device, but it would have to wait. They had arrived at the playroom. Charlie handed him his night-vision goggles. In the control room filled with computers and operators, an infrared-illumined fishbowl of naked men and women going at each other tooth and nail.

Charlie leaned toward Dr. Greenbaum. "A few big wheels are flying in tonight to see the night moves out on the mountainside before they play their own Most Dangerous Game tomorrow—you know, the human hunt. Out on the mountainside we'll see some play for real stakes."

Greenbaum grimaced, despising Americans for their crassness. Men hunting down national security females like Baby Rose offended his sensibilities, and yet it got the appropriations he needed for science. He made a mental note to call Sibelius as soon as possible regarding his geographic intuition about Saint-Germain.

28

Vicente Liputzli

I have used the term Celtic Church instead of Gallic Church to refer to the Christians in the south of France. I have done this deliberately as otherwise one forgets that the Church in Gaul and that in Britain were sister churches of the same family, having as their common tradition the fact that they were founded by St. Joseph of Arimathea when he came by boat to Marseilles with the Virgin Mary, Mary Magdalen, Martha and Lazarus, Mary Cleophas, Mary Salome, Maximen, Cleon, Trophimus, Saturnin, Martilla, Sedony, Eutrope and Martial.

–Michael Gabriel, *The Holy Valley and the Holy Mountain*, 1994

To give notice that the Modern Green-ribboned Cabal, together with the ancient brotherhood of the Rosy-Cross: the Hermetic Adepti and the company of Accepted Masons…

–Announcement, 1641

O cursed spite,
That ever I was born to set it right.

–Hamlet, Act I, Scene 5

It was one o'clock checkout time at the Wigwam Motel in San Bernardino and the Mexican maid was knocking at tipi number 19. She needed to clean. Inside, all the pilgrims but one—the Colonel being outside doing slow and easy laps in the pool—began righting themselves from the floor and beds to the vertical business of the day. Once the bus and Caddy were packed up, they joined the Colonel for a few laps and splashes, throwing the Frisbee for Sirius to retrieve. Southern California was already stovetop hot. They could hear a Phil Ochs song playing from someone's radio—

> *My life is now a myth to me*
> *Like the drifter with his laughter in the dawn.*
> *My life is now a death to me*
> *So I'll mold it and I'll hold it till I'm born*
> *So I turned to the land*
> *Where I'm so out of place*
> *Throw a curse on the plan*
> *In return for the grace*
> *To know where I stand*
> *Take everything I own*
> *Take your tap from my phone*
> *And leave my life alone*
> *My life alone*

As they sat down to tea, cinnamon and honey *tortillas*, and fruit, Mannie wondered about Phil's line *Take your tap from my phone*. It was then that the Colonel noticed a short young man with a huge pack walking east along Route 66.

"Maybe we could ease his burden for a while," he said, pointing.

Thomas glanced in the direction the Colonel indicated. "Good idea," he said, standing up, "let's hit it."

And that was how they met Vicente "Vince" Liputzli, the Mayan Timekeeper whose presence would change everything. Vince heaved his heavy pack into the back of the bus, Mannie moved to the Caddy backseat with Baby Rose, and Vince took his place next to Thomas.

His t-shirt was emblazoned with a cross dedicated to the Lord of the Four Winds and around his neck swung a *xiquipilli* or medicine bag. From his mother, he'd received his Mayan surname and a face like a dark full moon. His father, *por otra*, was a distant Castilian cousin of Queen Isabella. Throughout his childhood, he'd wondered how his paternal grandfather, a judge in the Corte Suprema de Justicia, could call Mexico home and yet send his son and daughters to *madre Espagne* for schooling and import Andalusians to tend his horses. The truth was that in his heart the old man had never left Spain and despised the dark indios who cooked his food, nursed his children, drove his car, and kept his gardens. That his only son Emilio set his sights on an *indio* woman, albeit from a respectable Chiapan family without an ounce of revolt in their blood, had surely been God's justice. The indignity hit the old man like the bus that paralyzed the crazy *puta* artist living in sin with the Communist pig Rivera. But when Emilio brought Esperanza (her confirmation name) to the *hacienda* for Sunday dinners and holidays while they were both still anthropology graduate students at the National University in Mexico City, the old man saw how hopeless it would be to resist. Her dark beauty and quiet ways had captured his son's heart so completely that all he could do was relent, reasoning that a little Mayan blood in grandsons might be politically advantageous by the time the *norteamericanos* merged Mexico with the United States and Canada.

Over the years, Vince had heard so much about his parents' wedding that he almost felt like he'd been there. All of Veracruz society was invited, and strange *anglos* in white suits came from Texas, Washington, DC, and Philadelphia. Relatives with fabulous gifts in tow arrived from Europe and South America by luxury liner, caviar was flown in from Paris, chefs from Madrid and Buenos Aires. A grand bullfight with a white bull from Venezuela was held in the large corral. Pico de Orizaba's snowy summit sparkled above a ring of cloud. Yes, the old man said to his guests, the old gods were smiling on this union of old Europe and old Mexico.

Emilio's family bent over backwards not to treat Esperanza and her family as poor relations, though everyone knew that was what they were. The old man's genius had been to hold the wedding not in the grand old church in Xalapa but in the chapel he and his father had built for the *campesinos*. He had had new vestments made for the priest and the stucco dwelling of God filled to overflowing with flowers. Emilio had been surprised by his father's beneficence and at first thought he had gone too far when he heard they would be married in the *campesino* chapel—he was, after all, his father's son—but when he saw how happy it made his bride and her family and the old servants he had known since he was a boy, he realized that his father had wisely exercised a democratic *gesture*, a show, really, a spectacle for the blink of an afternoon, worth the discomfort of Veracruz *patrones* who did not understand and still clung to the old fanfare and divisions and obeisance that earned them secret hatred and plots. The old man was no fool. He had studied how *el norte* people were made to feel free and equal with mere words and sentiment so they then paid and obeyed with little complaint. Anglo leaders glutted their people with cheap goods and cheaper Hollywood thrills, not dissimilar to what the Catholic Church had achieved for centuries. In Central and South America, Jesuits still handled agreements with *norteamericanos* and *británicos*.

So it was that the wedding between Emilio and Esperanza drew mangos from everyone's tongues, thanks to the old man's philosophy of *Cuando los hombres hablen mal de ti, vive de tal manera que nadie les crea* (When people gossip about you, live your life in a way that discredits what they say.) No one remembered that it was not a good match, only that it was a wondrous wedding and the bride so beautiful. So when the union bore the fruit of one girl and then another, people smiled and sucked their teeth, holding their breath for the Mayan woman with a face like a moon. With the birth of Vicente, everyone breathed easy again. Esperanza had proven herself, so it was a good match, after all. But the singular son with no plural caused the silence around her to deepen, like a fallow field birds no longer visit, and it was in that silence that Vicente grew until silence was mother's milk to him, a strange and loud silence that took him years to understand.

And when Esperanza's father spent more and more time with Vicente, the whispers turned to, *No hay peor cuña que la del mismo palo* (The worst wedge is that taken from the same tree). But as for being the worst wedge, the whisperers were wrong. Vicente was by far the best, and his maternal grandfather knew exactly who he was. Vince's Mayan grandfather had studied the 12-headed serpent at Chichén-Itzá in Yucatan, heads representing the Maya dynasties that had reigned for 18,000 years before the Can dynasty, Mayan calendars being nothing if not exact. The last King Can, according to the Troano Manuscript, lived 16,000 years ago. As the *Ramayana* said, *In olden times there was a prince of the Nagas whose name was Maya*. Prince Maya, according to the Calendar, lived 18,900 years before the present era and wrote the *Sourya Saddhanta*, the Indian treatise on astronomy.

Vince's anthropologist father Emilio taught his son that when the Catholic Church attempted to wipe from the face of the Earth the heretical Albigenses, Cathars, and Bogomils—remnants of the 3rd century movement known as Manichæism—their *perfecti* had gone underground or, more exactly, *understream*. Emilio had taken Vicente to a vast estate southeast of Mexico City, the home of a wealthy Spaniard whose library had its own fireproof building. There, he viewed machine-printed books from the 1200s on paper with elaborate watermarks, headpieces, and colophons. The 1200s were the era of European guilds, many born in the secretive Provence district of France. The German printing press would not be printing the Gutenberg Bible for the Protestant Reformation until 1450, but privately circulated books had been printed for centuries on the Chinese presses invented in 145 AD. *Understream* movements always have their own printing devices, the Spaniard told Vicente, as well as their own paper and watermarks. Cathedrals, libraries, and tombs received their own obscure markings from the traveling craftsmen. He showed Vicente scores of curious editions on alchemy, cabalism, magic, Rosicrucian histories, all written under pseudonyms or by *Anon Nymous*, with ornate ciphers, emblems and symbols. One watermark was a vase or jug, which the Spaniard felt referred to either the Holy Grail or the Waterbearer of the Aquarian age due in a thousand years.

The 13th century was filled to overflowing with troubadours, jongleurs, actors, Minnesingers, Meistersingers, peddlers and craftsmen all wandering Europe. *These heretic foxes*, said Pope Gregory IX, *have different faces, but they all hang together by the tails.* Many of the themes in the tales told, sung, acted, and finally printed revolved around how Death comes for us all, rich and poor, high and low, and how spiritual treasures are the only treasures that last. Pope and peasant, king and beggar dance to Death's tune. Robin Hood of the 14th century, like El Zorro of the 19th century, stood for the free life of honor that rights the wrongs meted out by the world's powerful.

"These tales were not contrived by individuals to be fictions for their own taste or career," the Spaniard explained to Vicente, "they were written with purpose by individuals tasked by secret societies to quicken in the people ideas about their dual mortal and immortal condition: the Aquarian urn at work. Thus were democratic visions fostered during feudal times—visions," the Spaniard looked meaningfully at Vicente's father, "shaped by secret societies to shape what is to come."

Grasping his friend's cryptic intent, Emilio had asked Vicente to go out to the car for something, and by the time he had returned with whatever it was, their discussion had reached its climax and moved on. Only a few months later would he learn from his father that he and the Spaniard had been plotting a troubadour mission for him. In fact, it was after that conversation that his preparation by his maternal grandfather and father had begun in earnest.

Vicente was schooled in all the religions, first by his grandfather and then by two shamans, male and female, of separate ancient schools, one the *nagualisme* path of the *brujo*, the other of the *curandera*. He did not have to become a *brujo* but had to grasp the worldview that was still alive and well, slithering on its belly through international politics and a degenerate Catholic Church. As for the art of the *curandero*, body and soul went together and he sought to know how to heal both from Nature's resources. Both shamanic schools of thought and practice counterbalanced his university studies in the history and sciences of the West.

The *brujo's* parentage was Brazilian and Austrian. From him, Vicente learned that most evil was the necessary outcome of forcing something that once served a good purpose in its own Time into another Time after its purpose had expired. The Catholic Church, *nagualisme*, and Freemasonry met that criterion. All had served human destiny in their time and now had sunk to evil, *satanisme*, due to the what all shamans worth their salt had recognized since the 1930s, namely that the cosmic Second Coming of Christ seeding individual consciousness was imminent. Continuing to corral the people within the strictures of decrepit hierarchic structures spelled the institutional evil of the Egregore. The challenge now was to help people transition from decrepit institutions to becoming individually responsible.

With so much freedom came so much spiritual responsibility! No wonder many were frightened and sought to cling to the old ways. Degeneration among the priests and governors—especially the pedophlia—exposed just how bankrupt the old was, and how necessary it was to institute new mandates for another millennium until the Sun's Vernal rising was no longer in the Fishes but in the Aquarian Baptizer. "We are living in a transition time and many errors will be made," Vicente's father insisted, "but just because the tailwind promises a bumpy ride is no reason not to take the airplane if it is moving in the right direction."

The *brujo* had then passed him along to other old ones from Mexico to Peru— Indian, Spanish, French, German. "Go and meet your people," his grandfather had advised on the telephone, "travel as they do, eat as they do, learn who they are and what they know. Honor them for being what they are but do not sleep or dream your way through them. Keep your sword of discernment sharpened by writing, and always ask yourself, *What is their source?*"

In the upper Amazon, he'd learned puma medicine and that the difference between good and evil shamans was not morality but *voltage*, the example being Christ, Who, the good shamans said, was the most powerful generator they encountered *up there*, and they pointed to space—not the docile Jesus taught by the churches, they stressed, but the cosmic Christ, the true galaxy generator. A Peruvian shaman taught Vince power songs he had learned *up there* with Christ, saying that despite their grumbling, shamans in his area had to admit that his *ayahuasqa* brew and songs produced the most powerful journey. With his songs, he was able to divert sorcery attacks, return spiritual darts to their origins, and neutralize his enemies' allies, all without killing or maiming them or their families. Those who chose evil hated his songs.

When a shaman fell prey to sorcerers, he had only to call on his galaxy generator. Yes, the Jaguar was still a powerful ally, but Christ was the ultimate defense. Everyone knew this, the teachers said, but some resisted it, which was why the spiritual war raging now had become particularly ugly. Some of the ugliest resisters, they whispered, are in the Catholic and Christian churches which did not want a real cosmic Christ, only a Jesus they could use for power over the people.

Early on, thanks to his Western university training, Vince had been in doubt about what the shamans taught and if Amazonian *chamanismo* had been tainted by Christian imagery. Nor had he at that time experienced the cosmic Christ they spoke of. *Learn who they are and what they know, and always ask, What is their source?* But surely a shaman knew more about invisible spiritual things than university professors. And if a *curandero* was still able to practice his ancient faith *and* call upon the cosmic Christ . . . To doubt those who had guided hundreds if not thousands into spiritual realms and kept them safe struck Vicente as foolish, so he cast his university bias aside. In spiritual things, all is possible. What if the Church was now actively *blocking the experience of the cosmic Christ? What had pedophile priests in a stale medieval Church to do with the mangod who could say Except ye become as a little child, ye shall not enter the Kingdom of Heaven?*

Vicente had partaken of *yopo*, the vine that had borne *vegetale* witness to everything from the beginning of Earth Time, whose DNA

35

could awaken DNA and share the Earth's memory—

Daime is Daime
The Professor of Professors
It's the Divine Eternal Father
And his Redeemer Son.

With *yopo's* assistance, he'd visited heavens and hells in *O Astral* and seen for himself how psychic states were warring over the human soul and that the human soul was to all sorts of beings worthy of holy warfare lasting millennia—worthy of the cosmic Christ's entry into it. *You are children*, a being with a gargoyle face explained to him outside the gates of one hell, *we make you strong by means of resistance. We too serve your species for the sake of free will. Remember us when you come into your kingdom . . .*

But on this first day with his new friends, Vince mentioned none of this. When Thomas asked where he was going, Vince said east. He had been in Lake Elsinore the night before to visit the therapeutic waters at the Crescent Bath House built by Freemason Franklin Heald in 1888. From his bulging pack, he extracted a bottle of the therapeutic water and shared it with Ray, Thomas, and Sirius. Actors had performed *Hamlet* in the bathhouse lobby, he said, with its aging oriental splendor of paneled walls and Turkish carpets. The play had moved him deeply, in part because it was performed at Lake Elsinore.

"I read in the program that the real Elsinore Castle was Kronborg Castle near Port Helsingør," Vince explained, "rebuilt by Frederick II, patron of Tycho Brahe."

"Tycho Brahe, the astronomer and alchemist?" Thomas asked, checking to make sure the two-way was on. Vince definitely had his attention now.

"The same. Frederick II's daughter Anne of Denmark married King James I of England—James Charles Stuart, King James VI of Scotland—who ascended the English throne in 1603 when Elizabeth I died." He looked meaningfully at Thomas. He recognized this *anglo* from another Time.

Thomas glanced back at him, surprised. "*Hamlet*, Elsinore, Tycho Brahe, James I—all were connected to the great Rosicrucian hijack by Freemasonry. Go on."

Vince took a breath. In the telling would be the seeing. "Exactly. A highjack that actually began in Italy before 1622, when Pico della Mirandola—"

Yes! Thomas thought. *The seen and unseen together constitute Nature.*

"—forsook the individual soul for the world soul, rejected scientific method for a Qabalist manipulation of symbols, and decided Moses and his Egyptian wisdom were superior to relationship with Christ."

Over the two-way, Mannie was carefully listening. Uncle Eli said the Red Sea was really the Reed Sea and Moses a great magus trained in Egyptian temples.

Vince went on. "Given the distortions of the Roman Catholic Church, it was understandable that Pico would long for the individual freedom to wield natural law in order to experience the forces behind Nature. Contemplating a Christ-embodied Earth far in the future was not enough for him. Pico's ideas appealed to thinkers grinding their teeth over how the Church had for centuries persecuted Neoplatonism and intellectual freedom. England had broken with the Church in Rome, Protestantism was on the move, clever Venetians were pouring Qabala mysticism and necromancy into England—all while the consciousness soul was struggling to be born."

"'Consciousness soul?'" Thomas interrupted.

Vince nodded. "The consciousness soul. Have you read the Austrian initiate?"

"Who?"

"The consciousness soul is the next evolutionary step beyond the intellectual soul that documents, analyzes, and files. The consciousness soul plumbs the depth behind facts, the patterns and what they *mean*. Europe then was gripped in a tremendous transition; what appeared to be, was not, and what had not yet quite appeared, was. Intrigue was rampant around Elizabeth I as various contenders, many of them Jesuit-trained, wrestled with the angel delivering the consciousness soul to humankind through the Anglo-Saxon nation."

Thomas was in awe of Vince's knowledge. "The consciousness soul out of England . . . It's hard to believe, given what it's become."

Vince was almost as excited as Thomas to have someone to talk to about the European side of his esoteric life. "Shakespeare is taught in schools but not the playwright Christopher Marlowe. Could it be because he was martyred on May 30, 1593—in the Julian calendar, that would have been 3/30 or 3/3/93—for revealing too much about the factions warring beneath the surface of the Renaissance over Europe's Faustian soul?

"As for the 'Rosicrucian hijack' you mentioned, new stars actually appeared in the constellations Serpentarius and Cygnus, portending the *Chymical Wedding* above and the royal wedding below between the Rhine and the Thames, between Frederick, Elector Palatine of Bohemia (now Czechoslovakia), and Elizabeth, daughter of James I and Anne. Like the peace movement arising today, the one in Bohemia was based on a true Christian ethos that welcomed all religious denominations *and* alchemical studies of Nature. Microcosm and macrocosm were both studied and valued and inductively conceived according to God's various earthly scripts, including mathematical-magical systems."

Thomas felt Vince's sadness. "Had the wedding between Frederick and Elizabeth been allowed to occur, imagine how society might be. Instead, materialism from the split between science and religion has engulfed us."

"So true," Vince lamented, "and four centuries before, Languedoc had been set upon by the Great Whore of Rome to wrest control of true Christianity from the reach of Christian initiates."

In the Cadillac, Seven, the Colonel, and Mannie were riveted on the learned Mayan. Languedoc! A utopic society sacred to Visigoths and Jews, Templars and Cathars—where Mary Magdalene was believed to have walked, where the language of the heavens was scribed in the

Earth, and all had hoped to live in peace and plenty.

Vince's voice grew sad. "And just as the Roman Church marched on Montségur in 1244 and destroyed the threat of a Christ-engendered peaceful community, so in Bohemia 376 years later—"

Thomas did a quick computation: the square root of 376 was 19.4 years, a Metonic cycle.

"—on November 8, 1620, Frederick lost the Battle of the White Mountain that began the Thirty Years War. James I was under the thumb of Francis Bacon and refused to come to the aid of his daughter and son-in-law."

"Bacon was the founder of the sixth great Empire of the Western world, the New Atlantis of America," Thomas inserted.

Vince went silent, overcome by his own words. A Hermetic cabalist, Bacon had wanted nothing to mediate man and Nature. Whereas authentic Rosicrucians viewed the human being as half if not more of the *Chymical Wedding* between macrocosm and microcosm and longed to redeem magic by merging it with natural science, Bacon sought to vanquish any taint of mystical experience with hard knowledge.

The Colonel's voice came over the two-way. "A high-degree Mason told me that Bacon's descendant Nathaniel Bacon brought a sequel of Bacon's *New Atlantis* to Jamestown in 1653. Nathaniel was the one behind the rebellion in 1676, fifty years after Francis Bacon's death and one hundred before the Declaration of Independence."

Thomas added, "My uncle mentioned that it was buried in Williamsburg beneath the tower of the first brick church in Bruton Parish. Bruton Vault, they call it."

"Everywhere we look, something or someone is secretly buried or cached for Freemason purposes," the Colonel groused.

Vince was ready to continue. "Through Bacon, England's most gifted man once Marlowe was dead, the British consciousness soul turned away from Central Europe's Bohemian Rosicrucian revolution and toward shadowy nationalism. Three hundred years later, under George VI and Elizabeth II, England would still be destroying Central

Europe and its Goethean 'otherworldly romanticism.'"

"And now through Tavistock and MI6, Freemasons all," Thomas interjected, "England still works to undermine, control, and divert the latest flowering of consciousness and community."

Vince was elated by the rare high level of conversation. "Few realize that Freemasonry and the British Royal Society arose from utopic ashes, Freemasonry from the inner, the British Royal Society from the outer continuation of Francis Bacon's legacy. Bacon left Dee to die in poverty in 1608, just as the equally magical Tesla was left to die 333 years later. But the worst was the despoliation of the Rose."

"Ah, Tesla," Thomas murmured, missing the Rose reference.

In the Cadillac, Seven softly touched the blue rose above her head in the sun visor.

"The power of the Catholic Church was formidable," Vince went on. "For example, in 13th century Toulouse Bible-reading by laymen was an Inquisitional crime. Gutenberg's invention of the printing press wasn't until 1453, and it wasn't until eight times eight years later on October 31, 1517 that Martin Luther posted his 95 theses on the door of the Palast Church in Wittenberg and challenged the authority of the Catholic Church over individual minds. Not two years later, the Catholic Spaniard Hernando Cortés was sent to Tenochtitlan, and the Catholic Charles V, the last emperor to be crowned by a pope, was twice crowned Holy Roman Emperor, first at Aix-la-Chapelle and then at Bologna, after which he speedily reestablished the Catholic Knights of St. John on Malta. Halley's comet skidded across the skies in 1531 and spawned the Portuguese Inquisition, war in Switzerland between Protestants and Catholics, and Henry VIII as Supreme Head of the Church in England. Enter the Catholic Spaniard Ignatius Loyola with a Knights of St. John mandate to counter the Reformation that undermined priestly power by allowing individuals to read the Bible for themselves."

Seven was thinking *Knowledge is the only real earthly power, not money*m, and *history is an intricate tapestry of truths, secrets, and lies* when the

40

20th century intercepted their brief hiatus in another Time with scraggly longhaired hitchhikers hoping for a ride. Thomas pulled behind her while the couple and their packs squeezed into the Caddy backseat with Mannie and Baby Rose.

The longhair in his late twenties lit a Winston and said he and his old lady just needed a few miles to the 395 cut off. Seven push-buttoned all the windows open. Oblivious, the longhair continued the threads of a dark conversation he and his high school-looking girlfriend had been engaged in while standing on the side of the road.

"No, the Manson thing didn't just 'happen.' From the start, it was set up to scare the shit out of middle class America." He looked at his girlfriend. "You don't remember that tabloid *Real Paper* paid for by the Process Church attorney hired by that Weld U.S. Attorney?" He gesticulated dramatically. "Vietnam was a bad moon on the rise, so the corporate media started selling pretty little flower girls like you as evil Satanic distractions."

His girlfriend grinned. "And beautiful Sharon Tate married to Mr. Rosemary's Baby."

"And Anton LaVey playing Satan while Rosemary's Baby was born June 15, 1968," her boyfriend grinned back.

She lit a Winston from his and sucked it deep into her lungs like marijuana, footnoting breathlessly, "And Sharon Tate's baby died August 8, 1969."

Baby Rose cringed in the corner of the Caddy's backseat, gripping Mannie's hand like death. Seven glanced at the Colonel, sorry she'd picked up the speed freaks in their own weird world, glad it would be a short ride.

The young man swept his dishwater blond hair out of his eyes. "Scorpio Charlie was Scientology, Process Church, Solar Lodge OTO, CIA, and MI6 all rolled up in a big nationwide Satanic network. He was Four Pi and the Grand Chignon was some rich LA doctor—a split, man, between the sensual Luciferians and the bloodthirsty Satanists going by the stars, with a fancy wooden altar and sacrificial knife with six blades.

I heard about it in the joint. Thieves, dope dealers, even killers don't go in for that weird Satanic shit or killing innocent chicks and kids, and they're heavy on guys who do."

"I heard Charlie had 150 hours of Scientology programming at McNeil Island Penitentiary in Washington State," his girlfriend said.

"Yeah, in '61. Poor bastard was in prisons his whole life, until the late Fifties and early Sixties when some kingpins got hold of him and suddenly he was studying Freemasonry and going to the prison psychiatrist all the time. Then he was cut loose so that de Grimston chick could teach him how to sculpt *fear* and introduce America to the triumph of the predatory Beast and calculated savagery. After he got out, he made a beeline for Scientology's Celebrity Center in Hollywood to contact two stars, the Beach Boy and Doris Day's son, all while undergoing heavy programming through The Process Church, the British offshoot of Scientology. Before the Sun sacrifices up on Sky Drive, Bobby Beausoleil—beautiful Sun, man—was shacked up with Kenneth Anger, and after the sacrifices he sat in prison and composed the music for Anger's film *Lucifer Rising*, then played Lucifer."

He took a drag and held the smoke down, speaking breathlessly. "All the time he was in Death Valley, Charlie was obsessed with the underground world of *vril* in Bulwer-Lytton's 19th century *The Coming Race*. Who taught him that, huh? Death Valley is the lowest, driest, hottest place in the United States. The Indians say it's a spirit-filled underworld. Stones move there. No, I'm serious—zigzags and swirls in the morning that weren't there the night before. Maybe wind, but huge fucking rocks? And what moves wind, anyway? Charlie tripped on Devil's Hole, a pit of dark water filled with blindfish. He had all of the Family on hole patrol looking for the hidden entry to the underworld." He exhaled and almost no smoke came out. "One Metonic cycle since Parsons and Hubbard cracked open the portal in the Mojave Desert. Charlie wanted one in Death Valley."

Mannie thought of George Reeves in *Superman and the Mole Men*. The longhair's girlfriend took a hairbrush from her bag and viciously brushed her hair. "*Weird* how he went to prison without laying a hand on those rich bitches. Charlie *Watson*, the mind-controlled fall guy from Texas, did the 44 stabs and wrote DEATH TO THE PIGS on the door. He was the set-up Man Son, wasn't he, honey?"

"Wat*son* and Man*son*, dig? Both Charlie's, W and M or just two M's for Mary Magdalene or Master Masons." He grinned, then leaned over the front seat gesturing toward the radio and commanded, "Turn on Mae Brussell, KLRB in Carmel by the Sea, 101.7. Turn it on, she'll be there." He leaned back, confident. "This is the magical desert, man."

Curious, Seven flicked the dial to 101.7 and like he said, there was Mae.

". . . the summer of '67 and something very big was coming to a head," the queen of research was saying. "Magnetic storms were buffeting the Earth atmosphere and cosmic rays were decreasing as admissions to psychiatric wards were increasing. It was a time of intense energy some people could handle, some couldn't.

"The cutting edge Sixties generation were high not just on psychedelics but on sharing housing, food, gas money, and rapping about everything under the Sun. It was a revolution not just in hairstyle, clothing, and non-cosmetics but in the values governing transportation and housing, an economic and sociological revolution affecting all of capitalism—the medical and grocery industries, land use, zoning. Many of the largest generation in history were living together, working together, sharing resources, giving each other rides, growing their own food, delivering babies, recycling and making their own clothes, refusing to eat animals and dairy industry products. They were meeting outdoors and breaking free of religion and generation boundaries. Divide and conquer was melting away like old film, beauty spreading as if the Bomb hanging over their heads didn't matter anymore. All that mattered was the moment and the day and each other . . ."

Like a summer storm, the hitchhiker's girlfriend broke into tears. "Tell it, Mae," she said, sniffling and wiping her eyes. "Those fuckers are picking us off one by one. It was too beautiful, too good, and they couldn't make enough bread off of us. They use our music and the Haight and make it sound like we're bringing ourselves down. They did Charlie. Fuckers!" she cried vehemently, her hands shaking. "They can't stand it when it's good, can't stand us getting it together, can't stand us *high*."

Her boyfriend folded her into his arms.

Mae talked about August 9 and the 44 stabs, the hairdresser Jay Sebring, Roman Polanski's friend from Poland Wojtek Frykowski and his coffee heiress girlfriend Abigail Folger, and Steve Parent, the 18-year-old caretaker's guest. The day after the grizzly murders, wealthy Leno and Rosemary La Bianca were stabbed to death in the Los Feliz section at 3301 Waverly Drive. Both crimes were military operations, Mae said. Nobody heard a sound, the dogs were quiet, the caretaker slept through the guns and screams. Someone had shimmied up the poles and cut the wires with precision. Hoods and ropes on their necks, signs and symbols laid out to scapegoat Black Panthers and hippies. No one saw a getaway car.

Ed Butler, tight with Lee Harvey Oswald, wrote the first article about the Manson thing. Ed wrote for Patrick Frawley of Schick Razor and Technicolor, a big far right supporter of Nixon. Gene Tunney at 52 Vanderbilt in New York was on the Schick board with Frawley. In the same building as Schick Razor and Technicolor was Long John Nebel's radio show. Nebel was married to Candy Jones, one of the early MK-ULTRA Presidential Models.

Mae reeled off December 1969 headlines: "3 Suspects in Tate Case Tied to Guru"; "Accused Killers Live Nomad Life with Magnetic Guru"; "Hypnotic Killers—Hippie Bands, They're Controlled by an Evil Genius"; "A Move to Indict God"; "The D.A. Asks Hippie-Cult Indictment"; "Inside the Desert-Cult Hideout— Family Members Talk of Black Magic, Sex, Murder"; "Charles Manson—Nomadic Guru, Flirted with Crime"; "Hippie Family Member Describes the Murder"; "Hippie Satan Clan is Indicted"; "Leader of a Hippie Cult Held in Isolated Cell"; "The Hippie Mystique"; "The Love and Terror Cult, The Dark Edge of Hippie Life"; "Manson's Race Theory Rested on the Beatles."

"Tell it, Mae," the longhair nodded, "Ed Butler played *agent provocateur* sent to spin the murders. Out at the Manson commune in Death Valley were lookout points, telescopes, walkie-talkies, 4-wheel drives—expensive, man, like the cameras and walkie-talkies, electronic devices, and security clearance Oswald had. And then there was that high-powered Beverly Hills attorney that met with Manson in '67 just before he got out of prison—same lawyer for both Charlie's, you dig? Charlie's fresh out of prison and overnight he has a big bus and credit cards and is friends with big Hollywood and Laurel Canyon stars. Who paid for the food for twenty or thirty chicks? Who paid for the machine guns, the walkie-talkies, the 4-wheel drives? Follow the money, man. Same with James Earl Ray: out of jail and a car and on his way to Canada." Vehemently, he tapped his temple. "No one *thinks* anymore, man."

He lit another Winston off his girlfriend's Winston. "And on the December 19, 1967 cover of *Life* magazine—not the Pentagon Papers or the suits or military brass up to their asses in Southeast Asia heroin deals, hauling it back in body bags. No, it's Charlie the ex-con scapegoat with mind-controlled crazy eyes—Charlie who hated being called a hippie. Sue Atkins made 150 fucking thousand dollars by turning state's evidence against Manson. Her lawyer was with the Warren Commission, and the lawyers who ran Sirhan Sirhan and Jack Ruby were in on the Manson thing, too. Shit!" He called out to the radio, "Mae, don't forget the Baroness Mama Cass Elliot and how deep into their drugs she got—Charlie, Pic Dawson's daddy-o was State Department—William Mentzer or Phil Benson, whatever his name was, the so-called Manson II with his buddy Marti, a former Argentine death squad leader. No wonder Mama Cass was killed for what she knew, going to Democratic Party functions saying she was thinking about running for senator. Is that what they baited her with?"

Mannie was puzzled. Mama Cass? When had she died?

The girl looked up, her mascara still running. "Didn't Mama Cass play the witch in that NBC movie 'H.R. Puff'n'Stuff'?"

Her boyfriend hooted. "Oh man, I loved it. They must have

45

been stoned when they did it. Remember Jimmy with the magic flute?"

"Yeah! Cass turned him into Robotic Jimmy—"

Her boyfriend turned robot. "'I'm a mechanical boy just like a mechanical toy. I follow directions, I do what I'm told, I never grow hot and I never grow cold. That's 'cause I'm a mechanical boy just like a mechanical toy. I never get older, I never can die, but I never can laugh and I never can cry.'"

The two looked at each other and laughed until the tears rolled. Happily, Seven had reached 395 and pulled over.

Back in the bus, Ray had only half-listened to the Mayan but had definitely listened to the speed freaks. Shamans, group experimentation with sensory deprivation, chanting mantras, and focusing on interior bodily sensations to the exclusion of outer stimuli weren't his bag. Some professor back East had an epiphany that he was the reincarnation of the fire god Vulcan, Jesus Christ, and Ulysses S. Grant all rolled into one and set up a commune called Minerva Nueva after the Roman virgin goddess of wisdom and war. It smelled like an intelligence operation to Ray Man.

But while listening, he'd recalled a rap he had with one of the Fugs at an LA party before the Tate-La Bianca murders. The Fug said a chick named Georgina "Jean" Bray gave Solar Lodge clones every psychedelic known to man—marijuana, LSD, Demerol, scopolamine, datura, jimson weed, ether, belladonna—not for consciousness-raising or grooving but for tests, man, and documented them like lab rats. When Ray asked what Solar Lodge was, the Fug said it was international—Order of the Solar Temple, *l'Ordre International Chevaleresque de Tradition Solaire*, aka Sovereign Order of the Solar Temple aka *l'Ordre Souverain du Temple Solaire*—all the same thing, and all *Crowley*.

The Riverside Solar Lodge of the OTO, Eye of Horus aka the Solar Temple Lodge, set up headquarters in Los Angeles near the University of Southern California campus in late 1966. In summer 1967, Bray assigned some members to the Mojave Desert while others continued running both the OTO book store at 1918 West Eighth

Street and the Rockfield gas station at 3401 South Flower. In the desert off Highway 95 between Vidal and Blythe, along the Arizona border, they began constructing an Ark while opening a tavern, motel, store and gas station in Vidal and a bookstore in Blythe. Drugs, sex, Masonic rituals, psychodrama and terror tactics programmed them for *inner circle* objectives, inner circle referring to military intelligence agents in Parker remotely directing the cult via the little transmitter-receivers two cult dentists at USC Dental School had implanted in their teeth.

On July 26, 1969, six-year-old Saul Gibbons was found chained to a cage on the Ark commune property. Two weeks later, the Manson Family murders occurred a few miles away. The trial for the eleven Ark commune members charged with felony child abuse opened in Indio on Halloween. But Bray wasn't there: the CIA had already whisked her to Ensenada, Argentina. Its name thus tainted, the Solar Lodge became the Velle Transcendental Research Association, Inc., a True, Universal Brotherhood paying homage to Freemasonry and magically invoking Thoth to call forth a tribunal before Horus, Lord of the Aeon, to protect their search for true freedom and understanding, etc.

At that point, some creepy-looking cat in black had come up saying some shit like As it is, so be it and the Fug shut up. Ray had seen cats in black like him in Haight coffee houses draped in old velvet curtains, dour longhairs sitting at second-hand tables with candles, John Renbourn and Pentangle records providing hip ambience, everyone drinking herbal tea while upstairs shit was going down in a black Sabbath red and black ritual chamber with a big leering Goat of Mendes on the wall. He didn't know if it was true or not but had no desire to find out; being tied up in the backroom of a voodoo front store as a kid had been enough for him.

So Charlie Manson strumming his acoustic guitar, chanting *Da da da da da* and singing about Lucifer, was Process. Manson, Crowley and his OTO, Hubbard and his Dianetics, the Beatles and their Maharishi, all tripping on Satanic Process shit. Even in 1930, Menninger in *The Human Mind* said that Satanists were holding Black Masses in big European and U.S. cities, not to mention Mexico. Ray knew one thing: evil was more than ignorance, though it depended on ignorance for maintaining power. Some thought Satanism was about rebelling against Western conventions and so joined trips like the Process or Church of Satan, listened to nihilistic rock, and took speed—but not Ray Man. Political was his middle name and he had a nose for intelligence operations.

The weird hitchhikers sent on their way, Seven still had the Caddy windows down, airing out the smoke and Manson talk. Mannie was reading a celebrity magazine he'd found at the motel pool. When Baby Rose pointed to the photo of psychic Jeane Dixon, he turned down the corner of the page. Thomas said they needed all the clues to Baby Rose's past they could get, at least until she started talking again. James Taylor was singing "Mexico" on the radio—

> *Way down here you need a reason to move*
> *Feel a fool running your stateside games*
> *Lose your load, leave your mind behind, Baby James . . .*

Mannie read on, humming the mellow tune. Dixon and her family had operated a gas station and grocery store right there in San Bernardino in 1919. Her birth name in 1904 was Lydia Pinckert. Born with a Star of David and a half moon on her palm, she was programmed by a German Jesuit priest in crystallomancy when she was eight. A conservative Catholic, she hobnobbed with Billy Graham and had a telepathic cat called MagiCat. Every morning she faced east and recited the 23rd Psalm, *Yea, though I walk through the valley of the shadow of Death,* then went to Mass. She'd syncretized the Zodiac with the Apostles: Peter was Aries, Simon Zelotes Taurus, James the Lesser Gemini, Andrew Cancer, John the Beloved Leo, etc. According to Dixon, Judas Iscariot was a Pisces.

Mannie was a Pisces.

At 22, she married a 37-year-old Swiss superintendent, then in the Forties moved to Washington, DC with yet another husband handler, James Lamb Dixon, a dollar-a-year man acquiring and overseeing warehouses for the government. Dixon did readings for President Roosevelt.

Hmm. Mannie marked that, too. Mrs. Franklin Pierce and Mary Todd Lincoln had sought out mediums. Even banks sought Dixon's psychic skills, and she was good at "foretelling" deaths: FDR, UN Secretary General Dag Hammerskjold, the three Apprentice astronauts, JFK in a vision she had in 1952. In fact, her last JFK prophecy was given on Long John Nebel's New York radio show. The year before Louisiana Senator Hale Boggs disappeared over Alaska, he received an anonymous letter about Dixon marking Democrats for murder or bodily harm.

Whatever else she was, she was a real moneymaker: an astrology column, New Year predictions, books on Jesus and horoscope cooking, dial-a-horoscope—all siphoned through phony foundations. Because she said 5, 7, and 9 were good numbers and 4 and 8 not, Nancy Reagan marked Ronnie's calendar accordingly with green ink for good days, red for not, and yellow for iffy.

Seven and the Colonel were listening to Vince over the two-way. During the intermission at the *Hamlet* play, he'd overheard a Spaniard and a Mexican priest talking about the difference between Jesuit and Rosicrucian paths of initiation—not the Rosicrucian degree shanghaied by the Freemasons but the *old* Rosicrucian path Francis Bacon had shanghaied.

"The Spaniard said a Rosicrucian initiation entails Imagination, Inspiration, and Intuition, whereas Jesuits use Imagination only to fill out a *shadow-counterimage* of Rosicrucian training so the acolyte's will can be controlled, broken, and re-fashioned for the Order's use, and all in the name of *King* Jesus. 'Many cry *Lord, Lord,*' the Spaniard insisted, 'but *which* Lord? Do we really know? The Jesuits have Jesus say, *It is my will to conquer the whole world and all my enemies.* Does that sound like the man of Golgotha?'" Vince's eyes shone. "The Spaniard was really sweating over the soul of that Mexican priest. 'Two streams of Christianity are pitted against each other: one Rosicrucian and respectful of the individual, the other Jesuit and interested in power through collective control.'" Vince shook his head. "Did I encounter a true Rosicrucian during *Hamlet* at Lake Elsinore?"

Seven and the Colonel shared a glance. Hesitantly, Seven asked over the two-way, "This Spaniard, what did he look like?"

Vince still saw him in his mind's eye. "Small-boned, dark hair and eyes, well dressed . . ."

Thomas and Ray got it. "Oh, man!" they both said at the same time.

"So who was he?" Vince asked, alert.

Thomas grinned. "Hermano, Ragoczy, Germain, an alchemist . . . Who knows? But a true Rosicrucian, Vince, and here for a reason."

29

Billy Joad

. . . And so, as the Pentagon Incorporated increases its imperialist violence around the world, the chickens have indeed come home to roost here in America in the form of a national security doctrine obsessed with domestic "insurgency" and the need to pre-emptively neutralize it. Its code-name: "Garden Plot."

−Frank Morales, *"The War at Home,"* 1999

In the days of Aztec supremacy, captured gods…were installed in an underground chamber at the heart of Tenochtitlan, where they were watched over by the earth goddess Cihuacoatl. Treated more like honored guests than as war booty, these idols were given offerings of blood and otherwise incorporated into Tenochtitlan's enormous schedule of ritual activities.

−Ptolemy Tompkins, *This Tree Grows Out of Hell*, 1990

Special Access adversely affects the national security it's intended to support.

−U.S. House Armed Services Committee, 1990

Just south of Victorville, a frantic bone-thin man looking older than his years flagged down the VW bus and didn't even wait for niceties but opened the sliding door and leaped in, slamming it after him.

"'Git goin' quick-like," he whispered hoarsely, his buggy eyes peeking outside the bus, then hitting the deck next to Sirius as a white van passed them. Thomas pulled out after the Cadillac. "Don't gawk!" the fugitive whispered fiercely from the floor. "Keep goin'!"

Once he bobbed his head up, he started right in. "I just come over from Palmdale where I seen a subcenter surrounded by a fence goin' on and on, with razor wire at the top pointin' *in*. The sign read, 'PEARBLOSSOM OPERATIONS AND MAINTENANCE SUBCENTER RECEIVING DEPARTMENT, 34534 – 116TH STREET EAST.' Across the street was the Palmdale Water Department with a fence doin' the same thing but razor wire pointin' out, and the railroad track beside the subcenter had three loadin' docks facin' the entry. I seen one like it in Brand Park in Glendale, and one in the San Fernando Valley by the Water District. Inside that one was a big building the guard said was a training range for police. But then there was new roads, new gray military-lookin' buildings, and a landin' strip."

Thomas passed a sign: "STATE OF CALIFORNIA TRESPASSING LOITERING FORBIDDEN BY LAW SECTION 555 CALIFORNIA PENAL CODE."

The bone-thin man sat up. "The ones in Manzanar and Tule Lake was used for detainment in World War Two, but these here are *new*. You might think they's part of that COG plan, continuity of government, with that Mount Weather and Mount Pony back east for all them government and Federal Reserve Bank people. But these here are *big*, and the fences are pointin' *in*, meanin' they don't want people gettin' *out*. So I say it's to do with Garden Plot and Cable Splicer."

He peered at the three young men and smiled. "You kids never heard them terms, did you? Garden Plot is to control the population wherever and however, and Cable Splicer is for

52

government takeover. They're gonna tell us that these 600 prison camps they got fully operational are for illegal aliens tryin' to get over the Mexican border"—he glanced uneasily at Vince—"but that's not what they're for." He shook his head emphatically.

"Race riots?" Ray asked from the bed where he was reading.

The man looked up sharply, not all that used to talking to Negroes, though he'd met a couple he'd liked. He shrugged. "Could be. Garden Plot began on July 29, 1967 with Executive Order 11365 and the National Advisory Commission on Civil Disorders. But the plan's bigger than that, longer in scope. I seen a camp 90 miles east of San Francisco on Highway 20, near Oakdale, that could hold 15,000. Another one at Vandenberg. They all got roads and railroad and airports nearby, and fulltime guards, even though they's empty right now. The Constitution's gonna be suspended like one of them slow-boiling frogs, mark my words."

"National emergency . . ." Ray mumbled, slowly getting the picture. "Are these prison camps and holding tanks all over the country, then?"

"Yep, that's what I hear." The man ticked them off his fingers. "The World War Two ones in Opelika, Alabama; Jerome and Rohwer, Arkansas; Livingston, Louisiana; Crossville, Tennessee; Mexia, Texas; McAlester, Oklahoma; Concordia, Kansas; Scottsbluff, Nebraska; and out west, besides here, there's Millard, Utah; Hart Mountain, Wyoming; Grenada and Trinidad, Colorado; Minipoka, Idaho; and don't forget Florence, Gila River and Yuma, Arizona. Yuma's on the edge between Mexico and the United States and named after *Juma*, the Tibetan god of Death that can read the past and future in a mirror like the one Tezcatlipoca the black magician had."

His meaningful glance at Vince passed a jolt through Vince.

Thomas glanced in the rearview mirror, surprised. "That's some memory you've got."

"Got to, I'm practically illiterate," the man said proudly. "If you got a desire to learn and you're illiterate, you damn well better have a good memory and pay attention.—Then they's the new ones at old forts: Fort McCoy, Wisconsin; Fort Drum, New York; Fort Benning, Georgia; Fort Chaffee, Arkansas; Elgin Air Force Base, Florida; Fort Huachua, Arizona—UN soldiers there—"

He went on like a teletype about bases and white vans, the Huey and small observation helicopter he saw north of Fresno outside Madera with no markings except for a white phosphorescent patch on the side. Underground installations were going in, U.S. Army Corps of Engineers deep works all under the Sierra Nevadas and southeast Wyoming, at the Book Cliffs, at Uncompahgre Uplift south of Grand Junction outside the gateway to Mormon Country, in the La Sal Mountains 20 miles southeast of Moab and at Rafael Swell west of Green River, then under Monument Uplift and Blanding Basin near Blanding and Mexican Hat, in west central Utah west of Minersville and southwest Utah west of Cedar City. Nevada was forgone, he said, pretty much an underground world, "probably where all them 'dead' and missin' scientists been taken," he surmised, under the Nuclear Test Site at Nellis, all around Tonopah and even northwest Nevada.

Just as he was about to dig into Arizona and New Mexico, they passed through Barstow where Earl Dorr discovered an underground river in the 1920s but could never find it again, and the bone-thin man switched tracks.

"Air Force Plant 42's in Palmdale where they's workin' on ARVs. Then they's a NASA Deep Space Network installation hereabouts, in Goldstone, with antennas able to track spacecraft more than ten *billion* miles from Earth, and a guarded airstrip separate from China Lake. I reckon they's trackin' alien saucers with infrared. Then they's NASA Satellite Control up at Sunnyvale west of San José, NASA Ames Research Center at Mountain View, and then the one up at Pilot Peak in Plumas National Forest between La Porte and Quincy even more secret. Oh, and the underground

COG facility near Napa with eight to ten microwave dishes." He glanced out the window. "Anyway, I'll be gettin' out in a couple of miles at Daggett."

"What's in Daggett?" Ray was agog.

"Mansion in the Mojave Desert belongin' to a group called the Augustan Society. Founded in 1957. More than that, I'm not at liberty to discuss. I'm on a mission, my friends, a mission of discovery, and if you ain't on a mission of discovery, too, then you ain't true Americans. This land is buried in lies and we need to be about the business of unburyin' the truth before we lose it all."

Thomas and Vince grinned at each other. Was the whole country on a quest or just hitchhikers?

The man pointed ahead. "Nebo Road, this here's my stop."

Thomas pulled over and the man shook hands all around. "You saved my butt back there. May God bless you on your journey of truth. My journey has been blessed with it, and I'm about to find more."

The pilgrims still had all sorts of questions for this raggedy compendium of knowledge. "You never told us your name," Thomas called as the collector of truth got out and walked back toward Nebo Road.

He stopped and turned. "Joad," he said, walking backward, "Billy Joad. My folks come west on this very road back in the dust bowl Depression days. My daddy was a union man who died for American labor." Tipping an invisible hat, he turned and walked on, then had an afterthought and turned back. "Don't forget, you're still in military territory—Edwards, China Lake, Fort Irwin. Watch out for them white vans." He gave the peace sign that for him might have been the Winston Churchill victory sign, then turned away singing an old Woody Guthrie song—

They say I'm a dust bowl refugee,
Yes, they say I'm a dust bowl refugee,
They say I'm a dust bowl refugee, Lord, Lord,
An' I ain't a-gonna be treated this way . . .

Once Thomas pulled back onto 66, Seven was beside herself on the two-way. "Billy Joad from Steinbeck's *The Grapes of Wrath*?"

Mannie and Baby Rose peered out the Caddy back window. "It's like he disappeared."

Billy Joad was right about California not being an entirely happy conjunction of ancient *oh-mah* dark watchers with a five-foot stride, exquisite national parks and monuments, Native American reservations, and Franciscan missions. From Tijuana, Mexico to the Lava Beds at the California-Oregon border where Captain Jack Kintpuash, a Modoc, held off the U.S. Army on January 17, 1872, and between military-Mafia-Mormon Nevada and the deep blue sea, the American military was everywhere. Round Valley, Red Bluff, north and west of Yosemite, below Kings Canyon and west of Death Valley, underneath Indian reservations at Tule River, Marango, Aqua Caliente, Capitane Grande, Manzanita, and Yuma—tunnels everywhere, from Long Beach through Camp Pendleton to San Diego and east to 29 Palms, Chocolate Mountain Gunnery Range and the Naval reservation at the US-Mexico border.

Even the original Jesuit-Franciscan missions were in the anaconda grip of bases and underground tunnels (including one to Hearst Mansion) snaking through the Hunter-Liggett Military Reservation that encompassed Santa Cruz, San Juan Bautista, San Carlos Borremeo de Carmelo, and San Antonio de Padua to San Francisco de Asis and the Presidio. Forlorn Nuestra Señora de la Soledad on Fort Romie Road was sick to death of rattling swords and sorcery winds blowing damp and bone dry, and the open eye of Shiva that made Hermano weep at San Miguel. Vandenberg Air Force Base—with its own launch facility since 1966, rumored to be connected underground to Camp Nelson, Edwards Air Force Base, China Lake, Fort Irwin, and 29 Palms—lay between San Luis Obispo de Tolosa and La Purisma Concepcion. Tunnels snaked beneath San Gabriel Arcángel and the bookends of Camp Pendleton at San Juan Capistrano and San Luis Rey de Francia to the very first mission in the Alta chain, San Diego de Alcala.

Edwards Air Force Base, before Tonopah Test Range and Area 51, was the most secret aircraft test site of all, covering a vast triangle from Long Beach through Pasadena and Lancaster and Palmdale in Antelope Valley to Tehachapi and Mojave, Edwards, China Lake, then back through Helendale to Long Beach. On the books, the Helendale facility was a radar cross-section (RCS) test range, but it was actually Lockheed's covert operations center. At Haystack Butte, the underground base reached thirty stories deep with electronic oval doorways. Tehachapi the Ant Hill included underground exotic propulsion craft hangars administered by Northrup. The Tejon Ranch at Tehachapi was dedicated to electromagnetic research overseen by McDonnell-Douglas, despite the sign reading "NORTHRUP CORPORATION — PICO RIVERA." Edwards also managed the 1.7 million acres of the Utah Test and Training Range.

China Lake Naval Weapons Station at Ridgecrest was northeast of Edwards. Adjacent to China Lake was Fort Irwin (the size of Rhode Island) with a major underground missile facility on I-15 between Yermo and Baker. China Lake was a military mind control-programming center working in tandem with Scotty's Castle in Death Valley.

Military acreage went on forever.

Nellis Range Complex commanded 2,000 roads and three million acres (the size of New Jersey) and included the Nevada Test Site (like Fort Irwin, the size of Rhode Island), Tonopah Test Range, and Area 51. At Nellis, the numbers got funny: Areas 1 through 26, then jumping to 51. The Office of Federal Investigations in Las Vegas (unlisted) did background checks for clearances to work at the Nevada Test Site or Nellis.

Along north-south Highway 395, the Three Flags Highway from Mexico to Canada, the town of Mercury was the only town on all of the 1,800 square miles of the Nevada Test Site. *Mercury*. First was Egypt's Thoth and his priest Hermes Trismegistus, then the Greek Hermes, and finally the Roman Mercury, god of commerce free to range the globe like quicksilver, able hermetically, magically, and alchemically to convert goods and labor into wealth on the cabal artifice called the computer. Hermes/Mercury was the fleet-footed, fleet-thought messenger zipping between gods and men; the god of merchants who trade in everything, including guns and lives; the god of cheats and thieves, lies, fortune, music, eloquence, young men, travelers and roads. Hermes/Mercury was the guide to Hades. The Germans called him Woden (Wagner: Wotan), and like the Freemasons' ibis-headed Thoth he bore secret knowledge from before the Flood, from Atlantis.

137 miles as the Crow-ley flies from Mercury is the town of St. George, tucked in the southwest corner of Utah. Between 1951 and 1962, the Nevada Test Site hosted 126 atomic bomb tests above ground and the Dirty Harry (Truman) bomb on May 19, 1953 blew a plume over St. George, so that when the movie crew of *The Conqueror* was filming there, actors Dick Powell, John Wayne, Susan Hayward, and Agnes Moorehead all ingested the radiation they would eventually die of, and 91 of the 220 cast and crew had developed cancer by 1980.

The Conqueror, indeed. Mercury had plenty of nuclear dead to lead to Hades.

Tests went underground. In 1976 alone, 54 bombs would be detonated at the Nevada Test Site, and by 1992 the tally would be over 800, with four tons of plutonium percolating in the soil.

The pilgrims were now deep in the Mojave Desert. Over the two-way, the Colonel talked about how General George S. Patton (1885-1945) had prepared a million men for the Sahara Desert in northern Africa here in 18,000 square miles of desert, basically southeast California and part of Arizona. For Thomas' benefit, he noted that the so-called *coso artifact*—an electronic capacitor or spark plug inside a geode dated at 500,000 years—had been found in 1961 just north of them up in the dry Owens lakebed west of Death Valley.

"Goes to prove that most of our discoveries are just re-discoveries," he finished.

"Amen to that, Colonel," Thomas responded, "and speaking of electronics, happy campers, I'd like to stop soon so I can make a couple of modifications to our radio equipment. How about after Ludlow?"

"Aquarius" began playing on the Cadillac radio as Seven radioed, "Roger, Captain America, over and out."

When the moon is in the seventh house
And Jupiter aligns with Mars,
Then peace will guide the planets
And love will steer the stars . . .

Thomas smiled. How he loved that woman.

30

Deus Terrestris

"You are right to be on your guard against magicians and impostors. I know that Cagliostro terrified you with an apparition which may be termed at least ill-timed. He yielded to the vain glory of showing you his power, without troubling himself concerning the disposition of your soul and the sublimity of his mission. Cagliostro is, nevertheless, no impostor; very far from it. But he is a vain man, and thus it is that he has often merited the reproach of charlatanism."

- Le Comte de Saint-Germain
to La Comtesse de Rudolstadt, 1847

Newton was not the first of the Age of Reason. He was the last of the magicians, the last of the Babylonians and Sumerians, the last great mind which looked out on the visible and intellectual world with the same eyes as those who began to build our intellectual world rather less than 10,000 years ago . . .

- John Maynard Keynes, *"Newton the Man,"* 1947

Black magic: where work is done with spiritual forces hidden within the earthly realm.

- Rudolf Steiner, 1861-1925

It was early evening when Sibelius received a message from Dr. Greenbaum that confirmed the Franciscan's story and caused him to forget his dinner.

Saint-Germain was back in America.

He went over what he knew. According to the chemical engineer Bergier, the alchemist Fulcanelli had been in France during the Nazi occupation, but not Saint-Germain. In 1710, Germain was fifty years old, but in the late 1800s in St. Petersburg he'd given Tchaikovsky a piece of music he claimed to have composed a century before. (Sibelius had seen the score in the British Museum.) From 1737 to 1742, he'd been in Persia studying the secrets of nature; in 1745, he'd participated in the Jacobite Revolution in England, in 1755 melted jewels in India, and in 1757 stayed with Louis XV at Château de Chambord. He discovered a secret regarding colors for oils, made pearls grow with water he specially prepared, made flax look like Italian silk. His father was said to have been Franz-Leopold of Transylvania, his mother a Serbian Tékéli, his aegis the last Duc de Medici.

Saint-Germain had taken many names over the centuries: the Marquis de Montferrat and Monsieur de Zurmont, in Venice Comte Bellamarre, at Pisa Chevalier Schoening, at Milan and Leipzig Chevalier Weldon, at Genoa and Livorno and Vienna Comte Soltikoff, at Schwalbach and Triesdorf Graf Tzarogy, and in Dresden the anagram Ragoczy. So many aliases would be ridiculous were it not for his habit of immortality, and because of the mysteries surrounding his existence, the name Germain had been tainted again and again by the vainglorious.

Sibelius wasn't all that surprised that the Wonder Man of Europe was still somehow miraculously embodied, but why now in America when so much was at stake? He'd been in Europe when the Jesuit Weishaupt was teaching in Ingolstadt and setting the Illuminati on their magical Masonry path, and that same Ingolstadt thread led directly to the present merger of occultists, organized crime, intelligence agencies, and law and order. The American Brotherhoods owed everything to Illuminized Masonry.

Still, he shouldn't worry: Saint-Germain had failed to prevent the French Revolution and he would fail again. Cagliostro's initiation into the Illuminati was in 1783, after which he'd discredited Louis XVI through the queen and the 1786 Masonic congress decided to assassinate both Louis XVI and Gustavus II of Sweden. The Marquis de Sade and Weishaupt had attempted to infiltrate the Knights of St. John the Baptist (Hospitallers, Malta) through Cagliostro after their Grand Master, alchemist Manuel Pinto da Fonseca, expelled the Jesuits from Malta, but had failed. Later, others succeeded by other means. Once Louis XVI and his Austrian bitch were guillotined in 1792, the divine right of kings was replaced by the Illuminati. Napoleon then waged a 22-year assault on England while the legacies of Saint-Germain, Goethe, and Schiller in central Europe were progressively undermined.

Still meditating on Cagliostro, Sibelius riveted on his *Necronomicon* on his oak bookshelf embossed with a rose, a cross, a triangle, and a death's head. His eyes moved to the *The Chaldean Oracles* by Julian the Theurgist, son of Julian called the Chaldean, from the 2nd century; then to Flamel's 14th century gold-embossed *ABRAHAM IBN EZRA THE JEW, PRINCE, LEVIT, ASTROLOGER AND PHILOSOPHER TO THE NATION OF THE JEWS, BY THE WRATH OF GOD DISPERSED AMONG THE GAULS, SENDETH SALVATION, Peter of Abano, translator*; then to Fulcanelli's *Le Mystère des Cathédrales* and *Les Demeures philosophales*, written in 1920; and finally *The Dawn of Magic*, translated from the French by Rollo May. He took it down and opened its pages.

Bergier's encounter with the alchemist Fulcanelli in June 1937 at the Gas Board in Paris had begun with a warning about the nuclear research then going on in Europe and America. By means of certain geometric arrangements of highly purified materials, he said, atomic forces would be released without recourse to either electricity or vacuum. Blasting through matter to antimatter would open a Threshold door it would be impossible to close.

Sibelius smiled. *Forces released geometrically*, like the ancient rituals and rites that could still invoke the Realm of the Father, of Number, Weight, and Measure, if done properly. Whoever Bergier had encountered clarified that modern physics did *not* arise out of early alchemy but was the creation of 18th century aristocrats and wealthy libertines. Science without conscience, he said incisively, is not what alchemy stands for. As modern physicists were discovering, the role of the observer's moral turpitude or excellence—or lack thereof—intervened in all experimentation. Sibelius had marked a particular passage—

> *The secret of alchemy is this: a way of manipulating matter and energy so as to produce what modern scientists call a 'field of force' that acts on the observer and puts him in a privileged position vis à vis the universe. From this position he has access to the realities which are ordinarily hidden from us by time and space, matter and energy. This is what we call 'The Great Work.'*

So taken was Sibelius by his own role in the Great Work that he glossed over the import of the final warning—

> *The essential thing is not the transmutation of metals, but that of the experimenter himself. It's an ancient secret that few men rediscover once in a century.*

Thus Fulcanelli, who, like Saint-Germain, seemed never to die but to disappear and reappear from time to time, had warned Bergier that nuclear secrets would transform not just physical life but moral life, as well. The Threshold would be breached, the door thrown wide, for which people were far from prepared.

Fulcanelli and Cagliostro had both been students of Saint-

Germain, and yet how different they were! Sibelius feared that if Saint-Germain knew where to find the present-day Fulcanelli, he would know where to find the present-day Cagliostro.

The telephone rang. It was Dr. Greenbaum.

"Did you get the message?" he asked.

"Yes," Sibelius responded.

"Send me your thoughts tomorrow via the same bearer." *Click.* Phone taps and satellite reconnaissance were sly and ubiquitous, so he was always brief. *The same bearer* meant Sibelius' very own MK-ULTRA slave with photographic memory, and *your thoughts* meant astral investigations. He would check with the Naval Observatory for tonight's aspects.

The Jesuit Sibelius kept his magical thoughts in his brain in his cranium in his copper-lined study beneath which he kept a hidden magickal chamber. When he conducted *Events* like the one in Mexico, he wore a bonnet much like John Dee's but closely threaded with DuPont Kevlar, well understanding the risks of this electromagnetic era. In other times, it was powers of magi or occultists from afar one had to worry about, but now it was computers, satellites, and remote viewers. Technology kept one on one's toes.

Late that night, he followed in Faust's footsteps and spoke the Words that would penetrate the present. BRAShITH ALHIM, *In the beginning, the Gods.* 3910, the years from the Fall to the birth of the Jewish Carpenter. ALHIM, permutations of *temura*, 3.1415 or *pi* to four places. BRA, *Ben* the son, *Ruach* the Holy Spirit, *Abba* the Father . . .

Magic and mysticism had always been the theoretical underpinnings for real science. Crick the genetics wizard had been on LSD when he deduced the double helix, the physicist Sir William Crookes, physiologist Sir Pierre Curie, astronomer Sir James Jeans, neurophysiologist Sir John Eccles—all knighted for their achievements. The list of mystic scientists, *Brotherhood* scientists, was long. A thin line existed between science and magic; once crossed, parallel realms opened. As Oppenheimer and sacred Hindu texts both knew, physical laws were appearances, surfaces, and shadows cast on walls of realities lying beyond that thin line. As Franz Bardon put it, magic is a metaphysics that deals with powers, matters, and substances of a more subtle nature, and is thus analogous but not identical to general consensus sciences. Hermetics preceded modern science by millennia. Its laws and applications in mathematics, chemistry, physics, and astronomy had not been lost due to war and cataclysm, as the profane were taught, but had been hoarded and cached by generational Brothers and institutions against the day that they might be optimally used.

It was Sibelius' destiny to live in such a time. The higher laws of energy, matter, and substance were now coming to fruition: laser, satellite tomography, plasma physics, high-powered microwaves, holography, electromagnetic pulse fields and devices, superconductivity, genetic engineering, mind control, remote viewing, weather engineering. Splitting the atom had opened Pandora's box.

19th century Brothers had concentrated on keeping lower-degree Brothers and *cowan* scientists under a spell of materialism, Darwin's evolutionary theory, and classical Newtonian science based on the Clockmaker model. Inside secret orders, the occult and science, magic and technology were still one. Finally in 1871, Bulwer-Lytton, Grand Patron of the Societas Rosicruciana in Anglia (and Philadelphia), released his book *The Coming Race* announcing the advent of *vril* and the hidden magnetic forces governing the Earth. Bulwer-Lytton had been the nuncio for the *electromagnetic* Mysteries that would make good use of the Second Coming's activation of the planetary ether, and once the instruments were ready, the 20th century would crack the Threshold and the 21st century would offer up the Earth plane to incoming psychophysical entities.

Earth forces and psychophysical beings were one and the same. Space overflowed with the luminous æther, plasma, electrical vapor, luminous magnetism, the all-pervading fifth element.

Occultists' crypts were filled with ancient writings and devices gained from countless apocalypses, wars and intrigues, all waiting in silence for the propitious century in which the electromagnetic work of Tesla and etheric work of Keely might produce power over the entire planet. *Scientia est potentia.*

Sibelius smiled. The Brothers had done well, despite their differences, when they had agreed that it was crucial to garner public excitement about anything but the Second Coming and the consciousness in the masses that it would generate. So they'd set to work doling out a believable mix of truth and propaganda through a controlled media network while other Brothers quietly controlled university physics programs. Since World War One, magical orders like Fraternitas Saturni, the Hermetic Brotherhood of Luxor, and *Reichsarbeitsgemeinschaft Das Kommende Deutschland* in Berlin had been stirring the scientific and magickal embers with one hand while quashing public knowledge with the other. They'd plied chosen JASON scholars with background on *vril, die Kosmische Urkraft* or *Raumkraft*, the ancient Atlanteans as *psychophysical dynamotechnicians*. They revealed how the Earth is an apple sliced vertically in two halves with the North Pole being the positive anode and the South Pole the negative cathode known as the *pit*; how the planetary body has an etheric body with seven *chakras* or energy centers linked to the human spinal *chakras*; and how the primal machine is man himself who, if his will could but be harnessed, might control all with mind alone. Man was a god in the making.

In 1914, young Franz Philipp flew with his *sonnenkraft-triebwerk* solar powered motor; in 1915 in Denver, C.E. Amman, 22, created an atmospheric generator that drew energy out of the air and drove his air-powered car around. Harry E. Perrigo invented a converter that extracted electricity from the air. In 1920, John Huston invented a condenser that could draw heat out of the air so hot the machine could destroy itself, and reversed, could create temperatures as low as -250°F. The U.S. refused to patent it, Canada and England promised to do so, but then like all the inventions and inventors, it disappeared and Huston was dead at 22.

The Magician laughed. "Nazi science" had been ridiculed at the Nuremberg show trials after World War Two, hiding the truth that the enlightened of every developed nation on Earth were willing to sacrifice their people and culture if they could acquire the magickal Nazi scientists who had wrested psychophysical secrets from *Natura*, secrets that would catapult humanity into a future long foreseen by Freemason occultists like Bulwer-Lytton. Sibelius had known Bulwer-Lytton in a previous life and hoped his old friend saw how his science fiction was finally fruiting—*tubes by which the vril fluid can be conducted towards the object it is meant to destroy, throughout a distance almost indefinite. And their mathematical science as applied to such purpose is so nicely accurate, that on the report of some observer in an air-boat, any member of the vril department can estimate unerringly the nature of intervening obstacles, the height to which the projectile instrument should be raised, and the extent to which it should be charged, so as to reduce to ashes within a space of time too short for me to venture to specify it, a capital twice as vast as London.*

The coming race was arriving.

Named for the Finnish composer, the Magician felt that he had played a small part in the attainment of the Cause by transposing Enochian music into blunt-fingered scientific language, like the cosmology of Hermes Trismegistus after his *visio smaragdina* inscribed on the Emerald Tablet had passed from Orpheus to Pythagoras to Plato to Apollonius of Tyana to Plotinus—

2. It attests: The above from the below, and the below from the above — the work of the miracle of the One.

3. And things have been formed from this primal substance through a single act. How wonderful is this work! It is the main [principle] of the world and is its maintainer.

5. [It is] the father of talismans and the protector of miracles,

6. whose powers are perfect, and whose lights are confirmed.

7. A fire that becomes earth. Separate the earth from the fire, so you will attain the subtle as more inherent than the gross, with care and sagacity.

This "primal substance," *fire that becomes earth*, referred to Æther, dark matter, plasma, the binding agent for all life soon to be weaponized for planetary power.

8. It rises from earth to heaven, so as to draw the lights of the heights to itself, and descends to the earth; thus within it are the forces of the above and below; because the light of lights is within it, thus does the darkness flee before it.

9. [It is] the force of forces, which overcomes every subtle thing and penetrates into everything gross.

Æther was the true messenger of the gods between the heavens and the Earth.

At an invitation-only conference, someone had asked Sibelius, "When it talks about the light of lights being within it, is it referring to electricity?" to which he had responded, "No. As Tesla made clear in his Colorado Springs experiments, 'the light of lights' is the æther, the medium without which electricity can do nothing, especially travel. Unlike æther, electricity and electromagnetism are entirely earthly. The physics of the 19th century viewed light as a magnetic wave, but early 20th century quantum physics revealed that the connection between light, electricity, and magnetic fields is far more complex. The Austrian initiate rightly said, 'The greatest contrast to electricity is light. To consider light as a form of electricity is to mix good and evil.' You and I might argue about what is good and what is evil"—chuckles greeted his sardonic smile—"but good science requires that we be entirely clear about the difference between etheric and electromagnetic, between light and electricity. As the good, albeit misguided, Dr. Wilhelm Reich detected, etheric and electromagnetic, *orgone* and *oranur*, are virtually antithetical and from completely different sources." He paused meaningfully and looked around. "To increase one is to decrease the other."

The Magician's eyes now wandered lovingly over his books, all the while thinking, *The value of agape is 93. Added to 3.1415 of ALHIM gives 3.141593—so sayeth Pico della Mirandola.* Henry Cornelius Agrippa of Nettesheim had made an unsurpassable version of the Hebrew tables of the practical Qabala with geomantics and planetary seals, sigils, and magic squares. *Three Books of Occult Philosophy.* The skeletal defrocked Dominican Giordano Bruno and Cardinal Nicholas of Cusa had given Galileo the idea of an infinite universe.

These were his true peers. Having to disguise himself as a businessman in a democratic consumer age was demeaning. To lie like a common thief when one had the power to command souls and the disembodied! And yet as the more worldly Brothers never tired of reminding him, the democratic impulse was from the gods' timetable and therefore could be thwarted only indirectly. Besides, this era presented an opportunity to do in one lifetime what once took many, and they owed it all to Catholic Italy for expatriating Bruno so he could go to England and loan his considerable talents to the Renaissance and the re-birth of magick. Between Bacon and Bruno, the Globe Theater was made into an early psyop that Bruno analyzed in his treatise *On the Composition of Images, Signs and Ideas.* Together, the two geniuses had heralded the Sorcerer State, *mundus imaginalis*, a transformation of the public mind by public relations firms, spinmeisters, and propagandists. How delighted Bruno would have been with telecommunications reaching millions of souls simultaneously!

Better a Kali or smiting Jehovah than a mewling New Testament Messiah. Better a return to the good old days of elite governance without all the subterfuge democracy required. The gospel of evolution meant *species* clear and simple, with divine individuality among the masses mere puffery and illusion. Leaders were gamekeepers on a vast preserve called society, groomed to keep species on track by silencing individual voices crying in the wilderness. Predation, weather, disease, starvation, war, and terrorism were the gamekeeper's tools of trade. I.G. Farben saw only a difference of degree between a factory and a concentration camp.

History books made the passage of Time sound like a long litany of kings and wars, when it was really the men behind a Rasputin or Hitler who made history happen. Philosopher magicians like Ficino and Pico, Bacon and Bruno, were the true creators of the Renaissance, which the hounds of heaven known as the Inquisition-loving Dominicans knew full well. Paracelsus, who said the Christ Infusion at Golgotha was *Iliaster* or star matter, died in a tavern brawl in 1541. Tycho Brahe drank fluids at the home of Baron von Rosenberg and politely held his urine until he returned home and found he could not urinate; after five agonizing days of delirium, he died on October 24, 1601, poisoned. That Paracelsus and Tycho Brahe and the great Bruno had been executed, whether discretely or publicly, was why modern magi like himself kept a low profile and became adept at deception even while guiding the *mundus imaginalis* on its way, including feeding the popular imagination Disney pablum like *The Sorcerer's Apprentice* and Simon Magus in Acts 8:18.

Renaissance *magisters* had navigated rich worlds in which phantasms became real until the Reformation and Counter-reformation crushed alchemical and metaphysical thought and drove them underground. Sibelius sighed. When the Renaissance magus Abbot Trithemius engaged in Secret Traditions, he did so *In Christ*, either for safety's sake or because pre-Advent solar cults in both Egypt and Ireland had centered their Mysteries on the cosmic principles known as the *Son of God*, considered essential to the Great Work, the Christ being the Philosopher's Stone, the Graal necessary to the *ars gothique*. Christ was Kant's *crux metaphysicorum* regarding not just Fallen humanity but the Mystery of Matter itself—the morsel of truth behind the misinformation campaign presenting Jesus as a Levantine magician. Oh yes, it was anything goes when it came to turning the people's gaze in any other, albeit ridiculous, direction. Sibelius sighed again. Nothing in America was too ridiculous for multitudes to buy cheaply.

But to the matter. He closed his books. He would enter the *Sigillum dei Aemaeth* with the 7 and proceed to where he had stored the desert elemental he'd shaped years before by means of the first Great Arcanum and given divine respiration by means of the third Great Arcanum. *There is no disappearance, annihilation or loss in spiritual beings and the part which seems separated, owing to its difference of phase, incurs no loss or deficiency whatsoever in the Upper Light.* In his hidden chamber, he would set the elemental on its Southwest mission.

31

"Soul-cracking" in the Mojave Desert

Very often, therefore, in human affairs we are subject to Saturn, through idleness, solitude, or strength, through Technology and more secret philosophy, through superstition, Magic, agriculture, and through sadness.

–Marsilio Ficino (1433-1499), *The Book of Life*

The year is six Kan, and the eleventh Muluc; in the month of Zac there occurred terrible earthquakes which continued without interruption until the thirteenth chuen. The country of hills and mud, the Land of Mu, was sacrificed. Being twice upheaved, it suddenly disappeared during the night, the basin being continually shaken by volcanic forces. Being confined, these caused the lands to rise and fall several times and in various places. At last the surface gave way and the ten countries were torn asunder and scattered in fragments: Unable to stand the force of seismic convulsions they sank with their sixty-four millions of inhabitants eight thousand and sixty years before the writing of this book.

–Troano Codex, translated by Abbé Brasseur, 1869

The cause of all your mistakes, gentlemen, is your unawareness of the direction being taken by civilization and the world. You believe that civilization and the world progress. No, they go backwards!

–Hernán Cortés to the Spanish Chamber of Deputies, 1549

Only the man of a great star, a great divinity, can bring the opposites together again, in a new unison.

–D.H. Lawrence, *The Plumed Serpent*, 1924

As Thomas searched for a place to pull off Route 66, Baby Rose stared out the Cadillac window at the late afternoon Mojave Desert, incapable of connecting it with her Pasadena dream journey about the Satanist and American military rocket man extraordinaire John "Jack" Whiteside Parsons, who had been out there at 34° N latitude, 118° W longitude with L. Ron Hubbard playing Edward Kelley to his John Dee, both subject to an American military cult Working via the Navy, NASA's Jet Propulsion Laboratory, and JPL's Theodore von Kármán. (*Hubard* in Enochian refers to living lamps.)

For eleven days, they'd invoked a Working of the Ordo Templi Orientis VIII° ritual, a homosexual ritual viewed as the secret marriage between gods and men *sans* intercession of the goddess-woman. Exactly 39 days later, they'd invoked the IX° to Goddess Babalon via Jack's redheaded elemental partner Marjorie Wilson Cameron, females being essential to the IX° ritual for creating a Homunculus or human embodiment of a force of Nature—what the MI6 man Aleister Crowley (brother-in-law to Sir Gerald Kelley, president of the Royal Academy) termed a Moon Child.

Scarlet Woman Cameron was of the same Wilson bloodline as L. Ron, a fact hidden by his father's adoption. She was an ex-WAVE who had been an aide to the Pentagon Joint Chiefs of Staff before being honorably discharged in Washington, DC nineteen days before L. Ron was discharged, after which both made a beeline for Pasadena and Jack—

December 5, 1945: L. Ron discharged from the Navy; moves immediately into The Parsonage

January 4-15, 1946: Babalon Working I; L. Ron "scries" Cameron's arrival, then leaves

January 19, 1946: Cameron arrives

January 27, 1946: L. Ron leaves

February 27, 1946: Cameron leaves for New York

February 28, 1946: Parsons returns to the Mojave Desert and channels *Liber 49*

March 1, 1946: Hubbard returns

March 1-3, 1946: Babalon Working II with Hubbard

March 13, 1946: Cameron returns

After the Babalon Working, Parsons was cut loose by the agencies that had made use of him. He and Cameron married on October 19, 1946 after L. Ron had absconded with Jack's money and his other Scarlet Woman, Sarah. The Parsonage was torn down. Jack quit his job at Vulcan Powder Company and worked for Hughes Aircraft without his government security clearance until March 7, 1949. Then Marjorie left him. On December 4, 1952, six months after his death by fire, L. Ron gave the Philadelphia Doctorate Course lectures. During a discussion of the Anti-Christ, he asked, "Who do you think I am?

It is for Man to be moral or not, to bend, break, or obey the laws etched into the universe by God. Such is the drama of future free will that all spirits are subject to, one way or another

Baby Rose didn't know or remember anything about the Mojave Desert or Death Valley or Nellis or Edwards or China Lake. For her, it was well and good to be traveling with people who imbibed the best of Sixties camaraderie and dreams. She leaned forward and put a hand on Seven's cheek. On the radio, Elvis was singing *If it weren't for the lighthouse, where would this ship be . . .*

Seven had come West because something ancient beckoned to her, something about old Asia and ghosts of old American civilizations. Her generation felt the Asian pulse thrumming from the West above and beyond materialism and sought it in *kundalini* yoga and gurus, Buddhism, the yin-yang of macrobiotics, acupuncture, shiatsu, tai ch'i, the *I Ching*. The pull of Asia had taken her as far as Hawai'i where she'd wandered the lush jungles of Maui and Kauai, wondering if James Churchward was right and Hawaii was the tip of sunken Mu, the Garden of Eden where her cycle of history began thousands of years before. She'd booked passage in exchange for cooking on a schooner bound for Australia and Asia, but they'd hit the doldrums somewhere east of Samoa and by the time they reached Tonga, the crew was unraveling. So she'd stayed, eventually flying back with a Tongan in tow. Vince verified that Tonga had once been the southwest coast of Mu, once his people's homeland. The *Ramayana* praised the Mayas for being mighty navigators and architects in ages so remote that the Sun had not yet risen above the horizon. Finally, Seven's Asian fever had lifted and she had turned with increasing curiosity toward the Western culture she'd been born to, little realizing yet the mysteries holding the Americas in their grip.

At twilight east of Ludlow and Siberia—both tiny Santa Fe Railroad water stops—Thomas finally found a scruffy little grove to pull into, followed closely by the Cadillac. Once they'd all gotten out of the vehicles and stretched, Thomas reminded them of satellite surveillance and not to look *up*. Vince shook hands with the Colonel, Mannie, and Seven, Baby Rose peeking from behind her. Seven liked the look of him, short and sturdy, older than all but the Colonel. *Wise beyond his years*, she thought, looking into his deep black eyes. He was the first Mayan any of them had ever met.

This being their first camp, there was much discussion about what and who should go where. Thomas and Ray got out the electronic scanner and tools while the Colonel took a little stroll, then set up his folding chair to smoke a pipe and watch the boys work. Seven, Baby Rose, and Mannie set up the cutting board and extra two-burner Coleman and began preparing brown rice and veggies. Vince found a little spot for his tent and made himself available to help when needed, producing herbs from his pack for Seven and copper wire for Thomas. Like Mannie's unique insights, Vince's cornucopia pack would become legend.

While dinner cooked, Thomas rigged the scanner he'd devised to intercept police channels but more importantly to intercept and descramble encrypted intelligence channels. Unlike Citizens' Band, it could scan the entire radio spectrum and record desired frequencies for future scanning, but it could also block interception. While he was at it, he explained how digital scanners monitor radio frequencies, and that the ultra-high frequency digital data link could be conveyed over a single standard military channel. After re-gauging the two-way frequencies so they were under the same block, he set the Caddy and VW radios in sync for the same stations. But it was when the test for the scanner came that Ray let out a long, impressed whistle. Clear as a bell, the dial could pick up dozens of channels, even air control towers. Ray volunteered to start logging channels and looking for communications with the tail Thomas was sure they had by now, maybe even with his brother along.

Vince built what he called an Indian fire—small and tight, unlike a white man fire—and with bowls brimming with good cell-building food free of animals, they sat in a circle around the desert-warming fire, ready to hear from the Mayan. As was proper, Vince began with Mexican history, pulling out his K'iché Mayan *Popul Vuh* Council Book he carried everywhere, about *Hunahpú* and his code for life. Christ was the Bread of Life, *Hunahpú* the Maize of Life, Vince said. Like the Persian Ahura Mazda, he was the aurora light that illuminates. *The first race of human beings were capable of all knowledge. They examined the four corners of the horizon, the four points of the firmament, and the round surface of the Earth*, said the *Popul Vuh*.

He regaled them with stories of his *Mayach* homeland east of the Isthmus of Tehuantepec toward the cobra's head of Yucatán. All the pilgrims knew about the lands south of the border was César Chávez and his migrant workers toiling in West Coast fields and orchards, driving beat-up trucks and living in dirt-poor camps like Billy Joad's forebears had done. They were stunned to learn that a civilization older and greater than that of ancient Greece once ruled supreme in the South. Vince Liputzli, Mayan chronicler extraordinaire, had actually been sent north to take notes, ask questions, record, and send his writings back to his father in Mexico. Vince said history was an intimate story going on here and now, if only one could open one's eyes and ears and learn the signs and sigils.

He described pyramids like the conical mound of Cuicuilco 370 feet in diameter and 60 feet high at the south edge of Mexico City. Archaeologists said the sediments below the lava flow under and around Cuicuilco dated back to 6050 BC, but the sediments covering the base to between 6550 and 28,050 BC.

"Dating the past has been a *political* issue since the 19th century," Vince said. "Ask any archaeologist at the Instituto Nacional de Antropología y Historia about the real age of Cuicuilco and you will probably be directed to the Smithsonian Institute. The old archaeologists may not have had radiocarbon dating, but they were able to estimate how long it would take to accumulate eighteen feet of sediment between the Xitli lava flow and the temple pavement, and on top of the Xitli—at least 6,500 years." He scrutinized his new friends' faces. "Remember the riots in major world cities in 1968?"

Ray laughed. "Yeah, we thought it signified that everything was going to come down. Instead, things are just tightening up."

Vince nodded. "In Mexico City, the Supreme Court of Justice to the Nation gave President Gustavo Diaz Ordaz a free hand to massacre leftists in the Tlatelolco district just days before the Olympic games. Tlatelolco was the Aztec religious and political center. Pyramids are buried there for when high-degree Freemasons tell the Smithsonian to finally 'discover' them." He hesitated. "My grandfather believes the massacre was a religious sacrifice before the Olympic games, like in the old days."

Everyone was silent until Seven haltingly asked, "Are you saying . . . that the Aztec religion may still be active on a *political* scale?"

Vince stared hard at her. "Yes, just as the Nazi religion is still active. Aztec from Mexico, Nazis from Europe, Satanists from America . . . "

"So the Smithsonian changes the dates of artifacts and civilizations?" Thomas was struggling to put together how *big* the picture of control was. *Scientia est potentia.*

Vince shrugged. "Yes. Control history and you control the present and the future. Keep previous American empires obscure by changing North American archaeological dates. Maintain the illusion that not much happened here until the Europeans and their Catholic religion and dynastic families arrived. The Smithsonian, American and European Freemasons, the Vatican in Italy, Jesuits in Japan." He laughed bitterly. "In Mexico, we are blessed with them all."

In fact, Vince said, there are *two* Mexicos, just as there are two United States, one in the north and northeast, one in the south and southwest. The demarcation in Mexico is the Isthmus of Tehuantepec. West of the Isthmus is Aztec Mexico, east is Mayach Mexico. East of Mexico City in Cholula, Puebla is a ziggurat three times the size of the Great Pyramid in Egypt, each side of the base measuring a half-kilometer. On the Mayan side is Chichén Itzá with its ziggurat Temple of Kulkulkan aligned with the light on spring and autumn equinox. At Palenque in the Chiapas Highlands, small portals in the palace align with Venus. Yaxchilán and Bonampak in Chiapas, Tikal and Uaxactun in Guatemala, Copán in Honduras are all lowland Mayan cities under rain forest jungle since the end of the Classic Period, about 1000 AD.

"While my grandfather and I were in Copán, I dreamed of the ball court there," Vince murmured.

Mannie loved baseball. "What kind of ball courts?"

Vince laughed. "In the underworld, where Gods play with a rubber ball for the cosmic stakes of life and death. The game that keeps the equilibrium of the cosmos in balance—not exactly the American pro's."

"What was your dream?" Seven asked gently, stroking Baby Rose's head in her lap.

Vince hugged his legs. "Six stone macaws are carved into the high sidewalls of the court, three in the east and three in the west. Macaws stand for the *nahual* or guiding spirit of the Solar deity captured by the stars and the planet Venus *Iko Kĳ nima chumil*. With the rubber ball, the six macaws make seven or *Ahpú*." *Seven*. He looked at Seven. Was her name a sign? He continued. "A statue of the hero Hunahpú stood between two giant rocks at the north end of the court in front of the entry to Xibalbá spinning like a top."

"Like the Greek Symplegades," Thomas said.

Vince nodded. "In the dream, I was standing at the south end of the court, mesmerized by the spinning. I knew that if I entered I would have to cross four rivers before coming to a black, red, white, and yellow crossroads— the sign of the god of Death, Mictlantecutli, a cross in a circle. I stood uncertain, wondering who my opponent was. The stands were filled with the Mimixcoa, countless dead ancestors suffering in the afterlife, and annihilated hollow-eyed zombies hooting and booing. Suddenly, I knew that before I could play I would have to use my psychic forces to go into the underworld and save the Solar deity—not the star we call the Sun, but its *nahual . . .*"

He looked around at the blank, dreamy faces etched in firelight. "Every cosmic body has a *nahual*," he explained, "a *Doppelgänger*. I began walking north toward Hunahpú, and it felt like a *Star Trek* tractor beam

78

reeling me in. I passed his statue and stepped inside the spinning opening to Xibalbá. Darkness enveloped me. All I could hear was rushing water."

His throat tightened at the memory. The pilgrims held their breath.

"It was this dream that convinced my grandfather and father that it was time for me to come to the United States."

"*El norte* the underworld," Mannie said.

"The Lords of Xibalbá in Washington, DC," the Colonel added.

Vince looked at the Colonel but said nothing.

"The trapped Solar deity—" Seven began.

"—and the human heart denied," Thomas finished soberly.

"Hey," Ray lit up, "Vince makes us *Ahpú* or seven."

Mannie beamed. "The Magnificent Seven."

"Seven Bodhisattvas," Thomas said, rubbing Seven's neck.

Vince looked at Seven. "Why you are named Seven?"

She shrugged. "Family nickname. Seventh and the last grandchild on my mother's side, the only child of my parents. I decided to go by Seven when I came to California. My given name is Lilya Columbia."

"District of Columbia," Vince smiled, "Columbia is the occult name for America."

"Really?" Seven wondered if her *roma* grandmother had known.

"'The Magnificent Seven,'" Ray said, puffing his chest out and pantomiming a gunslinger. "Our guns shoot *nahual.*"

As they all laughed, the bus radio burst into life.

"From the desert to the sea, to all Southern California, a good evening. This is your iconic news anchor bringing you The Big News on KNXT. Angelenos, the Watergate affair isn't about catching Tricky Dick at dirty tricks but about using him one last time as he has been used for years, this time to undermine the Presidency. Nixon's resignation will be just another reward for 33° Freemason Vice President Jerry Ford for his good work in chairing the Warren Commission cover-up of President John Fitzgerald Kennedy's assassination. Ford may be the first unelected president of the United States, but not the last.

"Soon to be former President Nixon must feel a little like Henry

IV on his deathbed, agonizing over how he usurped Richard II's crown—"

[British voiceover:] *God knows, my son*
By what by-paths and indirect crook'd ways
I met this crown…

"Watergate throws the water gate open for the completion of the *coup d'état* that began with the Killing of the King on November 22, 1963, and as with every *coup*, the mop-up continues. Since that fateful day, a gigantic struggle has ensued behind the scenes between those committed to the *coup*, those covering their you-know-whats, and those striving to retain the shreds of a noble document once known as the Constitution. Nixon will pass through the Watergate just in time for the nation's 200th birthday.

"Other news: getting around states' rights. A man who worked on FDR's Brain Trust and now works for the Ford Foundation is proposing that we have ten regional *Newstates* instead of 50 states in preparation for COG national emergencies. Meanwhile, a CFR member is writing 'A Declaration of Interdependence' for 32 Senators and 92 Representatives to sign on January 30 (1/30=13), 1976 during the nation's bicentenniel birthday party in Philadelphia—"

[Voice-over:] *Two centuries ago our forefathers brought forth a new nation; now we must join with others to bring forth a new world order,* NOVUS ORDO SECLORUM.

"Signing off, *angelenos*, for KNXT by way of KRMA, Akashic news station from *the other side . . .*"

The radio faded to off. The pilgrims stared at each other.

"What did you do to that radio, my man?" Ray asked Thomas.

That very first night under the desert stars, Thomas dreamed of sitting by the fire with Seven and an ancient Indian who said to them, "You poor kids have no elders to guide you. Someone has taken pity on you here in the desert and sent me to show you a thing or two. Don't be afraid," he tapped his left shoulder, "I'll be right here."

He took out his ceremonial pipe and tapped tobacco into it, praying under his breath as he offered it to the six directions. "This special tobacco will bind us together so you can see what I see. Inhale once and don't exhale until I do." He lit the pipe, drew deeply, then passed it to Thomas who inhaled and held the smoke down, passing it to Seven. He then beat his drum and chanted. From somewhere, other drumbeats answered. Purple, red, blue, and green drum vibrations wafted up and turned into a huge undulating serpent.

Thomas' abdomen lurched. In his left ear, the old one said, *Watch and learn.*

Thomas' body relaxed as the serpent entered his belly and slithered up his spine. *K'ulthanlilni,* the old one clarified—what you call *kundalini.*

Suddenly, Thomas saw two circles around a fire, the outer of tiny copper-colored men, the inner of women, fading in and out as they chanted *Indihuasca janayari, Curihuasca janayari, Ayahuasqa janayari.* The men passed a bowl and drank from it.

The serpent reached the summit of his spine and entered his skull. It bit his pineal gland and light flashed from between his eyes. The men's heads turned into yawning jaguar heads, their bodies soft yellow with dark spots. Thomas cringed, remembering Seven's story of the Jaguar priest. *It is not him,* the old one whispered.

A deep yawn overtook him. The old one said, *Quick, shut your eyes if you still can.*

But he couldn't; the serpent had awakened the eye that cannot be shut and therefore can be seen as well as see. A tall Jaguar man stood, intent upon Thomas, and into the circle pounced the two-headed jaguar *Mokokoneute.* Its yawn-roar vibrated throughout Thomas' body, catapulting him eastward at rocket speed along a *haecceidad,* a magnetic pathway. He had no idea where he was going or how or who might be following him, but when his aionic speed slowed down, he found himself in a bedroom bathed in a lurid yellow-green light. A clock was ticking very loud and he smelled something putrid. Hovering over a large bed, he looked down on a sleeping man. When he drew near the face, dead eyes opened and stared into his.

Thomas jolted back into his body that was still lying in the desert next to Seven. His body was breathing heavily.

Beside him, Seven asked sleepily, "Are you all right?" She placed her hand on his cheek, the sheen of starlight coating the darkness.

"I think so," he nodded, his heart still racing. "But where is the old one?"

He rolled away and fell like lead back to sleep. He'd *seen* a pair of frightening dead eyes in a face he didn't recognize but somehow knew.

32

The Trail Heats Up

The Malicious have a dark Happiness.

–Victor Hugo, 1802-1885

I am not happy about the rebirth of the Jesuits. Swarms of them will present themselves under more disguises ever taken by even a chief of the Bohemians, as printers, writers, publishers, school teachers, etc. If ever an association of people deserved eternal damnation, on this earth and in hell, it is this society of Loyola.

–John Quincy Adams, 1816

Hours before Thomas' dream, Agent Iff and Didy had checked the Wigwam Motel log and left. All the night desk clerk had seen was the Cadillac and a young woman registering as Lilya Eliade, who then left that afternoon after checkout time. Iff wanted to see the room and its garbage, but the maid had already cleaned. Iff asked her in Spanish if she'd seen anything unusual, but she indicated she spoke only Quiché. The truth was she knew Spanish but also what CIAs were capable of. In fact, she and her Sandinista National Liberation Front (FSLN) husband had fled to *el norte* to escape Somoza and his CIA thugs.

The stream of satellite intelligence so far supported only two hard facts and two strong possibilities: the Cadillac and VW bus were registered to two individuals who were probably in the vehicles, possibly with the black dissident Raymond Kofi, who at this point was a red herring. Given that the retired Air Force intelligence colonel was legally blind, it was safe to assume that Lilya Eliade was driving the Cadillac, as she had on many Sundays. The military couldn't believe that after so many complacent years their colonel had flown the coop. They suspected abduction. The problem was he *knew* things, the adjutant said. So Kofi was driving the VW bus? Infuriatingly, none of the photo recon so far showed who else was in either vehicle, and no one wanted to raise a flag by pulling them over. Was Reagan's escaped butterfly with them? Greenbaum kept asking himself, *What happened to her GPS implant?*

Another far-fetched possibility had been gnawing at him. If Thomas was responsible for disintegrating that cabin in the foothills above the Communist's house, was he in one of the vehicles? And what exactly had he been working on? What did he know? Photo recon revealed that the blue bus had made more than several trips to the cabin no longer there.

His instructions to Iff were basically under no circumstance to involve law enforcement. He was to stay well behind the two vehicles and not worry about line of sight; Greenbaum would feed him sat intel as he got it. Since the motel, the VW had picked up a hitchhiker at the motel, then stopped outside Barstow and again at an obscure road near Daggett, though no one was seen getting in or out. Greenbaum knew the obscure road well—the Augustan Society mansion—and wanted Iff to check out the stop en route.

"Inquire if anything unusual occurred on the mansion grounds this past afternoon," he told Iff on the satellite phone. "Tell the gatekeeper that Dr. Greenbaum sent you and show your credentials. I'll be available by telephone if you have trouble—and keep your eye on Didymus while there."

So Agent Iff and Didy headed to Daggett while Agent Iff continued to air his grievances to his built-in soundboard. Iff had wanted to infiltrate the left, not babysit an MK-ULTRA experiment. Throughout training, that's all they'd raved about, how the highest an intel operative could climb was to become an operations officer in right- or left-wing groups, and that the left was a lot more fun than the right. What was it that narcotics cowboy Captain George Hunter White said when he gave that talk at Langley? *I was a very minor missionary, actually a heretic, but I toiled wholeheartedly in the vineyards because it was fun, fun, fun. Where else could a red-blooded American boy lie, kill, cheat, steal, rape, and pillage with the sanction and blessing of the All Highest?* White had it made, running that Greenwich Village apartment with two-way mirrors and surveillance equipment, then in 1955 moving it all to San Francisco under Operation Midnight Climax. But Iff's "profile" wasn't right even for the right, they said, despite the fact that he was Mormon and as patriotic as you could get. As for the left, he didn't look "hungry" enough. Too urbane, one interviewer said. Too Pillsbury Doughboy, another said. So what did they have him doing? Driving an angelic moron around. "Oh, and keep an eye on Didymus while there." Christ.

And why hadn't he qualified for cryptozoology, the perfect cover? As cryptozoologists, agents could say they were going to the Highlands of Scotland to check on the Loch Ness sonar readings of University of Birmingham scientists. They could go in quest of the sauropod-like N'yamala in Gabon, the Mokele-Mbembe in the Congo east of Gabon, the pterodactyl-like Kongamato in northwest Zambia, Olitiau in Cameroon, Ahool in Indonesia, the Ogapogo in Lake Okanagan of British Columbia, the Kraken giant squid from Newfoundland to Norway, the Lusca octopus in the Bahamas. Throughout the 1950s and 1960s, when the CIA had "business" in China, cryptozoologists were humping it over the Himalayas. In the West Bengal city of Kalimpong, there were more cryptozoologists than inhabitants. In 1958, a fleet of B-26 bombers provided by the CIA turned into an anti-Sukarno coup in Indonesia, the same year cryptozoologists had been in the area claiming to be looking for the orang pendek.

Slick Airways and Flying Tiger Lines, Civil Air Transport

out of Kelly Field in San Antonio, Air Asia, Southern Air Transport out of Miami, and Intermountain Aviation were flying CIA and Special Ops in and heroin out. Tolstoy's émigré grandson had been part of an OSS team in Tibet until he settled in Florida and became general manager of Marineland. Teddy Roosevelt's grandson, Kim, had been OSS and running the coup against President Mossadegh in Tehran in 1953.

Right now, behind the 26,810-foot mountain Dhaulagiri, altitude 15,000 feet, Tibetan-speaking CIA agents were in Mustang, a little 750-square-mile Nepalese thumb sticking into Chinese Communist Tibet, a theocracy since the 1380s. When China overran Tibet, Mustang was spared due to a 160-year-old agreement that made the King of Mustang and his pure Tibetan culture (not Hindu at all) a tributary to the Hindu Gurkha kings of Nepal, paying 886 Nepalese rupees and one Mustang pony per year. A 1961 agreement brokered by the U.S. between the Chinese and Nepalese reaffirmed Mustang's inclusion with Nepal.

Iff could have been flown in from New Delhi to Pokhara, then 15 days and 150 miles into Mustang through the valley of the Kali Gandaki between Dhaulagiri and equally high Annapurna, to the medieval walled capital city Lo Mantang. (*sMon Thang* means the plain of prayer.) Sakya-pa sect Tantric Buddhist monks comprise 13 percent of the population, 23 villages and three towns. He could have been keeping an eye on the Chinese army from Mustang, but the CIA pulled out of Mustang in 1969, so he was shit out of luck for that assignment. He'd followed the extraction from Lhasa of Tenzin Gyatso on March 17, 1959. Now, the CIA was training Tibetans in covert warfare at Camp Hale in Leadville, Colorado under the name of ST Circus. Even that would be more fun than babysitting.

The International Society of Cryptozoology made more sense to him than the nonsense spouted by organizations like the Smithsonian and National Geographic Society. The ISC believed in "continuing species coexistence," not in sequential evolution.

Australopithecines didn't die out 750,000 years ago, nor *Homo erectus* 200,000 years ago, nor Neanderthals 35,000 years ago. Wild men were still seen in the wilderness everywhere: Sasquatch in North America, Yeti, the Almas in the Caucasus, the Wildman in the Shen Nong Jia Mountains of central China.

Didy listened while anxiously awaiting permission to turn on the radio.

"When you're the new kid on the block, Didy, you have to lay down in the mold. For the CIA, that was the OSS, and the OSS included British Intelligence *and* Nazi SS, namely Herr Reinhard Gehlen. You're talking bloodlines and hierarchy when you talk CIA, with the best at the top, the richest, the best positioned, best educated, the brains who do not give the lie to 'intelligence,' get it? That's the *left* hand of the government magic act. The *right* hand, the one you and I see, are the politically elected and appointees, the boys who worship greed and raw power. The left hand already has all that, so what's in the power game for them? *Refined* objectives, that's what—what most of us have been conditioned to think of as what went out with the Nazis. But for them, see, it's *real*, more real than another new limo or young girlfriend or secret boy toy, even more real than having to have someone killed, if need be.

"If you want to understand British Intelligence and the master spy Gehlen's European network, our Cold War models, you have to go back to John Dee and Queen Elizabeth I, then connect it to Himmler's Wewelsburg Castle in Westphalia. Ever seen it?" Not waiting for a reply, he turned contemplative. "Phil Agee is the latest Company 'defector.'" He laughed. "He's no defector, he's damage control, going to college campuses and giving the left a spy who came in from the cold. Real defectors wear cement shoes. I met Agee in Puerto Rico. He graduated Notre Dame where a Jesuit Freemason behind-the-scenes bunch troll for Company candidates. Agee set up the University of Mexico riots in '68, then publicly condemned them. He did so well there they sent him to Puerto Rico and then

Cuba, where he was supposedly turned by Castro's DGI." He shook his head. "Mumbo jumbo. Castro's a Jesuit Freemason like Agee. Liberation theology, the Second Vatican Council—it's all Marxist, all red. Jesuits in South and Central America, and the CIA is right in there because most of them, other than the Mormons," he laughed sardonically, "are all Knights of Malta spelled J-e-s-u-i-t."

His indignation slammed up against Didy's blank, friendly face. "You might well ask, what does Iff have against the Jesuits? It's fishy, that's what, and I don't mean the Christian fish. It's everywhere. Even El Maestro, Pedro Albizu Campos, the people's hero in Puerto Rico, was a Jesuit pawn; they ended up torturing him with microwaves in U.S. prisons. You know what microwave torture looks like? The skin swells and cracks." Iff's face registered disgust. "They let him out in '65 and he died." His hands gripped and re-gripped the wheel. "It's getting so Jesuit, Knights of Malta, Pro Deo, Opus Dei, Mormon mafia, and CIA are all synonyms. The CIA's some kind of occult bureau, Didy, like the Soviet KGB and the Nazi SS. They're arming guerrilla movements and propping up puppets all over South and Central America. What the hell's going on?"

Didy snuck a peek at his partner. Iff had a diadem of sweat around his hairline. The desert was definitely getting to him.

"Goddamn it, Didy, *is* the CIA some kind of religion? Am I missing something here? What about that fascist prick Francis Parker Yockey, born in 1917 in Chicago—classical pianist, BA at Georgetown's School of Foreign Service, law degree *cum laude* at Notre Dame in '41. Jesuits again. Immediately after graduating, he enlists in the Army and is assigned to a G-2 intelligence unit in Georgia. Then he disappears for two months in the fall of '42, then has a nervous breakdown when he returns to base camp. Honorable discharge in July 1943. The OSS turns him down. Briefly, he's assistant prosecutor for Wayne County, Michigan, then out of nowhere, he's appointed civilian counsel for the U.S. War Department in Wiesbaden for the Nuremberg Trials. Once in Germany, he begins agitating the fascist right all over the world. Where'd he get the money for all the travel? He was programmed and bankrolled, that's what he was, like Oswald and Ray and Sirhan and—" Iff glanced at Didy. "He wrote *Imperium* without notes, like Hitler wrote *Mein Kampf*, ha ha, and it was immediately endorsed by far-right extremists like Wehrmacht General Otto Remer who was teaching classics at the University of Illinois, if you can believe it. Then he potassium cyanided in a San Francisco jail at 42, my age. Carto, Mr. Liberty Lobby, visited him just before he popped the tooth pill.

"What was it that MI6 spy Crowley said? *Always tell the truth, but lead so improbable a life that no one will ever believe you.* Spies and ex-spies don't tell the truth, you and I know that. Maybe the CIA ought to be the COA, Central *Occult* Agency, like the East German Stasi, the Cheka, the Gru. Intelligence collection, analysis, counterintelligence, covert black ops—what some Company higher-ups like Angleton are already doing: torture with an *occult* twist."

Iff was right. Ever since CIA bacteriologist Frank Olson's death, two factions of the CIA—Technical Services Staff (TSS) and Office of Security—had been struggling over whether to use LSD for interrogation or destabilization? The Army was conducting experiments on all of its bases while the CIA was everywhere, including benign outlets like the Addiction Research Center of U.S. Public Health in Lexington, Kentucky, funded by the National Institute of Mental Health and U.S. Navy, where almost all of the inmates were black.

Food and cigarettes laced with tetrahydrocannabinol acetate had been given to "Wild Bill" Donovan's "dreamers" as early as '41 and Augie Del Grazio, a leader in Italian crime on the Lower East Side of New York City, spilled his guts about underworld operations to cowboy Captain White who then reported it to spychiatrist Dr. Sydney Gottlieb. Based on the information Del Grazio provided, the OSS/CIA was able to cut a deal with the Italian mafia through Lucky Luciano to help Patton's invasion of Italy in July 1943. Instead of serving 30-to-50, Luciano was released from the clink in 1946 and deported to Italy—to rebuild the heroin trade.

Agent Iff glanced at Didy. It was hard to believe, but Didy was quite the killer. Part of his training had been from the White Russians that Allen Dulles and Bill Casey had resettled in the South River, New Jersey area—the *Vorkommando Moskau* elite, the forward unit of SS intelligence on the Soviet front. And yet all Didy remembered were vague images of wrestling naked in the dark with other glistening young male bodies as taut as Spartans and a monstrous chorus of grunts, thrusts, moans, whimpers, and slurps.

Agent Iff had to admit that somewhere along the line he had become afraid of the future, afraid there would be no such thing as retirement, other than the one you didn't get up from. Men might retire from a corporation, but from a Brotherhood like the Company? Never.

Didy was being gnawed at and slowly digested by the future. When Agent Iff disallowed music so he could rant, part of Didy's mind recorded the rants verbatim while another part passed the time by reciting whatever bubbled up—songs, formulae, conversations he'd recorded. En route to Daggett, it was, *These are the hidden sayings that the living Jesus spoke and Judas Thomas the Twin recorded: Jesus said, If the flesh came into being because of spirit, it is a marvel, but if spirit came into being because of the body, it is a marvel of marvels. Jesus said, I have thrown fire upon this world, and look, I am watching it until it blazes.* Where he'd learned this, only Drs. Greenbaum and Gottlieb knew.

The Augustan Society had opened for business in 1954, two years after the Bilderberg Group had birthed the Enterprise and begun consolidating Brotherhoods. Greenbaum said the Augustans were a Knights of Malta front once based in Torrance, thus explaining the phrase, *When you hear a sneeze in Torrance, you hear a 'God bless you' on the Via Condotti.* The Augustans researched genealogy, royalty, nobility, chivalry, heraldry, etc.—in other words, bloodlines and eugenics, and were supposedly the only ones with the authority to award the Noble Order of the Rose to intelligence officers. The Augustan Society was in league with MK-ULTRA and the Black Rose Group, the symbol of the rose having been stolen from the Rosy Cross that originally referred to redemption of the astral, perhaps to what Yeats was referring when he wrote—

> *Surely thine hour has come, thy great wind blows,*
> *Far-off, most secret, inviolate Rose.*

The Austrian initiate called it *regressing evolution, the occult-astral, which interferes with the progressing one.* In medieval times, the Vatican opened bordellos named for the rose, code for prostitution and high-degree Jesuit abuse that prepared Catholic boys and girls to compromise priests, congressmen, dignitaries, men and women in power. Bordello girls wore rose crosses and tattoos. *To pluck a rose.*

The Order of the Rose, Noble Order of the Rose, Fourth Reich, and Aquarius were kinship terms in some mysterious way. Founded by Sir Rodney Hartwell and Ernst August Prinz zur Lippe, first cousin of the infamous Prince Bernard of the Netherlands chairing the Bilderberg Group, the Noble Order of the Rose was an esoteric Brotherhood of Catholic fascist power: Jesuits, Nazis, and Knights of Malta working together as they had for the ratlines at the end of the war. Soon, they would seat their own Pope on the Throne of Peter. Canada's prime minister was one of theirs.

The Qabalist had been sent to Haiti to observe Jesuit success in merging Santería with Catholic mind control, Haiti being America's Afro-Caribbean open-air lab under the Order of the Rose. He'd also accompanied Dr. Greenbaum to the Augustan Society mansion to pick up one of his Presidential models. It had reminded him of The Fellowship in Washington, DC, a "retirement-entertainment" center for elite intelligence types—old OSS, Skorzeny Nazis, Shickshinny Knights claiming descent from the Russian Grand Priory of the Order of St. John of Jerusalem. Patrons included Otto von Hapsburg of the old Austro-Hungarian Imperial House and Prince Victor Emmanuel of Savoy, Grand Master of the Vatican chivalric Order of St. Maurice and St. Lazarus—in other words, Dragon Court types.

Agent Iff sailed through the Augustan Society gates. He told Didy to wait in the car and almost missed how paralyzed with terror Didy was.

"What is it, pal?" Iff asked, careful not to touch him. (Greenbaum had stressed this.) Iff looked out the window at the mansion. "What do you know that I don't?"

The part that knew in Didy was buried alive beneath memories he couldn't access. Still, his body knew he'd been here with Baby Rose, and it was not a nice place.

Didy's assassin programming included verbatim memory of multiple conversations and names, which meant being taken to secret meetings purportedly as a bodyguard but really to mentally record every detail. Only those who knew the triggers could access the treasure house of data stored in him, or contrarily, bury what he had seen others shamelessly do.

Nor was Didy privy to how many industry and intelligence higher-ups were involved with the occult to one degree or another not for kicks but as a "binding" agent, i.e. blackmail. Rituals— homosexual, pedophile, death, pain, confessional—*eroticized* the Enterprise, binding everyone by drugs, sex, pain, and death, the prize being power and more power, political, social, personal, *magickal*. Many came in as skeptics, going through the motions because the club or Lodge demanded it and the prize was tantalizing. Others became believers because of what they saw or experienced— unbelievable things, the presence of blood, the possibility of death, the dire embrace of the forbidden, the dangerous, the possessing, the frightening, the exhilarating, all of which made them feel more alive than ever. Didy would be there guarding the door, seeing but not seeing the youths and children drugged, on their knees, bent over, sucking, fucking, cameras rolling behind the mirrors, microphones hot. Sometimes he would be called upon to participate in blow jobs, sodomy, whips, bondage, death, the cum flowing like rivulets, the men's conceit that their cum was the Philosopher's Stone, Mercury's cum, aborted metallic sperm, milk of the Virgin, pontific water.

Nor did Didy know that he had had the double misfortune of being born a twin leased to Father Mengele and his American Nazi-Jew clone Greenbaum in exchange for political favors to his own uncle. He did not know because he had been subjected to more *hsi-nau* experiments than anyone should endure, much less imagine, shattered and split like Humpty Dumpty, then put back together in layers he could not access. The mental faculties that were his birthright had been stolen.

And while he was plugged into EEGs being conditioned to kill people he didn't know, his identical twin was living a brilliant, privileged life. Had Didy known they were enacting *The Prince and the Pauper*, he might have felt toward his masters something other than mechanical obedience. But the leash was all he had ever known and feelings other than pain were out of reach, at least until that day in the foothills of Santa Barbara when he had seen Baby Rose. Now for the first time, a memory he could almost touch but not quite was quickening him back to life like Lazarus.

And he had already lied twice.

Out on the desert, the seven pilgrims were deep asleep when KRMA chose to switch on and melt a future news item into their unconscious.

". . . will be using longitudinal wave interferometers, also known as Tesla howitzers, to tap the Time domain—the very weapon Khrushchev spoke of in January 1960, a weapon that can initiate earthquakes and volcanic eruptions and engineer weather by marking the Woodpecker Grid for plasma orbs and instantaneous howitzer strikes that don't travel through 3-space but travel *around* it,

93

manipulating ripples and patterns in the spacetime fabric to create an energetic effect that then emerges from the spacetime vacuum.

"In exothermic mode, this Tesla weapon can produce a blast of heat of near-nuclear proportions to topple buildings, heat the atmosphere of discrete regions, destroy electronics and power grids, drop airplanes from the sky, destroy missiles in flight, etc. In endothermic mode, it sucks out energy and creates a blast of cold to freeze tanks, personnel, and equipment.

"As for mind control and psychoenergetics, one end of the longitudinal wave spectrum can drop everyone unconscious while the other can 'snap' the mind-body connection for an instant death. Without even convulsing, the body drops like a limp rag that won't begin to decay for 45 days. Between unconsciousness and death lies an involuntary trance, with the mind hypnagogic and susceptible to overriding commands.

"Perhaps most remarkable is how the weapon's destructive power is delivered instantaneously from the local vacuum at the place of the target. In other words, it's not about energy transmission through space via EM force fields; this is transmission through spacetime in the form of electrogravitational potentials. Protective Tesla domes or spheres can be made to emerge from the local vacuum to destroy missiles, whereas nesting domes can protect the domed area from nuclear radiation.

"Crop circles are the artistic side of interferometry. Marker beacons direct the satellite laser to 'draw' what the supercomputer dictates. Weather could be sent to grow crops in drought areas, nuclear waste could be cleaned up, global heat could be vented into outer space, but so far, this technology is being used to destroy and intimidate. What it will do to the Time domain remains to be seen. This is KRMA . . ."

The radio switched off.

During the broadcast, Baby Rose was cruising on the dreamtime *Nautilus* through deep canyons off the Bahamas.

Sometime before her escape (she didn't call it that because she didn't remember it and therefore couldn't call it anything), she had been on the atomic submarine *Nautilus*. Out the Captain Nemo window, she had seen roads, domes, and fluted columns on pillars of toppled buildings. Now, a statue of Neptune holding a crystal with little pyramids shooting rays of energy caught her eye. She knew it was Neptune because of her Little Mermaid programming. (Dr. Greenbaum had once burned an upside-down Green Empire triangle into her brain with a red laser aimed at her forehead, then electroshocked her before the next image, saying, *Go deeper, deeper . . .*) Suddenly, four divers appeared, waving as they swam down between two fluted pillars.

That's when she woke up to her brain replaying what KRMA had said about interferometry. She picked up Seven's dream journal and pen and automatic wrote it all down with her left hand for Thomas since obviously the broadcast was for him. Her stomach hurt a little because of that Nazi Alice, but writing with her left hand got her around Alice's executive function.

Her work done, Baby Rose wandered with Sirius around the desert until the other pilgrims surfaced from sleep.

33

The Bagdad Café

The British and other people around the world care about who killed Kennedy because we all are concerned that the greatest democracy may be crumbling without the American people being aware of it. Can you kill a sitting U.S. president and get away with it? Apparently, yes, you can.

—Nigel Turner, *The Men Who Killed Kennedy*, 1988, a 9-part documentary

I was given a mission and I tried to carry it out.

—Lt. Col. Oliver North, televised Iran-Contra Hearings, 1987

Let me be frank about what we are finding. There are instances where CIA did not, in an expeditious or consistent fashion, cut off relationships with individuals supporting the Contra program who were alleged to have engaged in drug trafficking activity.

—CIA Inspector General Fred P. Hitz; testimony before the U.S. House Intelligence Committee, March 1998

While Baby Rose with her owl eyes and Sirius were wandering around just before dawn, the Colonel was dreaming he was a boy again, standing at the airfield with his father watching the great *aerostiers* the Red Baron Manfred von Richthofen and Captain of the French Air Force Group 2-33 Antoine de Saint-Exupéry, *le petit prince* himself who went down in a Lightning on the morning of July 31, 1944, making a recon run from Bongo, Corsica to Grenoble . . .

He woke up to a thread of pink in the east. By habit, he rose early, but now it may have been due to diagonally squeezing his six-foot-something frame on the bus bed. Gauging by the half-lidded eye of the rising desert sun, he guesstimated he had time for a little walk. Maybe he'd even get lucky and find a good strong cup of coffee, though he doubted it. He stretched a bit, wrote a note about a quest east, cast a last loving look at the rumpled sleeping bags, and set off.

With his cane leading the way and his glasses already glinting in the sun, he walked and thought about how overnight he and his Caddy had become gypsies. Like his hero Patton, he knew there was much more after death, but one more adventure wouldn't hurt. The Bible-thumpers of all persuasions could have the Old Testament, including the military men who preferred violence and bitterness to loving kindness.

He squinted. *Baghdad Café.* He was in luck, and the red '64 Mustang convertible parked outside indicated it might even be open. Out back was a pristine 1944 Aerocoach.

In the entryway was a handwritten sign saying, *Average annual rainfall: 2.3 inches.* Inside, Hank Williams was singing "Your Cheating Heart" from the jukebox. The smell of bacon mingled with coffee made the Colonel melt onto the stool at the black Formica counter. It was tough traveling with vegetarians, though he knew it was probably good for him. Visions of sausages danced in his mouth. The coffee pot read *DRINK ME,* so he got up and got his own cup. One sip of the black gold told him it might be the best cup of coffee he'd ever had.

Through the order window to the kitchen, he could see the back of a young man in a muscle shirt at a sizzling grill who, with perfect timing, turned friendly-like and called out, "I know what you want, Colonel, it'll be right up," and winked as though the Colonel were a regular.

Before he could even blink, a short, trim, middle-aged Navy Admiral in full dress uniform strode out of the kitchen and poured himself a cup of coffee. *A sailor's sailor*, the Colonel thought admiringly.

"'Morning," the Admiral nodded pleasantly.

"'Morning," the Colonel returned, surprised when the Admiral sat down a stool away.

"You're Air Force, aren't you, Colonel?" the Admiral asked, sipping his coffee.

Looking down at his rumpled leisure summer shirt and slacks, the Colonel wondered what gave him away.

The Admiral grinned. "Oh, don't be alarmed, Colonel. From *this* side, we can see just about everything, and I've come to see *you*."

The Colonel's growing flummox was interrupted by the cook arriving with his breakfast, which was, as assured, exactly what he'd envisioned: eggs up easy, sausage, biscuits and gravy. On the cook's muscular arm was a U.S. Navy anchor.

"Thank you," the Colonel murmured, still thinking over the phrase "from this side."

"You bet," the sailor grinned, then eyed the Admiral. "Your usual, sir?"

"Not this morning, Mike. Just coffee."

The sailor looked back at the Colonel. "Admiral Boorda was my CNO, back when we were alive." He leaned on the counter. "He was murdered *by our own* because he was going to turn the tables on the Navy regarding what they were doing in mind control and brain warfare. See this?" The sailor pointed to a shaved spot on his close-cropped head. "I died of what they did to me. They made the Admiral's murder look like suicide, adding insult to injury." His broad face reddened as he turned back to the kitchen, mumbling, "Sons of bitches."

The Colonel hesitated over his beckoning plate. Murder was not his idea of breakfast conversation, nor was he sure the food was real, or for that matter what currency "real" had at the Bagdad Café. Maybe he was dead, too.

"Go on and eat," the Admiral laughed, "the food's good. You'll get used to the desert's 'open-door policy.'"

With a mouthful of perfect eggs, he glanced at the ghost seated beside him. "*Were* you . . . murdered?"

"Oh, yeah. The blueblood WASP admiralty hated that I was Jewish and achieved my rank the hard way—the only enlisted seaman to rise to Chief of Naval Operations in 200 years of Navy history. To them, I was just a political appointee coming in to kick their racist and sexist asses. When I pressed for female and ethnic minority promotions, they despised me. But that wasn't why they blew a hole in my chest a half hour before my scheduled meeting with two *Newsweek* reporters. I'd also set up an interview for a British news series entitled, 'Bosnia: The Secret War,' given that I'd been Commander-in-Chief of U.S. Naval Forces in Europe and of Allied Forces in southern Europe from 1991 to 1994—"

The Colonel set down his fork and stared at the Admiral. "1991 to 1994?"

The Admiral put a hand on the Colonel's shoulder that felt real enough. "Take a deep breath, Colonel. As we all know from this side, spacetime is one fabric of one geography.—I was about to go public with some highly controversial national security issues my Strategic Studies Group had uncovered—cognitive warfare, biological process control, chemical lobotomies, remote mind control using acoustical, optical, and electromagnetic fields to interfere with biological processes, including the brain—all boiling down to invisible kills from afar. While heading up the Strategic Studies Group, I did enough reading to realize that the enemy was a moving target, especially after reading Captain Tyler's 1984 paper, 'The Electromagnetic Spectrum in Low-Intensity Conflict," the conceptual basis for microwave beam weapons.

"During the Reagan administration, the Classified Information Procedures Act (CIPA) withheld evidence considered classified from those being prosecuted, along with SAMs or special administrative measures. Then at least 25 British defense industry computer programmers and engineers died or disappeared under suspicious circumstances, all connected in one way or another with the Navy, and CIPA made sure no one could find out what the Navy had to do with it. Five had worked for Marconi Underwater Systems, a major Strategic Defense Initiative (SDI) contractor. Malcolm Puddy was found floating dead in an English canal with a painter's palette tied around his neck; he had two pending patents for *stardrives* before the Brits and U.S. Navy tagged them as national security. His 'suicide' was like mine."

"Stardrives?" The Colonel stared at him, his mind trying to race ahead twenty years.

The Admiral returned his stare. "Well, that's the really big secret, isn't it? The UFO thing. The space thing. On December 27, 1980 at a BBCTV/Marconi complex near the U.S. Air Force Bentwaters Rendlesham Forest base north of London in Suffolk, everyone on duty saw UFOs—whirring, bright orange lights. That's when the Ministry of Defense formed its UFO S4F.

"Three years before, in July 1977—that's thirty years after U.S. disc technology was dramatically unveiled with harbor patrolman Harold Dahl and pilot Kenneth Arnold in the Pacific Northwest, and the Roswell Incident in New Mexico—bright round objects hung over the sea at RAF Boulmer in Northumberland, one of which shape-shifted into a body with projections like arms and legs.

"Even the 17 April 2005 *Sunday Times* was *still* mum on the thousands of UFO sightings over the past half century, including fantastic aerial maneuvers two years before my death over Edinburgh's Blackford Hill, where the Royal Observatory is. The question is not *are* the ships there—they are—but are they ours or are they 'theirs'?"

He sipped his coffee. "Oh yes, my Air Force friend, silent warfare behind the scenes is hot and heavy. Endless wars of distraction have been planned while nations are blackmailed into going along with a one-world defense scenario. You know the real action always lies behind the scenes, cloaked in 'national security.'

"Anyway, the motiveless 'suicides' were purposely made bizarre to inspire terror in the scientists who'd signed nondisclosure agreements: under bridges with puncture wounds, hangings, disappearances, lost time, plastic bags over their heads. Then there were the strange deaths of dozens of Sky TV technicians. Colonel, these new 'less-than-lethal' technologies can pipe speech, suggestions, and thoughts into the brain as well as read its thoughts. They can control voluntary muscle movement, emotions, sleep, dreams, wipe or replace short- and long-term memory.

"Two months before my death, the Air Force and Navy opened an investigation into allegations that the Navy had been involved in torturing at least 500 people with remote-controlled neuro-electromagnetic and radio frequency weapons. Heart attacks, suicides, assassinations, blackmail—weapons leaving no trace or evidence for a court of law, the ultimate criminal weapon."

His voice dropped so low the Colonel could scarcely hear him. Even talking about these revelations still caused pain to the man who had shuffled off his mortal coil.

"And you had no idea?" he asked the Admiral gently, mopping up his gravy with the biscuit that happily never seemed to get cold, savoring the coffee that remained eternally hot.

The Admiral took a deep breath. "When I read the testimony of those victims, I realized they'd been used as guinea pigs for a technology that had gone much further than I had imagined. I may have been the new kid on the block, but I was a quick study. First, a terrific increase in Navy suicides. Add the British Marconi deaths, the testimonies of 500 guinea pigs, and you get the picture." He looked hard at the Colonel. "You were career military. You know what it is to love what you *think* you're serving." His ghost hand white-knuckled his coffee cup. "Was it possible those young sailors didn't really kill themselves? That they were guinea pigs, too? Is there no decency left?"

He shook his ghost head. "But even that wasn't really why I was killed. I found out about the Omega Navigation System and what it's really about. The Australian oil engineer journalist Joe Vialls found out about it, too, and the Navy microwaved him for 20 years, then gave him a heart attack.

"I decided it was time to bring it all out in the open, 'fess up, lead the way for the rest of the military to come to their senses and be the military I swore to uphold. That's when they 'suicided' me. Shot me through the heart."

The Colonel shook his head. "No one commits suicide in the chest."

The Admiral laughed. "Exactly. I put up some resistance, so maybe they had to settle for however they could get it done."

The Colonel smelled roses. Blood was seeping through the Admiral's whites.

The Admiral stood up. "That's it, Colonel. I came to tell you my story because of your experiences during the trench warfare in the Great War. *Great War,* what a term, huh? You were used, I was used, but neither of us could have stopped it. By the way, that young girl in your party? She's one of theirs and they're looking for her. And the young scientist." He searched the horizon out the window.

The Colonel followed his gaze, but didn't see anything but desert.

The Admiral continued. "And I guess you know the military's now wondering where you and your Cadillac have gone."

The cook came out of the kitchen. "Time to go, sir. The Sun's climbing."

"Right, Mike. Give him the file for the young woman called Seven. Pass this on to her, Colonel. The short version of what happened to her father is: the Navy. Just like me." He winked.

The Colonel took the glowing manila envelope from Mike as the two ghosts saluted him. A lump rose in his throat as he saluted back. At the door, the Admiral turned and smiled. "Breakfast's on the Navy, Colonel."

They jumped into the Mustang and Mike accelerated, the Admiral keeping his eyes on the Colonel. *I'll be seeing you soon*, the Colonel heard in his mind. Then they roared off and disappeared into the thin desert air.

Making his three-legged way along 66 back to his young friends, the Colonel thought of Baby Rose, wondering who the hell would want to hurt a sweet kid like her. So the military was looking for him, too. Sure, he'd been privy to secrets, but who cared about those secrets now? He wondered how many JAG active reserves were still in the American court system keeping tabs on secrets like the Admiral's death.

When he turned for a final mental snapshot of the Bagdad Café, all he saw was rubble and cement blocks. Like the Mustang, the Aerocoach and café were gone. He glanced at his grandfather's pocket watch. Time hadn't moved. The Sun's eye was still half-lidded, like a still shot. But the glowing envelope for Seven was proof.

He remembered hearing about the murder of another Naval officer, Lt. Cmdr. William Bruce Pitzer, head of the audio-visual unit at Bethesda Naval Hospital where Kennedy's autopsy had been done. He'd seen something in the 16mm films of the autopsy that got him "suicided" in the right temple. (Pitzer was left-handed.) After Kennedy's assassination, Fort Bragg used the Dallas assassination as a classic for Special Forces being trained to kill heads of state.

On January 22, 1991, Colonel James Sabow would pay with his life for the big drug trafficking operation he and a mustang Marine working secretly for him uncovered at El Toro and Tustin air bases near Irvine in Southern California: unmarked C-130s landing in a remote part of the MCAS El Toro airfield known as Spook Corner and flown in by nonmilitary types in the middle of the night were carrying drugs and the makings of drugs like red phosphorus and P2. Raytheon's E-Systems in Greenville, Texas created sophisticated electronic gaps through which planes could cross the border without tripping warning systems. (E-Systems was directed by former NSA Director Bobby Ray Inman.) The drugs were then conduited through the Defense Regional Management Office (DRMO) and crooked National Investigative Service (NIS) agents.

El Toro had been the seat of operations for CIA contract airlines like Air America during the Vietnam era. Other facilities sprang up in Fire Lakes, Nevada, Joplin, Missouri, Iron Mountain, Texas, and Mena, Arkansas. C-130s, P-3 Orions, helicopters—all through the Department of Agriculture, U.S. Forestry division, to Hemet Aviation. Counter-Intelligence Terrorism teams (CITs), sleepers and sociopathic killers with access to all the uniforms they needed.

The 1994 *Eye-to-Eye with Connie Chung* television program blew it all wide open—Sabow's suspicious death, drugs being delivered on military bases. So the CITs were ordered to plug all the holes: a Marine who had loaded the drugs onto airplanes, the co-owner of T&G Aviation, the computer specialist who accessed records during the Inspector General shakedown before Sabow's death, and another colonel at El Toro after a *60 Minutes* segment ran on February 19, 1994 regarding the illegal use of C-130s. The El Toro sergeant who reported the wholesale theft of computer equipment (hundreds of thousands of taxpayer dollars) was court-martialed for his diligence of duty, but at least remained alive.

Semper fidelis. Once the Reagan-Bush-Cheney *troika* hit the big time, drug "bake sales" would grow like bad seed all over the United States. In Mena, Arkansas, for example, they would be run out of the governor's mansion with a direct line to the operations room in the White House, all intimately linked with the 6,100-square-foot command center on the sixth floor of the Justice Department. Thanks to the DOJ's stolen and enhanced PROMIS software, those under FEMA cover could track U.S. dissidents and make their way around the 1984 Boland Amendment to orchestrate combined military-DEA-CIA drug operations as funding for the *contra* war in Nicaragua and other black ops. Contra training would take place ten miles north of Mena in the Ouachita National Forest—old stomping grounds of the Knights of the Golden Circle—and the money laundered through Arkansas bond brokers. Air America veterans who once flew heroin out of Southeast Asia for Shackley and Generals Singlaub and Secord would fly for another CIA cutout, Southern Air Transport, and Project Donation would protect individuals who allowed their insured planes and boats to "disappear" in exchange for drug profits at the other end. Guns would be unloaded and cocaine loaded at John Hull's ranch in Costa Rica for the return trip to Mena. U.S. Attorneys were placed to defuse any legal threat and rewarded with appointments like Administrator of the Drug Enforcement Administration (DEA). Foxes running the henhouse while Americans were alpha-waved by their televisions.

The televised 1987 Iran-Contra Hearings under Senator John Kerry and the 700-page report that followed would serve as damage control. At every juncture, where real names and dates might be revealed, Senator Daniel Inouye (D-HI) would call for "national security" secret sessions and evidence would be shredded, given that uncovering the CIA drugs-for-arms connection would threaten future covert operations, not to mention the Enterprise as a whole. The star of the televised Iran-Contra Hearings—the faithful deputy director for political-military affairs for the National Security Council under the Reagan-Bush-Cheney troika—would be rewarded well for perjuring himself before Congress and being convicted of three felonies. Of course, his prison sentence would be suspended, after which he would become a Fox News reporter abroad. Strangely, Reagan's Knight of Malta campaign manager (rewarded with DCI for his role in the October Surprise) would die of brain cancer that same year, after which his replacement, William

Webster, Director of the FBI since 1978, would pass the gauntlet in 1991 to Robert Gates. After September 11, 2001, Webster would chair the Homeland Security Advisory Council and Gates would become 22nd U.S. Secretary of Defense under the 43rd President and continue under the 44th.

At the top of the drug heap above Shackley, Singlaub, Secord, Poindexter, North, Weinberger, Thomas Clines, and Chi Chi Quintero was the CIA's SAC in Dallas on November 22, 1963, the ex-DCI man of the hour at the October Surprise meeting in Paris before the 1980 election that made him Vice President and eventually 41st President and father of the 43rd President.

Between the 41st and 43rd Presidents would be the Arkansas governor whose drug operations would move from Mena to other ports of entry like Newport, Oregon. Behind the Newport airport manned by military and foreign UN training troops, drugs would be adulterated for experimental purposes before being put on trucks and shipped out Highway 20 to Boston to be dispersed along the East Coast; others would go out via Evergreen Airways (CIA) from Albany, Oregon. Many upstanding citizens in towns across the United States are NSA operatives ready to be called to duty and make extra cash.

I'm world weary, the Colonel was thinking as Seven waved cheerfully to him from her little Coleman. Ray was fiddling with the radio and trying to follow the chords of a Richard and Linda Thompson song called "Shoot Out the Lights" that wouldn't come out for twelve years—

> *In the darkness the shadows move*
> *In the darkness the game is real*
> *Real as a gun*
> *Real as a gun*

34

The Mars Men

This new bunch of barbarians – just as pagan as any BC Aztec witch doctor – are engrossed in ELF-zapped genes, single-phase, speeding DNA transcription, microwave radiation, reciprocal and effective mass tensor points, micro-pyramid structures in "Cu Metal Flakes," ionic crystalline structures, transduction of theta waves, videodrome signals, the earth's Power Grid Vortex, Fluxon, Spinors, Scalars, ULF effects on biosystems, and phase relationships in the wave of motions of radio frequencies.

—Dr. Peter Ruckman, *Black is Beautiful*, 1995

Dr.: Would you like to be dead, Arlene?
Arlene: I already am.
Dr.: Well . . . if you are, how can you talk?
Arlene: Why don't you die . . . and find out?

—Donald Bain, *The Control of Candy Jones*, 1974

. . . It must be known that even though these apprehensions can come to the bodily senses from God, one must never rely on them or accept them. A person should rather flee from them completely and have no desire to examine whether they be good or bad. The more exterior and corporeal these things are, the less certain is their divine origin. God's self-communication is more commonly and appropriately given to the spirit, in which there is greater security and profit for the soul, than to the senses, where ordinarily there is extreme danger and room for deception . . .

—St. John of the Cross (1542-1591),
The Ascent of Mount Carmel

In Washington, DC, Sibelius the Magician awoke. He had found Thomas. It had been easier than he thought; he had simply tuned in to the frequency of that condor in the dogwood in Coatzacoalcos. Greenbaum would be pleased.

And he had learned something else: Thomas had protection.

He got up from his bed, musing on how appropriate it was that *coatl* meant both serpent and twin, as in Quetzalcoatl the Plumed Serpent or Magnificent Twin, calling to mind the DNA double helix. In Mexico, the Amazon, Australia, India, Scandinavia, Sumer, Egypt, Persia, and Greece, androgynous creator gods had arisen as cosmic serpents, whereas the Hungarian chemist August Kekulé dreamed in 1862 of the *ouroboros*, the snake eating its own tail, like the ring shape of the benzene molecule that foretold a singular self. In 1913, the Dutch astrologer A.E. Thierens said that astral primal atoms appear to the inner eye as snakes, which was why the occult sciences of Egypt and India called them *Nâgás* or Masters of Wisdom. Eliphas Levi said that the astral light of the stars has always been called the Great Serpent.

Sibelius plugged in his electric kettle. In 3102 BC, before the Aryan conquest, Mayans known as *Nâgás* or Serpent-worshippers (*Danavas navas nagas nagual*) lived on the banks of the Saraswati in the Punjab. The later Brahmins learned cosmology and astronomy from *Nâgá* adepts (*Naacal*, the exalted) who raised the magnificent temple dedicated to the 7-headed serpent *Ah-ac-chapat* in Angkor Thom, Cambodia, later disseminated to Akkad and Babylon. Blue Vishnu sits upon the 7-headed *Caisha*. Mayan sacrificial victims were painted blue, as were the altars upon which they were immolated.

In *The Secret Doctrine* (1888), H.P Blavatsky tells how the *Nâgás* were from Patala, the antipodes of Central America. Dowson's *Classical Dictionary of Hindu Mythology* said the same. Both *Khan* and *Can* mean serpent, a title given to Prince Coh's Mayan dynasty due to the contour of the empire from the Isthmus of Tehuantepec to Yucatán looking like a cobra with an inflated breast. In fact, at the time of the Conquest, the Maya Empire was still called *Nohcan*, the Great Serpent. Egyptian rulers remembered their motherland by centering the asp on their crowns.

Before 500 BC, Zeus had been a serpent, but after 500 BC he became the serpent *slayer* by defeating Typhon, serpent son of Gaia. Consciousness was advancing from the reptilian limbic brain to the cortex, and reason (Athene) began managing the God-given *k'ulthanlilni* (*kundalini* or serpent power) coiled around the Tree of Life or spine, which was why the serpent, revered as divine wisdom for millennia, began taking on the aspect of *tempter*. Krishna—the god Vishnu in his eighth avatar—kills Anantha, Horus kills Apophys, Apollo kills Python. A serpent coils at the feet of the Virgin Mary, a dragon encircles the rock upon which the Japanese goddess Maya stands, in her hand a branch of the mangrove tree (her totem *Canchi*, the Mayan *Canché* or serpent wood).

Sibelius sipped his ginseng tea, staring at a wall map of Mayan Mexico. Myth left a clear trail of breadcrumbs to the fact that the Sun forces were birthing a cosmic human development beyond that bequeathed by the *k'ulthanlilni*. The Troano Manuscript shows the Maya Empire either as a mulberry tree rooted in the South American continent or as a serpent with and without wings. The tree and the serpent, like in Genesis. Quetzalcoatl, the feathered serpent.

Amaru being the Peruvian name for Quetzalcoatl, Amaru's land is *Amaruca*, America in the North engraved with serpent mounds and carved stone snakes. In the Victoria, British Columbia Parliament building, twin feathered serpents wind up a winged caduceus in a stained glass window entitled *HYGEIA*, like the Pythagorean pentacle of 5-sided darkness in which the living flame takes root. The Greek term *hygeia* is derived from *wedjuat* referring to the Eye of Horus, and its symbol is now the ℞ of modern pharmacology. (In Greek, *pharmakia* means sorcery.) The *hygeia* twin feathered serpents in the Victoria Parliament allude to the myriad affinities between the Nahuatlatolli language and Tsimshian Nootka-Columbian languages like Wakash, Ahts, Haidah, and Quaquiutl, all in British Columbia. High-degree Freemasons, silent keepers of the mystic past, know all of this. *Scientia est potentia.*

As for the DNA double helix and twin serpents, in the 1960s anthropologists took *ayahuasqa*, the rain forest tea made from leaves with dimethyltryptamine in them, and from a creeper that protects the dimethyltryptamine from stomach acids, and encountered entwined twin dragon-like beings claiming to be the true gods of this world. If they constituted the sacred vine of the double helix, the ladder of wisdom joining Heaven and Earth, then shamans specializing in *ayahuasqa*—*ayahuasqueros*—were communing with the molecular level of consciousness.

Greenbaum agreed that overcoming the serpent or reptilian brain was the next step in divine consciousness evolution. Doing so would develop what is specifically *human* and release humanity from subnature, as yet an avatar attainment. He said this while traumatizing reptilian limbic brains and implanting triggers in MK-ULTRA children. Dragon Court elites opposed *all* divine mandates and sought to bind human beings to subnature and a "hive mind" for remote manipulation, a temporal lobe hotline to the limbic lobe deep in the old brain. Dragon Court elites wanted mechanized slaves, not free will, divine human beings.

The Magician smiled. Merging occult practices with electromagnetic technology meant affixing serpent power to the human will for good. Both eyes and bodily fluids transmitted this force, particularly when yoked to the Earth's electromagnetic currents. Eyes still had the power to transmit an invisible *grasp* or apprehension over distance, such as the Huichol Ramón Medina Silva's shamanic balancing act of sending ahead his astral light from his eyes and fly along the Earth's magnetic roads.

As for fluids, the profane viewed the ritual ingestion of semen, blood, vaginal fluids, and urine as vile. But to the occult technician, such practices circulate the currents trapped in matter that once flowed as astral light from the *wedjuat*. Thus was astral light *liberated*. And as for transferring fluids, Alexander Graham Bell and other Freemason adepts made use of geographic places like Georgia's potent Jekyll Island for such *magica sexualis* Workings. Bell's ritual entailed standing in front of an upstairs window while a Freemason underling performed fellatio on him. Thanks to the "telephone line" of force connecting Jekyll Island with St. Simons Island in the northeast, vital energy was thus transferred from Bell to the underling via the law of correspondence.

(Note: Jekyll Island was also where the Egregore of the Federal Reserve was ritually founded by J.P. Morgan, John D. Rockefeller, Jr., and Paul Warburg of Kuhn, Loeb & Company representing the European House of Rothschild as Halley's Comet made its first appearance in the 20th century. *As below, so above.*)

Fluids act as serpentine, vitality-filled leylines. In *Fear and Loathing in Las Vegas* (1971), Hunter Thompson's attorney advised him to take a hit of adrenochrome, the fluid drawn from a ritual murder victim whose blood is flush with adrenalin. Such fluids are the means by which Brothers of the Shadow evade death and old age, keeping their own fluid leylines vital by "eating of the Tree of Life." Endocrine infusions from the desiccated glands of dead animals do nothing; only infusions from a live human being do the trick. Death by fluids—not to be confused with death by water— entails directing volatized poisons through space, as in the case of the murder of defrocked Abbé Joseph-Antoine Boullan in Lyons on January 3, 1893 during an occult war among Parisian occultists.

Between vitality and death, fluids of particular glands call up psychic abilities, organ imaginations once known as *belly* or *organ clairvoyance*. First, impulses enter the gland through the sense organs—for example, by watching someone being tortured—and trigger responses via the resistance of the layers of membranes that make up the organ. The gland then responds with a micro-combustion of secretion, a salt that the moment it falls into the body electrochemically releases an inner image, either emotional or instinctual.

Thirty years in the future, director Steven Spielberg would expose the public to a modern imagination of organ clairvoyance in the film *Minority Report*, based on the Philip K. Dick short story of the same name. In the film, three wired pre-cogs (precognitives) or *brothers of the 3 points* lie like spokes in a wheel in a viscous photon milk pool of nutrients and liquid conductors to enhance the images they receive from a future embedded in the slipstream of Time, images of which are then scanned by optical tomography. Dopamines and endorphins keep the pre-cogs in a dreamy, feeling-no-pain state while their electrode headgear reads and transmits what they see to computers that then display the visual images on monitors and record them. The best organ clairvoyants, the film informs us, are a female and identical male twins—a mere hint of the Mengele-style scientific torture that attends such occult technology. Whether one views the precogs as *pattern recognition filters* or Greek oracles, they are denied individual lives of their own. "We're more like clergy than cops," says one of the pre-cog cops. It is thus that the Dragon Court elite view their pursuit of glitzy glass and steel electrochemical organ clairvoyance.

As for stomach clairvoyance, Sibelius had seen for himself that the solar plexus, cecum, or stomach sends out not only infrared heat waves but the entire light spectrum. In ancient days, the cecum was known as the *monacle* of the large intestine, the seer of the body, the "gut reaction" that could issue a warning the bowels could understand. Gut waves are weak, and yet, according to radio astronomer John Pfeiffer in his 1956 book *The Changing Universe*, the 50-foot aerial at the Naval Research Laboratory in Washington, DC can pick up radio signals coming from a stomach more than four miles distant, the body being like a radio tower and the stomach area a major beacon. Greenbaum explained that all somatic cells are electromagnetic resonators capable of emitting and absorbing very high frequency (VHF) radiation. And because the nerves governing the stomach and duodenum issue from the solar plexus (third *chakra*), those who are psychically manipulated or attacked often have stomach problems, due to their solar plexus "receiver." According to Arthur Guirdham, MD, in his book *Obsession: Psychic forces and evil in the causation of disease* (1972), rapid emptying of the stomach coincides with being drained by others on the same wavelength.

During the early days of Artichoke, CIA and military intelligence doctors learned from the Nazis and other Satanists how to teach "alters" to enter the body through the solar plexus-stomach area. Bouts of excruciating stomach pain, sometimes cramping in the legs and feet, often indicate entry. Both the stomach and legs have corresponding etheric acupuncture points; one of the calf muscles is even named gastrocnemius. Candy Jones experienced it when Dr. Bernard Jensen called forth the spy alter Arlene Grant. Sleeper assassins like Sirhan Sirhan, Mark David Chapman, and David Berkowicz all complained of severe stomach pain, as did country singer Tammy Wynette. In 2000, Daniel Bondeson [*bond son*] would feed arsenic to parishioners at the Gustaf Adolph Lutheran Church in New Sweden, Maine, saying in his suicide note: *I had no intent to hurt this way. Just to upset stomach, like the churchgoers did me.* And in the jailhouse letter of Jessie Misskelley Jr., after an act he swears "he" didn't do, he says, *My stomache has been hurting me.*

How a *neuronal matrix* like Arlene Grant can radio in through the solar plexus receiver and take over Candy Jones' body and personality is a complex proposition that defies mundane analysis. The CIA used narco-hypnosis on Candy to produce a deep trance agent who could pass for normal and remember nothing of Arlene's activities. That the stomach is tortured during this mysterious transmission and transformation is a fact. Long ago, the shamans of Central America referred to *virotes*, invisible psychic darts they were able to implant over distance in an enemy's stomach. *Pharmakia* drugs can act as *virotes*, too, and open access through the solar plexus.

So secret is stomach clairvoyance that Western accounts of

the bloody rites of the Aztecs in the final demise of their civilization were revised to read *heart* incisions instead of *stomach* incisions. Only one sacred piece of sculpture called *Mictlantecuhtli* (*circa* 1480) remains at the Museo del Templo Mayor in Mexico City to tell the truth about this anything but mundane organ. *Mictlantecuhtli's* thoracic cavity is open, exposing the coveted stomach between the two lobes of the liver that open like the petals of a sacred *chakra*. The Nahua perceived that the *ihíyotl*, one of the three spirits of the body, resided in the liver, the head being *ilhuícatl* (heaven), *ihíyotl* the earth, and the entrails, including the cecum, the underworld and death.

Whole continents of history are often shifted so as to keep hidden the meaning and intent of occult matters. *Scientia est potentia.*

Later that morning, Sibelius met Dr. Greenbaum for a small invitation-only CIA conference on teleportation and told him about having found Thomas with the little group heading east. Greenbaum added that infrared photo recon taken at dawn had picked up a figure whose blond hair and walk were almost certainly those of Baby Rose. If it was her, and if Thomas was there, as well, it was uncanny had somehow found each other. But where was this little band of fugitives going? They had no idea. Anyway, the puzzle pieces were falling into place. As they settled into their chairs, Greenbaum asked if there was any word on Saint-Germain.

Sibelius shook his head. "Not yet. The Qabalist is setting up mediums." He hesitated and decided not to mention his thoughts about Vitzliputzli, nor the protection he'd sensed around Thomas. Saint-Germain and Vitzliputzli working together would be worrisome, indeed.

The presenter was a young physicist who worked for Science Applications International Corporation (SAIC). He began right away, apologizing in advance for a plane he had to catch.

"As we all know, the Soviets initially led the way in the quantum understanding of energetics of inert matter, biological systems (bioenergetics), and the science of mind (psychoenergetics).

Psychokinesis, telekinesis, levitation, transformation of energy, electromagnetic fields that affect the mind irrespective of distance or time—thanks to technology, we can now explore natural phenomena once thought of as supernatural—like the magnetic anomalies recorded in streaked or fogged film indicating the presence of occult and UFO phenomena. Like the telescope and microscope, our instruments now reveal vistas long limited to the purview of gifted occultists, many of whom, you may recall, were scientists."

He smiled and caught the Magician's eye, then continued. They had been friends at Georgetown.

"Teleportation works on the principle of *entanglement* on an atomic and subatomic scale measured in *qubits* with a *q*, atomic quantum bits. Make a measurement at one end and the characteristics of the object at the other end are instantaneously determined, no matter how far apart they are. Information in one object teleported to another is due to the qubits being in *superposition*, in both states at the same time.

"An experiment in the field might look something like this: We want to access someone in their home in an invisible way." He smiled an unlikeable smile. "Or we want to quietly bring a subject from one continent to another without all the logistics that generally entails. All we need is two sets of data: their quantum body specs, their *telepresence*, and the two coordinates of the exact locations, where the subject to be teleported is and where he or she is going. We then initialize their ground states, a satellite laser pulse looses the red or blue photons corresponding to each qubit state—entanglement— the physical body is knocked unconscious, and the quantum body is on its way.

"Ladies and gentlemen, the mind and all that is mental exist in Time but not in 3-space."

The room stirred. He waited for the marvel to sink in, then went on.

"Classical electrodynamics claims two transverse photons, but quantum field theory has discovered *four*: 1,2, the orthogonal oscillation polarization along the X-axis and Y-axis; 3, longitudinally polarized along the Z-direction of travel; and 4, the time-polarized or scalar photon oscillating along the Time axis. 1,2, blue-blue, red-red; 3, blue-red; 4, red-blue . . ."

A hand shot up. "Like the Doppler effect, the radiation moving toward the observer is squeezed and its frequency increases . . ."

"Blueshifted, yes," the physicist responded, "and moving away, it's stretched and redshifted. Only 1 and 2 are observable by our instruments in 3-space matter; the longitudinal and time-polarized aren't visible. Activate 3 and 4 in the time-domain so they exactly parallel each other and you'll get a spike of electrostatic scalar potential to superposition the two qubit states, and write into memory the information being teleported *around* 3-space.

"Could this mean mental 'body swapping'? Yes, it could. The brain is amazingly adaptive, even to incorporating the image of an external device like a steering wheel or joystick into its neuronal space."

Another question. "Could we augment our bodies in virtual space?"

"Yes, or include someone else's downloaded personality along with our own in one body. This is fifth-dimensional physics. Imagine a science fiction novel in which a serial killer takes victims apart internally from any distance by means of an invasive computer interface technology much like the teleportation technology I'm describing. Longitudinal and time-domain manipulation."

One of the few women in the room raised her hand. "What will this mean for the death process?"

An uncomfortable silence followed her question.

The physicist glanced at her, then at Sibelius, who made a mental note to check the identity of the woman.

"How close are we to this technology?" Dr. Gottlieb asked. He knew the answer but wanted to move beyond the question he surmised touched on "national security" issues.

The physicist smiled. "I'll put it this way: we're not worried about the Russians anymore."

As the meeting broke up, Sibelius made his way to his physicist friend and Dr. Greenbaum to Dr. Gottlieb. All four had been honored for their work in Artichoke, particularly their contributions to synthetic telepathy and what was being called *Soul-catcher* technology—virtual immortality, not real immortality; it was just a matter of time before an old man's memories could be downloaded into a younger body. Tiny videos in the retina linked to computer monitors had excited Greenbaum until he heard that it would take 300 megabytes to hold the memories of just 30 days of life. Once lives were mainframed, you could ask them questions and get answers. Soon, executives would be attending meetings via holograph; all they needed was more bandwidth. *Telepresence.*

Gottlieb had had a breakfast meeting with Pentagon brass about how to handle MK-ULTRA agent breakdowns as they approached midlife. Instead of eliminating them like any malfunctioning computer, they'd decided to monitor the breakdowns by assigning high-functioning MK-ULTRA agents to infiltrate survivor groups so they could study the kinks in the programming and learn which leaks to plug. Of course, more programmed psychiatrists and therapists would be needed. A nurse mentioned checking into already programmed cult specialists, and Gottlieb made a note to check with a colleague at the American Psychiatric Association.

Greenbaum and Gottlieb then switched to German to discuss the possibility that Baby Rose and Thomas were traveling together.

"Are outside influences involved?" Gottlieb asked. Unlike the speaker, he was still worried about the Russians.

"I don't *think* so," Greenbaum responded slowly, "but we're exercising extreme caution. My hope is to quietly re-acquire both of them, but if it gets down to a choice—"

"It has to be Baby Rose," Gottlieb said firmly. "Once re-acquired, we pull her files, back them up, reprogram her, check her Over the Rainbow parts, and prepare her for future use as a spiritual healer—lock in programs for independence, public speaking, writing, etc., to attract other agents and abductees breaking down and contain them. Include speaking out against Satanic ritual abuse and trigger words for sealing others' deep programming." Gottlieb looked meaningfully at Greenbaum. "By the way, the DIA is breathing down my neck about their retired intelligence colonel."

Greenbaum had hoped to avoid military attention. Too late. He glanced around as Gottlieb left. Across the room was Edwin Land, founder of Polaroid but primarily engaged with classified mind control under the CIA's Office of Research and Development (ORD) and his own Scientific Engineering Institute. Land reminded Greenbaum of Wilhelm Keppler, Hitler's personal economic adviser who'd ended up a Kodak man. Leonard Kille had co-invented the Land camera, but the CIA had implanted his brain with 80 electrodes and zapped him until he signed over his patents. Lesions in his amygdala, ESB by Sweet and Ervin at Mass General. *Unfortunate name, Kille*, thought the good doctor.

The Qabalist was also at an invitation-only meeting, proxying for the Magician who hadn't quite mastered being in two places at once. The presenter was a young Mars program astrophysicist.

"Given that I'm addressing JASON Scholars, I'd like to discuss the Mars you *won't* see through telescopes, or at least you won't *recognize* it there. First, the human vestiges from ancient Moon evolution living *in* Mars. 'Mars men' are subject to Mars magnetism the way men here are subject to Earth magnetism. Wedded to Mars soil and living *inside* the planet due to the cold and wind, they are much less cosmopolitan than we." He clicked a slide overhead. "Here, you see 50-meter resolution photographs of lakes on the Cydonia Plain—and yes, these are actual photographs of artificial structures no doubt built by Mars men. Subject them to photoclinometry and fractal analysis and you will see these are not fakes."

The room was abuzz.

"And those red bursts you see? Perennial strife due to strong astrality not tethered by an 'I'—human beings without an Ego but with prematurely advanced astrality. A Heinlein or Phil Dick science fiction story, huh?"

A smattering of uneasy laughter.

"Now imagine Mars men on Earth, particularly those of you who are digging endless underground bases to at last feel at home."

The audience didn't laugh.

"Christ on or *in* Earth, Buddha on or *in* Mars, how about that? Mars men there and here bent on defeating both of them. Mars men on Earth incapable of getting an 'I' so they take over the bodies and personalities of men who already favor Earth magnetism over the innate human spirit. How about *that*? Crazy, huh?"

The room was silent. Given that they hadn't been invited to a *Star Trek* convention, some had begun to think, others to turn to stone.

The young astrophysicist continued, undaunted. "What do I think about all of this? Well, with all the plasma ships and light orbs we're seeing in and above the atmosphere, I'm taking a serious look at a whole other way of conceiving the consciousness mix on Earth." He shot a razor look at the audience. "If you're not doing the same, why not? If Mars is a reincarnated ancient Moon as old as 19th century occultists said it was, and if those Mars men I described possess transformed ancient Moon consciousness, in human bodies they'd be supermen with uncanny abilities *and* uncanny aggression. Sound like anyone you know? Aggressive control technologies aimed at humans who *do* have an 'I'?"

A few listeners looked uneasily at those around them.

"One of our vector craft pilots told me about an encounter he had with dwarf-like phantoms on the Moon. 'Noisy little bastards,' I believe he called them while downing his third or fourth scotch." The astrophysicist leaned forward for emphasis. "What if there are beings on every planet and moon that have psychic access to human beings and seek to utilize their 'I' for their own ends?"

He grasped the podium and peered at his audience. "Thinking in such arcane ways will take some getting used to, and ladies and gentlemen, I'm here to say, *do it*. Many of you are familiar with Freemason lore that says human souls have been consorting with beings from other planets since the last of the Mu epoch when the Earth finally hardened."

The Freemason reference had guaranteed full attention.

"Stop thinking so much about making money and expand your consciousness to assess arcane realities before it's too late. The Americas, these Saturn continents, will continue to be driven by increasingly mind-boggling technologies as beings from other planets not bound to physical bodies and lacking an 'I' hasten to fill the vacuum of technology-saturated souls. Their offspring are either here or returning through the hyperspace portals being opened by our technology. Imagine that."

Briefly, he stared at his listeners and laughed. "Tonight, drive beyond Washington's light pollution and look up at the night sky, that great brain of which we and our planet are only thoughts. Consider other thoughts streaking through that brain, that giant psyche and nervous system, as the Desana Indians in the Colombian Amazon describe it, made up of two hemispheres, right and left brain, between which the Milky Way flows. Our very solar system points the way. We must learn to view the reality speaking to us through *both* hemispheres. *Outside the box*, my friends. Read or write science fiction as quick as you may before the gap between fiction and reality closes for good. Don't allow ignorance to scorn what you don't yet understand. Thank you."

35

Fey*

Whenever a feeling of aversion comes into the heart of a good soul,
It's not without significance.
Consider that intuitive wisdom to be a Divine attribute,
Not a vain suspicion:
The light of the heart has apprehended
Intuitively from the Universal Tablet.

–Rumi, 13th century

Precognition and premonition are themselves special cases of a more
general phenomenon: the anomalous retroactive influence of some
future event on an individual's current responses, whether those
responses are conscious or unconscious, cognitive or affective.

–Daryl J. Bern, "Feeling the Future:
Experimental Evidence for Anomalous
Retroactive Influences on Cognition and
Affect," 2010

By the time the Colonel had trekked back to the gypsy camp, the Sun was beating down on his back, everyone was sleepily moving about preparing breakfast and packing up for the day's drive, and Baby Rose and Sirius were back.

The Colonel sank into his chair and waited for the breakfast circle. Once everyone was seated for Seven's oatmeal, toast, and tea, he handed the still-glowing manila envelope to Seven and began relating what had occurred at the Bagdad Café. Discretely, he left out the Admiral's assurance that they would see each other soon.

Vince took out his notebook and pen while Ray wondered about the Colonel's senility, especially when he said he'd looked back and the café was rubble.

Seven held up the papers from the envelope. "These are about my father working as a scientist for the Navy in the Pacific theatre during World War Two."

"Mayans don't draw a hard black line between one Time and another, this world and others," Vince said. "To me, it makes sense that the Colonel would encounter a brave military man murdered by the military he gave his life to, and that he would have information about Seven's Navy father. My guess is we will all be meeting someone, somewhere, sometime, maybe alive, maybe dead, maybe a phantom with specific information we need."

Thomas was ecstatic and puzzled. "But Vince, what is going on with Time out here in the desert? Billy Joad and his Dust Bowl grandparents, Nixon and the water gate, the radio broadcasts, and now this . . ." After meeting Ragoczy, Thomas had given Time a lot of thought. "Deutsch's fabric of reality theory is that reality consists of large sets of complex entities, except that instead of each only being able to perceive entities in its own set . . ."

Ray was still puzzling over what Vince said. "But what did we get from Billy Joad?"

"The military being everywhere . . . ," Thomas began.

". . . the Augustan Society . . . ," Vince added.

". . . and how America's buried in lies and we need to find the truth before we lose it all," Ray finished, nodding. "I dig. And there may be other connections as we go along. Not so much the messenger as the message . . ."

". . . and what it's pointing to," Seven finished, passing the papers to Thomas. "When Faulkner said 'The past is never dead, it's not even past,' maybe he meant that Time is always doubling back on itself, layer by layer, so why isn't it doubling *forward*, too, despite how we sequence events with before and after? Aristotle said the 'now' is an unchanging substrate of ever-different nows. *Be here now*, Ram Dass said, meaning be self-aware, be aware of being in Time. 'Now' may not be an instantaneous boundary but continuous and reflective." She shrugged. "Maybe past, present, and future only exist so we can consciously experience life."

"Arab writers make no distinction between past and present," Ray confirmed.

"A billion minutes ago, Jesus was alive," Mannie said.

They looked at Mannie, wondering where that came from.

And it was 'now' then," Seven said, "and it's still 'now' for some people, seeing what the rest of us don't, like the Colonel seeing the Bagdad Café. Maybe everything that's happened is still happening on some plane, only under normal circumstances we can't perceive it."

Mannie nodded. "In 1477, they calculated that Genesis said Creation happened in 6985 BC."

Thomas nodded back. "Right, Mannie. Ordinals, cardinals, and calendars aren't Time, they're just a way of ordering it so our memory can order life events. Time is inexorable, like planetary motion, but calendars are more about politics than astronomical correctness, like trying to convince people that the world began in 6985 BC—"

Ray was suddenly excited. "Like after the French Revolution, they tried to change the calendar and it didn't work. In 1929, after the Russian Revolution, they tried to leave out Saturday and Sunday, but no matter how they re-shuffled it, people still computed Time the old way and took Sundays off. They finally gave up in 1940 and kept the old calendar."

Thomas laughed. "The Julian calendar was our Old Style calendar instituted in 46 BC under Julius Caesar. According to the planets, it was 11 minutes and 14 seconds off. When Pope Gregory

XIII instituted the New Style calendar in 1582, his astrologers dropped eleven days in order to catch up with planetary Time. One day it was October 4 and the next it was October 15. Where did those eleven days go?"

The Colonel added, "But Britain and its colonies—that's us—kept the Old Style Julian calendar until 1752, almost two hundred years after everyone else had been using the New Style Gregorian. And to make it more confusing, both calendars hearken back 6,000 years, the Julian to zero on 1 January 4713 BC and the Gregorian to zero on 24 November 4714 BC, when the 19-year Metonic cycle intersected the 28-year Saturn cycle. The practical Romans added an Indiction cycle, a 15-year tax cycle, as a third intersecting lock on Time, and the Gregorian calendar ended the practice of making years ending in 00 leap years."

Seven was puzzled. "But why does the international astronomical calendar measure Time in Julian days, ignoring differences in length of months, leap years, lunar tides, solar flares, seasons, religious observances, everything but days?"

"Cardinal," Thomas said absentmindedly, distracted by thoughts about Bohm's implicate or enfolded order that moment by moment creates our universe. To our brains, everything is nonlocal, especially consciousness.

"And why did Britain wait 170 years to adopt the calendar?" Ray asked.

"Anti-Catholic," Vince said. "British and American Freemasons still go by the Old Style calendar for their high holy days."

This got Thomas' attention. "Masons have high holy days?"

"Oh yes," Vince said, "most of which are pre-Christian, but not all, given that high-degree Masons well know what Christ's first Advent meant.—The heliacal rising of Sirius is on July 20, and the first half of their Celtic-Egyptian year runs from July 22 with Mary Magdalene to January 17 and St. Augustine, the second half running from January 23 to July 21, with five intercalary days from January 18 to 22. Then depending on the Lodge, the solstices and equinoxes; October 31 to November 1, All Hallow's Eve and Samhain; April 30 and May 1, Walpurgisnacht and Beltane; February 1, Oimelc, to July 31 and August 1, Lammas and Lugnasadh; August 13 and 31—inverted numbers— for Hecate. All mathematical, like Imbolc on February 2 being the 33rd day of the year and first day of the last 333 days."

"Ground Hog Day?" Mannie asked.

"Candlemas," Seven said.

"The Jewish year is now 5730," Mannie said.

"And the Masonic year now is—5970?" Thomas looked at Vince.

"Yes, and the Islamic year 1391, and the Chinese 4638." Vince grinned. "All political, with astronomical dates threading through them. The Mayan calendar is astronomical, and the old pagan high holy days and religious holy days are based on the motions of Sun and Moon. Come the beginning of November in *Mayach*, people will again make cakes from the finest corn and meat they can find and hang them on the branches of certain trees at crossroads, in forests and isolated groves, for the souls of the departed to eat. The cakes are *hanal pixan*, food of the soul, exactly like November 2 when the Sun is rising in Scorpio—All Souls Day, *El Día de los Muertos*, an ancient observance in Peru, India, Tonga, among the Australian aborigines, ancient Romans and Egyptians. Holy days maintain a uniformity of Time over a vast lapse of Time."

"Who still celebrates these ancient holy days?" Seven asked.

"Certainly the Freemasons who must always obey the geography of the spirits they hope to influence or control. In Europe, they followed Celtic practices; in America, it must include Aztec and Mayan because the Mexican civilizations were the very last vestiges of sunken Atlantis. Then there are the Satanists and pagans who have brought a hodge-podge of generational spirits with them from long centuries of practice in Northern Europe, Africa, India. Your First Amendment gives free rein to all manner of spirits and has ushered in a distinct *chaos* that my grandfather says is necessary but difficult for freedom. Add to this how most are conditioned to think of this world as singular and material and—" he shrugged "—secret societies can manipulate people right and left for the sake of the spirits they serve.

"The present world, according to the Mayan calendar that began its bar-and-dot notation on 13 August 3114 BC, is now speeding toward its end in 2012—not an apocalypse but the end of the world as we've known it. The spirits are taking the helm. More than any religion or system of thought I am familiar with, the Mayans and your Southwest Indians understood the powers operating behind Time and Space and used ritual to contain their dangerous, sometimes anti-human, energies.

"But now old priests have reincarnated and re-discovered how to pop open Pandora's box, thinking they will be able to control what comes out with rituals, ritual murders, drugs, hypnosis, weather engineering—anything and everything at their disposal, consciously and unconsciously. But my grandfather says they are in over their heads." Switching tracks, he smiled. "Space was created by Time, and it looks like your trip to Dallas to see where your leader fell—a long journey for the sake of the truth—is being affected by Time."

Baby Rose stared at Vince's moonlike face. She wasn't concerned about Time. In her programmed, diamond-shattered state, Be Here Now was all she could do, other than some part of her dividing Time into profane (when she had to undergo or do things for Dr. Greenbaum) and angelic (every other time). Seven had made it all angelic time. The Valkyries, Horae, and Apsaras could have thundered down from the sky or off the desert and it would still have been angelic time.

Vince made multiple concurrent worlds and Times sound so sensible and natural, a Bohm world of an enfolded order creating a perceived universe moment by moment, giving whole new meaning to Be Here Now. Were desert future frames inserting themselves Mobius-like between past and present, like the tachyons Philip

K. Dick encountered in the pink glow on 2-3-74 four years in the future? Tiny particles moving faster than light in retrograde Time bearing bits of information from the future that might save us, if recognized in time? Orthogonal Time perpendicular to linear time, in which whatever or whoever has happened still exists in a will-be and has-been and is way?

Far out. Far fucking out.

The Caddy and bus packed up, the Magnificent Seven and Sirius hit the road, hardly knowing anymore who or where or when they were, much less that they had active enemies on the move. Kate Wolf sang them an invitation to consciousness—

> *It's an unfinished life that I find lies before me*
> *An open-ended dream I don't want to wake*
> *I've crossed so many rivers in search of crystal fountains*
> *I've found the truest paths always lead through mountains*
> *I've seen water on the sky*
> *And fire burning on the lake . . .*

While Seven drove, thinking over what a mystery her father had been, Mannie scanned a glowing Van Nuys Valley Times dated August 2, 1960 that he'd found in a filling station bathroom. On the front page was the headline, "Saucer Ready for Flight" and an AP wire photo of the top half of a pilot sticking out of the cockpit of a circular flat ship with USAF and U.S. Army on its hull. The caption read Defense Department today released this photo taken in Canada of saucer-shaped aircraft being developed for U.S. Army and Air Force. Revolutionary craft is said to take off and land vertically on cushion of air. Mannie knew it would be a keeper for Thomas.

Glass skyscrapers were rising across America without a thought to energy conservation because the U.S. was swimming in cheap energy. Air conditioning, power gadgets, throwaway obsolescence, aluminum cans instead of tin, detergent instead of soap, oil-based synthetics instead of natural fibers, artificial fertilizers, petrochemicals. The welfare state, consumer society, and the Vietnam Conflict needed petroleum, so pipelines were getting bigger and tankers as super-sized as the oil mergers.

War games at Fort Bragg, Aberdeen Proving Ground in Maryland, Fort Benning in Georgia, Fort Leavenworth in Kansas, and Dugway Proving Ground in Utah. Men were being dosed with LSD to see how they performed at command post maneuvers, squad drills, tank driving, radar reading, antiaircraft tracking, meteorological and engineering surveys, etc. At Edgewood Arsenal, LSD *and* sensory deprivation was followed by hostile interrogation.

In Washington, DC, a Joint Chiefs of Staff General was having a snooze after two long morning meetings, one on MK-ULTRA and the other on teleportation, but his respite was being marred by the same Aztec dream that always banished peace and rest. As usual, he was Huitzilopochtli the Sun god of war, born from Coatlicue, the mother culture the Aztecs usurped. As the Sun battled darkness daily, he was battling his brothers the stars, decapitating his sister Coyolxauhqui, and tossing her body at the foot of Capitol Hill . . .

He escaped into wakefulness and stumbled into the kitchen to make a cup of chamomile tea that his wife said was calming. The question that had plagued him for years was still unanswered: *Was he living an alternate life in an alternate reality?* Thirty years ago, he'd read a letter in Ray Palmer's *Amazing Stories* from a man named Richard Sharpe Shaver who claimed to be *Mutan Mion*, a demigod from before the Atlantean Flood. Mutan Mion claimed that when the Sun's chemistry changed, Lemurians had retreated deep into the Earth. Bulwer-Lytton had written about underground people with advanced technology— electromagnetic rays, robots, telepathically guided ships, etc.—and the Nazis prophesied that the people of Agharti would emerge from their caverns in Central Asia and Tibet in 2029.

The General dunked his teabag, wondering what the

phantom bogies slipping from space into the atmosphere were. That CEO they called the Magician said they were scouts from "caverns in space," to which they could disappear in the blink of an eye. The Magician also said they were slipping in and out of animal and human bodies.

The General had seen a phantom ship or two from beyond the now-porous Threshold. Maybe he should visit the archaeological portals and re-read the old myths—Freemason, Opus Dei, Anthroposophy, Theosophy, Islam, Qabala, Hindu, native legends, all the Time-worn traditions hiding timeless facts in symbolic language. Maybe compare Lemurian and Atlantean technologies with the electromagnetic spectrum discoveries erupting now: genetic engineering, superconductivity, macroscopic weather engineering, EMP fields and their impact on cell structure, holographic projections from hundreds of miles up, synthetic telepathy and voice synthesis, laser, tomography. Technology was becoming unimaginably advanced. *What did it mean?*

He sipped his tea. They were naming the airborne tactical laser ATL in honor of the ancient weapon. It was a little frightening but not impossible to think that cutting edge technical and military minds had returned to do it *right* this time. Some believed it, chapter and verse. Was he from the Aztec stream, like Patton was from the Greek? He should get hold of that astrologer Greenbaum knew. Since World War One, military brass had been obsessed with death numbers. In Vietnam, they were staging large blood sacrifices, vast bloody initiations into chthonic regions that for the materially pampered and spiritually starved American officer and soldier would probably be the only direct contact with spirit they'd ever have this side of their own death. Certainly they'd never be the same again. Sacred violence was like that, with its ecstatic transformative edge that daily humdrum "reality" simply couldn't match. Warfare and sacrifice were becoming a way of life here, just as it was in Tenochtitlan. Some men he knew already equated violent death and sex with children with pleasure and ecstasy. He thought of his granddaughters and winced.

Aztecs had been obsessed with the moment of death and the charged moments leading up to severing the soul from the body, similar to the MK-ULTRA doctors concentrating on protracted torture and its psychic possibilities. For the Aztec mind, it was not about how one lived in this world but how one died to it; this was what determined one's fate, not the good or evil they did in life. This and not just how historical records would remember them was why Freemasons and Jesuits arranged deaths according to circumstance, means, time, place, and age. "Being as gods" entailed a heavy responsibility.

The General sighed, then gulped the rest of his tea. He'd looked in men's eyes as they died and felt them leave. *Holy.* One minute someone was in that body, the next they were gone and the eyes empty. But it was the killers that chilled his blood, mostly CIA types with dead eyes and still walking around. Maybe his eyes were like that and he hadn't noticed. He'd look in the mirror. No. He'd ask his wife.

In the shower, he thought about the spacetime experiments the Navy was running down in the Southwest desert and wondered what that rogue retired intelligence colonel had to do with it. Would Time experiments affect the chthonic regions that young astrophysicist alluded to? Intellectually, he knew Time was relative, but what could their devices do to it? He turned the water off. Probably just more wasted millions.

Naqoyqatsi was speeding across America.

36

Laurence Mulls Over a Pint of Bitter and Hiram Dines With His Actuary

This is a country of the mind which the author knows to be relevant to the Grail.

–Geoffrey Ashe, *Camelot and the Vision of Albion*, 1971

…Therefore, the silent weapon is a type of biological warfare. It attacks the vitality, options, and mobility of the individuals of a society by knowing, understanding, manipulating, and attacking their sources of natural and social energy, and their physical, mental, and emotional strengths and weaknesses.

–Hartford Van Dyke, "Silent Weapons for Quiet Wars"; in an IBM copier at a surplus sale, July 7, 1986

Laurence had returned to London and was having a pint at The Green Lion & Dragon. As he took the first mother's milk draw on the bitter, his eyes took in Old English script over the stone pit. *In magic, any act known and made public is lost.*

A nearby Anglican church rang out the passage of Time.

His mind was full of the tiny wizened Pict he had met outside his Edinburgh bed and breakfast that very morning. They'd joined step along the Royal Mile toward Edinburgh Castle and the Pict had led their talk toward the Stone of Destiny's return to Scotland. Of course, Laurence didn't hold with the general legend that Jacob had used the Stone as a pillow at Bethel, and its erection as a pillar sounded like a Freemason myth. What *did* sound true was how monks at the Abbey of Scone had hidden the real Stone at Dunsinnan Hill when Edward Longshanks came looking for it, and that they had passed off a sandstone from the Annety Burn for him to take back to Westminster.

"But there 'as to be a transfer o' power befor' it'll see its 'ome again," the tiny man nodded.

"Between England and Scotland?" Laurence asked.

"Aye, from the Grand Lodge to the Scottish Rite." He winked and then tried to give Laurence a secret handshake.

Laurence smiled sheepishly as the Pict withdrew his unrecognized hand. "Sorry, that's my brother's terrain, not mine. I never went beyond Third Degree."

The Pict brushed the incident aside. "Mark me words, once the Stone returns, Scots'll be the majority i' the House o' Commons an' the House o' Lords."

"Aye," Laurence said, getting into the spirit of his forebears, which made the Pict smile. Laurence had then mentioned that he would soon be heading south to France to see Notre Dame. "I haven't seen it since I was a wee lad."

"Well and good," said the Pict, puffing his pipe and thinking for all he was worth. "Begun in 1163 and not finished until 1345. Its three portals are Judgment, the Virgin, and Saint Marcel, secret names for the three great sciences of the Middle Ages: Mysticism, Astrology, and Alchemy. And while it's true the French 'ave wholeheartedly joined the modern era, especially with their nuclear alchemy"—he winked and smiled—"neither have they left behind the past, as some nations have tried to do." Laurence knew which nation he was referring to.

"Take Lyons, for instance," the Pict went on. "The mists roll up into the streets every mornin' from the Rhône, but hidden amidst the long avenues and wide boulevards, the delicatessens and silk and churches, to this very day is mysticism, enchantment. In

La Guillotière, you can have someone bewitched for a franc. Look up and there is another Notre Dame, Notre Dame de Fourviere, inside which are Assyrian, Roman and Gothic symbols—all Asiatic, not Christian in the least. Eugéne Vintras died there; he celebrated sex magick masses he called *celéstification,* either *unions de sagesse* with higher beings, or *unions de charité* with lower beings. Upside-down crosses and blood-stained hosts and the lot."

The whiff of sulfur drifting up from the little Pict's soul had blown Laurence's thoughts toward his brother and the Enterprise, neither of which he was ready to discuss with the obviously magically inclined Pict. After a few more words about the little church on the Cnoc nan Aingeal or Hill of Angels in front of Sithean the Fairy Mound on Iona, where photographs of ill people were still left (and people got better), the Pict had cheerfully left Laurence at the Castle gates and gone his way.

His talk of magic had stirred up a Macbeth brew of doubt and anxiety in Laurence's gut, so much so that after a cursory look in the Castle still awaiting its Stone of Destiny, he hastened to gather his things at the bed and breakfast and make his way to the train depot. Chugging south out of the rill-threaded land of William Wallace and Knights Templar, he'd been haunted by the Pict and Macbeth:

Say, from whence
You owe this strange intelligence? or why
Upon this blasted heath you stop our way
With such prophetic greeting?

Now at The Green Lion & Dragon, fortified by bitter, he cracked open a book about ancient Britain and read how around Lindow Moss and in central England the old festivals were still celebrated: well dressings, the Haxey hood game, sword dancing with ritual decapitations. Children were still warned about spirits lurking about wells and bogs and how the feeling of *dread* still alive must be appeased.

From Anglesey east across England was the old Druid gold road that began in Ireland in the Wicklow Mountains—probably from when the two lands were one long ago. In 1942, the Royal Air Force built an airfield close to the narrows that separate Anglesey from Holy Island and unearthed a massive slave chain with six neck rings, then used it to tow trapped trucks from the mud. Other finds were unearthed as well but sent to the National Museum of Wales under the supervision of Sir Cyril Fox. *Fox*, Laurence thought. Weren't foxes and witches connected in old lore?

The findings at Llyn Cerrig Bach, the lake of little stones, led to the significance of Watling Street, which runs through Mancetter in Warwickshire, once called Mandvessedum, the place of chariots, all the way to East Anglia and beyond by water road to Denmark. The Fosse Way—an entirely geographic Roman road running southwest-northeast, now mostly the A46—cuts across Watling Street at Vernemeton, 25 miles northeast of Mancetter.

Vernemeton was once a thickly wooded sacred grove, one of the greatest sacred sites of Celtic Britain now hidden where the boundaries of Leicestershire and Nottinghamshire meet, near the village Willoughby-on-the-Wolds. Leicester lies among Dane Hills, once sacred to the goddess Anu, now called Black Annis, the child-eating hag living under the hill. Here, the Black Field, charred by many a sacred fire, hides and hordes a noble (or ignoble) passionate past. The Romans purposefully built their roads through sacred sites, such as through the sacred springs further south at Bath.

Strange how churches and the military go hand in hand. Mancetter church sits where a Roman fort of Claudian date (43-54 AD) once sat, and where, before them, a Celtic sacred site near the beloved River Anker sat. And so it goes from era to era: Roman, Saxon, Viking, Norman, Angles—conquerors establish their spiritual and physical plants of power where those before have pointed the way.

Penbridge and Wall were two others taken over for Roman

fortification immediately north of Mancetter and south of Lindow, both once sacred groves. Wall was dedicated to the Celtic goddess Brigit and later to the Roman goddess Minerva. In Abbots Bromley eleven miles north of Wall, antler dancers still dance.

Back to Watling Street, an overlay of an ancient Celtic route made sacred by its holy groves along its way, at least before the Romans. After cutting through the River Trent-River Severn passage to Wroxeter, the Romans sent it north to Chester, around the coast of North Wales to Anglesey, linking Mancetter, Penbridge and Wall and wedging between Vernemeton and the Lunt, on the outskirts of Coventry where, again, Rome chose to build a fort.

Laurence drained the rest of his ale and looked about. He was the last in the pub and it was ten past eleven. Outside, a late spring drizzle was dampening London spirits, but Laurence felt the wet gratefully. He had received instruction from William Wallace in the north; tomorrow, he would visit the Round Church of the Knights Templar, then take a train to seek out Arthur in the south at Cadbury Castle in Somerset.

While Laurence was sipping bitters in London across the great pond, his brother Hiram was having drinks with his actuary Mr. Cohen at Mr. Cohen's club in Boston's Back Bay. Business as usual was being conducted at the club, such as the Quator Coronati Masonic Lodge member reporting for the Jesuit Superior General regarding leading *yeshivas* and Christian Fundamentalists under his watch. But that was elsewhere than Hiram's tête-à-tête.

The impeccably dressed Mr. Cohen had just returned from his annual trip to London for a conference put on by the Rothschilds. Both he and Hiram freely admitted to being in awe of the Rothschilds, or at least in awe of their well-deserved myth. It was, after all, Mayer Amschel Rothschild (1743-1812) who said, *Give me control over a nation's currency and I care not who makes its laws.* Mr. Cohen had studied everything Rothschild he could lay his hands on, and like a groupie hoped for an invitation someday to a Rothschild private gathering. Hiram had heard rumors of grisly Rothschild affairs and thought his actuary fortunate *not* to be invited. He himself hoped he would never receive an invitation that most certainly he could only turn down at his peril.

The club chairs were overstuffed leather, the mahogany deep and glossy, and Mr. Cohen was taking delight in tutoring Hiram about how brilliantly the Rothschild brothers had discovered and applied the passive component of economic theory known as economic inductance, which came into its own with the rise of the electric computer without which control of the world economy simply could not *thrive*. Hiram listened attentively to how the Rothschild minions wielded economics as a weapon of sociopolitical control, knowing that money and media were the 1-2 punch of the new silent warfare, the prize being the Enterprise.

Mr. Cohen was giddy with Rothschild appreciation. "By means of currency and deposit loan accounts, Mr. Rothschild acquired the *appearance* of power necessary to induce people to surrender their real wealth in exchange for the promise of greater wealth—real collateral from individuals, governments, and corporations for promissory notes. Once the overconfidence occurred, as it must, he then tightened the money and collected the collateral. Mr. Rothschild became the valve money had to pass through. He kindled wars and controlled currency to determine who won and who lost, then collected debts via foreign aid. By repeating this cycle, his descendants have gained extraordinary profit, but more importantly, influence and control over nations. Now, currency is lifting free of precious metals and the GNP." He paused to sip his Tokay. "Brilliant, what?"

Hiram smiled and nodded. He despised Cohen's British affectations but adored the Levite mind making him richer and richer.

"Rothschild made credit look like capital, when really it is

136

negative capital—look like service, when it is really debt. Was there ever a greater magician? Economic inductance instead of economic capacitance." He paused to marvel, then leaned toward Hiram and spoke in a hushed reverential tone. "And how would such debt be balanced? Not by increasing goods and services. Not by currency. By *war*, Hiram. By killing off the true creditors, the public duped into exchanging true value for inflated currency. By eliminating the useless eaters and thus falling back upon now-increased resources. By shifting economic inductance to situations encouraging the greatest instability, the world came to his door and gave him the leverage over wars that would cull the numbers of resource-devourers." His eyes shone. "With our higher and higher speed computers, Mayer Amschel's dream can now come to fruition. The necessary economic oscillations of the rapidly shifting, currency-free system he set in motion over a hundred years ago can now be monitored and controlled. And this present fruition all began at my alma mater." He beamed and raised his glass in a mock toast.

"Harvard?" Hiram was hardly surprised. So much had begun at Harvard.

"With the Harvard Economic Research Project in '48, the year I graduated." He glanced at Hiram. "You graduated Yale in '40, didn't you? Your brother was Harvard."

Hiram didn't respond. He didn't like being reminded of his vanishing youth, nor did he want to think of his spineless brother or how he was still grinding his teeth over losing Thomas and eating crow. Still, he probably wouldn't be sitting here enduring his pompous actuary without his spineless brother's sons having paved the way to his present career. *Silver lining, Hiram*, he reminded himself, nodding affably to Cohen.

Mr. Cohen continued his accolade. "With mathematical theory and computational computers, the Rothschilds realized they could control economic trends just like the trajectory of a guided missile by making an economy obey the same laws that apply to generating and controlling an electronic field. Imagine that, Hiram. Demand as voltage, supply as current, and the relationship between the two as admittance resulting from hindsight flow, present flow, and foresight flow. Foresight flow is stock or inventory, capacitance or stored charge. Present flow, input-output or the economic valve. Hindsight flow might be a pure service industry (inductor) whose money (current) creates a magnetic field or active human population. If the current diminishes, the magnetic field will have to collapse in order to maintain current flow. And the collapse? War, the economic inductor that then acts as a spark."

"Doesn't England use social welfare programs to maintain its current?" Hiram was getting the picture.

"Yes, but England doesn't have a volatile class structure like ours. Their class structure hasn't changed much since the Middle Ages: a small aristocratic class, a bit bigger tax-bound merchant class, and a large dependent underclass. We're reducing both farming and industry to almost nothing and using war as a stabilizer. They use social welfare, an open-ended credit balance system that creates a false capital industry. In return, the recipients become state property addicted to their monthly check. Of course, the public will have to pay later for this method of stabilizing capacitance, just as we will for war. In a sense, this might be the *fourth* law of motion: onset." Mr. Cohen smirked at Hiram. "I have it on good authority that we shall soon be eliminating our own social welfare system and resorting to borrowing from the future by printing money far beyond our GNP."

"Inflation," Hiram added unnecessarily.

Mr. Cohen shrugged. "Perpetual war will keep accounts balanced during the transition to a cashless society." Mr. Cohen admired his Tokay. The sweetness of the grapes in Tokaji Aszu was concentrated by a mold called *Botrytis cinerea*. Draining the glass, he announced, "Destroy the creditor."

"Benevolent slavery and genocide?" Hiram inquired.

Mr. Cohen had a think. "Yes, a quieter warfare to reduce

economic inductance. In the Third Worlds of Asia and Los Angeles."

The *maître d'* approached. Looking at each other, the two men stood. They were hungry.

After supper, Hiram retreated to his limousine and told his driver to take the long way back to New York. As they maneuvered through the evening traffic, Hiram peered out his one-way tinted windows at the people it was his job to manipulate. He didn't know which he despised more, the little Jewish prick he'd just spent two hours with or these objects, these targets that constantly had to be swayed, led, misled, drugged, fed, starved, killed, birthed, made sick, made well.

At a stoplight, an old beggar woman in the tatters of centuries past was pushing a shopping cart loaded with her personal effects across the street. *Why doesn't she have the decency to die?* Hiram whinged. Just looking at her turned his full stomach. Hitler had had the right idea: only the young, strong, fit, and useful should be allowed to survive. He was useful to the Enterprise, and *when they no longer needed him, they would do with him as they willed, being as gods.*

The words made him catch his breath. Where had he heard them? Perhaps in Freemason literature, or Crowley? He perpetually got the two confused, they sounded so much alike.

The car continued and the old offending woman was gone. He thought of his brother. What was the fishing lodge sojourn about? Would Laurence be his keeper when he was no longer useful?

Cohen preening his feathers had it easy crunching numbers for finance, manufacturing, insurance and government, all logically structured, bottom line mathematical projections, technical coefficients. Not so with his own domain. Psychological and sociological profiles, surveys, media and Congress errand boy for the Enterprise.

He knew something of mathematics. To study the consumer public economy or household industry, economic engineers used shock testing: increase the price on a staple commodity or availability of work, then watch the shock waves in advertising, purchasing, sales, other commodities, all the while gathering data to translate into prediction and control. The people were taught to think of the free market as making prices plunge or soar, but the free market was only a myth used to create faith in the experts. Shock testing like labor strikes in transportation, communications and public utilities created the chaos necessary to disrupt lives and create fear to further enslave them to an economic system that manipulated them like yoyos. Cohen was right. Availability of money and mass psychology went hand in hand. Skyrocket the price of gasoline and produce the final straw in an already economically burdened marriage or life. Violence was a gas tank away. Feed observations like these into a computer and probabilities lead to the predictable outcomes of just how vigorously the public money tree might still be shaken.

And while the economic engineers shook the money tree, Hiram's job was to deliver public acquiescence toward whatever the paymasters decided. Economic engineers handled the bread, he worked on the circuses. East Coast media, *New York Times*, *Washington Post*, CBS, NBC, ABC. Midwest and West Coast overseers. His team numbered about a dozen, and beyond their brains hundreds of contract agents from intelligence, entertainment, universities, crime syndicates, Congress, the State Department, Justice, industry, Nazi cults. Now that all the media that counted were big corporations, and all the airwaves privatized in the name of free enterprise, a web of influence was assured—not as mathematically precise as Cohen's figures, but close. Distract the public with endless entertainment, inundate them with news bytes, "debates," and talk shows at lightning speed. Disengage the mind, keep the brain in alpha, pour the pap in to confuse thought, keep them busy with the inconsequential and emotional development at about fifteen years old unto perpetuity. Encourage self-indulgence in the name of personal freedom. Amp up sex, violence, and war to stimulate the lower, more primitive centers and keep the neocortex stunted. Teach them what to desire and then give it to them in excess, depriving them of what they would need in order to develop into true, rational, emotionally mature adults able to reclaim control over their lives. Yes, Hiram had big shoes to fill. As the RAND man he reported to and received directives from put it, there is profit in confusion, and the more confusion, the more profit. Create the problem, then offer the solution. *True Hegelians,* Hiram smiled.

Recently, there had been some sort of shift upstairs in military or intelligence, it didn't matter which. Shock testing of the national psyche was now psyops for daily fare, and he'd become errand boy for that CIA psychiatrist Greenbaum. Well, whatever loaded the coffers. He glanced at a memo from a Lodge brother—

Hiram –

You asked for military updates on technology that could influence public psy ops. All I've come up with so far are scalar experiments going on in the Southwest from Southern California to Los Alamos and wherever the hell in West Texas that collider is. They're building an EM substructure detector—scalar communications, that kind of thing.

How it might look from this side is pretty science fiction. Scalar potentials alter time flow and everything existing locally in time, due to the stress effect. Scalar involves outfolding the inner energy spectrum of the Whittaker structure. That's probably Greek to you, but it boils down to altering the perception of time. Any more is beyond my security clearance.

Altering the perception of time in the Southwest . . . Wasn't that where Greenbaum said Didymus was on the trail of some black radical? He'd send this memo on to Greenbaum who demanded to know everything and ask about Didy being in the Southwest.

Who knows? Thomas was out there somewhere and maybe the twin magic Mengele promised would lead to him. If they were altering Time in the Southwest, why not? *It's a brave new world, Hiram.*

The next morning in London, en route on the Tube to Blackfriars station and the Knights Templar Round Church, a thought like a mantra kept running through Laurence's brain cells. *Wordsworth and Freud were right: The child is father of the man.* Schliemann found Troy because in boyhood he'd believed the tales of Homer. For years, like a closet alcoholic, Laurence had been secretly studying Arthur and the Grail legends he'd heard as a boy from his tutor. In his mind, Arthur and the Knights Templar were inextricably bound up with one another *and* the Grail, whatever it was. It was only now that he began to understand how he had loved these myths because he sensed they held solutions to life's mysteries.

Understanding Britain's role in Europe begins with geography. Long ago, the isles were connected to the Continent by two rivers: one with an estuary close to Norway that once ran along the bed of what is now the North Sea, and the other into the Atlantic from the bed of the English Channel. When the ocean rose, Ireland separated from the Scottish isles and the two rivers widened and became sea. Aristotle mentioned the two large Britannic islands Albion and Ierne, but long before Aristotle, the British Isles were underwater, some parts more recently than others. It was from this fact that the ooze of oceanic British mysticism continued to strain beneath a thin veneer of stuffy rationalism and pragmatism. Rivers, marshes, lagoons, even a sea route from Bristol Channel, shift from tide to tide, season to season, year to year. Shores there one year are not there the next, strange lights in the marshes, disappeared paths—that is Somerset. Such watery haunts are just that, points of contact and transition between this world and *Other* worlds, like Tir-nan-Og or the isle of Avallach, the apple orchard of Avalon. In fact, before and after the Romans left, coast dwellers along the peninsula of Armorican Gaul (Brittany) were still ferrying their dead back to Britain.

Malory's 15th century *Le Morte d'Arthur* signaled the weaning of individual power from magic, but those who should have noticed chose not to. When Merlin withdrew because it was now the Age of Men, all Britain could see was a nationalistic Arthur, not a Christ-like universal Arthur. For them, the Return of Arthur meant a return to empiric glory, not some cipher about the Age of Men. Thus it was that elites of many stripes, none very imaginative and most definitely of this world and this world alone, committed themselves and their sons and grandsons to re-obtaining the glory of what had vanished with Merlin. Instead of seeing the death of the old as the herald of the new, they set to moving hell and high water to bring back what was vanishing.

Their error in perception plagued the centuries after the Freemasons took over the throttle from the Templars, an error in Laurence's opinion that led inexorably to perdition at the will of those who would use anything to obtain and keep political or spiritual power. *Redeunt Saturnia regna*. Voltaire, Rousseau, Victor Hugo, Hegel, Marx and even the workers' revolution sought a reinstatement of an idyllic primitive communism redolent of the French Revolution's *liberté, égalité,* and *fraternité*. Napoleon, the Kaisers, Hitler, and the reinstatement of the Holy Roman Empire. From Canaanites to Palestinians and Zionists, *the ransomed of the Lord shall return and come to Zion with singing . . .*

At the Blackfrairs stop, Laurence climbed the stairs, studied the Thames river traffic, then made his way to the Temple, winding along the paths through the Inner and Middle Temples of barristers' chambers and courts before arriving at the Round Church. His footsteps on the walkways of power sounded muted beneath the perfect London pearl gray sky. He recalled his first trip to London as a boy and how Londoners had seemed to know exactly when to unfurl their umbrellas for a timely shower and furl them again seconds before the shower had spent itself. Even the weather had

143

seemed controlled in Britain. Fleet Street and the Temple Bar were still the citadels of Western power, but quietly so, letting the Bear and Eagle provide the spectacle circuses always needed.

A tiny eddy of weekday tourists trickled out of the church. When Laurence was at last alone among the Knights, it pleased him. Inside the quiet, he wound left into the Round where the effigies lay in repose. The Knights Templar had built the church in the round to recall the beloved Church of the Holy Sepulcher in Jerusalem and the churches they had built in Axum, Ethiopia where, it was rumored, the Ark of the Covenant lay. The Patriarch of Jerusalem had consecrated the London church in 1185. Henry II had been there, his infant son buried beneath the floor of the Chancery.

Slowly, he studied the nine marble effigies of the knights supposedly lying in a vault beneath the floor. Knowing the British Freemasons and how important the Knights Templar were to them, he guessed that the Knights' bones had been quietly moved, perhaps even to Freemason Hall. They were like that about bones— Geronimo's skull, Skull & Bones, etc.

There was William Marshall with his two sons. Laurence wondered if the crossed legs of some of the knights indicated their sworn chastity. Idly, he contemplated being buried beneath the floor of his house and smiled. The Knights of St. John the Hospitallers were eventually granted English Templar lands. The Great Fire of London in 1666 had stopped short of the Round Church, as though the Knights had held it back. But the Nazi *blitzkrieg* succeeded on May 10, 1941. After considerable reconstruction, it was rededicated in November 1958.

He looked about. Candidates seeking entry to the Templars would have entered the western door at dawn to be initiated and take their vows. Given that the church was still a *royal peculiar*, meaning under the monarch and not a diocese, Laurence assumed that initiations of some sort were still taking place during non-tourist hours. He shuddered. In one way he knew too much since his own initiation into the Blue Degrees, and in another—since Veracruz—not enough.

He felt *comforted* by the Round among the dead. Something deep in his chest was letting down, unwinding for the first time in decades. He sat on a bench with his back against the wall, took a deep breath and let it out. A voice from inside suddenly cried two words to the Knights: *Help me.* Laurence listened, as if the words had come from someone else. *I am neither Jerusalem nor like the One you loved. I am only a modern man who through his own folly and weakness has lost two sons and his wife and his grip on what it is to* be*, to really* be*. In mid-voyage, I am lost in a storm. Guide me, man to man, knight to derelict.*

His hands fluttered up to his face to feel his stubbled cheeks. They were wet. The someone inside he no longer knew was leaking heavenly dew. The last time he recalled tears was when he was nine and it was his turn to leave his nurse and home and submit to St. Alban's as his brother had. His dormitory pillow had been damp many a morning.

He heard someone entering the Chancel and quickly wiped his face with his sleeve. Incredibly, it was a boy about nine or ten in his choirboy white. His father stopped at the doorway and stood with arms crossed while the child made a beeline for the choir stall in the middle of the Chancel. After climbing up on something so as to be tall enough to sing into the microphone on Sunday or whenever he was to sing, he shut his eyes and sang in his British boy soprano an exquisite 18th century hymn by Thomas Haweis.

> *O Thou from whom all goodness flows,*
> *I lift my heart to Thee;*
> *In all my sorrows, conflicts, woes,*
> *Dear Lord remember me.*
>
> *When groaning on my burdened heart*
> *My sins lie heavily,*

My pardon speak, new peace impart,
In love remember me.
Temptations sore obstruct my way,
To shake my faith in Thee,
O give me strength, Lord, as my day,
For good remember me . . .

    The boy sang it through once, hopped down from his perch, ran back down the aisle, and buried his pleased face in his father's legs. Little did he know the surgery his song had performed on the American sitting in the shadows of the Round, wrestling with Death and Birth, becoming one the Knights would no longer call lost.

37

The Qabalist Seeks Out
the Hudson Oracle

*We shall unleash the Nihilists and Atheists, and we shall provoke a formidable
social cataclysm which in all its horror will show clearly to the nations the
effects of absolute atheism, origin of savagery and of the most bloody turmoil.
Then everywhere, the citizens, obliged to defend themselves against the world
minority of revolutionaries, will exterminate those destroyers of civilization,
and the multitude, disillusioned with Christianity, whose deistic spirits will be
from that moment without compass, anxious for an ideal, but without knowing
where to render its adoration, will receive the pure doctrine of Lucifer, brought
finally out in the public view, a manifestation which will result from the general
reactionary movement which will follow the destruction of Christianity and
atheism, both conquered and exterminated at the same time.*

- Illustrious Albert Pike 33°, Letter 15 August 1871, addressed
to Grand Master Guiseppie Mazzini 33°; British Museum
Archives, London

Crime once exposed has no refuge but in audacity.

- Tacitus (56-117 CE)

The enemy of my enemy is my friend.

- Arabian

The Qabalist was rapt in thought. Above his head on the
wall was a large painting of the Göbekli Tepe temple near Sanliurfa,

Turkey, built 11,500 years ago, 7,000 years before the Great Pyramid, 6,000 years before Stonehenge. Beside it was a gold-inlaid painting of a medieval chart with angels and demons flying about colorful words under the scripted heading, *Liber Rationum of Peter of Abano (1215-1313), translator, Padua.* Beneath the heading were the yet more ornate words—*From the short Qabalistic treatise De Septem Secundeis by Johannes Trithemius (1462-1516), Abbot of Spanheim*—followed by a list of Planets and Archangel Regents governing the world in a 354 year-4 month cycle among fluttering angels and demons, indicating that until 2233 AD the present time would be subject to the Regency of the Sun and Archangel Micha-ël.

PLANET	ARCHANGEL	3rd ROUND
Saturn	Oriphi-ël	245 BC
Venus	Ana-ël	109 AD
Jupiter	Zachari-ël	463 AD
Mercury	Rapha-ël	817 AD
Mars	Sama-ël	1171 AD
Moon	Gabri-ël	1525 AD
Sun	Micha-ël	1879 AD
	Thaumi-ël	

In the Qabala, Thaumi-ël was equal to the Supreme Kether and defined as the twin two-headed fallen angel representing dual contending forces. Thaumi-ël had no planetary association or date, given that he was ruled by Satan, Master of Dual Contending Forces, Lucifer and Ahriman.

The Qabalist returned to his list of mediums and astrologers: Dixon, Richter, Petchek, Doc Marque, the KGB's Georgy Rogozin, Hitler's and Himmler's astrologer the Führer, the Panama witch in the American sector of Amador, Eileen Garrett, Pieter van de Hirk; Gavin Arthur, descended from 21st President Arthur; Phyllis

Schlemmer, the O'Connor girl at Esalen. Sabin, Eastlund . . . He considered updating with Shirley MacLaine and Nancy Reagan.

He sighed. Greenbaum was right: the old abilities were waning. No more Copernicus, no more Cheiro. The English astrologer John of Eschenden had foreseen the plague of 1347-48, the German astrologer Lichtenberger the birth of Luther, the 16th century astrologer Carion the French Revolution—and yet had they really *seen*, or just been well informed? Stalin's astrologer, Yury Yammakin, was sent to a *gulag*, then reinstated by Khrushchev. As abilities born of blood receded like the Nile, they would have to make up the difference with technologies.

Under MK-ULTRA, they still turned to the old techniques: drugs, hypnosis, pain—and cold, of course—to pop the soul out of the body and readjust the brain; and the water torture that took *psychic warriors* (the term favored by the military) to the brink of death, after which they were brought back. Flotation tanks were new, with their carefully controlled temperature and IVs for modern Oracles of Delphi called *pattern recognition filters* and *remote viewers*. Technology constituted their greatest hope for accuracy and consistency. Already pattern recognition centers were referred to as *Temples*.

The Hudson Oracle, a woman born of French aristocracy whose atavistic clairvoyant capabilities had been genetically bred through intramarriage with the Stuart line, Merovingian priest kings, and before them Jesus' brother James. The fact that her blood still worked for belly clairvoyance while others from equally pure bloodlines didn't, the Qabalist surmised, must have to do with the Jesus bloodline. He had used her for years due to the fact that her consciousness was a *tabula rasa*, thanks to her family's assiduous early childhood practices. Her receiving and transmission capabilities were exceptional and therefore commanded the highest respect and fees. Her reception accuracy was eighty percent, her transmissions one hundred. She was kept in relative comfort *in vitro* in the Hudson River Valley family mansion built in the 1840s over a boulder submerged in a deep underground spring. The family, dedicated to the Enterprise, had resigned themselves to the Oracle's high fate and did everything they could to meet Dr. Greenbaum's strict dictums. She was not to be earthly in any way, other than lying in a bed. Real food had not passed her lips in years; she was IV-fed synthetics. What was in the drip at any given time was a mystery fathomed only by Drs. Greenbaum and "Black" and the nurse who never seemed to require sleep. Saline drip, MRI, EEG, near-arctic temperature-controlled environment—such was her life. A landing strip had been added to the old estate to accommodate the many dignitaries and luminaries with questions. When was the most propitious time for a wedding of state? Who had the latest scion been in his most recent incarnation? Why had Uncle Jeffrey changed his will? Which property should they purchase, the one in St. Tropez or on Capri?

But this aspect of the Hudson Oracle's job was only, in modern parlance, her cover. The Qabalist had other, more pivotal assignments for her requiring transmissions from beyond death, indeed, but beyond *human*, as well. Truth be told, it was in what the boulder in the stream had to say that Dr. Greenbaum and the Qabalist were often most interested. Her abilities, coupled with the close tabs the Qabalist kept on the heavens, ensured that the Enterprise from the American end was rarely taken by surprise.

For these most esoteric assignments, Dr. Greenbaum would administer a particular drip with a particular hormone in it, then put the question to her via electrodes and computer. For a face or place, the image would be either held in front of her closed eyelids—light hurt her pale eyes, so she rarely opened them—or fed to her brain's visual center via a monitor hooked up to the EEG. Her sense organs would then transmit image impulses to her nerves, then to her glands that resisted the sensations and secreted substances into her blood. Her membranes and skin, being primarily siliceous, then acted as capacitors that resisted the flow of forces and thus built a field around the organs that interacted with the conducting and resisting minerals in the buried boulder below. Thus would visions arise in 3D holograms that would go straight to the computer monitor. Yes, the Hudson Oracle was top form, all right, perhaps the last of her kind.

In a brown study, the Qabalist watched his wrinkled hand glide toward the new book he was reading, *The Christ, Psychotherapy and Magic* by Anthony Duncan, an Anglican clergyman. He was reading it because it discussed Christian mysticism and the Sefiroth. Books and the stars were his life, with people to put up with . . .

Ancestry was on everyone's mind. How often he had told the rich American *shiksas* and their husbands that even the blood of European royalty was no longer any thicker or richer or more gifted than anyone else's. Greenbaum even said the reason Jews and Teutons were so backward was that they mistook recurrent incarnations for bloodlines. Before the 10th century, bloodlines had made a difference, back when the Grail lineage ran in the blood of European nobility. But the royal Grail line had dried up, and abilities once ferried by the blood arrived less and less. Spiritual revelation, superior abilities, second sight—dried up. Not entirely, but certainly no longer assured.

Infuriating to the elite, abilities once cached in careful family alliances began showing up in commoners. The Qabalist knew who was to blame for this eugenic loss: the Messiah, the new Lord of Karma. His First Advent had changed everything, which was why methods of obtaining revelations and skills had become so desperate, even stooping to using pain, fear, infanticide, and necromancy. Even Qabalistic science needed "aids." Cosmic depletion meant fighting tooth and claw against the new Landlord's egalitarian, democratic insistence of developing the opportunity for freedom in any and every human being.

Thus more than ever the rich and aristocratic were preying upon commoners like vampires, scouring their children's test scores and family histories for exceptional abilities, leaching their life forces. Aristocracy stripped of the power of its blood meant vacuous lives falling like tares into the consuming fires of Satanism, the Dragon Court, darkened Illuminism and its bent, cheapened offspring. This downward turn was agonizing for the Qabalist but the very grist for the mill he must grind.

He would use the Hudson Oracle to find Saint-Germain and the new incarnation of the Mexican initiate Vitzliputzli. Sibelius was concerned that Saint-Germain might have come to work in tandem with Vitzliputzli. Then there was the Gardner boy now traveling east; he too had eluded Los Angeles and Santa Barbara clairvoyants, indicating that he had protection, possibly Vitzliputzli, possibly Saint-Germain.

The Qabalist turned back to his notes on astronomy and sidereal astrology. Earlier, he'd gone over Edgar Cayce's 1943 predictions regarding tectonic upheavals as per the JASONs' request. Cayce had referred to the number 76 but no more, so the Qabalist had plotted everything but the outer planet Pluto and discounting 1976 and 2076. But 76 years after 1943 was a possibility: 2019. Jupiter, Saturn, and Pluto would all ingress Capricorn in the 10th house in 2020, squared by Uranus in Aries. A cardinal mega-conjunction in the house of public affairs could mean either a pivot in power or starting over after a cataclysm. The last time Pluto was in Capricorn was from 1762 to January 1778—just as the United States of America was being birthed.

Pluto's difficult transformative powers could mean destruction, death, earthquakes, hurricanes, volcanic eruptions, drought, famine, atomic power, viruses. In a *plutocracy* sense, it could mean obsession, kidnapping, coercion, waste, underworld crime, mass manipulation, terrorism, dictatorships, obsessions, secrets. Pluto ruled Scorpio as the highest octave of Mars, and it was true that the plutocrats were seeking to quietly shift human consciousness by means of controlled chaos, orchestrated death, and alpha brain states under artificial intelligence (AI) control. Pluto's eccentric spin around the Zodiac takes 247.8 years, but takes only a Jupiter or

Saturn cycle through a sign. Right now, Pluto was 27° retrograde Virgo / the Sophia, and she reclines as many as 70° or one-fifth of the Zodiac. If Cayce's 76 did mean 2019, it could mean the downfall of the Enterprise, if not more.

It wouldn't be the first time that empire had ended in an Earth cataclysm.

The Qabalist yawned. Late nights were taking their toll. Tomorrow, he would check the Saturn-Pluto alignments and oppositions, the 33- and 16-year pulses. World War One, then a Saturn-Pluto square in 1932 for World War Two, then the National Security Act in 1947, the Middle East and Vietnam in 1965 under a Saturn-Uranus-Pluto conjunction. In 1604 (*had the conjunction moved into Saggitarius?* He couldn't remember), a nova had appeared where three higher planets were conjunct just as the tomb of Christian Rosenkreuz was discovered. Kepler had been ecstatic. He already knew that 2001 would be a big year to set something political in motion, then 2020—and not to forget the 133-year underworld pulse of Uranus and Pluto.

The Qabalist stepped outside the French doors for some fresh air and a look at the heavens he loved. None of Philadelphia's light pollution here. It was cold and clear, Passover finished, the Iyyar Moon and less than six months to Elul 26, tropical September 23, sidereal October 19, 1° Libra in AD 29, when the *rabboni* and the Baptist stood in the Jordan. What was it that clever Russian novel said? *In a white cloak with blood-red lining, with the shuffling gait of a cavalryman, early in the morning of the fourteenth day of the spring month of Nisan* . . . So Russian. The fourteenth day of Nisan, the twenty-ninth. Kepler was both an astronomer and an astrologer and computed the Jewish Carpenter's birth as 7 or 6 BC in the Fish or the Ram. Some things one never forgets . . .

He stared at the waxing Moon. Perhaps by the time its horns were new, he would know where Saint-Germain was. Christian Rosenkreuz died in 1484, that much was certain—the year the magnificent *coniunctio magna* of Jupiter and Saturn in Scorpio inaugurated the Renaissance, era of magic and science rising from the ashes of Uranus-Pluto in 1455 and Neptune-Uranus in 1479. *Nothing new under the Sun.* The printing press and the little prophet Martin Luther born in 1484 in Germany, the Scorpio country from which Pope Innocent VIII sought to purge occult sciences. The Qabalist smiled. But how can you purge occult sciences without purging science? You can't.

Five hundred years later, a Phoenix year, would be 1984. Warburg (his family ran the occult Warburg Institute in London) changed George Orwell / Eric Blair's book title from *1948* to *1984* because of the Phoenix year. By 1984, the Freemasons would have raised from the ashes their own Mephistophelean style of a Renaissance magic era. He shivered. Francis Bacon must be turning in his grave to see how *crass* his New Atlantis was turning out. The forces in America were far more vicious than those of Calaban in his *Tempest*, and there was the Masonic Maitreya yet to appear . . .

Long ago, two Mystery streams migrated from doomed Atlantis, one Northern, one Southern. The Northern sought the Sun mysteries in the external macrocosm and life after death, while the Southern sought the Moon mysteries in inner contemplation of the soul and life before birth. The autumn Sun mystery, the spring Moon mystery. Zoroaster struggled with Angromainyu or Ahriman and Buddha with Mara, then everything changed when the Christ abandoned the Sun sphere for the Earth. The ancient Atlantis Mystery streams no longer worked as they once did; they had become either evil or empty—honorless, either way. And what had happened to the Sun sphere?

Above, satellites like beads on an electromagnetic rosary were silently executing their circumnavigation of the Earth. The Hebrew lunar calendar was a night calendar, the solar calendar a profane day calendar, both based on the twelve signs of the sidereal Zodiac, both structured on the cross of two equinoxes (equal nights) and two solstices, beginning (as did the world) with the vernal equinox and dividing the days into 30 sidereal degrees as the Sun wended its way through the Zodiac again and again, sweeping us through our Zodiac lessons. Yes, the solar calendar keeps the Earth apace of the stars and planets, but it is the Hebrew moon calendar that is intimately concerned with the Earth and her atmosphere. The months of the lunar calendar—Nisan, Iyyar, Sivan, Tammuz, Ab, Elul, Tishri, Heshvan, Kislev, Tebeth, Shebat, and Adar (and in leap year a second month of Adar)—relate to processes and beings subject to the Earth's etheric body and aura, which was why magicians and occultists always turned to the Hebrews and their Qabala. During the Babylonian and Egyptian Captivities, magi like Moses learned of the deep and ancient past that had been lost over and over to water and fire, and of the laws opening the portals to knowledge of the Earth. The Hebrew G-d is a G-d of History, of *this* planet, *this* kingdom—not of gods and the solar system *out there*. Knowledge, not Love, as Christians harp on.

The Qabalist continued to stare up at the Moon, remembering what a scientist said at one of the insufferable *goy* parties he had to attend: that on the dark side of the Moon were craters named after Giordano Bruno, Leo Szilard, and John Whiteside Parsons. Crowley's *Amalantrah Working* had opened a portal in 1918; Szilard conceived the nuclear chain reaction; Parsons opened wide what the Bomb had only unlatched, having grasped the harmonic mathematics essential to determining the exact place in the desert for fine-tuning the Western magickal portal. Parsons had also developed the *intent* by which etheric-astral thought forms could be made electromagnetic enough to bridge the dimensions like a radio. What Crowley and Parsons began, lesser magician scientists were now Working in order to bind the planetary Double to their will, the Double being—*Thaumi-ël?* Intelligence agencies, religions, and behavioral-neural psychiatrists labored in the vineyards of others' greater discoveries.

He contemplated the American portal through whose gates long ago Og and Goliath had come, giant hybrids from the ancient tribe of Nephilim to whom the Books of Enoch, Jubilees, Jasher, and Testimony of the Twelve Patriarchs attested. Many demons now roaming the Earth were Nephilim souls who lost their physical bodies at the time of the Flood and now sought human bodies. Angelic half-breeds and hybrids were entering, aliens and their UFO forms from inside the Earth, walk-ins. The Illumined Ones of Enochian Fraternal Lodges, the invisible Kings of the Earth who ran oil, pharmacopoeia, and the nuclear industries had decreed it, and so it was. The design of the Pentagon, after all, was an Enochian magickal *sigillem ameth*. Theosophical luciferian doctrine plus survival of the fittest evolutionary philosophy have thus far constituted the syllogism that man can be God and the only God to worry about is man.

The Qabalist sighed. Jewish tradition said that two *maggids* or narrators, one good, one evil, accompany us on our walk through life. The *maggid* on the right (*dexter*) serves the conscience, but the one on the left (*sinistra*) is from the *Sitre Ahre*, the Other Side—our double or *Doppelgänger*. Our mission in life is to tell them apart, and what helps us do this is the double's secret longing for redemption. A proper initiation should help us to reclaim our divine memory so we can remember who we are and where we came from, and which is which. But there were very few proper initiations anymore—only that of quixotic life itself.

One of the Qabalist's *maggids* (on the left or right?) reminded him that once Mars stood beside Spica, the seed-bearing sheath of grain held by the Virgin, after the planetary contractions in 1980 and 1982, the birth of the manchild to rule all nations with a rod of iron would occur. And there was the Sun conjunct Mercury and Venus in the Fishes on Woden's day, April 3, 1985— pointing to the Good Friday on another April 3 long ago. Friday, Freia's Day. Yes, the Fishes opposing the Virgin's sheath of grain might portend a Mars birth. The signs weren't always amenable to correct readings, but they had to be attended to nonetheless. He would remind Greenbaum to monitor all male children born in 1983 or 1984, and not just from elite families.

War and iron. They must prepare an era that would welcome a man of iron as a savior. Halley's comet completes its exit in 2024 and they plan to announce planetary governance in 2025, despite starry agendas to the contrary. The merging of man as god and Shylock's necessity.

Wishing a good night to the Moon and her Sea of Fertility after which the Japanese novelist who had yet to immolate himself named his tetralogy, the Qabalist went inside for a few hours of much needed rest. It comforted him to know that for a few blessed hours his astral body would flee earthly complexities and return to the stars he so dearly loved. One night, not so long in the future, he would stay there and not return to the shackles of necessity gripping him still.

38

Crossing the Colorado

The physical metamorphosis of spilt blood can stand for the double nature of violence . . . Blood serves to illustrate the point that the same substance can stain or cleanse, contaminate or purify, drive men to fury and murder or appease their anger and restore them to life.

–René Girard, *Violence and the Sacred*, 1972

You know Proteus, he on whom it was conferred
To be able to switch shapes, to any and all,
Who shows everything and from everything
Revealing all from all.

–Giordano Bruno (1548-1600),
On the Composition of Images

In Needles, the pilgrims stopped for groceries and to do a couple of loads of laundry. While Thomas, Ray, the Colonel, and Vince went in search of groceries on the grocery list, Mannie and Seven loaded the machines while Baby Rose and Sirius gravitated toward the television perched in a corner. At first, *As the World Turns* was guiding Americans from desire to deceit to retribution and back again. But etched beneath the scene, Baby Rose could see the vague image of a man's face with dark eyes and hair parted like Hitler's. Words were swimming like salmon fighting upstream from his mouth and her immaculately programmed brain began recording. *There exists a group of people who set the tone for the development of mankind today . . . they wish to rule the earth by utilizing the mobility of the capitalist economic impulses. All circles of men . . .*

The screen went blank, then white noise. Somewhere, a tug of war over the airwaves was going on. The channel switched all by itself to a religious station. ". . . Guests today here on the *Hour of Power* in the Crystal Cathedral are Mikhail Gorbachev, now residing at the Presidio where a vast underground base known as the western White House . . ."

Seven slowly made her way toward Baby Rose as the channel changed again. A smiling Caucasian couple held up a plastic card. *AT&T. One world, one card.* Next, a flying saucer whizzed over the heads of field workers in a soybean field as a male voiceover declared, *If aliens are smart enough to travel through space, why do they keep abducting the dumbest people on earth?* A Winston cigarette logo appeared. *Winston. Straight up.*

The monitor returned to static and a machine-like voice claiming to be a representative of an extraterrestrial civilization announced its presence in the atmosphere, ending with, *We conveyed to Sir John Whitmore and to Dr. Puharich that we would interfere with your radio and television communication system to relay when the civilizations are coming close to landing on your planet.*

Seven didn't know who Puharich was, but she had seen him in Veracruz at the spine-chilling ritual.

The channel switched again. Now Mannie abandoned the magazines and dog-eared paperbacks and stood beside Seven, his mouth hanging open. On TV 3 New Zealand, big block letters read—

GEORGE W. BUSH
PROFESSIONAL FASCIST

Suddenly, it was CNN and the show banner *Millennium 2000.* AOL/Time Warner CEO Gerald Levin was speaking. "Global media will be and is fast becoming the predominant business of the 21ˢᵗ century, media being more important than government, educational institutions, and nonprofits. We're going to need to have these corporations redefined as instruments of public service, and that may be a more efficient way to deal with society's problems than bureaucratic governments. Corporate dominance is going to be forced anyhow because when you have a system that is instantly available everywhere in the world immediately, then the old-fashioned regulatory system has to give way . . ."

Then it was Cybersky, "television Web service of video feeds from all over the world." Cameras were trained on thousands of protesters in the streets of Genoa, Italy. The word *GENOACIDE* crept across the lower screen as a British voiceover explained. "Here in Genoa, in preparation for the G-8 meeting of economic world powers, 20,000 troops have been mobilized, 15 helicopters, four planes, seven naval boats, tear gas, water cannons, rubber bullets, body bags, rooftop watchers and satellite surveillance. In this latest chapter of global class war, one youth has been shot in the head and crushed beneath an armored police vehicle, and seventy activists clubbed while sleeping in the offices of the Genoa Social Forum, the floor littered with blood and broken teeth. Seattle, Philadelphia, DC, Prague, Davos, Gottenberg, Genoa—the military response to public protest grows, going all the way back to Operation Garden Plot . . ."

"Garden Plot. What Billy Joad talked about," Seven mumbled.

The channel kept switching. But Baby Rose was now picking up on a *sound* outside. Protective Sirius followed her. Far above Needles, an EC-130E Commando Solo was beaming earthward and Baby Rose's brain was picking it up.

Mannie pulled his eyes away from the mesmerizing monitor. "Seven," he said, sprinting outside.

Thus it was that Baby Rose, Sirius, Mannie, and Seven all did what Thomas said not to: they looked up to where Commando Solo's cameras were whirring far above. All that Mannie and Seven saw was blue sky, nor could they hear what Baby Rose and Sirius were hearing.

When laundry was done and the pilgrims had reconvened, Seven recounted how the laundromat television had behaved and how Baby Rose had gone outside and stared up, but she and Mannie had seen nothing. For Thomas, that they had turned their faces skyward did not bode well. As they left Needles, he encouraged Ray to speed up his mapping of radio frequencies.

In the backseat of the Cadillac, Mannie scanned the *Watchtower* he had liberated. Beside him, Baby Rose silently tabulated the subliminal Satanic and Masonic symbols in the pictures. *Only the Anointed Class are born again; the Great Crowd cannot look to Jesus as their mediator. Only the Anointed can take bread and wine. The problem is that less and less Anointed Ones are alive—to be exact, less than 9,000 of the original 144,000, and half of them are women and therefore ineligible for leadership.*

Seven and the Colonel were discussing Genoa and Operation Garden Plot. The two-way was on, of course.

"Reminds me of what Ray's mystery man in the bus station was talking about," the Colonel said. "Maybe Synarchy comes into its own with G-8. And the televised anarchy in the streets sounds like the old Hegelian one-two punch of control the conflict to control the resolution still working in the future: uppity crowds to justify more law and order. Fascist and Synarchist interests struck common cause a long time ago but lacked the global communications. Even Orwell's *1984* played a role. The Pan-European Movement in 1922 was a first step, financed by Max Warburg, banker and director of the infamous chemical cartel I.G. Farben that backed both Lenin and Hitler. Max's brother Paul directed the American I.G. Farben as well as the Federal Reserve Bank of New York, and Frederic Warburg was *1984*'s publisher—three brothers serving the fraternity that finally publicly revealed itself in 1954 as the Bilderberg Group."

Ray whistled over the two-way.

The Colonel explained what the Allied defeat at Arnheim

Bridge in 1944 signified for the delay in getting Nazi wealth out of Germany before war's end. "That was the year of the infamous Bretton Woods meeting up in New Hampshire, when Nazi and Japanese Synarchists tantalized Western powers with their scientists, technology, and Black Eagle Trust as collateral for rebuilding Germany and Japan. The first Bilderberg meeting in 1954 at Oosterbeck—just a few kilometers from Arnheim—celebrated the quiet Synarchist coup at the expense of nations still playing by the rule book."

Into the two-way, Thomas said, "Wasn't getting Nazi wealth what the Dulles brothers were working on so feverishly?" He'd heard about his uncle's Dulles heroes for years.

"Exactly," the Colonel said emphatically. "After the Bretton Woods meeting, West Germany was returned to sovereign nation status, and on May 5, 1955 (5/5/55) German corporations, many still run by Nazis, were freed from Allied control. The assets of corporate families like Thyssen, Krupp, Wolff, Dornier, Warburg, Pinay, Gubbins, etc.—many of whom were instrumental in creating the Bilderberg Group—were ferreted out of Germany through various accounts, and gold by Vatican ratlines protected by Gehlen's Organization, British and American intelligence—including the infamous trip to Scotland by Rudolf Hess that ended in his being scapegoated. MI6 agent Crowley was involved. Pearson's 1966 biography of Ian Fleming goes into it—the British edition, not the expurgated American. But only some of the assets returned to rebuild Germany."

"And the rest?" Ray asked, glancing at Vince in the back, scribbling in his notebook as fast as he could.

The Colonel shrugged. "Here's your renamed G-8 of the future on their way to global empire. Synarchy types have used war hoards throughout history to expand their power. Nazi gold, the Golden Lily gold the Nixons will take to Madame Mao in 1976—it will all probably go into supporting the next Committee so it will move China away from nationalism and toward a more *corporate* model of world power, and the rest will support the Third Reich here in the Americas, given that income from debt interest, drugs, arms deals, and taxes aren't enough." He studied the Air Force Academy ring on his finger.

"They'ill create more wars to acquire more hoard money," Ray added over the two-way. Frighten the Americans with the Communist bogeyman while Synarchist fascists set up shop and Synarchist Crowley founds his OTO. Like that speed freak said, Charlie Manson probably got his race wars idea from OTO programming, along with sadomasochism, drug dealing, blood drinking, child rape, and murder, with Jean Bray being the daughter of an Air Force colonel stationed at Vandenberg."

Ray thought back to the night he went looking for his father. *Devil worship*. He listened to the Colonel talking about the Order of the Temple of Astarte, OTA, run by a Green Beret and cop, everyone on military time. OTO, OTA. Pentagon, military, CIA. The Man and his psyops were everywhere.

Ray didn't care if he ever saw the Haight and its Victorian tenements again. The mercury vapor lamps they were putting in spooked him almost as much as the Lie Man's column in *The Avatar*. Fag or not, Ray was sure the Lie Man had crept out of the same CIA cult skin bag that Manson had. Superspade had been murdered, put in a bag, and thrown off a cliff north of San Francisco. Sure, Satanism was a good-is-evil-is-good medieval rap, but it could just as well be used to intimidate and control not just believers but society at the other end of the media stick. Crowley had been British intelligence, so why wouldn't the CIA be into mindfucking and cults?

There's heavy kid mind control at the Solar Lodge, a street brother said. And an LA street sister told him that a couple of kids had been riding their bikes outside the new little incorporated Orange County town Villa Park when they found a pit half full of skeletons and desiccated remains of a couple dozen big dogs. Satanic underworld in Southern California . . . And the Rolling Stones' free Altamont concert last December, when the Hells Angels killed that kid named Hunter. Multiple stabs, like Charlie's creepy-crawlies did to Sharon Tate. The Manson murders were the counterpoint to the Summer of Love, just like Altamont was to Woodstock. Ambrosia had become a witches' brew that felt and smelled like an orchestrated psyop intent on bringing down the political Sixties, like that speed chick said. Next step was more law enforcement and a crackdown on youth and all that youth stands for.

Yeah, the mental light bulb was glowing brighter and brighter. Easy drugs, easy sex, the endless party, free speech on street corners—all of it watched by the Watchmen making their lists. Cults and experiments, bring in the gurus and roshis to run the alpha brain trips. Peace, enlightenment, and love. Flood the streets with CIA LSD, then bad acid, heroin, and speed. Send in the Rolling Stones and Doors, love-ins, be-ins, anti-war and civil rights, pop the Three Kings, then cameo the radicalized Weather Underground.

Anton La Vey—high priest of the Church of Satan, author of *The Satanic Bible*—embraced a world without God and blamed the Catholic Church for inventing the seven deadly sins that were just natural. Werner Erhard and est pushed *Gestalt spiritual assertiveness* with its no victims and choosing our fate and being ultimately responsible for whatever happens to us. Ray hated that shit because it left out political manipulations. How could what happened to him as a kid be something he created? And the Zodiac killings—how did those victims create their fate?

He and Seven had gone over the Zodiac articles. She'd noticed a similar female-male pattern in Florence, Italy, beginning August 21, 1968 in the midst of all the revolts in Chicago, London, Paris, Berlin, Prague, Mexico City—exactly a year before the Manson murders in California on August 8, 1969 and 81 years since the Jack the Ripper murders in London that began on August 31, 1888, Hecate's holy day. In both the Zodiac and Monster of Florence killings, couples were shot at point-blank range, and secret service SISDE agents protected the Monster while he extracted vaginas and left breasts for Tuscan high society Satanic rites. Seven's conclusion had been, "The same repression that leads to the tabloid fix on the Zodiac and Manson is what led to the pornographic literature and imagery of witchcraft and the Inquisition." *And the photographs of Vietnam atrocities*, Ray had added silently.

Throughout her readings about the Russian Revolution and the two world wars in the 20th century, Seven noted how socialism and the occult seemed to run in the same harness. Lenin, Hitler, Mussolini, Franco . . . Occultism wasn't necessarily Satanism, but Satanism was occult. Occultism could be made to swing either way, good or evil, though she never heard much about its good side. Socialists were dedicated to an ideal State, and most occult fraternities were wary of individualism and seemed dedicated to the collective. Marx and Engels' dialectic sounded atheist but was actually a 19th century occult mix that the Synarchists simply turned into an atheist religion.

Were serial killers occult psyops? From the late 15th to 18th centuries, nine million witches were burned at the stake across Europe. The fewest were burned in Italy, home of the Vatican. Seven surmised that both the witches and their persecutors were victims of acute child abuse and dissociated to one degree or another, making them easy to program—ritual scapegoats to relieve the private and public psyches torn asunder by rampant childhood abuse. She wondered if the *Diagnostic and Statistical Manual of Mental Disorders* (DSM) today would diagnose the priests and good citizens who incinerated all those people as borderline personalities projecting their dissociated alters onto dissociated "witches."

Pump out rhetoric about democracy and transparency so the superficial intellectual level doesn't probe too deep, and meanwhile blast the public on a subliminal, unconscious level.

The number one enemy of the Catholic Church and its

Inquisition has always been the rogue imagination or *phantasy*, such as that of Manichæan Christians. The Church's double game is to feed the masses dogma and faith while giving free rein to gifted scholastic Jesuit priests tasked with studying everything they can about *phantasy*, the telephone line between the dimensions, after which their findings are stashed in the Vatican archives for a propitious day. To control sorcery, it was made a *crimen exceptum* in 1468 and a black line was drawn between 'natural' magic (physics) and 'transnatural' demonic magic that depended upon *phantasy*. Dominican Giordano Bruno went too far by preempting the secret plurality of worlds, and sometimes priests still go too far in arousing their chthonic appetites. *Scientia est potentia*.

Vince said that even Cristóbal Colón was buried in a Franciscan frock and had belonged to multiple Brotherhoods: Knights Templar, Johannites, and the Albigensian heresy whose leaders had sent him to open the Blessed Isles of the West. Lorenzo de Medici had financed the expeditions, and even Leonardo da Vinci had been involved. History books consistently lie. Seven said that Longfellow's "Song of Hiawatha" was based on the secret that the Iroquois League was led by Deganawida the Great Peacemaker and his disciple Hiawatha. Why not just tell us?

As they crossed the snaky Colorado River that Vince said was the gateway to the Cliff Dwellers whose roots were in Mexico— its trunk along the California-Arizona border, its branches spread throughout the Four Corners states all the way up into Wyoming and even Idaho—the pilgrims grew silent, each in their own way contemplating what they were leaving behind.

Vince thought about the California of brown men and women and children laboring in the fields—pickers, hoers, bundlers, their backs bent like commas punctuating the long straight rows, heads bobbing, arms moving hour after hour, a fine film of sweat on their brows and dripping from armpits, hearts and lungs pumping, fingers toughened but nimble, giving themselves to the gentle rhythm of the work like responsive lovers. Per bushel, not per hour, was their wage. Small children fanned babies in the shade, carried buckets and ladles through the fields. Larger children followed the adults, looking to the horizon to tell them when they were done for the day, when they could escape from the present they didn't choose to a future they did or someday would or could, *Madre de Dios.*

Now and then, a Ford or Chevy sedan would pull onto the shoulder of 101 and park and one or two men in short-sleeved white shirts and blue jeans would get out, their black hair smooth and glistening as helmets, their faces clear and brown and round. The words *union* and *Chávez* would tumble over the field, heads popping up to look, then swinging toward the white *poncheador* sitting in his pickup in the shade of the field's perimeter, listening to music on the radio. The union men, respectful of the fact that the field was private property they were not welcome on, would study the workers, count the children, and write on their clipboards. The *poncheador* would get out of his truck, hitch up his pants and spit, then raise his binoculars to make note of the union men's license plate and scan the rows of workers for just one wetback not bent to his work. Meanwhile, big trailer trucks pulled into the field to load up heads of lettuce or artichokes.

Were they thinking at all while their bodies moved to the rhythm dictated by the work? And the work, where did it go? into the lettuce on the trucks? into shopping carts and bellies? No, the people's labor was not lost between their bodies and the pittance of money they received for it. Vince imagined it wafting up into the atmosphere, joining the breathing out and breathing in of the vegetation in and around the fields, in the one thousand watts of sunlight arriving from the cosmos, the winds gathering and dispersing, moving the leaves and dust, the water beckoning skyward from ponds and rivers and swimming pools. The people's labor merged with, added to, transformed the Earth and beyond it the cosmos itself. *Millions of years,* he marveled as the VW bus engine revved to haul them up an incline.

Vince thought of what Mannie had told him about his Uncle Eli's story of a German farmer who divided his land into four equal parts, prepared each plot the same, then gave the same seed to four different people to sow, each on a separate plot. *Just to sow,* his uncle had stressed. When the plants broke through, they were not at all the same. On one plot they were thin and weak, on another strong and healthy, on another short, on another long and spindly. *All different,* his uncle had nodded sagely, eyeing his nephew to see if he got the point.

Vince had gotten a ride with two National Farm Worker's Association *chavistas,* one older, one young, the older one with Indian features and skin, the younger one more European. *El viejo* had worked with César Chávez since the early 1960s, after the National Farm Worker's Association was founded in Fresno and La Causa began. In 1966, he'd walked the 340-mile UFW *Peregrinacion* to Sacramento after Schenley sprayed strikers with agricultural poisons. Two years later he wept when Martin Luther King, Jr. was shot down like a dog and feared that César would be next. Then Robert Kennedy had come to Delano to join 8,000 *campesinos* and supporters, had celebrated mass with César when he broke his 25-day fast to strengthen the commitment to nonviolence. Robert Kennedy had been next. Recently, the *chavista* had been cutting his teeth on the strike against California grape growers now about to pay off in contracts for *campesinos,* he told Vince. Next, they would strike for lettuce.

The younger *chavista*'s dark eyes fired as he listened attentively to the union veteran's history of the entire Mexico-United States border agreement to guarantee cheap labor for agribusiness growers. In 1951, the informal Bracero program became Public Law 78, stating that no *bracero* (temporary worker) could replace a domestic worker but meaning the exact opposite. By bringing together unions, churches, and community groups affiliated with the civil rights movement, Chávez pressured politicians to end the Bracero program in 1964. Wages, however, had remained low, grape pickers being paid ninety cents an hour plus ten cents per lug, less than the working standards of slaves.

During their ride together, the radio had played Tennessee Ernie Ford singing—

> *Some people say a man is made out of mud,*
> *A poor man's made out of muscle and blood,*
> *Muscle and blood, skin and bone,*
> *A mind that's weak a back that's strong.*
> *Sixteen tons, what'll you get?*
> *Another day older and a-deeper in debt.*
> *St. Peter, don't you call me 'cuz I can't go,*
> *I owe my soul to the company store.*

The older *chavista* said there were no portable toilets. Workers had to drink from the same cup and pay a quarter for the honor, and pay two dollars a day for unheated corrugated sheds with no cooking facilities, no plumbing. Tough luck if they were injured. The average life expectancy of a *campesino* was 49 years old. He said their first break was the year after the Bracero program was ended. A new agreement between Mexico and *el norte* paid farm workers a dollar and twenty-five cents an hour but only for the grapes in Coachella Valley that ripen first and must be moved quickly. But when the farm workers who had worked Coachella demanded the same wage north of Bakersfield and were refused, the NFWA joined with Filipinos, Chicanos, Anglos and Negroes in AWOC, the Agricultural Workers Organizing Committee.

The *chavista's* eyes shone. "I remember that day, at Our Lady of Guadalupe Church in Delano, hundreds of us. *Viva la Huelga!* we shouted. Even when the growers brought in Chicano scabs, we did not weaken. We set up roving pickets and picketed a field a day,

169

there were so many ranches. We stayed off the fields but shouted to the scabs to leave the fields. Many of them joined us. But by the time the growers conceded the dollar twenty-five, it wasn't enough for us." He laughed and poked the young *chavista* in the ribs. "We had remembered the jaguar's teeth. Chávez called upon people not to buy grapes without a union label. The hippies, those young white middle class kids with everything handed to them, were the first to stop buying grapes and wine. Some even joined us in picketing supermarkets that continued carrying non-union." He had winked at Vince. "Take your allies where you find them, *muchacho*, however they look, whatever their race or class or religion. That's what King did and look where it got him."

Vince had hesitated. "Dead?"

The older man nodded slowly. "That, too. *Angloamericanos* allow their good, great ones to be killed. No, I mean pride in people of color, those of us who have forgotten the beauty in the earth colors of brown, red, and black because everywhere the white ghost blinds us like fog, like flour in our eyes." He looked out the window. "This is as far as we go, *muchacho*. There are Rael and the others."

Vince had gotten out and lingered while the two *chavistas* greeted their union cohorts. In a few months, Walter Reuther, the most powerful, incorruptible labor leader in the country next to César, would be killed by American corporate wrath. The small Lear Jet landing in Emmet County Airport in Upper Michigan through thick mist would burst into flame and plow into the treetops. Reuther and his wife, two other UAW associates and the two-man crew, all dead. "Accident," they called it.

As they crossed the Colorado, Seven was thinking over something Hermano had said that night at Wheeler Springs. "The Colorado is now the Rhine. World War Two was a Manichæan war in which Hitler served the *other* world of black magick. Now, another war between Light and Shadow is underway in America under the secret auspices of what your government cunningly labels 'national security.' Certainly this war is a struggle against fascism, but beneath fascism is something else. As the British author C.S. Lewis imagined in his prescient 1938 science fiction book *Out of the Silent Planet*, it is a war between the human soul and the forces that would devour it."

The Colorado is now the Rhine.

She contemplated the thousands of people caught in cults, asleep to the manipulations of a Synarchist "national security" assault upon the soul. Hermano said an awake imagination—not one hypnotized by television, films, and drugs—was the key to waging spiritual warfare.

"True esoterics require cross-pollination among traditions, and true religion is not a matter of dogma for the intellect or blind faith but of something deeper that leaves people free to grasp what comes toward them in this particular Time. Once the doors to your own individual perception open, Lilya, you will know what to do. This is the essential first step for any true spiritual warrior. Then hindsight will teach you where the trail leads."

Hermano's words were cryptograms, but she knew that the old Chumash woman had activated something dormant in her. Maybe her friends and the Will Rogers Highway and KRMA and the laundromats and the mysteries of Time would help that door to stay open so she could discern the secrets and non sequiturs and esoteric correspondences Hermano indicated were everywhere. Manly Palmer Hall said there was a Great Plan, a Great Work overseen by vast organizations acting as world guardians bearing priestly obligations. *If ambition or selfishness breaks the bond, the privilege of guardianship is forfeited. The Plan then passes to the keeping of other groups and other ages.* Had those world guardians failed the Eternal Commonwealth that America was part of? *And mark in every face I meet Marks of weakness, marks of woe*, the poet William Blake wrote of 19th century industrial England. The earliest Great Seal of the United States had been a phoenix, not an eagle—*the phoenix rising from ashes of its cataclysmic Atlantis past for a cataclysmic future?*

On the Atlantic shore, Dr. Greenbaum was examining a file marked *FOR YOUR EYES ONLY*, regarding the California Zodiac killings and media coverage, part of a COINTELPRO campaign going better than expected. He'd contracted with the FBI under the CIA's Operation CHAOS to use one of their Process cults for the public fear they needed.

Oct. 30, 1966 [*Walpurgisnacht*]	Female	Riverside
Dec. 20, 1968 [*Solstice*]	Female and male	Lake Herman
July 4-5, 1969	Female / Male lived	Blue Rock Springs
Aug. 8, 1969	??	
Sept. 27, 1969	Female / Male lived	Lake Berryessa
Oct. 11, 1969	Paul Stine, cab driver	Presidio
Oct. 22, 1969	"Sam" at Napa State Hospital talked to attorney Melvin Belli on KGO Channel 7 talk show	
Dec. 11, 1969	Leona Roberts	
March 3, 1970	Cosette Ellison	Ravine

March 5, 1970	Patricia King	Ravine
March 13, 1970	Marie Antoinette Anstey	Lake County
March 20, 1970	Eva Blau	Gulley

Female on Walpurgisnacht in '66, male-female on winter solstice in '68, then six in a row from Independence Day to the end of '69 with the Belli chat (a nice touch), and four so far in 1970 with the promise of more from vernal equinox to the end of the year. Lass and Hilburn in the fall. *Hill burn.* He liked the name touches: Lass, Leona for lion, Cosette for victorious people, King, Marie Antoinette, plus the death-by-water and ravine themes. Winter solstice '68 to spring equinox '70. They were using a team Greenbaum might have to share. Their patsy would be Arthur Leigh Allen. *ALA.* Later, they'd send more letters to the *Chronicle* and add Santa Rosa and Northern California.

Greenbaum sighed. Zodiac, indeed. The *Mikado* Lord High Executioner, indeed.

The red light on the phone began flashing: an incoming fax. He waited patiently over the machine, realizing it was an aerial photograph. At last, he tore it from the roll of thin paper. Black and white, but the close-ups were clear. There she was: Baby Rose. Beside her were the VW owner, a dog, and what must be yet another passenger. How many were there? He would forward this to Agent Iff and Sibelius. Thomas, the Air Force colonel, Lilya, the black dissident, this young man he must find out about—and Baby Rose. Were there more? And where were they going?

39

Southwest Sword of Damocles

You know, those crop circles are amazing, I don't know where they're coming from. We had places out in Nevada, there were no crops, it was sand and low bushes, with crop circles identical to those at the test site. I can tell you one thing, at the test site, it wasn't some prank. In England some say it was some pranksters, but at the Nevada test site [Nellis] it wasn't a prank. There are no pranks out there.

–V.C. Custer, August 1995

Aliens were the muses of rave culture at its peak, and a lot of rave veterans still believe, oh yes.

–Cintra Wilson, "Space Odyssey," *Image*, 1995

Bottom line, any argument condoning, or even seeming to condone, UFO/ET abductions on the basis of 'it's for our own good' or 'they mean us no harm,' etc., is morally unacceptable and political suicide. It will incur the wrath of the majority of the world's population and the opposition of . . . important organizations as a clear violation of the UN Charter and Declaration of Human Rights as well as the Declaration of Independence upon which America was founded. Let there be no ambiguity about this.

–Jack Sarfatti, quantum physicist (1939-)

The petroleum bloodstreams of western North America were on the move. Truckers had been pushing it all night, stopping only to tank up at Ruby's, The Pit, Grandma's—swapping reds, yellows, polka-dots, a whole apothecary guaranteed to get them to Milwaukee by Thursday, Cincinnati by tomorrow. Pay-per-trip meant time is money, money is time. No time for scenery, got to be home by Johnny's baseball game, Christine's confirmation. Sheri's period is late, one more mouth to feed. But not to worry, just pick up another load on the sly on the return trip, hope the chicken coop between Antelope and Donner Pass is locked up. Not caught yet but there's always a first time. Just a little extra cash when deadheading, where's the harm?

The word *harm* had a few raw edges for Al booking it south on 93 to Kingman to catch east 66 for home. *Harm* felt like razor wire in the shadows of the mind because it reminded him of a night run with his old partner Bob who'd insisted on stopping at dusk for a girl hitchhiking outside Chicago. He could still see Bob's predatory eyes and the sheen of sweat around his hole of a mouth with its pink, clit-like tongue. The three-day stubble and stink of him all came back in a rush. She was a young thing, jiggling with the roll of the highway, foolish to be hitchhiking alone. She'd sat between them, Al driving and sneaking peeks at her clear child's profile, her cheeks still babyish, reminding him of his daughter Gracie, his little girl. But Bob was thinking *piece of meat* while talking crap, pretending to be interested in her. When she yawned, he said, *Go ahead, take a nap in the bunk, we'll wake you when we get to Springfield.* Al felt more than saw her considering the offer as he kept his eyes on the white line down the middle of the road with the yellow streaks screaming *Don't pass! Don't pass!* Breathless, he felt more than saw her glance at him as she examined his profile in the twilight of the instrument panel. And after she'd crawled into the bunk behind them, he'd tightened his grip on the steering wheel and cursed himself for stopping, cursed himself for ever agreeing to team up with this twisted bastard who liked them young. Bob was silent for so long that Al thought it might be all right after all, that he'd missed the streak of decency in him, that he was all talk, him and his toilet mouth about teenaged girls no older than his Gracie.

Now with his hands on a different wheel, he shook off that tired old trail of thoughts—sewage under the bridge—and forced himself to think of pleasanter things, like last night before—well, before whatever had happened. He'd taken the detour down Extraterrestrial Highway 375 so he could go through tiny Rachel and have a couple of beers at the famous Little A'Le'Inn.

Tikaboo Valley. Groom Lake. Freedom Ridge or Area S-4 at Papoose Lake, seven miles south of Dreamland, Skunk Works in Burbank. He'd read everything he could lay his hands on and chatted with other truckers with CB ears about weird military facts and myths, he never knew which. At Skunk Works, there was going to be a night show far more flamboyant and informative than the Las Vegas shows 94 miles southeast. Maybe a third generation *delta*-shaped Aurora after the CIA's SR-71 Blackbird would make its debut down the 11,960 x 140-foot runway at Area 51 going Mach 8 (770 mph x 8). Plugged into Keyhole and Lacrosse reconnaissance satellites, two-man Auroras could get real-time electro-optical, infrared, radar, and electronic intelligence from anywhere on Earth in four hours and deliver hypervelocity weapons. His plan had been to see it from Rachel, 150 miles north of Sin City.

Humming, *Rachel, Rachel, I've been thinking, what a queer world this would be if the men were all transported far beyond the northern sea*, he'd ruminated on the born-again trucker telling him about the Bible Rachel's tomb being on the way to Ephrath (Bethlehem), adding something about the entrance to the Garden of Eden and the entrance to the Tabernacle in Solomon's Temple being in the east, while the Masonic Temple, being inverse if not perverse, had its altar in the east and entrance in the west. Al figured the trucker for a born-again Mason.

Anyone who knew how to get to Rachel could stand at the black mailbox on 375 in the Jumbled Hills and watch unorthodox flight patterns doing multiple g's. The U.S. Air Force would grab an additional 89,000 acres for F-117A tests in 1984, then firebomb 21,000 acres of wilderness adjacent to Nellis in an effort to get people to leave so they could have those acres, too. Public viewing at Freedom Ridge and White Sides would then become history.

Seventy percent of Nevada airspace was militarized and irradiated. Sonic bombs ripped limbs from cadavers, and in 1988 a pregnant woman in Smokey Creek Valley would miscarry when a Nevada Air National Guard jet swooped too close. On 95, Al had seen F-15s and F-16s and B-52s practicing carpet-bombing. When they strayed outside Nellis airspace, their combat overpressure wake could rip up private planes, homes, and barns. Western Shoshone land was now the American Armageddon, the Virgin of the Fields become Beast.

Area 51 lay at the eastern end of the Nellis Range Complex on the southern shore of the dry lake called Groom. Built in the 1950s to test Lockheed's U-2 spy plane, it was now a flight and weapons test facility for the Air Force, Navy, CIA, and National Reconnaissance Office (NRO). Restricted Area 4807 disallowed flyovers; wander in and you'd be shot or forced down. Wackenhut Special Securities ran perimeter security while Edgerton, Germeshausen & Grier (EG&G) took infrared photos of UFOs hovering over Area 51. (In 1999, EG&G would sell its government services division to the Carlyle Group.) USAF Police, Navy Seaspray and DOE Special Response Teams handled the vector craft hangars, the *vimana griha* hangars with 22 floors below them. A good buddy in an 18-wheeler with the handle Off-World and a kicker told Al that Groom Lake—Area 51, S-4, S-2, Dreamland, Paradise Ranch—had 18,000 employees and nine underground bases covering four cubic miles.

In the 1960s and 1970s, the CIA and Los Alamos Scientific Laboratory, Lawrence Radiation Laboratory, and Sandia

Corporation used Area 51 for *black* tests, like the Red Hat program in 1967 testing Soviet and Chinese aircraft, then the U-2, the F-117A Stealth fighter loaded with LIDAR (laser radar) and computer-enhanced imaging radar with a resolution of one inch to 30,000 miles, the SR-71 Blackbird, and UACVs (unmanned aerial combat vehicles).

Al had gotten up at dawn in hopes of seeing a Janet 747 fly employees into or out of Area 51 from Las Vegas-McCarran Airport, but no go. All things secret went on there over the years, from DEWs (directed energy weapons) to genetic splicing and mind control. In the 1980s, it would be discovered that Area 51 employees had been exposed to dioxins and dibenzofurons from the black smoke of Stealth byproducts burning in trenches—byproducts from making smooth surfaces and the ultrablack coating that absorbs rather than reflects radar pulses, reduces heat emissions, and thwarts infrared. The smell was nauseating, eyes and throats burned, and rashes developed as livers gave up the ghost and employees quietly died far from the world press.

The Tonopah Test Range in the west sector of the Nevada Range Complex in Great Smokey Valley was far more isolated than Area 51. Administered by the Department of Energy through Sandia Labs in Albuquerque, its Tonopah Electronic Combat Range tested radar invisibility and other electronics. The Northrop TR-3A Black Manta at Tonopah had laser capability, and unmarked MH-60G Pave Hawk helicopters in drab black had infrared sensors and radar. Entry to the range was at Cedar Ranch off the Extraterrestrial Highway just before the Queen City Summit.

Al wasn't interested in being gunned down by unmarked Pave Hawks, but he *was* interested in catching a CIA show. Maybe an SR-75 Penetrator would take off on runway 14-32, said to be 18,750 feet long with a 4,950-foot extension into a dry lakebed. Or the pure and simple Penetrator, a ghostly luminous triangle with a 75° wing sweep, climbing to 90,000 feet, then launching an XR-7 Thunder

Dart powered by two after-burning turbojets and two PDWEs (pulse detonation wave engines) that throw off a loud low-pitched roar with a rhythmic pulse at a hypersonic Mach 7. The Thunder Dart's wake would spill donuts-on-a-rope from special liquid methane ZIP fuel circulating and cooling the jet skin and ceramics before injecting the engines. Its mission: reconnaissance, hypersonic experimentation, and HSCT (high-speed civil transport).

Black Cadillacs and BMWs with tinted windows were parked outside the Little A'Le'Inn when Al had pulled in around nine. One BMW pulled out, maybe with Men in Black in it with sallow faces and slant eyes, leaving a cloud of radioactive dust. He'd heard that people came and went from Rachel with inexplicable bruises, nosebleeds, and lost time.

When Al walked in, trance dance music was playing. The television in the corner of the bar was set to KLAS-TV, first television station in Nevada, started on July 22, 1953 by Hank Greenspun, owner of the *Las Vegas Sun* he sold to Howard Hughes. Al sat down next to a coffee-stained copy of the *Las Vegas Mercury* with a garish headline about the Skinwalker Ranch in northeast Utah. Over in the corner, two science types were playing Celestial War, a proto-chess game with the Milky Way dividing the board. On the wall was a framed magazine article about Area 51 dated August 8, 1993. One sentence glowed: *More than 7,000 UFO sightings are reported annually in the United States alone. A 1990 Gallup poll indicates 47 percent of Americans believe UFOs are real.*

Tapping his cigarette ash into a flying saucer ashtray, Al ordered a Pabst and gawked at the tranced-out blonde casting news for KLAS, her bow lips tight like Rod Serling's lips on *Twilight Zone*. Probably an ass-puckered Mormon.

". . . compass covered with ancient hieroglyphics discovered by hikers in a canyon in a northern New Mexico state park in 1972, code-named 'Ancient Arrow' by the NSA," she droned. "Rockslides in the state park have exposed a hidden cavern with tunnels and

23 chambers carved from solid rock." The camera panned around one chamber filled with wall paintings, pictographs, hieroglyphs. "Ancient Arrow includes arcane technologies that have archaeologists puzzled. The cavern has been placed under the jurisdiction of the Advanced Contact Intelligence Organization, a secret NSA department headquartered in Virginia with personnel in Belgium, India, and Indonesia . . ."

As Al ordered a burger and fries, then a cute space bunny in go-go boots asked him for a quarter for the jukebox, then . . . Time just vanished.

He woke up in the sleeper at dawn, pounding the steering wheel with his palm. *Damn!* He turned on the ignition and looked around. Where was he? Furrowing his brow, he struggled to remember. He was past Sin City, he knew that. Sin City wasn't even one of his stops. Vaguely, he remembered backing up to a loading dock just blocks from where casino money laundering was going on at the Frontier, Stardust, and Binion's Horseshoe—guys entering with dirty money, buying chips, gambling a little, then cashing the chips in for clean money. For dirty CIA payoffs, the reverse was going on with casinos going through Shamrock Overseas Disbursement Corporation to pay off CIA contract agents. *Had he unloaded there?* He checked his watch; he must have been at that Las Vegas depot for—he had no idea. What the hell?

He turned off the ignition and put his emergency blinkers on, hopped out of the cab, went around to the back, and opened the doors. Clean as a whistle, except for his little moneymaker stash. He hopped up and walked through the trailer. Clean as a whistle. Jesus, Mary, and Joseph. His heart was pounding. He checked his wallet: the cash amount for a few beers and a burger was gone, but otherwise everything was there. Jesus, Mary, and Joseph.

With lost time on his mind, Al could be forgiven for almost missing the turn onto 66 east at Kingman and ill-manneredly wedging between a pale yellow Cadillac and a blue VW bus. Kingman was the Golden Triangle of methamphetamines; in 1991, a bank account there under the name of Nayaad would conduit millions of dollars from the Bank of Iraq via the SWIFT international banking system in Brussels.

Thomas slowed down for the 18-wheeler. "He's what truckers call a Willy Weaver."

"I'd like to give his Willy a weave," Ray fumed. "We could have hit him."

Thomas leaned over to turn up the latest KRMA broadcast that spaced-out Al was also tuning into.

". . . Richard Wayne Snell, a mind-controlled patsy run out of The Covenant, The Sword, and the Arm of the Lord (CSA), an intelligence-sponsored cult in Elijah, Arkansas similar to Christian Identity in Elohim City, Oklahoma. Snell had been in on a plan to truck bomb the Alfred P. Murrah Federal Building in Oklahoma City as early as 1983 in revenge for the murder of the militia movement's Gordon Kahl. The cult's leader 'King' James Ellison was handled by Richard Butler of the Aryan Nations in Hayden, Idaho and had ties to Jack Oliphant of the Arizona Patriots in Kingman, Arizona."

Ray slapped his thighs. "Kingman, man! We're in Kingman!"

"In 1983?" Mannie added over the two-way.

"After a four-day standoff," the newscaster continued, "the CSA finally surrendered to 200 federal agents on April 19, 1985. Snell was arrested and sentenced to death while King James turned state's evidence and walked free. Eight years later, the feds chose the same date, April 19, for the final grisly chapter of the televised 51-day siege of the Branch Davidians outside Waco, Texas, then chose it again two years later in Oklahoma City when the Murrah Building was finally brought down twelve hours before Snell was executed at the Arkansas Department of Corrections. One hundred and sixty-eight people federally bombed to hell and high heaven . . ."

"The future sure doesn't sound like the Age of Aquarius," the Colonel commented grimly.

Yes, America was still the Wild West.

Drs. Greenbaum and Gottlieb knew why Didy was as super quick at technology as his twin Thomas in the VW bus ahead of him on the Mother Road. Didy had never *studied*. What he had was genetics and a programmed antenna scanning for how every technology under the Sun worked. Agent Iff couldn't count the times Didy had straightened out surveillance and tracking equipment at AT&T hubs.

As usual, Didy was fiddling with the radio dial, for a while finding Peter Gabriel's "Signal to Noise" somewhere in the future—

> *. . . send out the signals deep and loud*
> *man I'm losing sound and sight*
> *of all those who can tell me wrong from right*
> *when all things beautiful and bright*
> *sink in the night*
> *yet there's still something in my heart*
> *that can find a way*
> *to make a start*
> *to turn up the signal*
> *wipe out the noise . . .*

Neither Didy nor Iff paid much attention to a radio bulletin about an Omnibus Counter-Terrorism Bill 25 years in the future, but when the newscaster mentioned that the FBI had subpoenaed call-detail records for 66,000 calls, Iff perked up and whistled. The FBI did computer matching of telephone records all the time, but that many? *Traffic analysis*, the announcer called it, utilizing Automatic Number Identification or ANI artificial intelligence software. *Artificial intelligence?* Wow. Didy was all ears, too.

Sidebands called Signaling System 7 or SS7 had been designed into telephone numbers to carry incoming or outgoing information back and forth between both ends of the call. The FCC was backing the FBI's demand that telecommunications corporations bow to the technical standards of CALEA, the 1994 Communications Assistance for Law Enforcement Act.

CALEA? Iff had never heard of it, and the date 1994 went in one ear and out the other.

"Digital technology is about to burgeon into mobile and cell phones, pagers, Internet, and all manner of wireless electronic messaging," the announcer said, "all by way of saying that cellular providers will use embedded global positioning (GPS) to determine location by *ping*s that triangulate with the base station and antenna nearest the caller. Typical CALEA installations on Siemens ESWD or Lucent 5E or Nortel DMS 500 run on Sun workstations directly connected to the Internet down at the phone company. No firewall, no Secure Solaris. Basically, everybody who knows how CALEA works can hack into it.

"Before CALEA, the FBI spearheaded ILETS in Europe, International Law Enforcement Telecommunications Seminars, until a similar resolution on International Requirements for Interception (IUR) was finally adopted by the European Union in January 1995. Now, comprehensive interception devices are built into all Western telecommunications systems.

"Not only does SS7 make Caller ID and Return Call possible," the announcer boasted, "but it also allows federal surveillance equipment to record telephone numbers of every call like lightning. For a demonstration of SS7 and ANI, call 1-800-MY-ANI-IS and a voice synthesizer will read the number you're calling from."

Though the dates seemed off, Simon Iff was glad to see traditional wiretaps go, *if* it was true. He was tired of searching through trillions of copper wires to attach his clips and headset. Phone companies had to help, of course, but without a court order— and that was most of the time—Iff was on his own.

The announcer droned on. "From the Communications Act

of 1934 to the FCC-backed Digital Telephony proposal that became CALEA, electronic privacy has been an elusive butterfly. CALEA requires that all providers of electronic communications—computer and telephone networks, software manufacturers— design systems that will accommodate wiretapping. Digital and fiber optics make finding one phone call among thousands traveling a single cable impossible by the old method. Now, AT&T, MCI, and Sprint have legally bestowed their gateway switch codes upon the NSA. Court orders are passé. Dragnet surveillance is underway, lists are being made.

"Section 702 of HR1710 will set up the Attorney General's Telecommunications Carrier Compliance Fund to pay telephone companies to install secret surveillance equipment. And what has the FBI Director to say about it?"

Another voice came on. "These are not new authorities. These are tools with which to use our current statutory authority, all—in my view—well within the Constitution."

Simon Iff was incredulous. That voice!

"That's not J. Edgar!" he cried to his idiot partner.

And when he pulled into a little filling station in Chambless to get a soda and call Greenbaum on the satellite phone about the weirdos at the Daggett mansion not knowing anything, Iff was still wondering if CALEA and all the rest were really happening or if the radio show had been one of those "War of the World" spoofs. After all, they were in the Southwest where rightwing militia rants were a dime a dozen.

While he was on the satellite phone, Didy found a pay phone by the bathroom and dialed 1-800-MY-ANI-IS. Sure enough, a machine recited the pay phone number back to him from the future.

40

LUCIFER and Glastonbury

In the technocratic society the trend would seem to be towards the aggregation of the individual support of millions of uncoordinated citizens, easily within the reach of magnetic and attractive personalities effectively exploiting the latest communication techniques to manipulate emotions and control reason.

–Zbigniew Brzezinski,
Between Two Ages: America's Role in the Technotronic Era, 1970

The giant Albion was Patriarch of the Atlantic; he is the Atlas of the Greeks, one of those the Greeks called Titans. The story of Arthur are the acts of Albion, applied to a Prince of the fifth century.

–William Blake, 1809

At South Cadbyri standith Camallate, sumtyme a famose toun or castelle. The people can tell nothing thar but that they have hard say that Arture much resortid to Camalat.

–John Leland, 1542

The future was being quietly constructed in America.

As low-energy cosmic ray flares disrupted the Earth's fields, IBM's Blue Gene computer was processing 10^{14} operations per second with six orders of magnitude more wattage than the human brain, Blue Gene's Hierarchical Temporal Memory (HTM) having been modeled on the human brain's 10^{13} operations per second.

FedEx trucks loaded with vials of anthrax, flu *Brucella*, tuberculosis, salmonella, E.coli, and West Nile virus were rolling over the highways bound for 4,000 secret military-contracted research labs. Water treatment plants that hadn't been designed to filter nanoparticles designed to make it through the blood-brain barrier were sending water downstream filled with cosmetics, food dyes and preservatives, and prescription drugs (arthritis, contraceptives, psycho-stimulants, tranquilizers, antidepressants, etc.) to be recycled from urine to drinking water.

Sterilization that had been going on in Indiana since 1907 was still going on. So far, 65,000 people in thirty states had been given state-authorized vasectomies, tubal ligations, etc., and women were being paid $10,000 for egg retrieval.

Blood was still taking 13 minutes to circulate.

U.S. Chamber of Commerce and military contractor attorneys were sabotaging and spying on government critics with *Discredit, Confuse, Shame, Combat, Infiltrate, Fracture* tactics. Small USASOC robot helicopters and unmanned John Deere R-Gator jeep-buggies were delivering electro-optical/infrared and audio synthetic telepathy to unsuspecting Americans.

Massive agribiz corporations like Cargill, Archer Daniels Midland, Bunge, and Monsanto were plotting mood foods and *eugenetics* with Kraft (Nabisco), PepsiCo (Frito-Lay), McDonald's and Yum! Brands (Pizza Hut, Taco Bell, KFC, etc.), while 368,000 Americans were dying of obesity compared with 14,000 from illegal drugs. Depression and anxiety were climbing steadily in America.

Foxes in the chicken houses of AT&T Wireless, Verizon Communications, BellSouth, AOL Time Warner, Computer Sciences, OAO, Intel, Lotus, Netscape, and Microsoft were busily dragnetting telecommunications traffic straight to the NSA supercomputers under Pioneer Groundbreaker. NSA sensors were already tucked into company networks and at Fix East in College Park, Maryland and Fix West at NASA Ames Research Center in Sunnyvale, California, at Mae East and Mae West, CIX, and SWAB, at Sprint's NAP (network access point) in Pennsauken, New Jersey, AmeriTech and Bell Communications Research in Chicago, Pacific Bell in San Francisco. Sensors and routers were as plentiful as apple-pie intelligence agents dedicated to national security, but try to call them on it and the 1953 state secrets doctrine is invoked.

Thomas' Uncle Hiram was en route to an AT&T meeting in New Jersey, 49 miles from where the World Peace Solution computer would soon be whirring at the Pope John Paul II Center for Prayer and Study for Peace in the Elmer Bobst mansion at 1711 Ocean Avenue in Spring Lake. "Peace" for Knights of Malta, Opus Dei, and Jesuits means communicating with world capitals via satellite about preparations for the imminent *novus ordo seclorum*. Around the world, computer-savvy Catholics would eventually be logging on to make their confessions to software ranking and recording their sins.

From the backseat of his limo, Hiram tried to call his brother but got no answer. *Damn, where was he?* Dead weight, that's what he was, a blight on Hiram's standing among the Brothers, a wet blanket, rain on his parade. Laurence would never do anything on his own; Hiram just had to make sure no one else used him. That he had betrayed Laurence by kidnapping one of his twin sons at birth remained deeply buried beneath where a conscience should have been. His only regret was that Thomas had escaped the Stuart genes blind experiment and Greenbaum might take it out on *him*.

Hiram sighed and turned to the day's agenda. Under the war on drugs cover story, AT&T was eavesdropping on the little man. AT&T, the NSA, and Echelon listening stations encompassed the U.S., Great Britain, Canada, Australia, New Zealand, Norway, Denmark, Germany, and Turkey. *The Nine*, he smiled. Encryption corporations associated with these nations (like German-owned

187

Crypto AG in Switzerland) shared algorithms and codes with the NSA and Echelon so they could intercept and decrypt all computer, telephone, and fax communiqués of any nation installing their encryption technology, which was most nations. Eavesdropping on sensitive communiqués generally spelled blackmail to one degree or another, as did the Hot Network and sex videos with "live all-American sex not simulated by actors" being piped into four- and five-star hotel rooms.

Propaganda and entertainment had been huge successes, and now it was to be general electronic surveillance. But Hiram's need-to-know status was so low that no one had spelled out why the little man's ridiculous self-important phone calls even mattered. Except for the occasional disgruntled dissident or citizen group easily infiltrated or listened in on, what was all the hubbub about domestic citizens? Debt and entertainment kept the masses comatose, and soon it was to be a web of invisible rays . . .

Hiram looked up from his notes. *That's* what it was all about: domestic invisible rays! While liberals worried about information privacy, a whole other privacy—much more important than information—was about to be pinioned, plucked, and plundered. Done right, it would be absolute; done wrong . . . Hiram guessed they were preparing for either contingency. Like IBM and ITT, AT&T was much more than a telecom corporation in that it was locked in tight with the NSA's encryption-scrambling movements of power. Appearances are deceiving, and plaintext easier to read than encryption.

Hiram had already heard the rumblings that would blossom like a dark flower into Watergate. True, Nixon had been pretty faithful to the Enterprise, but he knew more than was good for him, such as details about the Kennedy assassination and that the U.S. War Department had continued to sell weapons to Hitler throughout the War via Continental Oil, the Nazi oil cartel Kontental Ol AG ("Konti") aka ConocoPhillips in Houston, fifth largest private sector energy corporation in the world. U.S. Naval Intelligence had sent Naval officer Nixon to review captured Nazi documents and cover up the fact that Karl Blessing, a Reichsbank officer and then President of Deutsche Bundesbank (1958-1969), had headed up Konti and was partners with I.G. Farben. Dulles needed Blessing to not be a Nazi in order to protect German oil interests in the Middle East, given that Konti was the Nazi link to Ibn Saud, King of Saudi Arabia, and Aramco, Arabian-American Oil. As a reward to Nixon for lying, Allen Dulles financed his congressional campaign.

While Senator Eugene McCarthy accused the Truman administration of housing "pinkos," Nixon and the fourth CIA director Gen. Walter Bedell Smith diverted investigations away from intelligence agencies while Dulles and British MI6 busily scrubbed Nazi records under the State Department's Office of Policy Coordination. Inoculating American conservatives with Communist fears eased the way for Nazi fascists to co-opt the wealthy Republican Party. This was how it was done:

After the 1952 Eisenhower-Nixon win, immigration laws were changed to admit not just German Nazis and SS but Croatian, Caucasian, and Bulgarian, as well. In 1956 and 1957, while President Eisenhower was ill (a question in itself), Vice President Nixon and CIA Director Allen Dulles (1953-61) made covert fascist hay at home and abroad. The unexpected election of John F. Kennedy in 1960 threw a monkey wrench into their plans, but with rightwing backing was taken care of. Nixon's 1968 presidential campaign promise to create a permanent ethnic council within the Republican Party began with the appointment of Laszlo Pasztor, ex-diplomat of the pro-Nazi Arrow Cross government in Hungary, to chair the Heritage Groups Council and Nationalities Council loaded with Nazi collaborators, former Fascists, Central and Eastern European Nazis, and home-grown German-American and Russian Fascists whose hearts beat for one hope: to get back into power in their homelands via the anti-Communist Trojan horse in Third Reich America. Back then, few Fascists swung Democratic. To Nixon, a Nazi alliance meant ethnic backing and a ready bulwark of "freedom fighters" on the new Eastern front against the Soviets. His 1972 reelection would convert the Heritage Groups Council and Nationalities Council into a permanent decision-making branch of the Republican Party. In fact, during the Nixon years, virtually every World War Two Fascist organization had Heritage Group representation in the Republican Party, even the Nazis who had fled to Argentina.

Nixon and his handlers had established their own Berlin Wall of advisers with German names: Haldeman, Erlichman, Krogh, Kleindienst, Kissinger, Weidenbach, etc. Many hailed from Orange County fraternities at the University of Southern California (USC) and University of California at Los Angeles (UCLA). Americanized Nazis were America's tar babies. Hiram surmised that AT&T was full of them, given that Nixon had given carte blanche to the military-embedded telecommunications industry.

During Watergate, the National Bureau of Standards (NBS) would publish a May 15, 1973 ad for *Cryptographic Algorithms for Protection of Computer Data During Transmission and Dormant Storage* in Federal Register 38, No. 93. Three days before the President's resignation on August 6 [Julian 6/6], 1974, IBM would present its LUCIFER algorithm. Together, the NBS and NSA would approve LUCIFER as the new DES (data encryption standard) on July 15, 1977 [Julian 5/15=1/3=13], one day and 188 years since the considerably less discrete Freemason *coup d'état* in France.

Adhering to the LUCIFER name, AT&T would eventually split into three companies, one being Lucent Technologies, formerly Bell Laboratories, a telecom tangent of Lucis Trust, formerly Lucifer Publishing Company, affiliated with the UN, Theosophy, and Skull & Bones. Lucent Technologies would headquarter at 666 Fifth Avenue in New York City. Its *Inferno* Operating System would include *Limbo* programming language and the *Dis* virtual machine, and its communications protocols would be called *Styx*. Inferno would connect ATMs, Internet, television, radio, voice and video networks, telephones, etc.—a virtual electronic Tower of Babel. Lucent's secure electronic transaction protocols for Mondex and Mastercard would be known as *SET*, with gateways in the Philippines, Poland, Argentina, and Brazil. A program named *Byzantine Hades* would be cyberattack gatekeeper. After purchasing Mondex/Mastercard, Lucent would merge with Alcatel SA of France, exclusive provider of land-based optical network equipment and a global undersea cable network (Project OXYGEN).

Hiram closed his notebook, as ready for the meeting as he'd ever be. As the parkway slipped by, he leaned forward to dial his FM radio, landing on Patti Smith singing "Birdland" in the future—

> *...And then the little boy's face lit up with such naked joy*
> *That the sun burned around his lids and his eyes were like two suns,*
> *White lids, white opals, seeing everything just a little bit too clearly*
> *And he looked around and there was no black ship in sight,*
> *No black funeral cars, nothing except for him the raven*
> *And he fell on his knees and looked up and cried out,*
> *"No, daddy, don't leave me here alone,*
> *Take me up, daddy, to the belly of your ship,*
> *Let the ship slide open and I'll go inside of it*
> *Where you're not human, you are not human"* . . .

The song summoned up his grandfather's wicked face. Quickly, he spun the dial.

". . . Since organizations superseded nations, kings, and potentates, co-optation of corporations already up and running has become the preferred method of expansion, and the older and more accepted the organization or movement, the better. Meanwhile, global crisis management is the preferred method for ushering in the New Atlantis."

New Atlantis. Hiram was suddenly all ears.

"Now fifteen years since the Declaration of Interdependence

was signed by 32 Senators and 92 Representatives, the Brandt Commission, also known as the Fifth Socialist International, has revealed that the term 'new world order' refers to the supranational authority now regulating world commerce and industry. According to the McAlvany Intelligence Advisory, this authority oversees world energy production and consumption, currency, the World Bank and International Monetary Fund, Interpol . . ."

The news faded. Hiram was bewildered. *Declaration of Interdependence?* He jiggled the dial but got nothing.

When he finally walked into the AT&T lobby in Bedminister, not just his ears but his eyes were now playing tricks on him. Inscribed on the wall was *Holy Roman Empire – Slave nations pay tribute.* He blinked. It was gone. The Doric columns must have reminded him of the Parthenon.

Several hours earlier in England—the morning after the Knights Templar and Green Lion & Dragon—Hiram's brother Laurence had rented a car and headed southwest for Somerset. How much *lighter* he felt! He even looked younger. Adventure was coursing through his veins instead of grief. He knew there would be more grief, but at least it wouldn't be *just* grief. *Thanne longen folk to goon on pilgrimages,* Chaucer said. His pilgrimage had begun. First stop today: Glastonbury.

For almost a century after Caesar withdrew in 54 BC, all was quiet in the British Isles, but it was the quiet of waiting for the other Roman boot to drop. Teutonic Celts held off Rome's legions at the Rhine in Germania, but all of Gaul was already Romanized. When they did finally return with the Roman Church in their wake, they were amazed: Christianity had already taken root among the Britons and their Druids. How could that be?

Before Christ, Druids had long awaited the birth of the new King of the Elements, the new Lord of the Dance promised by the stars. This new Lord's sacrifice would institute a new age that would revitalize the elements and save their people from the blunt-minded Romans. Some had tired of waiting, however, and like the Mayans had sought out the old equation of despair and sacrificial blood. Night and day, it seemed, the triune gods clamored for blood— Taranis the Thunderer, Esus the All-Powerful, and Teutates, god of all the far-flung Celtic tribe that had emigrated long before from their homeland in Central Europe. Taranis' fire devoured more and more prisoners of war hung in giant wicker cages; Esus called for more and more human fruit to hang from his sacred trees; and Teutates clasped more and more beloveds to his watery bosom in the sacred wells and pools throughout western and central Europe. The *teuta*, the people, were at risk.

Still other Druids, particularly on the *insula sacra* of Ireland, did not falter, so deep was their trust sown in the starry heavens, so acutely could they still see the prize of human destiny, the promise of the gods. Their sacrifice lay not in blood but in training their neophytes in the sciences and arts, in patience and readiness, and at last they were rewarded with a sign. A prince of the Green Isle had been undeservedly banished over the Irish Sea to Albion with his foster child, the wee lass Bridhe, only to have his boat dash on the rocks of sacred Iona off Scotland in the black of night. Who should save them but the Archdruid Cathal, arriving at dawn to light the sacred fire as he always did on the holy hill overlooking the shore, so that the first rays of the Sun might impregnate the flames and therefore the land. In a vision, Cathal recognized Bridhe as the castaway child of the King of the Elements on his way back from the stars and trained her in his Druidic arts. Every day, clad in white with a wreath of rowan berries about her head, Bridhe watched her teacher light the fire and memorized the thousands of prayers and invocations to the King of the Elements whose advent had long been expected, even as the Jews in Palestine had cried out to their desert god YHWH to send a Messiah to save them too from the Romans—

At Tara today in this fateful hour
I place all Heaven with its power
and the Sun with its brightness
and the Snow with its whiteness
and the Fire with all the strength it hath
and the Lightning with its rapid wrath
and the Winds with their swiftness along their path
and the Sea with its deepness
and the Rocks with their steepness
and the Earth with its starkness
All these I place
by God's almighty help and grace
between ourselves and the powers of darkness.

Finally on Bridhe's midsummer 21st birthday (so said the Archdruid Cathal on his deathbed), a white merle led her through cloud and mist, water and light, until she was walking not on Iona's green crags but upon desert sand into a village where no rain fell. There, she met an old man bent with age and a woman heavy with child in a mantle blue-bright with stars, and when the child was born, the rain fell and flowers bloomed in the desert, and Bridhe held the child so his mother could sleep. But Bridhe must have slept, too, for when she awoke, mother, child, and man were gone and only a path of moonlight remained to guide her back through white sands to verdant Iona. While she'd been gone, her teacher Cathal had *seen* her with the King of the Elements lying peacefully on her breast. Cathal had then slipped away into the Otherworld to rest between lives, like Simeon who had seen the infant Jesus on Mary's breast, as reported by the Greek physician Luke.

Over the next three decades before the Romans returned, legends grew from slender facts much as pearls form around grains of sand in the oyster's belly. It is said that some time after his 12th birthday Jesus came by way of France to Britannia, to Gloucester, with his merchant uncle Joseph of Arimathea. Auspiciously, his uncle came to trade with the Druids so Jesus might confer with them and bless their Western Isles. The fierce British visionary William Blake alluded to this visit—

> *And did those feet in ancient time*
> *Walk upon England's mountains green?*
> *And was the holy Lamb of God*
> *On England's pleasant pastures seen?*
> *And did the Countenance Divine*
> *Shine forth upon our clouded hills?*

Thus when the Romans and their Church finally returned, native Britons kept silence and hid their Celtic priests, both old Druid and Christianized Druid, as well as the wondrous secret they shared with Gallic Celts, a secret whose *Angleterre* heart lay at Glastonbury Hill as its French heart beat among the Sancte Baume mountains of Provence. Romans less savvy than Julius Caesar interpreted their silence as bovine stupidity and let it pass. A Welsh triad named the three great British monasteries Glastonbury, Amesbury, and Llantwit Major, each once graced with a perpetual choir singing around the clock. Glastonbury was considered *the* center of Celtic Christianity, due perhaps to the sacred burials in St. Joseph's and St. Mary's Chapel. Welsh apostles had radiated out from monasteries ruled by abbots, not dioceses ruled by bishops; monks and hermits had set the tone, not hierarchy.

The Christianity of the Celts had thus been *Other*, transiting the worlds between which the ever-elusive, Nature-fused Holy Grail had taken root in the individual quest, not in hierarchy and obedience to Rome. In Time, the cauldron in the custody of the nine Avalon maidens who had borne Arthur's body away had fused with the Cup of the Last Supper brought to Britain by Joseph of Arimathea, as reported in the 3rd century by Maelgwynn of Landaff who read the epitaph, *I came to the Britons after I buried Christ. I taught. I rest.*

When Laurence arrived in Glastonbury, the commercial Age

of Aquarius had commandeered its shop fronts. Late-sleeping longhairs greeted him from among the brambles, their young faces untrammeled by life. During his breakfast of tea, eggs, toast, and beans, he tried to imagine the town in its soggier Neolithic period when Joseph of Arimathea with his boatload of Jerusalem survivors arrived over the flooded Somerset Levels. According to the Benedictine monk Cressy, St. Joseph of Arimathea, Paranymphos of the Virgin Mary, died at Glastonbury on 27 July 82 AD. Joseph's saint day was left out of the Roman calendar so as to erase the fact that the Celtic Church had preceded the Roman one.

After breakfast, Laurence strolled through the ruins of the Abbey. Monks in 1191 had found the graves of Arthur and Guinevere south of the Lady Chapel, strengthening Geoffrey of Monmouth's 1130 claim that Glastonbury was Avalon. Arthur had fallen to Saxons at the Battle of Camdann in 537, pierced through his thighs by a lance. His remains disappeared with the execution of the last abbot in 1539 during Henry VIII's Dissolution, surely the beginning of a Freemason assault not just on the Roman Catholic Church but also upon Celtic Christianity, Joseph of Arimathea, and a Christian Arthur, all in one fell swoop.

Laurence peered into a dark well tucked in the side of the Lady Chapel ruins. Nearby was a stone table like that of Aslan's sacrifice in C.S. Lewis' *The Lion, the Witch, and the Wardrobe*. He shivered. The Holy Thorn Tree of Joseph had been chopped down during some war or other, though sprigs of the present hawthorn had been sent to the Right Reverend Henry Yates Saterlee, first Bishop of Washington, DC, in October 1901. The tree that one of the sprigs became grew outside of St. Alban's.

On Tor Hill, he came into his element, sighting Wells Cathedral on the horizon, one of the Rose Line rosary beginning at Roslynn Chapel, as his wife's Royal Arch Mason cousin had indicated. Glastonbury was within the Wells constituency in the House of Commons and the Wells Archbishop's domain.

Laurence felt exhilarated while standing on the famed dragon lines running through Tor Hill. How *island-like* it felt! In winter, the surrounding moors still flooded, the teashop owner had assured him proudly in a broad accent. Southeast twelve miles was Cadbury Castle, built to blend in with the hills. From Camelot to Avalon and Avalon to Camelot, the Matter of Britain wove a spell regarding the return of Arthur like a messiah. Thousands of pounds were donated annually by unnamed sources to the Matter of Britain. Geoffrey of Monmouth said Arthur was descended from a long line of British monarchs back to Brutus well before 1000 BC—back, in fact, to *oceanic* antiquity.

By one o'clock, Laurence was on the road to the tiny village of South Cadbury. After St. John's Eve, midsummer 1966, the Camelot Research Committee had begun digging in earnest at Cadbury Castle, an Iron Age hill fort that the British dark ages king Arthur may have refurbished in about 500 AD. Archaeologists and graduate students on both sides of the Atlantic had rushed to help, and 5,000 visitors labored up to the summit each six-week excavation season, buying Chesterton's *Short History of England*, Trelawney Dayrell Reed's *The Battle for Britain in the Fifth Century*, and of course Geoffrey of Monmouth at the tiny gift shop. Arthur slept in a cavern closed by the iron gates of the Age of Man, but on St. John's Eve the ground purportedly rang with hoof beats as Arthur and his knights rode the old track through the village to the spring beside Sutton Montis church, where, it was reported, they watered their horses.

Schliemann found Troy because he believed Homer. The English could say what they liked about why digs were again occurring at Cadbury Castle, but Laurence thought they were looking for a bit of old glory now in tatters after all the dishonest dealings of two world wars. Cadbury Castle was their neolithic Troy, and they were hoping that their long-ago glory was but muted by silt. *Pax Britannica* might be gone, or it might just be that Britain's power machinations had become more serpentine. London was still the world's financial center, wealth and title still opened doors, and high-degree Freemasonry still ran all that was important.

Laurence parked just past the church in South Cadbury in

the little parking space the teashop owner had mentioned. He passed Arthur's Well, feminine portal to the Otherworld. Toiling up the hill, Laurence thought about how Gandhi had once offered England some redemption, just as Martin Luther King had tried to do for America. Both had been martyred. Ralph Waldo Emerson and Henry David Thoreau read the *Bhagavad-Gita*, Mahatma Gandhi read Thoreau, Martin Luther King read Gandhi. The British elite had had a hand on the gun that murdered Gandhi as surely as the American elite had a hand on the gun that murdered King. *Give the masses someone to look up to,* Hiram had smirked after Kennedy's assassination, *but make sure he's dead.*

From the crest of the hill upon which Arthur's Palace once stood, Laurence could see Glastonbury Tor rising above Avalon like a Mexican pyramid. Below the hill ran the old well-worn track to Glastonbury. The palace had been an Iron Age fortification long before the Romans evicted the British Celts, built their temple, then left. Then the Celts had built over it, then Arthur's timber hall over that in which his warriors met, feasted, and planned. Layers in Time.

He could see the various sectioned off digs that had been going on. Thus far, they had discovered a gatehouse and a cobbled road, and cuts in the hill indicated ramparts and breastworks. In the southeast corner of the ramparts, a human skeleton had been found of a perfectly formed young man curled up and rammed head-down into a pit, Celtic sacrifice for Vortigern's stronghold.

The image of El Greco's *Pietà* arose in Laurence's mind—the Dead Christ surrounded by the tight little group of His Mother, Mary Magdalene and Joseph of Arimathea while ominous slate clouds portended in the background. He'd seen it in Philadelphia and hadn't known what he was looking at. Gethsemane, the portentous garden, came from the Hebrew words *gat shemanim* or olive press. Olives need pressing for oil to flow forth, the philosophy that once justified sacred violence. Arthur, Christian or no, had been subject to Druid rites and priests like *Myrddin Emrys*. Not much had changed, really, Laurence decided, thinking of his Freemason brother . . .

41

Hi Jolly and the Sheikhs

They were remote places for news that he traveled in and in those uncertain times men toasted the ascension of rulers already deposed and hailed the coronation of kings murdered and in their graves . . .

- Cormac McCarthy, *Blood Meridian, or The Evening Redness in the West*, 1985

[The people north of the Pyrenees] are of cold temperament and never reach maturity. They are of great stature and of a white color, but they lack all sharpness of wit and penetration of intellect.

- Abu el Hassan Ali el Saïd, Merinides ruler of Morocco, 1331-1351

This is a political age. War, Fascism, concentration camps, rubber truncheons, atomic bombs, etc., are what we daily think about, and therefore to a great extent what we write about, even when we do not name them openly. We cannot help this. When you are on a sinking ship, your thoughts will be about sinking ships.

- George Orwell (Eric Blair, 1903-1950)

The East had come soul seeking in the West. Youths, thirsty for spirit, were gathering around gurus and smiling detached monks in saffron robes, their dark eyes hinting at mysteries. Youths were chanting mantras and making mudras in quest of foreign gods that still shone, old wine in old wineskins that for them looked new and as exotic and soft as Western religions and philosophies never did with their pews and pedophiles and hallowed halls of learning now cold and dead, hard-edged as Occam's razor, rotted by hypocrisy and logic. All that was Western looked like folly, decay, and deceit.

In fact, American youths knew nothing of Western Mysteries that had survived the Holy Roman Empire, tucked away by Brotherhoods anxious to use and abuse them for power over people under the spell of matter. Sleeping Beauty was to continue her sleep, buried beneath Lodge hoards, sigils, and astrologies, the brambles grown thick around her while old men slept fitfully in their armor, swords crossed over their silent breasts, their loyalties misplaced, their once great hearts now arrested by Isis of inundated Atlantis.

What the American youths didn't know was that the East too was becoming anachronistic and so came shopping in the West for middle-class souls sick of sterile suburbs, Vietnam slaughter, public assassinations, death and more death, race, hypocrisy, billboard litter, television mindlessness, Hollywood cults, rags of the soul, quagmires of shiny, seductive commodities in bed with the double-headed devil of desire and debt. Hindus and Tibetan Buddhists flew on Western wings of steel to America to gather in its parched youths yearning to nurse at the breast of anything that looked spiritual. The Dust Bowl that was the American soul salivated for a few drops of dew from what Whitman sang just before the railroad and oil barons glutted America, before banking families bought and sold America, before Woodrow Wilson and Colonel House peddled America like a whore, before FDR dosed it with the grey of State socialism.

When Thomas slowed down for two Middle Eastern hitchhikers in sunglasses, *dishdashahs*, and *ghutras*, Seven pulled the Caddy over, too, and everyone got out to stretch their legs. The two men, one young and one old, touched their foreheads and gestured invitingly toward a shady copse of Afghan pines and were overjoyed when the Colonel addressed them in Farsi.

"Allow me to present the Egyptian cleric Dr. Omar Abdel

Rahman and his young Bedouin disciple Ahmed," the Colonel translated. Baby Rose had received Farsi programming in her wired sleep at the Defense Language Institute, Presidio of Monterey, and dutifully began recording every word.

Seven spread a bleeding madras on the ground and the pilgrims began laying out their offerings of fruit, chapatis, cheese, miso, and peanut butter while their hosts like Ali Baba magically produced a feast from their *dishdashahs* and the older man's voluminous *bisht:* stuffed sweet peppers and dates, spicy chickpeas, pita, babaganoush and hummus, cucumber and mint and yoghurt. The Colonel set up his chair while the others sat in a circle, passing water for drinking and cleaning hands and faces.

Sheikh Rahman was blind. Smiling from behind his sunglasses, he bowed to the Earth and said a prayer, then politely began conversing as everyone dug into the desert lunch they weren't sure was real.

"Hell is a sunlit sky and Heaven a moonlit sky," he intoned as the Colonel translated. "The Sun is a shriveled old hag who dries up everything, whereas the Moon is an energetic bountiful young man who guards the nomad while he sleeps and dreams, guiding him on his night journeys, providing the dew that feeds the buried cisterns throughout the desert."

The Colonel responded in kind. "*Le desert est monotheiste,*" to which the Sheikh nodded, thanking the one God Allah.

Sheikh Rahman explained matter-of-factly that his body was presently asleep far away, thanks be to Allah, but he and Ahmed had been able to enter this extraordinary desert Time pocket to share something. Ahmed handed the Colonel a cassette tape sparkling with piezoelectricity and asked him to play it. The Colonel passed it to Thomas who got up and slipped it into the Cadillac tape player, turned the volume up, and left the door open. An interview was in progress.

"Emad Salem," explained the Sheikh in *sotto voce,* "was a former Egyptian Army intelligence officer recruited by the FBI after the 1991 assassination of Rabbi Meir Kahane. Salem infiltrated my inner circle and sold information to the FBI—$1.5 million worth—while recording more than one thousand of his conversations with his Bureau handlers over a year and a half as his life insurance policy—like this:"

> [Salem:] . . . If that's what you guys think, fine, but I don't think that because we was start building the bomb which is went off at the World Trade Center. It was built by supervising supervision from the Bureau and the DA and we was all informed about it and we know what the bomb start to be built. By who? By your confidential informant. What a wonderful great case! And then he put his head in the sand I said 'Oh no, no that's not true, he is son of a bitch.' [Deep breath] Okay. It's built with a different way in another place and that's it.

As the desert sun inched over parched Arizona, Salem revealed that he had driven the van with the bomb in it to the World Trade Center garage on February 26, 1993. He had requested phony explosives, but the FBI denied his request and the blast had damaged his ears and forced him to check into St. Clare's Hospital.

When the tape was over, Sheikh Rahman said, "I am now an FBI target. Salem will be paid to make me and my followers take the fall, as you say, for Salem's crime. He will testify against me for inspiring the bombers with my sermons and I will be sent to prison in Springfield, Missouri."

Ahmed was beside himself. "And all because Sheikh Rahman is an Islamic hero. His unjust imprisonment will incite the terrorism and counterterrorism necessary to those Brotherhoods pulling the strings behind the international scene."

The Colonel mopped his brow, the Sun bouncing tiny filaments of light off his thick lenses. "And this is what I fought two world wars for."

Just then, three Arabian camels magically materialized out of the desert. The two riderless camels sank to their knees as the rider on the third bestowed a *Salaam* and called out in English, "Greetings, 20th century friends. I am Hadji Ali, but you may call me Hi Jolly, the last rider of the magnificent U.S. Camel Corps—unless you count the ghost rider on the camel called Red Ghost. Beware of him." He nodded south, laughing. "My bones are buried in Quartzsite. The Freemasons gave me my own pyramid."

The Sheikh and Ahmed mounted their snorting camels that then rose with their loads. Like the Three Wise Men, they headed southeast, waving goodbye with all good wishes. Sheikh Rahman called out something only the Colonel's hairy old Buddha ears could hear.

"What did he say?" Thomas asked.

The Colonel smiled. "'You are fortunate to have entered the Hadj.'"

"What is the Hadj?"

The Colonel mopped his neck. "The Sacred Journey that all men seek, some men pray for, and no man can avoid. Travel and travail . . ."

Ray squinted, determined to see where the ghostly camels went. Almost immediately, they wavered and vanished, as did the magnificent repast leftovers and glowing cassette tape. Scanning the seamless wavering horizon, Ray murmured, "I'm hungry."

Thomas stared after the phantoms, recalling the officers' clubs and hallways of the Pentagon behind sealed doors opened just enough to allow a colonel or general to confer briefly with Sheikhs in Arab garb and Chinese, Soviet, and European brass.

They ate more of their earthly food, then packed up, climbed into their noble metal steeds, and once again cruised the sweltering asphalt thread of 66, discussing what the sheikh had indicated about future psyops and returning to the all-consuming topic of Time and KRMA.

"So if the 5,000-year Kali Yuga ended in 1899, we're now in . . . ?" Seven asked the Colonel after making sure the two-way was still on.

"Satya Yuga, from 1900 to 4400, the Age of the Second Coming," the Colonel answered. "The Piscean Age ends in 2375 when the vernal point enters Aquarius and remains in Aquarius until around 4535. Two Time pulses will overlap by two degrees of precession, 4400 to 4535."

Seven worked it out slowly. "So each pulse follows a different

Will of Time?"

"Something like that," the Colonel nodded, "each epoch resonating to a different theme on Earth." He looked closely at her and grinned. "Maybe this epoch's theme has themes that attracted, some sort of knowledge or experience you need for your evolution."

Seven recalled a guest speaker in her religious lit class talking about hidden threads that link ideas to an invisible Will of Time. "To you young Americans, it is perhaps insulting to think that you might be acting roles directed by some impulse other than your own. But the play *As You Like It* told you that 'All the world's a stage, And all the men and women merely players: They have their exits and their entrances; And one man in his time plays many parts . . .' Are we not acting on the world stage of 20th century America? *And who is the director?*"

She remembered how he had paused before continuing.

"Perhaps you expect me to say 'God' or Richard Nixon." Everyone laughed. "But I cannot, given that 'God' is now a word like 'love,' signifying nothing because it excludes nothing. 'I love America,' 'I love peanut butter,' etc.

"To even entertain the idea of an invisible Will of Time, I must turn to my five senses, my imagination, and my intellect. Without the images provided by my five senses, my intellect can comprehend nothing, and with the images, I use my imagination like a sense organ to apprehend the presence of invisibles like the Will of Time operating through themes that my era seems obsessed with.

"And where does *mind* fit in—more comprehensive than intellect or imagination or senses, an amalgam of all three, invisible translator of the soul?" He stepped away from the podium. "Since the Renaissance, imagination versus intellect, phantasmagoria versus rationalism, magick versus science has been unfolding in Time. And behind them all, a relatively new question of *responsible freedom* intended by what I can only call the present Will of Time . . ."

When Seven had relayed the gist of what the visiting lecturer had said, Vince said, "In the Mayan calendar, certain themes return again and again in a spiral . . ."

". . . or mobius strip," Thomas said excitedly, "or lemniscate turning back upon itself and meeting itself at crossing points of eras that will take the theme another evolutionary step."

"So Time is not linear but cyclic, rhythmic, a pulse with a certain frequency theme," the Colonel said. "Occult Brotherhoods know this secret of Time and therefore recognize that our present era is recapitulating Atlantis themes of world government, air technologies, electromagnetism . . ."

". . . and minus the new Will of Time thrust toward *responsible freedom*," Thomas grimaced, knowing something of such Brotherhoods. "Instead of a recapitulation that could move humanity forward, the Brothers seem resigned to a mere repeat."

"Yes, Thomas, a repeat of the catastrophes both Mu and Atlantis ended in," the Colonel said. "This is our problem."

Gram Parsons began singing "Return of the Grievous Angel" over KRMA from the future—

We flew straight across that river bridge last night half past two
The switchman waved his lantern goodbye and good day as we
went rolling through
Billboards and truck stops pass by the grievous angel
And now I know just what I have to do

And the man on the radio won't leave me alone
He wants to take my money for something that I've never been shown
And I saw my devil, and I saw my deep blue sea
And I thought about a calico bonnet from Cheyenne to Tennessee . . .

From then on, discussions of KRMA broadcasts included what the Will of Time and its *responsible freedom* might want them to learn and why. They'd decided that KRMA was like an Akashic history and truth all in one, *alitheia*—the ancient Greeks having no word for history—their job, like that of the oracles at Delphi, was to interpret and put it all together. They went back and forth about the transmissions being random or specific to their little soul ships, but one thing was certain: history was no longer a boring string of battle dates, winners and losers, broken treaties, and patriotic hype. *Real* history seemed to be an ongoing battle between truth and lies, good and evil, going on behind events and words. KRMA was *real* news, wherever it was coming from.

Mannie pictured KRMA coming from a run-down transmitter in a tiny desert town of a dystopic future where *Fahrenheit 451* and Fifties Beat survivors had taken refuge. Ray had a similar picture but with Wobblie types. Thomas pondered the dry desert air as a perfect conductor for transmissions of an on- or off-planet resistance getting the truth out. Seven sensed that the transmissions were linked to the Akashic Chronicle of ancient Hindu cosmology, an atmospheric library of everything that had ever occurred or been thought or imagined, eternally registering in the Astral Light of the ether. Vince made notes but said nothing, certain that somewhere, sons and daughters of Light were broadcasting the Mirror of Karma. As for Baby Rose, she was not yet even aware of Time.

The Colonel sensed a definite correlation between KRMA broadcasts and the Time manipulation they'd been experiencing. Surely DARPA or some other military agency was tickling the æther state of matter connected to the 4th dimension of past, present, and future. The men who had slaughtered the Three Kings as sacrificial lambs were bearing down on the future. That the pilgrims could reap knowledge from even a military experiment was an inverted blessing at best, but then the desert was a cathedral in which angels armed with insight and knowledge could just as well be riding KRMA radio waves like the Zen Trappist monk Thomas Merton perceived—

And the deep ferns sing this epithalame:
'Go up, go up! this desert is the door of heaven!
And it shall prove your soul's frail miracle!
Climb the safe mountain . . .

Seekers, the dry desert air, Route 66, and Time glitches were all in the seamless zone mix with KRMA.

Soon, they would be in the Four Corners, the most sacred landscape in North America—in fact, more of a mindscape than landscape that the military, nuclear, and mineral industries were assaulting. Fiery elemental clashes generated by mineral barons and nuclear high priests were assaulting Indian Country spirits of place and forcing native dancers whose job for millennia had been to appease subnature forces to dance harder. Underground nuclear "tests" pounded at the doors of previous worlds, and Southwest skies were saturated with as much fire as air, vestiges of primordial days when the Earth was still cooking.

Just outside Peach Springs, a talk show fading in and out piqued Ray's incarnational interest in Sixties politics.

". . . Remember the Houlihan Report from the study commissioned by Ronald Reagan when he was governor of California? It was more of a plan than a study of how city and county governments could be restructured into medieval fortresses of law and order. Reagan's kitchen cabinet came up with its own version of C4: collapse, crisis, catastrophe, and corruption. Sound familiar?

"In the California of the Sixties, political terrorism was used to bring the enemy home to the leftist dissident *Kulturkampf* in order to expand surveillance and countersubversive intelligence. The Baader-Meinhof cells, Italian Red Brigades, PLO, Weather Underground—dig under any of them and you'll find intelligence funding and planning."

Ray was riveted.

"California has always been a separate, crooked DEA jurisdiction. Most of the banks in California are owned by the Japanese Yakuza—Wells Fargo interlocks with Household International, the Vatican-owned Bank of America took over Continental—"

"And the Federal Reserve and Wall Street won't allow full disclosure," the interviewer added.

"Not in a million years," the guest agreed. "Then there's C4's 'neutralization' program—not just apprehension or death, as in

207

the case of Fred Hampton and Mark Clark in Chicago, but political incapacitation, intimidation, bad jacketing . . ."

"And what is 'bad jacketing'?" the interviewer asked.

"Making someone appear to be a police informer, infiltrator, or provocateur when they're not. Discreditation. Like Mumia Abu-Jamal (Wesley Cook), once the information officer of the Black Panther Party—he'll spend years on death row for a crime he didn't commit. At the very least, the cost of political activism will be judicial railroading."

"And what constitutes an informer?"

"Well, there are several types. The planted informers who hang around, observe, listen, and collect documents but don't get directly involved; the sleeper who absorbs information for an active role later; and the novice who builds trust by doing humble tasks and not taking initiative. In the unpaid category is the unwitting informer, usually a disgruntled activist who can't keep a lid on it, or an activist who's been quietly picked up on petty drug charges and wants to save his skin, which is why illegal drug use can be so compromising. Meanwhile, the distrust and paranoia generated in the group assures C4's success . . ."

The interviewer cut in. "Like this one?"

A scratchy, excited newscast cut in. "National Guard troops have opened fire on student war protesters at Kent State University (KSU) in Ohio and have killed four students and wounded nine others. Barely two months after the Bank of America burned to the ground in Isla Vista, the student housing compound of University of California at Santa Barbara, the Vice President uttered these words—"

> *[Agnew:] There is a group of students committed to radical change through violent means. Some of these may be irretrievable; all will require very firm handling. This is the criminal left that belongs not in a dormitory but in a penitentiary. The criminal left is not a problem to be solved by the department of philosophy or the department of English—it is a problem for the Department of Justice.*

Ray leaned forward and stared at the radio. "This is going on now——"

The newscaster continued. "On Friday May 1, students buried the Constitution in the KSU Commons. That night, there were 14 arrests and 47 broken windows . . ."

"What day is today?" Ray was frantic. "If we drove there, could we stop it?"

The Colonel's voice came over the two-way. "Ray, I don't think that's how this KRMA time thing works. If we really are in a 'time capsule' here in the desert, we don't really know what day this is and if it's before or after the events we're hearing about. For all we know, Kent State is history being related from far in the future. Notice the use of the past tense."

". . . On Saturday, the mayor of Kent declared Civil Emergency, established curfew, and banned the sale of alcohol, firearms, ammunition, and gasoline. Some students threw lit matches through the Reserve Officer Training Corps (ROTC) building and started a small fire that went out by the time they left, and yet when they returned an hour later, the entire building had burned to the ground. Both the Bank of America and ROTC buildings were well insured, and both incidents provided an excuse to bring in the National Guard. At KSU, the Guard was ordered to exchange their rubber bullets for live ammunition.

"On Sunday, Ohio Governor James Rhodes, then seven percent behind Robert Taft in the polls, spoke of Nixon's grudge against Ohio antiwar activists and how they had shouted him down at Akron University in October 1968—

> *[Rhodes' voice:] These protesters [pounding] are the worst type of people we harbor in America, worse than the brown shirts and the communist element . . . We're going to use every force of law that we have under our authority . . . We are going to employ every weapon possible. There is no place off limits. There is no sanctuary and we are going to disperse crowds.*

"Nearly one thousand armed National Guardsmen were now on campus. Against curfew, students attempted to gather and were bayoneted and tear-gassed. Sixty-eight arrests were made.

"On Monday, as classes let out for lunch, 2,000 students gathered. A bullhorn ordered them to disperse.

[Sound of bullhorn voice.]
[Students chant:] 1, 2, 3, 4, we don't want your fucking war!

"Troops threw tear gas canisters, students threw them back. Troops corralled demonstrators and held back TV and news correspondents. Then an FBI *agent provocateur* created a diversion with a .38-caliber revolver. Seventy seconds later, thirteen Troop G Guardsmen turned, aimed their M-1s, and opened fire on students 275 feet away. No verbal warning was given.

"Thirteen seconds and 76 bullets later, Jeffrey Miller, Sandra Scheuer, Allison Krause, and Bill Schroder were dead. Schroder was ROTC, just there trying to figure out what was going on. Days before, Allison Krause had put a daisy in a Guardsman's rifle and said, 'Flowers are better than bullets.' Her father had this to say—"

[Arthur Krause:] Have we come to such a state in this country that a young girl has to be shot because she disagrees with the actions of her government?

"In these two weeks, Nixon has bombed Cambodia, four students are dead at Kent State, and over 100,000 Americans are heading for Washington, DC to protest the war . . ."

As the show faded, Seven was crying so hard she had to pull over. Thomas pulled over behind her as Ray went ballistic and leaped from the bus, yelling *Motherfucker!* over and over. Soldiers shooting students! How could it be? Baby Rose put her head on Seven's shoulder, and Mannie sat numb. Seven had a friend in Tucson involved in the SDS who had recently written about a Yippie Free Store opening there and Jerry Rubin coming.

Cars and trucks whizzed by as they all got out. Seven sought refuge in Thomas' arms, the others milled around, upset. *FBI agent provocateur . . .*

In mid-afternoon, they cruised into Peach Springs, tribal headquarters of the Hualapai Indian Reservation. Once they'd parked and gotten out, Thomas took one look at Seven and folded her in his arms again. The Kent State broadcast had thrown them all.

Quietly moving in rhythm with the Colonel and his cane, they walked along the tiny main street, finally stopping by a Winnebago parked beside the trading post. Emblazoned on its side was *RACIST PROPAGANDA AT ITS BEST! LAST COPIES!* Over the open door was a hand-painted sign that read, *Forgeries, Lies and Truth Book Store* and beneath it in script, *Can you tell the difference?* Ray ventured up the steps with Mannie, Thomas, and Vince, while Seven, the Colonel, and Baby Rose went into the trading post to ask about camping spots.

No one was inside the Forgery, Lies, and Truth Book Store on wheels. On a shelf was a photographic triptych of writers George Bernard Shaw (1856-1950), Israel Zangwill (1864-1926), and Israel Cohen (1879-1961), "Founders of the Fabian Society, Friends of Karl Marx." Zangwill's 1908 play *The Melting Pot* ("Played at New York's Metropolitan Playhouse March 2006!") was there, as was Cohen's 1957 book *A Racial-Program for the 20th Century.* Beside them on the wall was a framed quote from the June 7, 1957 *Congressional Record* (Vol. 103, p. 8559)—

We must realize that our party's most powerful weapon is racial tensions. By propounding into the consciousness of the dark races that for centuries they have been oppressed by whites, we can mold them to the program of the Communist Party. In America we will aim for subtle victory. While inflaming the Negro minority against the whites, we will endeavor to instill in the whites a guilt complex for their exploitation of the Negroes. We will aid the Negroes to rise in prominence in every walk of life, in the professions and in the world of sports and entertainment. With this prestige, the Negro will be able to intermarry with the whites and begin a process which will deliver America to our cause.

Mein Kampf, The Protocols of the Elders of Zion and *The Rise and Fall of the Third Reich* were in a red and black box, "THREE FOR THE PRICE OF ONE!" Another book, *The Apocalypse Watch* by Robert Ludlum, promised "Post-World War Two Nazi research into implanted chips." Ray kept muttering, "Uh huh, uh huh," while Vince scribbled book titles and authors in his notebook.

Seven popped her head in with barely a glance, having had enough in-your-face politics for the day. "Let's go, I've got a lead on a place to camp and Grand Canyon Caverns are dead ahead." She and Thomas loved caves.

Exiting, Mannie asked, "That book store's not connected to the trading post, is it?"

"No, I asked," Seven said. "They said some white guy leaves the Winnebago here and returns for it later. The Hualapai don't interfere. As the woman behind the counter said, 'There's a lot of kooks out here in the desert.'"

Back on 66, they spotted a bumper sticker that read, *Pray devoutly. Hammer stoutly. The Fabians.* Burma Shave signs were pointing the way to the Stargazer Drive-in.

"Did the directions include a drive-in?" Thomas asked over the two-way.

Seven was puzzled. "She didn't say anything about one." Drive-ins to Seven meant fending off pawing high school boys.

Thomas laughed. "Neither Vince nor I have ever been to a drive-in. Maybe we need a little light entertainment."

"I've never been to one, either, or a cave," Mannie said, excited by the prospect of both.

"Ditto here," Ray said.

Thomas had done spelunking years before in the Appalachians.

Seven glanced at the Colonel and he shrugged. She called out, "All right, Captain America, we'll set up the tents by starlight. First the caverns, then the drive-in."

A cheer went up as they pulled into the little gas station-laundromat combo at Grand Canyon Caverns to fill up. The older Native man washing their windows and pumping their gas turned out to be a World War Two Navajo code talker. He and the Colonel talked about how the Japanese never broke the code, then about the big power plant on Navajo land after Holbrook. Seven had to drag the Colonel away, promising they would return after the caverns to do a load of laundry. They dug out sweaters and jackets, Thomas commissioned Sirius to keep an eye on the vehicles, and they headed for the little trade store tour.

As the rickety elevator plunged into the Earth, the savvy Hualpai guide explained that bacteria csn't live more than three days in dry caves, and that during the Cuban Missile Crisis the American government had stored enough food and water down in the caverns to last 2,000 people for a few weeks. "But this elevator shaft entry isn't the real entry," he added quietly. "The real one is through a sacred burial ground." He and Vince shared a glance. "And there's caves and rooms not open to the public—space exploration experiments, including a cosmic ray telescope under 126 feet of solid limestone."

"Sounds like NASA is studying the penetration of solid rock by interstellar cosmic rays," Thomas surmised.

The elevator opened into a lit cavern with no stalagmites or stalactites as big as three football fields. Baby Rose clung to Seven, sensing the presence of spirits. When Thomas asked about the breeze wafting from the south, the Hualpai looked at Vince and pointed down.

"From there," he said in a soft small voice.

"Why is it called the Grand Canyon Caverns?" Seven asked in an equally soft voice.

"Military scientists burned red smoke flares to find out how far the caverns went. Two weeks later, red smoke came out Grand Canyon walls near Supai, sixty miles northeast. The real name is Yampai, *gateway*. Medicine men say it's a Mongolian word."

Walking through the giant stone cathedral, his soft voice echoing, he talked about how 345 million years ago all the American West was ocean, his flashlight illuminating thousands of clam impressions, scallops, and sea turtles buried in the limestone walls.

"So many little bodies," Mannie murmured.

"Little bodies pushed up and up to over a mile above sea level," the Hualpai went on, "split the crust, water in the caverns . . ."

"Then acid rainfall," Thomas added, "seeping through cracks and caves, carving out the Colorado River. And when the water evaporated, calcium deposits," he gestured broadly, "and over Time, this beauty."

"Cold, crystalline beauty," Seven shivered, sensing the otherworldly in the shadows and hugging the trembling Baby Rose.

"At the sacred entrance," the Hualpai pointed vaguely, "there's an 18,000-year-old giant ground sloth skeleton from the woolly mammoth and saber tooth tiger days. Sloth probably weighed 2,000 pounds and stood fifteen feet."

Mannie shuddered to imagine an underground encounter with a giant sloth.

They wound through tunnels of helecite, selenite, and red-wall limestone until they came to a cache of canned goods from the Cuban Missile Crisis days.

Seven sidled up to Thomas and wrapped her arm around him, her other arm around Baby Rose. "Thinking of creating your own rainy-day cache?"

He smiled. "Might come in handy, given how the future is looking."

On the way back up to the surface of the Earth, Seven was already missing the intimate feeling of the womb-like darkness pregnant with shy spirit shadows. But *living* in an underground womb, no. As St.

Francis said, Brother Sun illuminates the soul.

It was late afternoon, so Seven ran just one load of wash she would hang out to dry overnight when they camped after the Stargazer Drive-in, which, by the way, no one at the caverns or gas station had ever heard of. The Colonel and code talker conversed while Vince, Mannie, Thomas, and Ray listened. The code talker explained how *Hozho* meant balance and *Hocho* chaos, and how he'd come back from the war filled with chaos and had to undergo the Enemy Way Ceremony to get the ghost sickness out of him. About that, he said something peculiar.

"At one point, they had me out on an atoll in the South Pacific where the French were using nuclear bombs on something they called the *hyperdimensional grid* to probe the Giza plateau halfway across the world. That really shook the soul out of me," he finished, shaking his head.

Thomas didn't say anything, but he took in *hyperdimensional*.

Mannie wandered out back of the filling station where a sign promised *Desert Flora and Fauna*. No sooner had he entered a little dry garden than he felt a wiry hand on his shoulder. There before him stood St. Anthony's twin in a loincloth, replete with desert wrinkles, long stringy hair, ancient sandals, and a faded Old Black Dawning Frank Black t-shirt. His skinny sun-darkened legs and arms were like those of a Maasai herdsman.

"Don't worry, son, the counterculture won't die," St. Anthony said to Mannie. "It will live on transmogrified. You know what transmogrified means, son?"

"No, sir." The old man's hand was zapping him with an energy transfusion.

The wiry phantom of hot days and cold nights peered at Mannie from its left eye. "It means the form of what was here yesterday and today will *look* different tomorrow but its essence will be the same. That's the beauty of this planet, son. All you have to do is learn how to *look*." He winked like an ancient tortoise.

Mannie nodded, his consciousness shifting but he didn't know how or where to.

St. Anthony's other hand pointed south. "That's where I'm from." He looked pointedly at Mannie. "Ever hear of Oracle or Biosphere II?"

Mannie shook his head.

"Smithsonian Institute? National Center for Atmospheric Research? Yale School of Forestry and Ecological Science? New York Botanical Gardens? U.S. Geological Society? University of Arizona Environmental Research Laboratory? NASA? Johnny Dolphin?"

Mannie stared, mesmerized.

St. Anthony squeezed his shoulder for emphasis. "Well, don't go near them, they use people." He pointed east. "And if you're headed for Santa Fe, watch out for the commune at Synergia Ranch, too, and the in-between underground bases north of Seligman, near Holbrook, Ash Fork, Williams, under the Black Mesa Basin on Navajo land." His cosmic eyes flashed. "And don't be taking any of those ha-ha drugs." He leaned close, as though they were in a roomful of listeners and he didn't want anyone else to hear. "They want you to take those *soma* drugs, those brave new world drugs, because they want you in the palm of their pharmaceutical hand. Be truly radical, boy. Fool them. Become *aware*, awake. Protect it. You know not when the Bridegroom cometh." The old tortoise winked again.

Mannie was surprised that the old desert rat's breath smelled sweet, like roses. Surely he had not brushed with Colgate or Pepsodent for years. In those wrinkled tortoise eyes was hard-wrought wisdom coupled with lonely madness and a dried-out hint of what once might have been blue, brown, green or gold. He had been transmogrified into a book of life, a library of the same purity of fire that once drove the Essenes and Desert Fathers.

The messenger lifted his head to listen to something only he heard. "And the last three trumpets sound! The fifth trumpet sounded upon the Earth between the 17th and 19th centuries and announced the first woe. The sixth trumpet sounded the second woe in 1841 and continues to sound even now, unto the beginning of the third millennium since Christ. Then shall the seventh trumpet sound the third woe, the climax of the spirit battle raging above and below the surface of the Earth, the outcome of which will decide which direction we humans take." He looked straight into Mannie's eyes. "Will we head toward the machine-like, or the Christ-like?"

Suddenly, the messenger's body was wrenched by something invisible and his face was bleached by terror. "I have seen the ghost of the Roman Empire!" he cried like prophets of old. "Prepare ye, children of Whitman and Emerson, to deal with the storming of the Threshold! Beware the men of science. Live anonymously so you do not attract their pernicious attention. Eat only from what Nature grows in Her living body. Eschew medicines, drugs, and animals reared and butchered inhumanely. Live by the medicines of the past, not the future—of the fields, not the laboratories. And should you have visions and out of body experiences, confirm them slowly, as their genesis might be a manmade machine or devolved beings and not the Organic Light."

And so saying, St. Anthony put his hand upon Mannie's head, blessed him, and strode back into the ever wise desert.

Walking back to his friends, Mannie contemplated St. Anthony's words and a question that had nagged him his whole life: Why did Jews and just about everyone cool and hip hate Christianity so much? It had first hit him first while reading P.K. Dick's *Valis*. It wasn't Fat who was having the vision of the pink girl with a silver fish hanging from her neck, but Dick himself. And when Mannie read the Latin words

Ex Deo nascimur
In Christo morimur
Per spiritum sanctum reviviscimus

he'd experienced his own flash of light. Thirteen million Jews in the world and yet how many really believed that Jahve (*Yod-Hey-Vav-Hey*), the great Jehovah, lived in all of Nature—in the thunder and lightning, the motion of cloud and star, the springs and rushing streams, the birth and growth of plants, animals and human beings? Fresh out of Babylon, the Jews *saw* Jahve as a serpent, perhaps the *kundalini* or the intertwined serpents of living, fire-breathing strands of DNA. For the first time, he understood the yearning for a Messiah: humanity could never be complete if it only relied on Jahve and His laws to give them their second birth, the resurrection that would make them conscious of being spiritual beings *in* Nature but not *of* Nature. Jahve and laws were not enough.

He felt guilty. How would his Buchenwald grandmother sleeping in her grave view such thoughts?

In Christo morimur, per spiritum sanctum reviviscimus! The words were a formula of some kind for something more, something beyond the desert law of guilt and fear. Human beings needed a metaphysical *gnosis* birth of their own not transmitted by priests and rabbis and dogma. All the priests and the rest did was *maybe* keep you safe until you were ready to slip over the edge where the *real* Holy of Holies was waiting for you.

Mannie leaped for joy. That was it! The spiritual war he could see everywhere was not about who was right, or if Muhammed was the equal of Yeshua, or how many angels danced on the heads of pins. The *real* war underneath all of it was between those who wanted to keep power over people through priests and rabbis and imam, dogma, sins, and repentance—whatever kept people in line and in fear—and those who wanted people's freedom beyond law. *Responsible freedom.* Was that why they'd hated Yeshua so much? Because he said there were only two laws? Mannie could feel something or someone beckoning and it frightened and exhilarated him, maybe like what lived in Yeshua after the Essene Baptist baptized him in the river.

Mannie was hit by another insight. The Sanskrit root of *sacrifice* was *Shak-* for Shakti and Shekinah. The heat of spiritual warfare. *In Deo nascimur* he had understood his entire life. *In Christo morimur* and *Per spiritum sanctum reviviscimus* remained Mystery equations. He wondered how they would be revealed, what they would look like. It was a relief that he wouldn't have to deal with a church or Jews for Jesus, as Uncle

Eli had tried to tell him. *Transmogrification*, St. Anthony had said.

No one noticed the difference in him that his epiphanies had made. Vince the language savant was busy talking in Spanish with a couple of skinny, ragged pubescent brothers gesticulating emotionally as they relayed how they had made it all the way from Guatemala to cross the border at Nogales through a tunnel and had to fight off homeless kids known as *Bajadores* (undergrounders) sniffing soda cans filled with metallic paint. Those kids attack illegals with rocks, lead pipes, brass knuckles, and homemade shanks. One brother pulled up his shirt to show the shank cuts. In Tucson, they'd gotten a ride north and walked most of the way off road to get as far as possible from the border and toward Route 66 that would take them west to Los Angeles where their parents worked.

The Guatemalan brothers ate with them and Thomas slipped them a few dollars, then they all took a swim for a dollar each in the Caverns Inn outdoor pool. The Colonel set up his chair under a scrawny mesquite with Sirius at his side and Baby Rose perched on the edge of the shimmering pool as Thomas, Ray, Vince, Mannie, and the two boys clowned around. Thoughtfully, Seven dove in the deep end, wishing for the thousandth time that Baby Rose would talk, haunted by the phrase *Seneq Peak is she who burns* and the strange, disparaging Alice voice. Ancient Egyptians believed the seat of the soul was in the tongue, the rudder or steering oar for making one's way through life. The phrase *run amok* came from Southeast Asian men's murderous rage followed by amnesia. Norse warriors went *berserk*, and the Fertile Crescent of the Middle East spoke of *zar*, spirit possession with dissociative laughing, shouting, and singing. In Turkey, *akil hastaligi* was a dangerously aggressive schizophrenia, whereas *ruhsal hastagi* was a disorder of the spiritual or inner self and not dangerous to others. If Baby Rose had been tortured, was her disorder of the spirit?

It was almost dusk when the pilgrims said goodbye to the two Guatemalans and got back on 66 to follow the Burma Shave-Stargazer Drive-in breadcrumbs. As sunset splayed over the red Earth, they paid their car admission beneath the flashing psychedelic *Stargazer* sign, got their cardboard 3D glasses, and pulled up side by side at speakers. Thomas backed in so he could flip up the bus rear door for Mannie, Vince, and Ray, and Seven and Baby Rose clipped the stereo speakers to the windows while the others went to the concession stand for popcorn and drinks. At last, Thomas was sitting happily in the Caddy front seat between Seven and Baby Rose munching popcorn and slurping Dr. Pepper while the Colonel stretched out in the backseat. Their 3D glasses on, the screen lit up.

Hours later, the pilgrims found themselves off-road and the Stargazer Drive-in nowhere in sight. *Lost time.* In a daze, they went through the motions of setting up camp. Seven heated up some leftovers to ground them, they lit a fire and ate, all the while trying to patch together what had happened. Their 3D glasses were proof that they had truly been at a drive-in, wherever "there" and "when" was. The screen had lit up, then sophisticated camera work and so real, so *out there* narration and music like a great *OM* on the cosmic sound system, but as far as the actual *film*, all they remembered were random scenes and words fused with strong emotions.

Thomas recalled the palpable density of dark space. He remembered squeezing Seven's hand hard at the moment he realized how *contrived* the Big Bang theory was. Long ago, he'd grasped the reciprocal relationship between the solar system and the Earth and recognized astrophysics' mathematical place, but had always longed for a science that would include *soul* (for want of a better word), foreshadowed by Heisenberg's uncertainty principle.

Mannie recalled the planets being connected to a huge spectral Mother body before slowly, musically separating from her and galactically dancing their way to individual orbits, like he had been doing since leaving Brooklyn. Somehow, it now made sense that the Earth had once been connected to the Sun, and that Mercury and Venus had kept some of the Sun nature but Mars and Saturn, being reincarnations of the ancient Moon, had separated from the Earth because of beings that couldn't evolve further. Jupiter was different; it was populated by beings of a future cosmic evolution not yet here. Mannie swore the thoughts came after the Stargazer Drive-in.

Ray remembered each phantom planet spinning away from the Sun and remaining spectral until the tension of opposing forces hollowed out a place in the dark pudding of space so each planet could have its own physical body. He was sure the narrator had said, *This hollowing-out, separating or breaking off from the actively streaming creative life force of the planetary spheres becomes an opposing entity that is dark, bounded, and substantial. And yet each entity shares the state of cosmic consciousness.*

The Colonel recalled the narrator saying, *Before the Moon separated from the Earth, during the great Earth Winter, everything became so hardened that many human souls had to make do with other planets. But after the Moon departed, Earth substance became finer and softer and souls gradually returned, embodied in the descendants of those who had been strong enough to remain. Atlantis arose, guided by Initiates of the various planetary Oracles . . .*

Seven remembered much the same, but especially, *Now most human souls come and go from the Earth, but those remaining on other planets have no Ego. This is especially problematical on Mars, which the Greeks rightly named the god of war. Wars can only be waged by embodied beings bound to the soil, like Mars men . . .*

Vince recalled Gautama Buddha's death and the globe of light that was somehow still the Buddha speeding up the Great North Road of the Milky Way all the way to a stunning stream of light Vince could still feel in his chest. The Buddha's light had hovered over the birth of Jesus and various members of the Grail stream, until it journeyed to Venus and then to Mars to work on the Mars men. *As Christ is for the Earth,* the narrator intoned, *so Buddha is for Mars.*

Baby Rose said nothing but remembered all.

The pilgrims stoked the fire and went through one memory after another, beginning with the Big Bang theory that Vince said he'd never believed. "Instruments say the universe is expanding, the story being that a primal state smaller than an atom exploded, beginning Time and expanding in Space, then differentiated in chance combinations of matter that somehow ended up as life." Vince laughed. "It doesn't fit gravity or entropy. It's a myth contrived to eliminate the divine."

Thomas wondered aloud. "And maybe to tweak the tail of what the Stargazer Drive-in showed us—you know, the free-floating quarks and gluons compressing into a tiny ball held together by forces before bursting and splintering into thousands and millions of stars and planets—quarks and glutons like water, atoms like ice, so you have to 'melt the ice,' which is what cyclotrons and betatrons do by colliding nuclei to release heat hotter than the center of the Sun. Protons and neutrons release quarks to produce a plasma or primordial soup, maybe like the Mother body . . ."

Vince laughed. "Sounds like the Egyptian myth about Atum's fiery ejaculation impregnating Nun's watery chaos and enormous clouds of water succoring stars like our Sun."

Seven asked, "Didn't alchemists and astrologers claim that planetary intelligences work together for our birth?"

"Divine intelligences are definitely involved," Vince agreed, "working in tandem with the karma seeking to evolve consciousness—from Lion heart intelligence to Water-bearer head intelligence, which may be why our nerves and senses are being assaulted with television, movies, and computers. Tesla's alternating current leads us deep into subnature and plays havoc with our nervous system receiving antenna and prevents us from forming spiritual thoughts."

"Hm, alternating current," Thomas mused, "I hadn't put that together."

"And subnature is . . .?" Mannie asked.

Vince shrugged. "The forces of *Xibalbá*."

The Caddy radio clicked on. The pilgrims listened to the Talking Heads singing "Wild Wildlife" from the future—

> *. . . I wrestle with your conscience*
> *You wrestle with your partner*
> *Sittin' on a window sill but he spends time behind closed doors*

Check out Mr. Businessman, he bought some wild wildlife
On the way to the stock exchange, he got some wild wildlife
Break it up when he opens the door, he's doin' wild wildlife
I know that's the way you like it, living wild, wild
Peace of mind, it's a piece of cake
Thought control, you get on board anytime you like . . .

"I'm trippin'," Ray said for them all, not sure he'd ever get used to being so hooked up with a talking universe. Before this trip, all he'd wanted was to go somewhere like Ecuador and lose himself in *ayahuasqa* with the Jivaro and Shuar Indians and bypass the pain of black and white America. He'd vomit up the *natema* with transdimensional properties that Vince talked about and see into the real reality under Indian guidance and finally not be on his own. But now the universe was coming to *him*.

"*Xibalbá*," Thomas repeated. "Like the song says, subnature is wildlife—UFOs, ball lightning hugging the ground, the *bardos* of our dreams. Here in the desert, I really feel like we're *threshold* surfing."

"Get your kicks on Route 66," Ray sang as he headed into the darkness to urinate.

Vince laughed. "Before, only shamans and initiates passed through the Veil of the Threshold, and now here we are on Route 66, undergoing direct sense perceptions of invisible realms."

The Colonel said, "It's like an opportunity for self-initiation, isn't it? First it was priests, shamans, and magicians, then clans and Brotherhoods, and now they're all being phased out, which is why they're pulling out all the stops to misdirect us with false self-initiations."

Vince agreed. "Aquarian Age self-initiations replacing Piscean Age priests. You're right, Colonel: power-lovers are bent on dragging seekers down into an asuric astral realm, a real but unphysical *counter*-sphere, a *counter*-Devachan for which materialistic Westerners are ill-prepared."

"Quick, come here!" Ray called from the darkness.

223

Seven helped the Colonel up and they all groped their way toward Ray's voice.

"Look!" he cried, pointing up.

Seven points of light were moving in an arc against the starry backdrop. Suddenly, they broke formation and turned in a circle as if playfully chasing each other. Then one by one they sped in all directions and blinked out. The entire spectacle took no more than a half a minute.

The pilgrims were speechless, then babbled all the way back to the fire. The Colonel mentioned the foo fighters he'd seen in Europe in 1944-45, spheres of light and fireballs, and how Sonderburo 13, the Luftwaffe special study group, had investigated UFO sightings.

Thomas thought the lights disappearing one by one was because space is curved and metric whereas Time is fractally structured. "Imagine every level reflecting a sequence, like the *I Ching* and its 64 x 6 = 384 structure. Or DNA based on 64 codons, a sequence of three adjacent nucleotides, 64 possible combinations of four base pairs, with the structure of each hexagram being two tri-grams in a sequence of 64."

Vince stared at him. "Their correspondence has to be Time. What else could 'prophetic' mean but understanding the laws and structure of Time and using them to locate events in Time?"

Thomas stared back. "Fractally structured, each level reflecting the sequence. So the ancient Chinese recorded it in code in the *I Ching*—"

"—having inherited the knowledge from older civilizations," Vince mused.

Tingles rippled up Seven's spine. "So fractal structure is how the *I Ching* reads what's in the process of unfolding in Time?"

Back by the fire, Thomas gesticulated. "Plotted, the fractal spiral would get smaller and smaller as we move through history, until . . ." He stared at a smiling Vince.

". . . until 2012, when one history ends and another begins," Vince said quietly. "If what we just saw were plasma UFOs and not U.S. Air Force or Navy UFOs, then they might be riding the Time wave as the Threshold thins."

224

"Wow," Mannie said, looking from Vince to Thomas.

The conversation then spiraled back to the alchemy of self-initiation and Vince's grandfather. Humans being experimental free will beings, the Philosopher's Stone that so many alchemists had obsessed over pointed to the Earth being pivotal to developing that free will. *Translinguistic matter.* Suddenly they were back in the Stargazer Drive-in galactic clusters, galaxies, solar systems, Earth, *I Ching*, and UFO geographic locales Thomas called *condensations*, with the law of correspondence connecting them all in their consciousness. *As above, so below.* Wow.

Through it all, Seven stroked Baby Rose's dreaming head in her lap, gently checking the healing of the wound behind her ear, sad that their Sleeping Beauty could not participate more in their cosmic conversations and self-initiation.

The fact was that as the pilgrims tripped on the universe and galactic clusters, a part of Baby Rose was cruising high above the atmosphere, communing with the Harmonies of the Spheres, the singing of untold beauty surrounded by fluid substances dissolving and resonating, answered by whales from the ocean deeps. Like Apollo's 12-stringed lyre— a perfect reverberating instrument of 12 semitones interspaced in 7 whole notes resounding in the seven Greek modes back through the seven planetary spheres—the twelve pairs of cervical nerves in Baby Rose's spinal marrow were resonating with her human birthright melody. While her friends drank *cota* and pored over the challenges of their Time, Baby Rose consorted with angels on inner dimensions.

The pilgrims discussed science fiction. Thomas had devoured the 1897 *Across the Milky Way; or Frank Reade, Jr.'s Great Astronomical Trip With His Airship* by Louis Senarens, the American Jules Verne of Cuban descent born in Brooklyn. It was published around the time of the 19th century airship wave from November 17, 1896 to April 1897, just before the great Philadelphia inventor John Worrell Keely died on November 18, 1898, the very day Aleister Crowley was initiated into the Order of the Golden Dawn. Europe wouldn't have their wave of powerfully lit *scareships* until 1913, the year after Keely's patron John Jacob Astor IV went down with the *Titanic*.

Thomas had done his homework on airships. He'd even visited the old mining towns of Sonora and Columbia to learn as much as he could about the Sonora Aero Club, a West Coast offshoot of the New York Zodiacal Motor Association or NYZMA, both bankrolled by Astor. The first airship sighting was in Sacramento, given that most of the airships had been assembled near Oroville, Stockton, and Berkeley. Like the rockets and Jack Parsons' Suicide Squad, GALCIT and Caltech, the Sonora Aero Club provided an out-of-the-way proving ground where technical genius and money could meet. While Keely spun the ideas in Philadelphia, Astor provided an international team of engineers and aerotechniks, everything on the hush-hush. Thomas was certain the airships were powered by Keely ether motors (*NB gas* and *supe*) put together by a man named Peter Mennis who died by fire like Jack Parsons, both being Illuminati Philosophers of Fire. After Mennis, other Sonora Aero Club members died strange and violent deaths.

"The press never mentioned Keely," Thomas said. "I heard from an old timer at the library in Sonoma that Charles August Dellschau, a German engineer who arrived in Sonora in 1850 and fled to Houston in 1886 fearing for his life, composed scrapbooks and manuscripts filled with cryptic notes and hidden messages, skulls and crossbones, ciphers that spelled out *todt*, which is death in German. Dellschau died in 1923 at 93."

The Colonel said, "I never heard of Keely, but skulls and crossbones—I guess we know what that cipher refers to. As a boy, I heard about the airships and wished I hadn't missed them. Back then, everyone assumed they were Freemason spectacled."

Thomas poked at the embers. "The West was still *terra incognita* then, at least to Americans in the East, Midwest, and South. Maybe that's why the magical display showed up out here."

"And again in the mid-20th century disc wave fifty years later," Vince said, scribbling.

"Keely described his aerial navigator as being driven by 'depolar repulsion' and not dependent upon air," Thomas explained, "which meant it could potentially fly in the interstellar vacuity of deep space by manipulating polarity shifts between planets."

"'Depolar repulsion' sounds like antigravity to me," the Colonel said.

Thomas grinned. "Keely's 1889 planetary system engine was composed of three gyroscopes, a *1-ton* metal plate, and tubes producing tones that made the gyroscopes produce vibratory ratios to attract and repel and thus move the ship. Weight didn't matter—like the vibration used to move the Stonehenge stones. Keely did mention helping *a* 'gentleman in California' with the problem of lifting heavy weights."

Seven was thoughtful. "So the *Titanic* . . ."

Thomas looked at her. "Sunk to shut Astor up about the planetary system engine."

Everyone stared at him.

"Wow," Mannie said.

Such were the mysteries of consciousness that one needs more than a microscope or telescope or EEG to perceive.

As Thomas drifted to sleep, he continued thinking of Keely. He'd first heard of Keely from one of his uncle's Freemason Brothers. While visiting his parents in Philadelphia, he'd gone to the West Laurel Hill Cemetery on Arch Street to see Plot 313 in the River section: *John Earnest Worrell Keely, Born September 3, 1837, died November 18, 1898*. Keely had been the grandson of a German composer who had conducted the Baden-Baden orchestra. *Baden.* Thomas' mother's family had something to do with Baden. He'd stood beneath the boughs of the hard maple and stared at the little grave coated with ivy. A 'widow's son,' Keely at ten had watched the windows vibrate long after a noisy wagon had passed out of sight; he'd observed how the drums of drummers driven inside by a storm had continued to roll in rhythm until the windows cracked from sympathetic vibration. His childish discoveries had dominated his entire life—how the vibration in everything can be made to communicate and exert a dynamic force double that of steam. Keely was the midwife of the re-birth of acoustic physics, and the energy barons had forced history to bury his name.

In New York City, Thomas had been invited to visit a J.P. Morgan underground vault to see Keely machines with their glistening metal tubes, wheels, and moving parts, everything contrived to maximize surface area, semi-circle upon semi-circle of copper rings, discs, revolving drums, all lifting, disintegrating, pressurizing without electricity or steam or coal, only oscillations—of what? The Keely Motor, the Compound Disintegrator, the Vibratory Globe Machine, the Resonator, the Rotating Globe that worked through human magnetism, Vibratory Discs, the Spirophone, the Pneumatic Gun, the Vibrating Planetary Globe, the Planetary System Engine, the Vibrodyne or Vibratory Accumulator, the Sympathetic Negative Transmitter.

"Vibrations of trapped and conducted æther," the university scientist Brother had confided when Thomas asked what ran the glistening machines they were strolling among. "Born too soon," the Yale man in the impeccable suit explained. "At that time, Keely couldn't be allowed to perfect his re-discovery of what the Atlanteans once termed *Mash-mak*. Nor did we yet have the technology by which to mass engineer it, so it couldn't be allowed, it's as simple as that. We like to guide our inventors and inventions. Edison refused an invitation from Keely in 1878. Edison was always our man, but Keely and Tesla, not so much; both were foreign, both had to be managed and so were not allowed to meet. Tesla was in Philadelphia in 1893 and 1895 to meet Edison and Bell, but on Tesla's behalf, Keely's invitation was refused. But Keely was dispatched honorably at three o'clock in the afternoon on November 18, 1898, and his devoted patron Bloomfield-Moore dispatched a little less honorably two months later. Tesla's funding was then transferred from Morgan to Astor, and Hearst ran the cover story that Keely's machines were frauds." The polished Brother chuckled. "As Charles Fort put it, people of all eras are hypnotics and almost all their beliefs are induced by—well, *us*." He had then planted a paternal hand on Thomas' shoulder.

But Thomas had insisted upon asking, "How was Keely

'dispatched'?"

"Poison, I think. He had Bright's Disease, and his doctor was our man. An old tactic. Wilson's physician, Hitler's, King George III's porphyry—all ours." His steel-blue eyes took Thomas in. "It might strike a young man as ruthless that the powerful retain the right to own another's lifespan, but history has ever been written by those who take this right as necessity. Such dispatches are done with great care; they are not sordid crimes of passion. The stars are consulted and the rites formulated so as to reflect the person's contributions to history." Thomas kept his face attentive and impassive as the man examined the effect his words were having. "We are the high priests of our day, Thomas. You will see the wisdom of these practices as you proceed."

Later, the polished Brother would tell Hiram that it was at this moment that he realized Thomas did not have what it took to be a dependable *left-handed* candidate.

At Keely's graveside, Thomas had pondered the two-ton iron sphere buried under Keely's workshop and the wire attaching it to a little remote device he carried, even to sleeping with it. The Sympathetic Transmitter had been "responsive to the touch," like the musical scale to a tuning fork. Intricate tubes and plates resonated with the seven distinct vibratory sounds and moved a drum exceedingly rapidly. Thomas thought of the Chladni plate he had bowed in grade seven at the Steiner school in New York City. Once he bowed a pure tone, the fine sand on the plate collected along the nodal lines of a geometric form—the higher the tone, the more intricate the form, B-flat, D, and F in one direction, F-sharp and A in another. Unlike the mechanical process of the bow, Keely had wrought a human-machine interface: the iron sphere was somehow activated by the vibrational frequencies inherent to his touch.

Keely had kept refining his machines, taking them from 22 tons to no bigger than a 3-inch thick dinner plate, then even a silver pocket watch that linked the air with the magnetic polar currents enveloping the Earth like a giant orange rind peel. He observed the behavior of triune celestial streams of magnetism, electricity, and gravitational sympathy that percuss on the dense atmosphere of the Earth at infinite velocity and release the latent energies we call heat and light. The *etheric force* he was able to liberate from air and water was the result, he said, of "interfering with this magnetic rind." One quart of water produced 54,000psi of pressure. No heat, electricity, or chemicals.

Thomas pondered the *etheric vapor* that Keely's phosphor bronze Liberator and Disintegrator derived from a pint of water. A pint of water to drive a train from New York to Philadelphia or a steamer across the Atlantic. Keely said the compressed etheric vapor from a bucket of water could move the Earth off course. Steam was derived from heat or combustion, but etheric vapor was spontaneous, needing only vibration and the rotary motion of the ether. But the engines had to be crafted perfectly.

After 1882, he worked with air instead of water by vibrating hydrogen. *The specific gravity of the ether is about four times lighter than that of hydrogen gas, the lightest gas so far discovered. The vibrations of ether are far more rapid than those of light.* Objects made to sympathetically vibrate together in the ether, whatever the distance between them, could exert a force—

It was at that moment that Thomas had grasped the occult university's interest in him: they wanted him to weaponize Keely's sympathetic vibrations of the ether! That's why they were exposing him to Keely's secrets. Keely and Tesla had unlocked Pandora's box of ether and electromagnetics respectively—unlimited free energy—and their inventions had been buried until such time as the means could be controlled. That time was now and the Brothers were wondering if Thomas might be part of the means.

Thomas despised their ignoble intentions. His uncle would say this was because he was young and untried, but Thomas would say it was because he was a moral being, despite the best efforts of his uncle and grandfather. Still staring at Keely's grave, he wondered, *What saved me from them?* His father had not lifted a finger for his son or his wife. Something in Thomas himself had prevailed to protect himself from the law of the jungle that had devoured his family. *Self-initiation.*

As Fournier said, "Where inventions are concerned, woe to the first-comer, and glory and profit to the one who comes after." Keely had needed hefty funding for his perfect machines of many moving parts of iron and copper—ever the pivotal dilemma for the inventor who wished to offer up his work to humanity. Sometimes, Keely had to scrap a $40,000 piece of machinery because of one imperfect part or joint or bolt hole that had to handle pressures of 25,000psi. Even steel pores could leak. With his trust fund under his command, Thomas would not have to go Keely's perilous route, though it was also true that the Brotherhoods had absconded with all of Keely's and Tesla's research and were now beginning to put it to use— now that they had the wherewithal to mass produce it, and now that the Second Coming was activating the etheric.

Keely knew he was harnessing ether, the universal life force the Chinese termed *Qi*, the Japanese *Ki* or *chi*, the Hindus *prana*, the Polynesians *mana*, the Greeks *pneuma*, Hermes Trismegistos *telesma*, Paracelsus *munis magnum*, Mesmer *animal magnetism*, Eliphas Lévi and Madame Blavatsky *astral light*. Wilhelm Reich, the occult university scientist had added dryly, called it *orgone*. Dragon Pulse or Serpent Power leylines were different: electromagnetic. The Soviets saw ether weaponized as bioplasmic and electromagnetics weaponized as psychotronic.

Science and the occult were combining forces, the university scientist affirmed, just as they had on Atlantis half an equinoctial precession ago. "We are the generation, Thomas, in which all the hopes of these scientists will be fulfilled," he had said, his arm cutting a swath over the vault filled with odd creations. Thomas had barely listened, so rapt was he in thoughts about Keely's triune theory and ether's role. Much of the electromagnetic spectrum's radiation was unfriendly to the human bio-organism, and yet by confusing the differences between electromagnetism and etheric-orgone, Brotherhoods were able to buy time until it would be too late to untangle the mess. Reich said the distinction spelled life or death. Necrophilia versus biophilia, Fromme might have put it. Whatever the occult university's professed dedication to science and technology, Thomas discerned weapons, death, and domination, not healing, life, and service.

He'd lingered over Keely's grave for some time, an intention beginning to percolate deep inside.

Far above the sleeping pilgrims, out in what is technically known as the Local Group, our convergent field of 24 galaxies whirled through space like the twelve dancing princesses and their phantom princes beating measured Time on their way past the demon star Algol, between Parsival's legs beneath his groin, and on toward their rendezvous, their destiny. The Milky Way held Andromeda and danced the night away. Strains of a Strauss waltz intermingled with the pulse of "Shine On, You Crazy Diamond" beneath the resonant *Om* penetrating the pregnant silence so silent and rich and full and dark that the pilgrims might have heard a sigh, a whisper, a stellar *Hosannah!* as they drifted away.

42

The Nines

*For many spirits dwell in [the body] and do not permit it to be pure;
each of them brings to fruition its own works, and they treat it abusively
by means of unseemly desires. To me it seems that the heart suffers in
much the same way as an inn: for it has holes and trenches dug in it and
is often filled with filth by men who live there licentiously and have no
regard for the place because it belongs to another.*

−Valentinus, 300 CE

*America is where it's at . . . Everybody heads toward the center; that's why
I'm here now. I'm here just to breathe it. It might be dying or there might be
a lot of dirt in the air, but this is where it's happening. And you go to Europe
to rest, like in the country. But it's so overpowering, America, for me, and . .
. I can't take much of it, it's too much for me. I'm too frightened of it. It's so
much, and people are so aggressive. I can't take all of that, you know? I need
to go home. I need to look at the grass . . .*

−John Lennon; interview with Jann S. Wenner,
Rolling Stone, January 7 and February 4, 1971

*This nation is under attack. We, the people, are under attack. And the
enemy in this case is not an Islamic radical hiding in a cave in Afghanistan
but a cabal of truly evil men and women at 1600 Pennsylvania Avenue
and on Capitol Hill aided by carefully picked, law-ignoring appointees
at the Hoover Building on Pennsylvania Avenue, a black glass-walled
building at Fort Meade, MD, and a complex in Langley, Virginia.*

−Capitol Hill Blue, June 1, 2006

It was Sunday and 63 million American Catholics were either going to mass or not, Italian-American, Irish-American, Spanish-American, Mexican-American, German-American, Polish-American. However they'd arrived at believing in Mother Church, they knew little of the *romanita* She was embroiled in, the geopolitics of the pending new world order, the *fantapolitica*. For them, Francis Joseph Cardinal Spellman was a holy man, as was Cardinal John O'Connor, and they didn't want to know that 83 percent of what supported the New York City Archdiocese came from local, state, and federal taxes.

That Italian Prime Minister Aldo Moro would be kidnapped on March 16, 1978 and murdered and dumped in Rome 55 days later—and that Henry Kissinger would be implicated on Italian TV and radio five months after God's Banker Roberto Calvi was found hanging from Blackfriars Bridge in London with £23,000 in cash in his pockets—well, that was politics, not religion. And that the Vatican Bank had processed Nazi loot melted down from wedding rings and dental gold, and that after the war God's Banker Michele Sindona had invested Mussolini's 1929 *donation* of $89 million to ensure Vatican neutrality, and that the Vatican had ratlined Nazis to South America—well, that was a long time ago. The War and everything to do with it was what everyone wanted to forget. As for the aftermath of corporate, intelligence, and crime alliances, good Catholics prayed that Santa Rita who grants the impossible would just make it all go away.

But it wouldn't go away. Despite all the confessions and Hail Marys and Our Fathers, in 2006 the Mafia, good Catholics all, would make £21 billion from extorting 160,000 Italian businesses. And when pedophile priests proved to be not just a few sick apples but an epidemic, American bishops in full knowledge continued shuffling them from diocese to diocese, denying and quietly settling with families as counselors told victims to hush, hush. And *still* parents sent their sons and daughters to Mother Church and called it faith.

234

It was Sunday for Catholic Dr. Greenbaum, too, and he was devoutly contemplating what the Austrian initiate had said: that we're returning to how we were on old Atlantis, our etheric bodies stretching out again. He thought of his MK-ULTRA methods as hurrying the stretching along before Mu rose again and the ocean returned, as Blavatsky had promised.

To distract and divert youths not conditioned by the old religions but who were in genuine quest of the greatest event of the 20th century, an endless conduit of Cold War money and expertise was being diverted into cults and religions to reframe and redefine the Second Coming phenomenon progressively leaking out all over the place. Mormons and seers like Jean Dixon were prophesying a soul battle with the Beast from the Abyss by 2040. Billy Graham was swearing that Christ would come physically. Sun Myung Moon and his Unification Church would soon announce that Sun Myung Moon himself was the Second Coming. Alice Bailey's World Goodwill merged Buddha and Christ and promised a Maitreya. *Technical* clairvoyance was being prepared to upstage natural clairvoyance— no more Austrian initiate or sleeping prophet, both of whom had *seen* that the Christ would come exactly as the original disciples had watched Him go: *in the ether.*

The Brotherhoods had bound the two world wars together with a Metonic cycle to assure 30 years of non-stop carnage, topping it all with the Jewish Holocaust to ridicule the blood He had chosen as His "chosen people" vessel. The Etheric Advent meant keeping Israel seething, and the Massacre of the Innocents called for desecrating as many children as possible. Hatred and derision of Him and His Christianity had to be at their zenith.

Greenbaum needed to know more about the Mexican connection Sibelius had explained to him—the Mayan boy of the Timekeeper lineage, his mother Mayan, his father Hispanic, born the day Japan bombed Pearl Harbor to provide 2,350 sacrificial dead. With Saint-Germain sniffing around, he could prove to be a problem. Was he too traveling with the strange little hippie troupe? If he was Vitzliputzli come again, what he did in 33 AD must not be allowed to happen again.

Sibelius had tracked down the university records of Vicente Liputzli, but there was no photograph. A model student, brilliant, well liked, a born leader—still, it was his lineage that spoke volumes. Eyes and ears in Albuquerque and Rancho de Taos reported he'd come north for the winter dances and then hitchhiked south and west. Only time would tell if the young man now in his Saturn return would be a problem. All the same, terrorist operations were being stepped up in Mexico because the Qabalist was certain that Israel and Mexico would again be a pivotal axis during the Etheric Advent. Two World Wars had taken care of Central Europe, but Mexico . . .

Greenbaum scanned his wall map. With 0° Greenwich as the fulcrum between Mexico and Israel, Dallas and Jerusalem were at almost the same latitude. If Liputzli was with Thomas en route to Dallas, it could be worrisome . . . He needed a photograph of Liputzli. Thus far, the Magician had been unable to *see* him—some sort of blocking was going on.

His mind drifted to Jerusalem. Two lunar eclipses, one before Herod's death in 1 BC, the other on April 3, 33 AD, darkness from noon to three, earthquake, blood red Passover Moon that Friday-Saturday, Pontius Pilate, Procurator of Judea 26-36 AD . . .

He reached for a Tums.

North and west of the pilgrims now at Mount Tenabo and Horse Canyon in Nevada, Shoshone horses were being seized and Barrick Gold's Cortez Gold Mine was gutting 5,242 acres of Western Shoshone traditional land that Washington, DC now deemed "public land." Barrick Gold, Oro Nevada, Placer Dome, Bureau of Land Management (BLM) were busy destroying 5,000 acres with an open-pit cyanide heap leach mine, dewatering at 70,000 gallons per minute, and detonating all the L-A-W-S of land, air, water, and sun, leaving behind the highest mercury concentrations in the country (4,600 pounds of mercury per year) so that fish from the Wild Horse Reservoir could no longer be eaten. And what was the Inter-American Commission on Human Rights doing? Nothing.

In the near dawn, Seven's eyes opened and beheld a naked man with several out-of-focus bodies wrestling in his one crouched body. Perched on his haunches like in a Fuseli painting, he had long *rasta* hair and appeared to be watching the pilgrims sleep while holding his own counsel in whisper mode. Seven rubbed her eyes and looked again: yes, Legion was crawling around inside the man's psyche and soma.

Looking further, she saw that the Colonel was already in his lawn chair having a morning pipe. She nudged Thomas awake and nodded toward the *rasta* man. "What should we do?" she whispered.

Thomas blinked at him. "Fix breakfast and see how things go," he whispered back.

She sighed, kissed his forehead, and crawled out of the sleeping bag, bent on rinsing her face before anything else. On her way by, she greeted the naked man, then the Colonel, pausing to whisper, "When did he arrive?"

The Colonel shrugged. "He was here when I got up."

Thomas rose and began stuffing sleeping bags in stuff bags. "'Morning," he said to the *rasta* man and Colonel on his way to the bus.

Seven got the oatmeal and tea water going, Mannie and Ray rolled up their bags, Baby Rose stood in front of the naked whisperer and stared, Vince wandered in from wherever he'd slept. As they all sat down to eat, the *rasta* man amped up his whispered soliloquy, his hands serving as punctuation.

"Kill a black cock and mutilate a lamb, fast and pray, confess and to Mass, it's 1629 and the spirits must be commanded! These are the days of Noah. Angels are being judged, some chained to Tartarus. The seas and waves roar, the powers of heaven quake, three-leggeds are pulling us down down into infinite depths. Be careful, Abramelin spirits bite. Pick them up on the radio, light a cigarette, and there they are. Nature talks in signs, spirits in images, Freemasons in numbers. The left eye of the dreaming self whispers to the right eye of the waking self. Intentions from the dreaming mind." He leaned forward to furiously whisper, "*Doppelgänger* replaced my dreaming and waking selves and is now controlled by invisible underground entities."

The pilgrims ate their oatmeal and listened as they would to a sage from another world.

Rasta man looked west. "The Föhn are coming! In and out of the body like a *Star Trek* station, drawing out ectoplasm! Katie Kings for William Crookes! Trading energies in the body, in and out." He pointed up. "Do you hear their ether engines? Don't let them take me! Pre-Adamic water spirits, animal phantoms, shapes with no inner mobility. Follow the water road to the worlds below. Deep lakes are the elevator down, rivers and streams the windows."

Suddenly, horror seized him. "Green fog is coming! Quick, call the green man! Put poppy seeds in my grave! Boil my head in vinegar! Chain me with wild roses to my grave! Bury me at the crossroads! Infrasound wants to carry you away! *Denn die Todten reiten schnell . . .*" He fell to his knees and began stirring something invisible.

Ray mumbled, "Man, he is *gone*."

"Can't we do something?" Mannie asked.

"Like what?" Thomas asked over the Tom O'Bedlam din. "In the Middle Ages and native America, the possessed wandered from town to town with messages from other dimensions and were fed, clothed, and washed in humble regard for their sacrifice."

"Baal, Bel, Baalzebub, Beltane," *rasta* man shouted. "He is coming back, you know." He stared at Thomas. "Hilarion says protons are escape points from 4D into 3D. When their potential is exhausted, their rotation reverses and we perceive them as electrons that then attempt to escape from 3D to 4D. You know, Thomas—

proton, electron, 4th dimension, proton, electron . . .”

Thomas was flabbergasted. “He knew my name. And Hilarion . . .”

Baby Rose had refilled her bowl with oatmeal, laced it with honey and milk, and now walked toward Tom O'Bedlam. Like a tender mother, she crouched in front of him and slowly brought a spoonful of oatmeal up to his twisted lips. Patiently, she waited until he opened his mouth, chewed, and swallowed, wiping the milk that had dribbled into his filthy beard. When he had eaten it all, Mannie filled the bowl again and Baby Rose fed him again, then poured water on his grimy hands, gently soaping and washing and rinsing them, then served him tea, placing the cup of warm mint and honey liquid in his now clean hands, bidding him drink, which for her he did.

The pilgrims gazed in awe. Tears coursed down Seven's face. Baby Rose in her innocence had done what she had been afraid to.

When he finished his tea, Tom O'Bedlam stood. Struggling like Ophiuchus with the beings torturing his body, he reached for Baby Rose's hands and forced his mouth to say, “God free you.” So arduous was his effort that his hands flew from her as he once again gave himself over to the Legion devouring him. Twisting grotesquely, he leaped and yelled as he raced back into the desert, shouting, “Believe nothing the spirits say! They lie. Many different worlds and dimensions move through you like a river. Qabala calls them *qliphothic* entities, Christianity demons, Tibetans *tulpas* in black, Indians coyotes. Crowley opened the door! Beware, beware . . .”

Later in the morning, the pilgrims were cruising into tiny Ash Fork when Vince cried, “Stop!”

Thomas pulled over and the Caddy followed suit, after which they all gathered in front of the post office window where the film *Flight of Apollo 11: The Eagle Has Landed* was looping on a television monitor.

“Good eye, man,” Thomas said to Vince. “Now, the question is: Did the U.S. actually go to the Moon? Watch the astronauts' shadows and blue-sky footage in deep space. How could astronauts in spacesuits walk on the Moon in full sunlight and absorb 256°F surrounded by a vacuum? NASA assures us that the Moon has no atmosphere and therefore no molecules bumping around. Neither air-conditioned nor water-cooled spacesuits would work in a vacuum because a vacuum is a perfect insulator. Why didn't they cook like turkeys in foil? NASA will probably backtrack with something like the astronauts found ice in the Moon craters, almost as absurd as water-cooling spacesuits, given that fresh water weighs 62 pounds per cubic foot. Later, they complained about how cold they'd been, probably due to the AC units on the movie set.

"And where is the engine inside the Lunar Lander?" he railed. "No, this footage was filmed in the Lunar Lander training simulator. If we were at the Smithsonian, we could measure an astronaut suit and the hatch. And those gloves. NASA claims the spacesuits and gloves were pressurized at 5 psi over 0 psi vacuum, but the gloves in the film weren't pressurized because if they had been, the astronauts couldn't have used their hands and fingers normally. On the *real* lunar surface surrounded by vacuum, they should have decompressed and died.

"Look at how perfect the lunar surface beneath the landing module is. Where's the evidence of 10,000-pound reverse-thrust rockets? And footprints result from weight-displacing air or moisture in dirt, dust or sand. And when the LEM leaves the Moon, zero exhaust. And what's this about stars can't be photographed in space? Yuri Gagarin said the stars were astonishingly brilliant."

The Colonel stood watching, pounding yet another nail into the coffin of his years in the military. The Apollo program had obviously been an elaborate cover for military R&D and deployment of space-based weapons. Bases on the Moon would be advantageous, but no way would the military *he* knew make such acquisitions public. Thomas was right: the Apollo program had been a circus for the masses. And there was von Braun laughing and congratulating himself.

Over Ash Fork, a geostationary satellite was blinking intelligently as it recorded the pilgrims' odyssey.

The pilgrims decided to splurge on a Sunday afternoon dinner at the Escalante Hotel in the train station. Walking toward the hotel, Ray sang—

> *Do yuh hear that whistle down the line?*
> *I figure that it's engine number 49,*
> *She's the only one that'll sound that way*
> *On the Atchison, Topeka and the Santa Fe.*

In the restaurant, tourists and locals having Sunday dinner were chewing over bits and pieces of Americana. Two men with crewcuts were comparing notes on the archæoastronomical observatory at Casa Grande south of Phoenix near Coolidge; a geologist was checking his U.S. Geological Survey charts of ancient Hohokam Salt River canals; a husband and wife were puzzling over the swords and crosses near Tucson with Latin and Hebrew inscriptions reading, *Jehovah, Peace, Mighty Empire*; a German woman was reading a brochure about Arizona Territory and how Texas John Slaughter heard a buzz in his head whenever he was near danger, his guardian angel having promised he'd die in bed and not in a gunfight, which he did in 1922. Reporters from the Arizona Project and Investigative Reporters and Editors were heatedly discussing the murder of *Arizona Republic* reporter Don Bolles, blown up on June 2, 1976 for sniffing around the state racing commission and Senator Barry Goldwater's involvement in drugs and land fraud.

After ordering, the pilgrims eavesdropped on three generations at a nearby table.

"As I recall," the oldest man was saying to his grown son, "once the North American Union was on its way, a new Constitution was rolled out, obviously written beforehand in 1970 in Santa Barbara, California at the Center for the Study of Democratic Institutions—"

Thomas and Seven raised their eyebrows at each other.

241

"—calling for ten Homeland districts with appointed governors subject to an overarching President whose powers were considerable, now that he and his Cabinet would serve a 9-year term." He began ticking off changes on his fingers. "Then there was the regulatory branch that shared governance with private industry; no more Supreme Court; Senators chosen by the governors, not elected; two Vice Presidents, one for general affairs, the other for internal; and no more Bill of Rights."

"Passed in the dead of night," his adult son shook his head.

"When was that?" the boy asked.

The boy's father and grandfather looked at him from a great distance, recalling the crisis that had followed from the shock doctrine of disaster capitalism squeezing the last drops of lifeblood from the American people.

The grandfather ran his hand over his grandson's tousled head. "Just after you were born. You're going to live in a different world and it's our job to prepare you for it." He grabbed the check from his son and the three got up and left.

The eavesdroppers across the aisle realized that the three must be from the future and until their food arrived talked a mile a minute about what a North American Union might mean.

Private industry and government running the country out in the open! Ray recalled a conversation he'd had in Oakland after a Black Muslim meeting with a brother in Malcolm X glasses. They both had reservations about Communism, but the brother had taken his thinking a step further. "The ghost of Trotsky hovers over Washington, DC in the link between a Bolshevik left and a Republican corporate right. What is Communism but militant internationalism, Ray? CAPINTERN = COMINTERN, my man. Trotskyites believe in the permanent revolution that the United States and its post-World War Two affiliation with Nazi International have been undergoing since 1952 . . ."

CAPINTERN = COMINTERN. With the NAU piece, Ray

could see how it would transition. The Central Committee would be First World nations in a big trade organization with fat cat global corporations manipulating money and taking over; the National Security Agency (NSA) in league with Interpol and an international star chamber posing as an international court would take the place of the KGB; non-government organizations (NGOs), foundations, and brain banks would be the subordinate committees. fear and coercion "democratic"-style would begin with a manipulated media, deception, and psyops, and only gradually graduate to outright fear and coercion.

As the paradigm changed, the Constitution would become increasingly irrelevant. Already, business-minded Trotskyites in the Republican Party were showing their internationalist permanent revolution and war—not so much the local beer-belly guys hoping for some teenage titty and a leg up in their careers, but certainly militant utopian Synarchists with bloodlines back to the Jacobins and Stuarts. *Illuminists*, like the man in the San Francisco bus terminal said—Freemason magicians transforming the chaos they engineer into the order they want. *Ordo ab chao*, corporate power employing controlled chaos. Communism and socialism were just two more tools in the Illuminist tool bag to merge under capitalism's banner. Boards of directors and Chairman Mao wrapped up with a neat little bow of democratic rhetoric.

Militant internationalism like that of Trotskyite James Burnham who left the Socialist Workers Party (Social Democrats USA) and joined the rabid CIA, then wrote for the *National Review*. Soon, Republican extremes would spring from Social Dems. SDUSA today, ultra-conservative tomorrow. Thesis, antithesis, synthesis—the end justifying the means. Trotskyites in conservative masks digging one Third World enemy after another out of the woodpile, all the while waging perpetual revolution and war. Change flags, not goals. From left to right, get it? *Technique*. Communism as Satan, mortal enemy of democracy today, but tomorrow China would be bosom buddies with the Western powers that paid for their revolution, just as they paid for the Russian revolution. Now, Socialist Workers Party were the good guys in the antiwar movement, but that was just technique, too. Influence, money, and power transform black into white and white into black. Nothing new under the Sun.

Ray got up and strode out of the restaurant. The pilgrims looked at each other and shrugged: he was moody. Mannie got up to go and look for him while the others watched out the window as the *Hassayampa Flyer* steamed into the station.

Mannie found Ray leaning against the wall outside the kitchen back door, toking up with the Black Indian line cook.

"Nines, man, look for the 9's," the cook was saying as Mannie leaned against the wall beside Ray. "John Lennon was born on October 9, 1940, and his and Yoko Ono's son was born October 9, 1975. John met Yoko on November 9, 1966—that's 9/9/66 in the Julian, four 9's, get it? Lennon met Beatles manager Brian Epstein on November 9, 1961—that's two 19's and two 9's—and *Rolling Stone* ran his picture on the front cover of its first issue on November 9, 1967, then re-printed it 33 years later on November 9, 2000. Three times three is *nine*."

Mannie was spellbound. He watched the cook inhale while talking.

"*Revolution No. 9* followed Paul's repeated refrain in 'Cry Baby Cry,' *Can you take me back where I came from?* Then comes endless backmasking of symphonic pieces, violins, mellotron, opera. When chanting *number nine* fourteen times is played backwards, it sounds like *Turn me on, dead man.*—You know: Paul in '66. Yeah." He finally exhaled.

Mannie heard someone in the kitchen whisper, "*No news is good news and this is your golden handshake. This is hallucination and these faces are in a dream. A computer-generated environment a fantasy island you can dooooo anything and not have to face the consequences. This is your golden handshake. You can put us in freeze frame, you can touch whoever you want, you can move us around into compromising positions, strip us naked, screw whoever although technically we will be frozen to the touch and SIT BACK DOWN AGAIN AND PRESS PLAY LIKE NOTHING HAS HAPPENED.*" Mannie peeked around the corner into the kitchen. No one was there.

The Black Indian cook inhaled again and passed the joint to Ray. To Mannie, he said, "That's Radiohead in the kitchen, man, telling it like it is.—So there's the Church of Satan Council of the Trapezoid or Council of Nine, the Order of Nine Angles, and of course the Argenteum Astrum or Silver Star—you know, with the two A's and two dot-dot-dot pyramids, and three times three is nine, right? And the Silver Star is Sirius and its number is 9, and the Secret Chiefs maybe from the Masonic Lodge called the Brotherhood of the Golden Dawn that first said *Sieg Heil! Sieg Heil!* All of them connected with Sirius and appearing astrally as hawks.

"So take your pick for the Nine! Order of the Quest, the JASON Society, the Roshaniya, Knights Templar, Knights of Malta, Knights of Columbus, Jesuits, Masons, Ancient and Mystial Order of the Rosae Crucis, Illuminati, Nazis, Bolshevists, Zionists, Executive of the Council on Foreign Relations, the Group, Brotherhood of the Dragon, Royal Institute of International Affairs, Trilateral Commission, Bilderberg Group, Open Friendly Secret Society, the Russell Trust, Skull & Bones, Scroll & Key, Book & Snke, Wolf's Head, Berzelius, Porcellian, the Order . . . All outposts of the European Synarchy movement."

He exhaled before beginning a little military New Age history. "The Council of Nine directed from France endorsed the Fraternitas Rosae Crucis doctrines. One of the Council of Nine was Arthur Young, inventor of the Bell helicopter rotor. He played taped revelations about aliens in secret bases in San Francisco at a parapsychology research meeting. And Gay Luce founded the Nine Gates Mystery School for working on the energy bodies, affiliated with the Institute of Noetic Sciences and Stanford Research Institute. From the Round Table Foundation in '48 to Nine Gates. *Star Trek: The Motion Picture* in 1979 came from the Nine. So did episodes of *Deep Space Nine* and *Star Trek: The Next Generation.*

"And guess what? They were all connected to the Kennedy assassination. Ruth Forbes Paine was married to Arthur Young, and Michael and Ruth Hyde Paine were Oswald's benefactors." His black eyes shone as he counted on his long fingers. "Remember Henry and Claire Boothe Luce? Henry Luce and Allen Dulles were lovers of Mary Bancroft who was best friends with Ruth Forbes Paine and probably *her* friend Dimitri von Mohrenschildt.

"Then there's the Egypt thing." He flicked through his fingers. "Atum, Shu, Tefnut, Geb, Nut, Osiris, Isis, Set, and Nepthys. Egyptair Flight 990 on Halloween 1999 crashed off Massachusetts at Newport, Rhode Island 50 miles south of Nantucket at 1:19, en route from New York to Cairo. Eighteen crew dead, 199 passengers. Fifty-four elderly on board on the *Grand Circle* tour.—Get it? 6 times 9, two nine's." He grinned. "The Heliopolitan Ennead is the *Aurea Catena*, man, the Golden Homeric Chain of wise men linking Heaven and Earth. Masonic Satanic, man, sacrificial offerings to Old Saturn, Father Time, the old millennium reborn." He grinned, toked, and passed the roach to Ray.

But he wasn't done yet, not by a longshot. Looking up and down the alley, he gestured to Mannie to come close. With terrible marijuana-onion breath, he exhaled. "Fuck the Secret Chiefs. There's other 9's I'm more worried about, like the Commission on the Ballistic Missile Threat to the United States—*nine*, man. And the Secretary of Defense and NSA working for the Navy's MITRE Corporation, SAIC, Lockheed Martin, generals at Aerospace Corporation, Booze, Allen & Hamilton, Smiths Industries—British—SY Technology, Scowcroft, Vulcan. Big military contractors have run this country since 1939, when Niels Bohr said the United States would have to be turned into a factory in order to build an atomic bomb."

He took a last hit from the roach. "*Nine* directorates with friendly names like Field Activities, Counter-intelligence and Law Enforcement, Behavioral Sciences." He winked. "Budget and size classified, no congressional oversight. They're the new

COINTELPRO data-miners deciding about all the Talon spy reports—Threat and Local Observation Notice 'dots'—on suspected domestic terrorists, contributors to charities and causes, activist and anti-globalist organizations. They read the Air Force Eagle Eyes reports and run real-time Joint Protection Enterprise Network (JPEN) intelligence and law enforcement shit. Then it goes to NORTHCOM and everybody else." He jabbed Mannie in the ribs. "*Enterprise*, man, get it? It's *them*, watching *everyone*. And don't bother whining about the Privacy Act of 1974. All that is *gone*, man." He whipped out a little black comb from his back pocket and held it over his top lip. "Heil Hitler."

Mannie smiled wanly, not sure if he was joking.

The cook looked around again, then leaned in for a final bad-breath whisper. "But it's not just the listeners accessing your phone calls, reading your email and your mind. It's the dogs of war coming to your house—FBI, military intelligence, it doesn't matter anymore—men in black with guns who don't need to wave a piece of paper in your face saying they can charge you with treason, terrorist sabotage, economic espionage, whatever. MIBs are just one long continuum of professional terrorists since the zobop in Haiti zomming around the back roads in black *auto-tigre* cars, motor-zobops projecting a blue beam to entrance their abductees." He gripped Mannie's arm. "Blue beams mean they don't even need to come in your house anymore. Remote mind control, man, via digital and microprocessor-based systems run by Homeland Security's *nine* federal contract research centers like RAND, MITRE, Lincoln Laboratory, and ANSER Institute doing R&D through the Homeland Security Institute. They're *all* the Nine, man, and MITRE runs the JASONs." He looked up to the heavens. "You hear me, Saint Lennon?" To Mannie, he said, "Tell your Mayan friend to mark my words in his Book of Memory."

Mannie stared at him. How did he know about Vince and his chronicle?

The cook gobbled the roach and started back inside, his dope break over. Mannie looked around for Ray, but he was gone, and when he stepped back into the kitchen, the cook was gone, too, and the grills were spotless. On the wall over the stove was a grease-stained Richard Brautigan verse from 1970—

33-1/3 sized
lions are roaring at the black gates of Fame
with jaws that look like record company courtesans
brushing their teeth
with would-be rock and roll stars
in motel bathrooms
with a perfect view of hot car roofs
in the just-signed-up
afternoon

Just too, too trippy, Mannie thought. He'd ask Ray about the cook but already figured Ray hadn't even been there. Route 66—inverted 9's—was trippier than trip.

Later, after they'd all finished feasting on food they weren't sure was real at the Escalante Hotel and were on their way out of town, Mannie freaked out over the movie theater marquee reading *Gene Roddenberry's Deep Space Nine*. As he rapped about what the Deep Space Nine phantom cook had said and Vince in the bus took notes, Syd Barrett sang "Long Gone" from the radios—

And I stood very still by the windowsill
And I wondered for those I love still,
And I cried in my mind where I stand behind . . .

They reminisced about Syd flipping out when he'd been experimenting with the sonic possibilities of dissonance, distortion, and feedback.

248

Ray got out his Zippo lighter and plucked a few notes to "Long Gone," doing a rendition of Syd's technique of sliding the lighter up and down the fret-board but through an old echo box or Binson delay units to create the otherworldly sounds Pink Floyd was still known for. "Strange how Syd went to Cambridge High School along with Roger Waters and David Gilmour," Ray said, "and his mother ran that boarding house that became the Cambridge University hangout. Syd returned there when the cuckoo bird moved into his screen door mind for good."

"Yeah, sad," Mannie said over the two-way. "The 1967 American tour was the first and last for Syd." Then he added quietly, "And Paul is dead."

All the talk about Syd made Seven think of Barbara and Rhea and wonder if they were all right.

In the bus, Ray diddled with the radio until he picked up KMUD in Humboldt County where a calm male voice was expounding on Groom Lake in the 1980s. ". . . Bob Lazar's physics clearance was said to be 38 levels above Q. Bob worked in Los Alamos in the Eighties before being transported from Groom Lake in a bus with blacked out windows to work at Area S4 on Nellis Air Force Range, Papoose Lake area. Lazar claims that vectored craft technology works on the principle of amplifying gravitational waves. In May 1989, he appeared on KLAS-TV and spilled the beans about Gravity A and Gravity B and an element called *moscovium (Mc)*, a synthetic heavy metal with the atomic number of 115 and a melting point of 400°C or 750°F. Apparently, part of the weightlessness essential to antigravity technology is a chilled superconducting disc that levitates and revolves over magnets. Depending upon the size and velocity of the superconducting disc (5,000 revolutions per minute minimum) and the weight of the disc to be lifted, gravity's effect can be virtually cancelled—so-called gravitational shielding.

"Hundreds of discs a few inches in diameter have been found in places like the Wonderstone Silver Mine in the Western

Transvaal, South Africa in a layer of pyrophyllite rock at least 2.8 billion years old. Made of a nickel-steel alloy, the discs discovered were at one time able to rotate on their own power.

"Publicly, Boeing and British Aerospace laugh at antigravity, but *Jane's Defense Weekly* writer Nick Cook knows better. In his 2002 book *The Hunt for Zero Point*, he says that the absence of discussion about antigravity aircraft in present day science indicates the presence of a vast black world, not that such devices don't exist or only exist by virtue of 'alien technology.' They're out there, folks, and they're ours."

The voice the pilgrims had already come to associate with KRMA signed off with, "Thanks to KHUM for transponding our KRMA signal." And off the radio went.

Ecstatic, Thomas cried "2002!" and stepped on the gas to pass the Caddy. Vince scribbled and Ray howled, leaning out the passenger window to make the peace sign to Seven, the Colonel, Mannie, Baby Rose, and the world at large. "KRMA spells *karma*!" he shouted. "We're on the hiiiiiiigh-way, yeow!"

Later in the afternoon, they sighted the shiny glint of a vectored craft bobbing and weaving in the Southwest sky before zipping straight up at out-of-sight velocity.

They're out there, folks.

43

The Threshold Beckons

It's true we used the same methods as the Mafia
But you know there are people who think
Yitzhak Rabin was a kind of Messiah
Like King Shaul Mashiach Ben Yosef, Mashiach Ben Yosef.
The Messiah is coming,
The Messiah is on the phone.

- David Orbach, "Who Murdered Yitzhak Rabin?" 2002

There exists a shadowy Government with its own Air Force, its own Navy, its
own fundraising mechanism, and the ability to pursue its own ideas of national
interest, free from all checks and balances, and free from the law itself.

- Senator Daniel K. Inouye, former chair U.S. Senate MK-
ULTRA hearings, 1977; during Iran-Contra Hearings

I still feel that the UFO phenomenon represents a manifestation of a reality that
transcends our current understanding of physics. It is not the phenomenon itself
but the belief it has created that is manipulated by human groups with their
own objectives.

- Jacques Vallee, *Messengers of Deception*, 1979

According to the 3rd century BCE Egyptian historian Manetho,
The reign of the Sages of Atlantis was 13,900 years ago. Ever since, Egyptian
souls—ever loyal to their illustrious founders—had been flying westward

on the wings of their *ka*, seeking the portals of Atlantis today known as the Hudson River, the Lawrence, the Potomac, the Mississippi, the Coatzacoalcos. For them, these were the Elysian Fields, the Sacred Western Isles where mighty corn grew, where the dead fed Earth forces. The Egyptian priests who wrapped the dead in linen knew they had no more need of physical bodies but were still in need of *soul* bodies. Thus mummified skeletons of Egypt retain their form while those found in the Indian mounds from the Great Lakes to the Gulf crumble to dust once exposed to the air.

On the wings of their *ka*, the dead entered the old outposts of the great colonial empire that once ruled the Earth before sinking beneath the waves long before Egyptian greatness. Some chose to enter the great birth canal of the Potomac where Freemasons founded their capital city of the New Atlantis, the District of Columbia, to establish themselves as Gatekeepers of the eastern entry to the New Atlantis. Other newly dead sped into the great G of the Caribbean Sea and up the Mississippi River, the great southern birth canal that Mound Builders and Phoenician copper merchants followed into the interior of the Atlantean outpost. Up the Mississippi to the Missouri and Yellowstone Rivers, east into Ohio, west to Oregon, souls flying upriver to Mounds of the dead in the Dakotas, Minnesota, Iowa, Illinois, and Indiana, where the Mississippi and Ohio merge; flying to Cahokia between Alton and East St. Louis, a mound as large as Cheops, rising 97 feet with square sides 700 and 500 feet, its summit flattened into a platform.

In Ohio alone, there are 10,000 tumuli. The mounds are not cones but pyramids with sides pointing to the cardinal points; in Hopetown, a walled square and circle, each with an area of exactly twenty acres. Fort Ancient on the Little Miami, between four and five miles in circumference with an embankment twenty feet high, could have held a garrison of 60,000 men and their families. From Southern New York through Central Ohio to the Wabash River, the Mound Builders built chains of double-walled fortifications. The combined pyramid-cross earth structure in Newark, Ohio, made with sun-dried brick and rushes, is two miles square. In Ohio, sculptures of manatees and toucans, seashells from the Gulf, obsidian from Mexico, pearls from the Atlantic. Did the Mound Builders then migrate south to Mexico? Were they the Nahuas who called the Mississippi Valley *Hue Hue Tlapalan*, the old, old red land?

Agent Simon Iff and his partner Didy were unaware of the dead all around them, but Iff had certainly known more than his share of death dealing. Driving deep in the north Arizona desert, he was thinking of all the counterintelligence presentations he'd sat through. Initially, he'd been surprised by how well organized public assassinations were, how they too followed a protocol with nary a hitch or a glitch. Since then, when he heard about an assassination like Lamumba or a domestic hit like Malcolm X or the Kennedy brothers or King, he could listen to a few news broadcasts and read *US News & World Report* and pretty much tell whose fingerprints were on the hit—the Agency, Mob, Big Oil, or DISC. Mossad, Kidon, Shin Bet, and the military intelligence unit Aman were all Agency, too, given that Israel and the U.S. swapped favors. Mossad Zionist hotheads were hard to work with, but their motto was bold: *With clandestine terrorism, we will conduct war.* Far more truthful than *And the truth shall set you free.* The OSS/CIA and MI6 set up Mossad in the early days and now the child had become the teacher.

Suddenly, the radio went all scratchy. Didy smacked it with the heel of his hand a couple of times and a British broadcast wriggled through the white noise some said was star transmission noise.

". . . I repeat: Israeli Prime Minister Yitzhak Rabin has been assassinated by Yigal Amir, a young man affiliated with Eyal, a radical anti-government organization with only one member, leader Avishai Raviv, who, it turns out, is a Shabak officer assigned to infiltrate right-wing movements. Despite Raviv's close association with Amir and his connections to Hamas, an extremist Arab organization, and despite the fact that Raviv was at the rally where Rabin was shot, the Knesset has announced that Raviv will skate free. It is the old lone gunman story no one should believe, given that the first words Amir uttered when apprehended were, 'Why are you handcuffing me? I did my job, now you do yours.'"

Agent Iff noted the synchronicity between his thoughts and the broadcast. The assassination followed the counterintelligence handbook to a T: blame a programmed military patsy handled by a "cult leader" undercover intelligence officer while the real shooter was probably waiting in the limousine. (A high-level kill was never left to an amateur, no matter how well programmed.) Next would be intimidation of witnesses, a tight rein on the press, removal and destruction of sensitive data, etc.

The British voice signed off with ". . . and gratitude to KRMA from BBC Israel, 5 November 1995," after which a hard-edged Hebrew song began.

Iff's brain kicked in. *1995? Yitzhak Rabin?* But the prime minister elected last year was the Iron Lady Golda Meir. Who the hell was Yitzhak Rabin? He glanced at his almost useless sidekick who was listening closely to the song, recording every note and word as he had been programmed to do, his feet tapping. *1995.* Iff couldn't radio anyone from out here in the middle of nowhere, but in the next town he'd call the Bureau or Agency for a reality check.

"What's the song say, Didymus?" Didy knew more languages than he could count.

Didy translated in perfect pitch. "'But you know it's the law of democracy, the law of sod-om-ocracy. I didn't want to kill Yitzhak, Oh please don't kill me. Who killed Yitzhak Rabin? And oh my G-d, why did he go to Heaven?'"

The inconspicuous sedan rolled along 66 through the desert of mysteries, in quest of a town and a phone. The spook had been spooked.

West of Flagstaff, Thomas was contemplating the non-local universe that he, unlike Agent Iff, felt depended upon him in some mysterious way to evolve, his job being to unlock the signs and wonders

254

now zapping him with unbelievable velocity and self-reflect. *Thought* was critical to evolving a well-aligned self-reflection of the non-local universe. Thinking's matter-as-energy nature converted pulse frequencies to meaning. This seemed to Thomas to be the highest manifestation of human psychic activity. Next to him, Vince was scribbling away in his notebook; behind him, Ray was reading *The Origin of Russian Communism* by Nicolas Berdyaev. Briefly, Thomas thought of the havoc that a dedicated satellite pulsing his body like a radio tower could do to his thinking.

Out here in the desert with almost no distraction, KRMA was guiding them like a pillar of fire through superspace worlds stitched together at nodes, moving in wavelike sync. Classical physics had been concerned with outer laws, not inner laws, until being blasted open by the Einstein-Podalsky-Rosen observation that the outcome of experiments are affected by the observer and his preconceptions. Thomas contemplated quantum phase entanglement. Yes, the universe of matter and energy was certainly entangled. Gamow posited that a billiard ball could go into two pockets at once in the 3rd dimension and in the 4th dimension. Separate particles A and B, send B to Chicago or Timbuktu, and whatever the observer does to A will happen to B faster than the speed of light, their only bond being that at one time they were together. Then along came the Irishman John Stewart Bell's theorem and *voila!* the non-local universe was born in the minds of thousands of scientists.

It was thus shortsighted to assume that all life exists only at the very bottom of the atmosphere on the surface of the Earth. The oxygen-carbon dioxide exchange was limited to this range, but what about other life forms not dependent upon that exchange? Above the skinny little troposphere was the 30-mile stratosphere and the ozone layer absorbing UV rays to keep *biós* creatures from percolating into a scorching death. Then the ionosphere 37 to 620 miles above the Earth, *iono* from the Greek *ienai* meaning *to go*, like the electrically charged atom, *ion*. To go where? Beyond the ionospheric winds into the magnetosphere and velvety dark space. The Earth was a gigantic magnet capturing charged particles from the Van Allen Radiation Belt extending 4,800 to 32,000 miles beyond the Earth; Explorer 1 had confirmed this in 1958, about the time the Van Allen Belt was being nuclear blasted to kingdom come.

Thomas reviewed the points of light they'd seen turning in a gyre, then blinking out. Before he'd turned Skull & Bones down, he had gone everywhere under his uncle's wing and had believed that war was a necessary evil waged to protect American freedoms. Air Force intelligence was in charge of "the UFO thing," Navy intelligence of psychological operations, Army intelligence of consolidating police and military at home and abroad. War was a blood-soaked international business. Phantom or no, Sheikh Rahman had spoken the truth.

Thomas had never seen discs in hangars on Air Force bases, but he'd gotten his first whiff of them when his uncle took him to a talk given by a Harvard psychiatrist at Wright Patterson Air Force Base—"one of ours, through MIT," his uncle had confided. Thomas had wondered how a full-grown man could belong to others, but one day he would know only too well. As they had walked away from a Rockefeller he'd introduced Thomas to, his uncle had whispered that "Rockybucks" were behind the research going on "downstairs." He'd then flashed his top security day pass and guided Thomas to the back row, nodding to various MIT and Massachusetts General Hospital MK-ULTRA people, a JASON Group rear admiral and MITRE Corporation man. Further up front were NICAP (National Investigations Committee on Aerial Phenomena), UFO special interest groups, and Project Blue Book brass like Major General John Samford, Director of Air Force Intelligence, who in 1952 had said in UFOs they were seeing "parallel spiritism," and Commander Randall Boyd from Wright Pat who sent jets to intercept the plasma discs that invariably faded when approached.

Thomas remembered the terms *Stargate, abductees, ETs,* and *ecopsychology* from the Harvard psychiatrist's speech but little else. He noted the presence of other boys his age and older and the occasional girl—a new generation under construction. Some of the girls looked tranced-out like Baby Rose, and he'd been puzzled by the reference to abductees being like "endangered species" that had to be moved to a safe place and "hurt for their own good." No one was laughing or shocked.

But it was for the meeting *after* the lecture that most of the illustrious attendees had come. The first Pugwash Conference on Science and World Affairs was about to convene in India, and UFOs were being taken very seriously. Apparently, ancient chroniclers reported that when Alexander the Great invaded India over 2,000 years ago, he'd been attacked by flying fiery "shields," and when Mohenjo-daro in the Indus Valley was excavated, they'd found black lumps of fused glass—like what was found at Hiroshima and Nagasaki post-1945. The November 21, 1950 Smith Memo would certainly be discussed. Wilbert B. Smith, a senior radio engineer with the Canadian Department of Transport, had proposed to the controller of telecommunications that a formal study on the harmonics of the Earth's magnetic field was needed because UFOs were using it for materialization, propulsion, and de-materialization. Smith stressed giving UFOs a higher classification than the H-bomb, given that the saucers were connected to "mental phenomena."

While Thomas was thinking about all of this from years before, in the Cadillac Seven began telling the Colonel about the dream she'd had the previous night. The two-way was open, of course, given that she hadn't had the opportunity to discuss it with Thomas, what with Tom O'Bedlam and all the rest coming hot and heavy:

She and Baby Rose had been cruising over a phantom Washington, DC. Various geomancy shapes inscribed into city architecture by founding Freemasons were lit up, perhaps even for her aerial benefit. First was a *Square* marked by the Washington Monument, the obelisk that was the 14th temple of Osiris—the phallus Isis sought in the Nile Delta now in the swampy Potomac site of the New Atlantis capital on Chesapeake Bay. (Alexandria, Virginia was named after its Egyptian namesake.) On the west side of the Capitol Dome, two

Romanesque women in marble huddled together: America weeping on History's shoulder. At the top of the Capitol Dome stood Freedom with her sheathed sword, shield, and laurel wreath, her eagle helmet not so much Native American as representing the warrior goddess Athena, patron of the Achaean rulers of the Mediterranean before Rome's ascendancy. The Dome, once called the Temple of Liberty, made a *Circle* like that of St. Peter's Basilica in Rome.

With the center of the Circle as a Compass pivot, Baby Rose and she circumscribed an Arc from the White House in the north to the Jefferson Memorial in the south. Within that arc, a T-Square ran from the Dome west along the Mall and past the Washington Monument before cutting north to the White House, the Mall being the Ruler measuring both Madison and Jefferson Streets, and Constitution and Independence Streets from 3rd Street to the Lincoln Memorial, with a blip at the Smithsonian Castle. *Madison and the Constitution in the north, Jefferson and Independence in the south . . .*

Pennsylvania and New York Avenues cut an X through the White House and created a common apex for two isosceles Triangles or Pyramids, the Mall being the base of one and K Street between Washington Circle and Mount Vernon Square the base of the other. The Ellipse at the southern entry to the White House grounds looked for all the world like an eye, while another eye looked north from the White House, a diamond-like eye with four points: the White House, Washington Circle, Mount Vernon Square, and the National Geographic Society six blocks north of the White House on 16th. The same whisperer she had encountered in Veracruz whispered, *The eye before the White House, between the State and Justice Departments, is the outer eye that sees outer things, but the all-seeing Eye of Horus sees what is* inner.

In the dream, Seven studied the diamond configuration. Due south of the White House and the National Geographic Society, equidistant from both the Washington Circle and Mount Vernon, was the Jefferson Memorial in the Tidal Flats. The three points made another isosceles Triangle or Pyramid, only inverted. What if the State and Justice Departments were the base of yet another Triangle or Pyramid, with a *northern* apex aligned with both the Jefferson Monument and National Geographic Society. Where would such an apex be?

She aligned the Jefferson Monument with the National Geographic Society and looked north. There it was, thirteen blocks from the White House: the majestic, illuminated Masonic House of the Temple at 1733 Sixteenth Street Northwest, guarded by two Egyptian Sphinxes. Architect John Russell Pope had designed the Jefferson Memorial, too. *This* was the site from which the never-sleeping Eye of Horus oversaw the measure of the nation's capital; *this* was the capstone of the present Pyramid of power. Together with the inverted Jeffersonian pyramid of the past, it made a Hexagon, a six-pointed Star of David.

So the measure of the nation had been taken with Circle, Compass, T-Square, Ruler, Triangle, Pyramid, and Hexagon. But where was the Pentagram? She looked southwest. Near the Jefferson Memorial was the 14th Street Bridge, and over that bridge was the Pentagon built in the fires of World War Two, as was the Jefferson Memorial. From the air, its size was mind-boggling. Why, the Capitol Dome would take up just one of its five sectors. In the apocalyptic light of the dream, its steel-reinforced concrete and copper shimmered like a five-sided saucer powering up to lift off at any moment.

"No wonder the Yippies and 50,000 people tried to levitate it," Seven chuckled. Mannie was leaning forward to hear every word.

In the dream, she and Baby Rose had gone deep beneath the Pentagon and into a large dimly lit chamber. *You're beneath the War Room,* the whisperer had clarified. There she saw twelve ageing men standing like pillars in a circle under a domed planetarium whose points of light emulated the great warriors ever-moving with the starry heavens: Perseus in the north, Taurus snorting below him on the Ecliptic, the tiny Pleiades riding his back, Orion on the northeast horizon. In the east and west of the chamber stood two statues of handsome youths in tunics with strange little hats with forward-curving peaks, their legs demurely crossed. Both held torches, one high in the east, the other low in the west.

The standing old men had aligned themselves with the cardinal directions: in the east, three in Middle Eastern garb; in the west, three in the togas of Old Rome; in the north, three in Waffen SS uniforms; in the south, three in American military Class A's. None noticed Seven's dream presence, so transfixed were they by a battle in progress between a huge bull and a youth in the strange little hat with seven glowing stars on his flying cape. The youth was circling the pawing bull, the glint of a knife at his belt. The bull snorted and bellowed and at last lunged. Unfazed, the youth parried and continued to wear the bull down, proving that size and superiority of strength alone can never withstand individual human cunning, agility, and speed.

At last, the youth obtained the moment he had been seeking. With north to his right and south to his left, he wrestled the bull to the ground and leaped upon him, his left knee bent, his right leg extended. Pulling the great head back toward himself with his left hand, he plunged his dagger into the jugular with his right, all the while looking over his shoulder into the East. As one, the twelve old men cried, "Mithras! Sword of Aries, sign of Mars! Bull of Taurus, sign of Venus! Opener of the seven gates! *Pater! Heliodromus! Perses! Leo! Miles! Cryphius! Corax!* The eighth awaits our effort!" And with that, they set upon the bull slayer with daggers and clubs, and beat and stabbed him until he, like the bull beside him, was slain.

Seven gripped the steering wheel and shot a glance at the Colonel. "It was brutal, Colonel. I felt every blow, every thrust, and doubled over with the pain of the steel sliding in and out of my soft flesh again and again, all the while hearing my cracking bones. I remember thinking, *How cold violence is, how it cracks the heart like ice.*" She shot another glance at him. "Why kill the hero, the bull slayer? And in the Pentagon. What did it mean?"

While listening to her Mithra dream, the Colonel thought of how World War One had lasted four years three months and eleven days. Eight million soldiers were killed, twenty million civilians, twenty million soldiers seriously wounded, three million permanently disabled. Twenty million dollars a day for four years three months and eleven days. He shrugged. "Mithra was born from a generative rock now called the Pentagon. Mithra the Bull-Slayer, intermediary between Ahriman and Ahura Mazdao the Sun God. I'll tell you all about Mithra, but not now." He pointed. "Better slow down; Thomas is pulling over for a hitchhiker."

He was right. She pulled over, content to wait for the bus and the Colonel's exposition. She thought about the Mars men, and now her dream had added Bull-slayers. She pulled the Caddy back onto 66, following the bus.

The lanky blond hitchhiker lugging his electric guitar case turned out to be a Dutchman whose heavily accented command of the King's English was better than that of the pilgrims. Immediately, he rolled a joint from his stash, took a long drag, then offered it around. As usual, Ray was the only one who responded.

Grinning at Ray, the Dutchman said, "You'll like it. It's from Amsterdam." A master at holding down the sweet smoke while talking, he began rapping at lightning speed. "I *love* America. Back in the first days of American rock-and-roll, when country crossed over into blues and rock, there was Robert Johnson, the first 27 Club casualty."

"27 Club?" Ray asked, coughing. "Wow," he intoned weakly, staring at the joint.

Smiling at the prospect of cluing Americans into their own history, the Dutchman took another toke. "Okay, so it all started with Robert Johnson, the black blues man from Hazlehurst, Mississippi, named after the chief engineer for Illinois Central Railroad, who recorded on Columbia's Vocalion label in 1936 and 1937. His music has influenced Bob Dylan, Eric Clapton, the Stones, etc." He shook his blond tresses and exhaled. "A music publisher in Glendale, California now owns the copyright—bought it for next to nothing in 1974 from Johnson's naïve half-sister.

"Robert played all along the Mississippi Delta during the

Depression on both sides of the river, but especially in the juke joints of Helena, Arkansas, where Little Boy Blue, Robert Nighthawk, Elmore James, Honeyboy Edwards, Howlin' Wolf, Calvin Frazier, Memphis Slim Chatman, and Johnny Shines all played. Oh yes, I know them all. But every young man and woman with a gift run the risk of being discovered by men who want to use that gift to their advantage. Ike Zinnerman became Robert's handler, his 'devil' who sent Johnny Shines everywhere with him." The Dutchman nodded sagely while drawing deep on the joint. Holding his breath, he passed it back to Ray.

"Zinnerman was the one who spread the word that Robert had learned to play guitar by sitting on tombstones and had made a pact with the devil. People laugh, but if you substitute 'cult,' 'voodoo priest,' 'psychiatrist,' or 'record corporation' for 'devil,' and then consider his behaviors and lyrics, you have to ask yourself, was that young black man crying for help while people smiled and applauded?" He shook his head sadly and exhaled.

"Robert could hear a tune once and play and sing it to perfection. He never had to practice. Sober, he was moody and erratic, pensive, his strings cut, but after a drink or two he was the life of the party. Sometimes, he would get up and leave in the middle of a performance, as if forgetting the personality who was playing. Was he a voodoo slave? Translate 'sold his soul' into modern terms and what do you have? Bondage to the rock, country, and blues industry, like a lot of musicians today."

The radio kicked on with Martha and the Vandellas prophesying *Nowhere to run, nowhere to hide*. The young men laughed uneasily at the synchronicity, the Dutchman's words ringing true. Ray had cut his chops on Robert Johnson singles and began strumming and singing,

> *I went down to the crossroads and fell down on my knees,*
> *Asked the Lord up above for mercy, save poor Bob if you please.*

West African religion believed Esu to be the guardian of

crossroads, and in the old Celtic religion the unsanctified were buried near crossroads outside of towns. Johnson was buried outside of Greenwood, Mississippi in the Little Zion graveyard off Money Road, a mile from the Three Forks juke joint where Honeyboy Edwards claimed Robert was poisoned—at 27.

The Dutchman fastened the roach clip and lit up. "So Robert is the founder of the 27 Club. Three times nine, 1-3, thirteen, and 27 reversed is 72, a full lifetime. On the Continent, it's common knowledge that cults use numbers as a cipher language, an *argot* that only those in the know or paying attention can read."

Ray exhaled the last toke of Amsterdam he could take, feeling like he'd excarnated. "So Jones, Hendrix, Joplin, Morrison . . ."

The Dutchman said, "Yeah, sure, they all died at 27. I'm surprised you didn't know, unless . . ." His stoned brain got it. "Oh my God," the Dutchman exhaled, "I'm dreaming." And with that he and his guitar and the roach vanished. Poof.

The dreaming Dutchman had been right about Robert Johnson. Demonbreun Bridge connects downtown Nashville with Music Row. The Hank Williams, Jr. Museum on Demonbreun Street housed the 1952 Cadillac convertible in which Hank Williams died. People say the name Demonbreun came from Jacques-Timothée Boucher, Sieur de Montbrun (*Sir Brown Mountain*), first citizen of Nashville. Like crossroads, bridges are associated with spirits, nixies, demons and devils, like in "The Three Billy Goats Gruff." In Yorkshire, England, Dibble's Bridge used to be Devil's Bridge. Anyway, Demonbreun Bridge leads to Music Row, where musicians learn to play and dance to the devil's tune.

Hank Williams first sang at the Grand Ole Opry on June 11, 1949 and was dead at 29 on the Druid feast day of January 1, 1953. Clutched in his hand was his last song, the last line pointing like a finger to *But that's the poison we must pay*. He died at Oak Hill, West Virginia, and was buried in Oakwood Cemetery in Montgomery, Alabama—Celtic oaks like the ones teen idol James Dean had a fatal encounter with at Paso Robles on September 30, 1955.

The $2.8 billion country music industry is rife with crime syndicates and CIA cults. Southern Jurisdiction Freemason Knights of the Golden Circle and Old Time Religion families offer up their golden-throated offspring for tours that double as delivery systems for cocaine, black and white slavery, mind control—whatever makes a buck, with the mayor and sheriff running Nashville's corruption from The Stockyard dinner club.

One has only to look at the shack in which Elvis was born in 1935 in Tupelo, Mississippi, and at the Lodge affiliations of his paternal grandparents in the shack next door that finally led to his handler Colonel Tom Parker and RCA Victor Records' pup listening for its master's voice from the Victrola and the country music syndicate falls into place. Elvis' non-Presbyterian swivel-hips and natural love for people of all colors bridged black and white and opened the door to black performers, bless his Southern heart.

As the devil gave Robert Johnson uncanny guitar skill, he gave Elvis an uncanny two-and- one-third octaves voice, from full-voiced tenor high B on down. Robert could hear a tune once, Elvis could assimilate styles. One black and one white, both born in shacks, both born performers, both isolated and used and murdered. Where'd they get the training that has to shape even native genius? Who lurked in the shadows from their very beginnings to their premature ends? Who sucked them dry until they were unable to make it up and over the hills of loneliness anymore without dosing themselves with alcohol and drugs? Between 1969 and 1977, Elvis gave 1,145 performances. In the end, Dr. Nick's pharmaceuticals got him—Dilaudid, Quaaludes, Amytal—and he died on August 16, exactly 39 years after Robert Johnson, both poisoned by those who figured they own Southern boys and girls born in shacks, black or white.

Tammy Wynette was also born in a Mississippi shack on 5/5/42 and died at 55. She was eight months old when her father died and she was taken from her mama to be raised by her Old Time Religion maternal grandparents who bequeathed to her lifelong stomach pains, painkiller addiction, and hospitals tweaking the golden goose with the golden throat. In her luxury bus *The First Lady*, she toured fifteen days a month, 100,000 miles a year, her Pittsburgh "physician" plying her with drugs, her husband-manager abusing her.

Far above the pilgrims, spy satellites were standing at their revolving posts, communications satellites were bouncing signals, research satellites were spewing data through military channels, and long radio waves were catching rides with AM and FM radio waves like desert air pintos. Whatever Thomas had installed under the dash was doing its magic in the lower and upper frequencies whose carrier waves were delivering military and police bands, international and entirely other, far out stations. Around Los Angeles, it had been a mash, but out in the no man's land of wavering highway mirages, the clarity was uncanny—hundreds if not thousands of transmission bandwidths.

Meanwhile, futuristic America was caught in a Time warp between *now* and the coming War of the Machines. Electronic and magnetic systems were surfing the American GENI (Global Environment for Network Innovations) and European FIRE (Future Internet Research and Experimentation). Lockheed's Commando Solo EC-130E, L3 Communications Integrated Systems' EC-130H Compass Call, and Boeing's RC-135 Rivet Joint were pulsing S^4 (Silent Sound Spread Spectrum) over AM, FM, HF TV, and military bands, broadcasting frequencies of fear and hopelessness in emotion signature clusters. The acoustical heterodyne Medusa was busy broadcasting voices, thoughts, and precognitive dreams to biotelemetric persons on government and corporate lists. Misty would be launched in 1990 by NASA's Atlantis shuttle STS-36 mission to beam voices and thoughts contrived by CIA paranormal orgs to New Age channelers, meditators, and MUFONs. Holosonic Research Labs and American Technology Corporation would direct the satellite "voice of Allah" via Brooks Air Force Base Research Laboratory's Human Effectiveness Directorate into the heads of the latest Middle East enemies via U.S. LRADs rolling through Third World streets. At Marina del Rey, what would become

University of Southern California's Institute for Creative Technologies (ICT) was already busy developing more and more synthetic experiences and mind-fucking mimeses for satellite dissemination.

With the disappearance of the Dutchman, Jim Morrison began singing *The End* on KRMA as Thomas pulled over for another hitchhiker who looked to be no more than fifteen—

Ride the highway west, baby
Ride the snake, ride the snake
To the lake, the ancient lake, baby
The snake is long, seven miles
Ride the snake . . . he's old, and his skin is cold
The west is the best
The west is the best
Get here, and we'll do the rest
The blue bus is callin' us
The blue bus is callin' us
Driver, where you taken' us . . .

It was evident that the new hitchhiker had the intuitive wherewithal to know he was out-of-body dreaming. He looked approvingly around the bus. "Sixties, right?" He laughed, delighted. "A Dutch dude asked me to cruise in to finish up the 27 Club story. I'm from the Nineties—you know, post-Eighties and Reagan? *X Files*?" He laughed again.

Thomas sighed. "Lay it on us."

"Right," the dreamer said. "Brian Jones, Janis, Jimi, Jim Morrison, all 27 and dead in 1970."

Ray stopped picking out tunes. "What?"

Seven recalled how all four had been gathered around Norma Jeane's bed and John Lennon had whispered, *Some of us are dreaming, but we'll all be like Norma Jeane soon.*

The dreamer ticked off more. "Then Clarence White of the

Byrds was 29, hit by a car with a glassy-eyed guy named Yoho Ito behind the wheel in Palmdale on July 14, 1973. Gram Parsons just short of 27 on vernal equinox 1973. The day after Gram, Jim Croce at 29. On July 29, 1974, Cass Elliot of the Mamas and the Papas at 32. Phil Ochs, 35, electronically harassed for his politics, then NSA suicided on April 9, 1976. Elvis in '77, including his alias Jon Burrows. Then John Lennon—"

Mannie was aghast. "Not Lennon."

"—gun shot, December 8, 1980." He looked at Ray's devastated face. "Let's stop there."

"Not yet," Ray said as if he were standing in a windstorm. "Bob Marley?"

"Dead at 36, May 11, 1981, injected with a cancer-producing virus by the CIA. Peter Tosh, other Jamaican radicals . . . too many more." His dream frequency began wavering.

"Wait, don't go," Vince said, writing fast. "What about your time?"

"The big one for me was Kurt Cobain of Nirvana, whose death reads like an *X-Files* script. They found him on April 8, 1994 with three times the normal dose of heroin pumped into his system and a shotgun blast to his head. He'd been dead for three days, which meant on Easter Sunday. Police said overdose and suicide, just like the others." He scoffed. "He'd escaped from the Exodus Recovery Center, a drug rehab in Marina del Ray where Beach Boy Dennis Wilson drowned and the University of Southern California's Institute for Creative Technologies 'manages perceptions,' you know what I mean?

"Cobain's wife Courtney Love was Hank Harrison's daughter, Mr. Grateful Dead with Phil Lesh. When she was little, she'd played with Jerry Garcia's little girl, then somewhere between six and sixteen went multiple and started working for the big, bad Lockheed kind of boys. Harrison used to work at Lockheed, which points to a lot.—Anyway, Courtney hired a Beverly Hills private eye to find Kurt, some say just to make herself look like a concerned wife. Like Yoko and Lennon, she'd married Cobain as a handler. Harrison said she'd watched the Frances Farmer story 32 times.

"Cobain wanted to break away from her and the Star Machine controlling them, so a month before that fatal Easter Sunday, he'd OD'd on Rohypnol and lived. The OD gave the killers the suicide handle they needed.

"And why did he want out of the music industry so bad? In 1999, an NSA engineer threw a document up on the Web—you know about the Web, right? Internet. Computers all over the world connected in a vast information-gossip-disinformation flow—"

Thomas nodded. "Yeah, we know about it: the public version of the military Arpanet. It's not here yet, but even when it comes, the military will keep their own channels for themselves and use yours for surveillance. Don't say anything you don't want them to know on the . . . Web."

The dreamer got it. "Thanks for the tip. Hope I remember when I wake up."

"Hey," Ray nudged, "Cobain."

The dreamer pursed his dream lips. "So the 1999 document details how the NSA's remote 'self-initiated execution,' suicide, works, saying Cobain was a casualty of MK-ULTRA and was terminated because he was writing clues about his victimization into his songs, like Lennon did about McCartney's 1966 death. The engineer who wrote it said that once the NSA torques up the highest level of brainwashing pain, the subject quickly expires. Cobain and probably every other rock star chained to the Star Machine used heroin to numb and slow down the NSA suicide process."

Mannie's mind replayed Radiohead's *technically we will be frozen to the touch and sit back down again and press play like nothing has happened.*

"Did they have that technology when Syd Barrett went under?" Seven asked over the two-way, thinking of Syd singing *And I cried in my mind where I stand behind.*

"Sure. The military's at least one generation ahead of what the public knows."

"Radio implant and satellite?" Thomas asked, pointing up and thinking of the Ludlum book at the Forgeries, Lies and Truth Book Store.

"Yeah, but a doctor in Finland says fully coded electronic brain stimulation, EBS, can pulse signals into the brain in voices and visuals the coders want the target to hear and see. They don't need implants anymore. They just hack right into the brain. All they need are the right frequencies for your brain signature."

"That NSA engineer who tried to let people know," Seven said, "is he still alive?"

The dreamer shrugged. "I don't know. The NSA could have wanted to brag a little on the Web where it wouldn't be taken seriously, the Web being a mix of weirdness and truth. You'll see; you'll have to develop a whole new discernment."

Ray sighed. He needed that new discernment now. Was this dreamer real? Were their minds just picking up his dream frequencies out in the desert?

The dreamer continued. "The night after Kurt was found by an electrician—nice touch, huh?—the lead singer of the Blind Melon on the David Letterman show had drawn a big question mark on his forehead about Kurt's death." He shook his head. "Every big singer or group's got to know they'll be next if they try crying for help."

"Buddy Holly, Ritchie Valens, the Big Bopper, the day the music died—" Seven said.

"—Paul McCartney, Syd Barrett—" Mannie went on.

"No end in sight," Ray choked, swallowing his grief and fury.

The dreamer had all but faded. "Sorry about the bad news. Maybe you can change what's coming, I don't know. Layne Staley of another Seattle group called Alice in Chains was administered an NSA 'suicide' exactly eight years to the day after Cobain for sneaking hints into his songs about how he was a satellite slave like Radiohead. Layne used heroin too to dull the pain." Fading, the dreamer sang—

My gift of self is raped
My privacy is raked
And yet I find
And yet I find
Repeating in my head
If I can't be my own
I'd feel better dead

The dreamer gone, Phil Ochs was finishing a song on the desert airwaves—

Way down in Santiago where they took away our minds,
We cut off all their money until their blood would flow like wine,
Maybe we should ask the question, maybe shed a tear,
But I'll bet you copper pennies it cannot happen here.

"Could we warn them?" Mannie asked over the two-way.

Thomas shrugged. "All of them? I doubt that this Time corridor grants us that kind of authority."

The Rolling Stones were next on the desert airwaves—

I look inside myself and see my heart is black
I see my red door and it has been painted black
Maybe then I'll fade away and not have to face the facts
It's not easy facin' up when your whole world is black . . .

"Man, were the Stones caught in that NSA frequency, too?" Ray was exasperated.

The pain of knowing was getting to them all. Thomas considered turning off the radio, but knew he wasn't in charge of what came through. Was that because they were already committed to learning what the desert had to teach, pain or no pain?

Brian Jones had been in the top three IQ percent of the

British population, a lad Tavistock eggheads would definitely have been interested in. His younger sister Pamela had died when he was three. During his early teens, the artsy Mrs. Filby at 38 Priory Street in Cheltanham brought in jazz musicians for the dear young people, much as Syd Barrett's mother had in Cambridge. Later, Brian's father would say that a peculiar change came over his son once he started going to Mrs. Filby's: he'd turned dark and unruly and at eighteen headed for the Continent to incubate in Germany and Sweden for nine months. By the time he returned to England, he was a "bad boy" guitar player whose Elmore James style had been engraved on his psyche much as Robert Johnson's was engraved on his.

In 1962 at nineteen, Brian met the future Rolling Stones at the Ealing Club. Mick, Keith, and Dick loved his slide guitar. During the next seven years with the Rolling Stones, the bright Cheltanham boy went even more peculiar as down into the Tavistock rabbit hole he went. *The brighter the specimen, the harder they fall.* Like Syd Barrett, Brian eventually became a liability and earned an entry ticket to The 27 Club: just before U.S. Independence Day 1969, he was drowned in the swimming pool on his Cotchford Farm estate where A.A. Milne had written *Winnie the Pooh.* A generation later in the Nasty Nineties, a Scientology-connected band called the Brian Jonestown Massacre put out CDs like *Methodrone, Their Satanic Majesties' Second Request,* and *Thank God for Mental Illness,* as down, down into the rabbit hole American rock went.

Knowing about the rock assassinations and CIA "suicides" shrouded the pilgrims in an unnatural silence, each of them buried in a brittle mix of thought and feeling. They would never listen to the music they loved the same again. Music corporations weren't just about greed and business as usual. Their beloved bands and singers were stumbling into fame as innocents and finding themselves trapped in Hell.

Finally, Ray said, "Jimi's gonna die and I can't do shit about it."

"And Janis, and Morrison," Mannie added.

Seven murmured, "Jim Morrison is Dionysus, like a Shelley or Keats." She recited—

271

The breath whose might I have invoked in song
Descends on me, my spirit's bark is driven
Far from shore, far from the trembling throng
Whose sails were never to the tempest given . . .
I am borne darkly, fearfully, afar . . .

"Shelly was dead at 30," she added, "Keats at 25. Shelley's boat bow was stoved in by the Italian authorities. They're both buried in Rome, one in the New Protestant Cemetery, the other in the Old . . ."

"Like bookends," Mannie said.

"'Here lies one whose name was writ in water'—that's what Keats' tombstone says." Seven glanced back at Mannie. "Like Brian Jones and Jim Morrison. Death by water. Shelley and Keats called poets the unacknowledged legislators and antennas of the race."

"Like our political singers," Mannie murmured.

Thomas was wondering why Plato banned poets from his republic.

"Shelley and Keats lived at the beginning of the Industrial Revolution, didn't they?" Ray laughed darkly. "The machine calls and poets need not apply." He strummed a discordant chord.

Vince finally spoke. "After two world wars, we're owned by a mystico-military machine systematically doping and killing our poets. I'm sure it's to drag us down into despair, like the Three Kings assassinations."

Thoughtfully, Seven said, "Shelley wrote, 'Poetry strengthens the moral nature of man like exercise strengthens a limb.'"

Ray laid his guitar on the bed. "That's it, isn't it? Bureaucrats and brass and CEOs don't have any real imagination and can't stand ours because it strengthens our moral nature."

Seven was stunned. "That's it, Ray and Vince. Control, or kill, the Imagination."

"So poets and musicians do drugs and alcohol to anesthetize

their pain of being controlled by The Man," Ray said.

"And their fear," Mannie added sadly.

KRMA burst in with news from 1994. "On November 14, while crossing six lanes of traffic on Wilshire Boulevard on his way to a meeting with gangbangers in South Central Los Angeles, Sixties activist Jerry Rubin was struck by a car. After remaining in a coma for two weeks, he died on November 28. Rubin went from guerrilla theater to Wall Street. At the time of his death, he was planning to return to activism by organizing demonstrations against Indian and Pakistani nuclear tests. Supported by a small stipend from the Alliance for Survival, he was ready to reignite the push for disarmament.

"Abbie Hoffman preceded his old sidekick in death by 5.5 years. On April 15, 1987, Abbie, former President Carter's daughter Amy Carter, 13 Western Massachusetts college students, and lawyer Leonard Weinglass won a class action suit filed against the CIA before the Supreme Court. (With William Kunstler, Weinglass had defended Abbie during the Chicago 8 trial.) Twelve of the 15 defendants had been arrested on November 24, 1986 for occupying a University of Massachusetts administration building after the university refused to ban CIA recruiters from campus. Weinglass put the issue succinctly: *Was this lawlessness on the part of the defendants, or were they acting to stop the lawlessness?* By drawing upon CIA involvement in Nicaragua and calling a series of credible witnesses to testify about how out of control the CIA was—including Daniel Ellsberg who released the 43-volume *Pentagon Papers* about U.S. atrocities in Vietnam to the *New York Times* in 1971 and Boston University professor of history Howard Zinn—Weinglass contextualized the student desperation that caused the commandeering of the UMass building. Ellsberg testified that in 1969 he had wept for an hour after hearing that Randall Kehler, a young anti-draft protester, was going to prison. The Deputy Assistant Secretary of Defense under Johnson testified that the CIA consistently violated the Congressional Oversight Act of 1980 and the Boland Amendment of 1984. The jury released the defendants and found the CIA guilty."

"Wow!" Mannie crowed.

The news broadcast continued. "Ten months later on February 6, 1988, Abbie spoke to 650 student representatives from 130 of America's 5,000 colleges and universities at the National Student Convention at Rutgers University. His book *Steal This Urine Test: Fighting Drug Hysteria in America* was selling like hotcakes. He spoke from hard-won experience to student organizers, warning them about how the Left tends to devour its own with all of its -*isms*, false dichotomies, and narrow issue orientations. "Decision-making has been a problem on the Left," he admonished students. "In the sixties we always made decisions by consensus. By 1970, when you had 15 people show up and three were FBI agents and six were schizophrenics, universal agreement was getting to be a problem." The crowd laughed, then grew serious when he cried, "It's up to you to save America. Reagan and the CIA are traitors, they sold America to the Holy Financial Empire." He spoke of students in the Gaza Strip, in Johannesburg, El Salvador, the Philippines, reminding everyone that it's the young who make change with their daring, creativity, imagination, and impatience. Keep unity, he begged, be bold and daring. Seize the day to save America. And the students loved him for it. They needed the old Sixties activists to speak to them.

"But the old COINTELPRO and CHAOS forces heard him, too, and didn't want him to resurrect youths' hope. Mae Brussell, the brilliant and courageous researcher and radio diva, would be dead by fast-acting cancer in eight months. Someone up the CIA food chain decided to add Abbie to the list, then pick off other Sixties holdovers who still might infuse youth with a vision of the America that would no longer be allowed."

Pink Floyd's "Shine On, You Crazy Diamond" played as a voice read a litany of names—

Mae Brussell, 66, 'fast-acting cancer,' October 3, 1988
Abbie Hoffman, 52, 'suicided by manic depression,' April 12, 1989

Jerry Rubin, 56, hit by a car and hospitalized, death November 28, 1994

Jerry Garcia, 53, 'heart attack' in rehab center, August 8, 1995

William Kunstler, 76, 'heart attack,' Labor Day, September 4, 1995

Mario Savio, 53, 'heart attack,' November 6, 1996

Anita Hoffman, 56, breast cancer, December 27, 1998

The announcer returned. "In *Operation Mind Control*, Walter Bowart documents what he calls the Mental Telepathy System (MTS), a CIA psychotronic hell method now known generically as *voice-to-skull (V2K)* and *synthetic telepathy* technology. One of the CIA's V2K experimental victims, Bernie Nelson, tells how he was being relentlessly zapped in an Austin, Texas hotel room, when suddenly the voice beaming into his head revealed that Abbie Hoffman was being bombarded at the same time in his converted turkey coop near New Hope, Pennsylvania.

"This is KRMA . . ."

Back east, Dr. Greenbaum had his feet up in his Walter Reed Army Institute of Research office after having spent the morning with Gottlieb and a few hand-selected MK-ULTRA cybernetics researchers and psychiatrists discussing and mapping the Time-polarized nonphysical mind as it couples with the biological 3-space material body and its ongoing longitudinally polarized set of electromagnetic operations. The coupling hinged on the many endings and voltage spikings of the dendrite cells and had required a careful, detailed analysis of thousands of case studies.

The meeting had ended with a small celebration of MK-ULTRA's role in producing a living mind *sans* physical body that could then be linked to any properly designed 3-space biological body created in the lab or commandeered from an already existent body whose mind had been—well, disengaged via computer. For the latter situation, they would first duplicate the mind of the target, alter it for different behaviors or personalities, then download it into another subject to obtain the perfect spy, acquiescent national leader, Hollywood star, newscaster, etc. That the altered mind would still "pick up" thoughts of the original mind like radio transmissions was intriguing. Up on a monitor, they would be able to adjust the altered mind, if necessary. They owed it all to MK-ULTRA, Gottlieb's baby. One day—not yet, due to national security—history books would praise Gottlieb and Greenbaum, along with Soviet psychoenergetics.

At exactly the moment Greenbaum was thinking his vainglorious thoughts, KRMA captured his attention from somewhere down the Walter Reed hall, just as it had in his home.

". . . The methodic and secret torturing of children under Artichoke has led to greater insight into the temporal lobe of the brain. In fact, it appears that Hitler's Parkinson's disease symptoms were actually the temporal lobe epilepsy caused by undergoing repetitive remote psychic abuse.

"On August 26, 1976, while fishing at the Allagash Waterway in Eagle Lake, northern Maine, four men were engulfed in a cone of light projected from a large glowing colored sphere hovering two to three hundred feet above them. Hours later, they watched the sphere ascend and disappear, remembering nothing of what occurred in the hours between. Thirteen years later, in 1989, one of the men had a temporo-limbic seizure. Were the two distant events connected?

"In 2006, the National Institutes of Health (NIH) awarded a 5-year, $10.3 million grant to the Neuroscience Program at the University of Wyoming to discover how to prevent the brain anomalies that end not in the Superman that Nazi eugenics researchers once hoped for but in abnormal brain functions that cripple adult lives. What the NIH proposed was not that pain induction mind control should stop, but that the pathways relaying the pain should be blocked.

"This is KRMA . . ."

As the broadcast faded, Greenbaum was on his feet and out of his office searching for KRMA's genesis, the phrase *the brain anomalies that end not in the Superman that Nazi eugenics researchers once hoped for* playing over and over, with the dates 1976, 1989, and 2006 slipping away. He found no radio, nothing.

Unsettled, he returned to his *CIA CULTS* portfolio of New Age-Vatican creations. Gittinger had been at the meeting, the personality assessment man, deviser of the PAS (Personality Assessment System) for the CIA's Human Ecology Fund. At Columbia University's College of Physicians and Surgeons Psychology Department, Saunders and Thetford had used the PAS on Helen Schucman, a Jewish atheist professor of medical psychology. In 1965, Herbert Spiegel, an expert in hypnotism and Korean POW brainwashing, had produced Ω waking dreams and a *voice* ("Jesus") in Schucman, similar to what Tavistock and British Intelligence did for Eileen Caddy in 1953 at Glastonbury and then at Findhorn, Scotland. For seven years, Schucman would channel A Course in Miracles (ACIM), known in MK-ULTRA circles as subproject 130. Originally, ACIM was designed to infiltrate the Association for Research and Enlightenment (ARE), the Edgar Cayce outreach organization, but by 1972 Cayce's son Hugh Lynn Cayce would see through Schucman's "scribings," at which point her NSA handlers would shift to beaming their remote *synthetic telepathy* upon the Urantia Brotherhood.

Spiegel's remote technique coupled hypnosis with early RHIC-EDOM technology (radio hypnotic intracerebral control – electronic dissolution of memory), then split the brain by entraining different frequencies in each ear with a hemi-synch device to produce vivid 3-D hallucinations with stereophonic sound effects. The RHIC stimoceiver implants post-hypnotic suggestions while the EDOM via a particular frequency remotely stimulates acetylcholine to block nerve impulses to the brain for selective amnesia. In 1968, Gittinger wrote the Condon Report to cover up the UFO abductions he and Saunders and others working for the CIA and Tavistock Institute were conducting and inducing.

Another CIA cult fish on the line was Jim Jones. They'd gotten him as a dissociated child from a Ku Klux Klan family and programmed him for communism, racism, and religion for a deep surveillance operation in Guyana. Forbes Burnham, the Marxist prime minister of Guyana, was sponsoring a covert Soviet missile base seventy miles northwest of Temehri Field, and Cuba was home to the Soviet Union's Caribbean submarine fleet. The Negro programming was because Burnham was a Negro, as was Guyana's population of slave generations. Finally, the religion programming was because it worked for political cover, thanks to the U.S. First Amendment. The staged event had to be seen as non-military so as to provide cover for any casualties airlifted to Temehri Airfield out of what they were already calling Jonestown. Helicopters would have to fly over the Soviet complex, so a religious cult debacle would work perfectly; they could land military forces and give the Soviets a message without fear of retaliation, given that the Soviets wouldn't want the world to know what they had been up to.

A CIA sleeper, Jones would move his flock there in summer '77 and everything would happen under Scorpio just before Thanksgiving. The Pentagon would announce a routine naval exercise 50 miles from Cuba. After the "mass suicide," forces would have to land to deal with the carnage while 75 miles away U.S.-British joint attack forces would surround the Soviet base and the Battle of Guyana would ensue while American attention was on Thanksgiving. Because Jones represented a considerable investment, he would be extracted via the Essequibo River. To account for the additional body bags, the "suicide" numbers would be adjusted. Thus far, Jones had chartered his Peoples Temple Christian Church Full Gospel and been to Brazil for additional programming. While the CIA set up the rest of his "career," he was kept in Northern California near Ukiah. Greenbaum thought they'd gone a little far in having Jones believe that he was the reincarnation of Jesus, Mahatma Gandhi, Buddha, Lenin, and Father Divine. But the CIA was like that: they had to have their jollies.

Then there was the Korean CIA's Reverend Sun Myung Moon who would be Jesus Christ reincarnated, too. Moon and his "love-bombing" and three-day weddings would be brought to the U.S. the following year.

Greenbaum turned the page to "Six Quick Conversion Techniques":

Isolate, intimidate, deprive, indoctrinate
"Sell It By Zealot"
Wear down resistance and increase tension
Generate uncertainty
Jargon
Humor (release) disallowed, then encouraged

Thus far, establishing cults had been easy, given the First Amendment protection and thin line between religious belief and brainwashing. After isolation and non-stop "service" to push subjects through an intense emotional threshold and prep them for subjection to the charismatic leader's will, fear and guilt deluged the weaker wills and wiped brain slates clean for new programming. Meanwhile, group hypnosis continued the process with soft tones of argumentation, the more people the better. The key, though, was the charismatic personality of the "living master," the wise man, the one who knows and has the will to implement it. Charisma. Will. The larger well-funded cults were already using infrasound at gatherings.

Brainwashing didn't have to *look* like religion, just *behave* like it. Military induction, human-potential seminar weekends, business seminars worked just as well—anywhere that actions had to be predetermined. Both military and intelligence cults from boot camp grunts to Knights of Malta, Freemasons, and Mormons grasped the power of shamanic initiations to "rend and reintegrate the human psyche," as the Roumanian mythologist Mircea Eliade put it in his *Shamanism: Archaic Techniques for Ecstasy.* Tear the boy apart, then put him back together the way you want him, just as Osiris was torn apart by Set and reassembled by Isis.

They'd studied everything, seeing themselves as ancient priests and initiates come again to guide others through the painful 20th century initiation into the Third Reich new world order. They saw themselves as engaging in shamanic rites, beginning with rending the personality with drugs, pain, fear, and trance states, all the while carefully studying Nazi research into the old Mystery religions: *yogis* who prescribed *arshti* drugs to open acolytes' perception, Egyptian and Eleusinian Mystery schools, Æsculapian priests of ancient Greece, the rites of the Oracle of Triphonius. From British psychiatrist William Sargant's *The Mind Possessed* to the 18th century Church of England preacher John Wesley, whose all-out assaults on the emotions and early use of Leyden jars for electroconvulsive therapy (ECT), they took what they needed.

They were particularly indebted to Pavlov for moving the shamanic toward the predictable science of the washed brain. Pavlov broke through transmarginal inhibitions by triggering emotions that increased suggestibility while decreasing cerebral judgment, then intensified the state with isolation, fasting, radical or high-sugar diet, physical discomfort, interrupted sleep patterns, tight scheduling of events, regulation of breathing, mantra repetition in meditation, special lighting, sound effects, incense, drugs, fear, doubt, etc. In the end, the brain slate was wiped clean for new programming.

Conversion was far more powerful than hypnosis. For individual spies, group hypnosis acted powerfully to lower the will before building a somnambulistic, hysterical, or hypnoid trance that could manage normal behavior, too. Perhaps they should have done it with Baby Rose. He sighed.

Music—whether hymns, Indian ragas or rock, ideally in the range of 45 to 72 beats per minute—moved the brain from beta to alpha. Long ago, singers with a certain vibrato were disallowed from performing publicly because listeners would go into an altered right brain state, often sexual in nature, due to the simultaneous release of enkephalins and beta-endorphins, both chemically similar to opium.

Then of course there was the cult leader's charismatic voice roll modulated at 45 to 60 beats per minute while gesturing with the left hand to access the right brain. Greenbaum particularly liked watching Billy Graham work a big arena while a 6-to-7 cycle per second frequency was being pulsed in through the air conditioner or sound system. Shock and confusion would distract the left brain and send people into an alpha state, making them highly suggestible and easy to manipulate. Thanks to whatever was done to his temporal lobe, Hitler had been masterful— similar to the interior mantra employed as an astral leash, an ancient technique that satellite computers would soon imitate with pulses. Holy songs or inspiring words were essential to moving the emotions toward the hive mind—miraculous events, healings, etc. It was all part of decognition, reducing alertness so the mind goes "flat."

Access the right brain by distracting the left. As in the fairy tale, a "yes set" of three truisms was embedded, followed by what the charismatic leader wants the subject to do, along with other commands. Or there was the *interspersal technique*, saying one thing with words while subliminally implying the opposite. Television advertising and the music industry were employing subliminals and would soon be delivering a Beta-endorphin fix every night of the week, though Greenbaum doubted it would improve Mr. and Mrs. Smith's sex life. Instead, Mr. Smith would find himself lusting after younger and younger pretty things, as television and magazine and billboard images programmed him to do.

Dr. Greenbaum closed the portfolio. He agreed with the Soviets: rugged individualism, personal determinism, imagination, and creativity were willful and unaligned enemies of the State, illnesses producing the disaffection and disunity that could collapse the hive consciousness necessary to maintaining a worldwide State. Lower black magic or *psychopolitics* was the solution. In America, the two pillars of psychopolitics were an obedient Mockingbird corporate media and the television-washed brain through BASK dissociation (behavior, affect, sensation, knowledge). His and Gottlieb's field was higher black magick, methods of removing (not just manipulating) parts of the soul that serve individuality at the expense of the State.

One of the hurdles was finding enough *normal* personalities to experiment with. Military hospitals and private psychiatric clients provided some but not nearly enough. Schizophrenics, the severely depressed, and obsessional neuroses in mental hospitals were at home in the unconscious and so were poor subjects. Multigenerational incest cult families were excellent for programming dissociated personalities, but only the normal were optimally ignorant of the unconscious and truly amenable to being subjected to hypnosis and manipulation.

Under cover of the Sixties "spiritual quest," the CIA had lit upon cults as optimal field labs while putting more and more drugs in the streets so as to multiply OD'd lost souls in hospitals and drug rehabs. Marijuana possession had been made a felony so that bright, young, inquiring personalities could be removed from the population and made accessible in prison away from family and public inquiry. These venues were at last providing enough normal personalities.

All was going well, except for the two escapees. Greenbaum would call Agent Iff to see how surveillance was progressing, then talk with the Defense Intelligence man about military plans for their rogue retired intelligence colonel. Picking the little troupe off one by one might serve them both.

44

No Place Like OM

Kantner: [Stargate] was a somewhat fictionalized account of a project I did for the U.S. Space Command at Cheyenne Mountain two years ago. It was supposed to be hush-hush, under wraps, all that sort of thing… Well, the Stanford Research Institute down in Palo Alto asked me to participate in some discussions. I thought it was all civilian academic. Turned out that two of the people in the white coats wore blue ones underneath. So then in 1991 I was asked to come out to Colorado Springs. It was supposed to be a seminar sort of thing at the Air Force Academy, but when I got there, they took me up to the mountain, and then things got weird. Michael [Aquino] was there; he knows.

–Interview with Paul Kantner of Jefferson Starship, *Scroll of Set*, 1994

External stimulation of the brain by electromagnetic means can cause the brain to be entrained or locked into phase with an external signal generator.

–U.S. Patent #5,356,368, October 18, 1994, "Method and Apparatus for Inducing Desired States of Consciousness," Inventor: Monroe, Robert; Assignee: Interstate Industries, Inc. EPI286

We have a new weapon, just within the portfolio of our scientists, so to speak, which is so powerful that, if unrestrainedly used, it could wipe out all life on earth. It is a fantastic weapon.

–Nikita Khrushchev, "To the Presidium," 1960

Across America, 12-atonal rock music was pulsing through lower *chakras* being enhanced by psychedelics, marijuana, cocaine, speed, and heroin. Everyone was grooving and not paying attention to how electronic music with its heavy repetitive beat was advancing hand in glove with drug use in the name of freedom and heightened awareness.

That evening, having experienced miles of Arizona desert and two phantom hitchhikers, the pilgrims had just pulled off-road and were setting up camp when they spotted a man and woman with packs on their backs walking west and invited them to share supper.

Ander and Lotke turned out to be Czech virtuosos of the *dvojnice*, a double-barreled flute. As the meal ended and the burnished sunset was vanishing, Vince lit the night's fire and the two Europeans insisted upon giving an impromptu concert. Seven sat in a half-lotus with Baby Rose lying with her head in her lap, the Colonel gently snored in his lawn chair with Sirius at his feet, and Ray, Thomas, Vince, and Mannie zoned out on their sleeping bags as the double-barreled flutes produced strange polyphonies with beat pulses in an octave so low that it was as if a phantom voice was vibrating their spines, their *chakras* the finger holes, their bodies the flutes.

The concert was mind-blowing and otherworldly. The Colonel and Sirius were deep asleep.

Afterward, Ander explained how the tones were like vowels. "The *Ah* opens the sinus chambers and lights all of the soul petals in the pineal gland, heart, and head."

Lotke played an *Ah*.

"The *O*," Ander continued, "closes the resonance chamber of the sinuses and forces the resonance into the larynx, solar plexus, and spleen."

Lotke played an *O*.

"*Om* is the first of the seven diatonic *and* the first of the pentatonic, meaning it vibrates the lowest center of any created being. *Om* is *Do* as in *Do re mi fa so la ti do*. The *M* of *Om* shifts the frequency from the larynx down into the stomach to activate the third *chakra* of the solar plexus. Five vowels, five major centers with two minor, and you have the flute of the human soul playing on the human body."

"I see intense reds and blues when you play," Seven marveled.

Lotke said, "Lovely. Though we play in fourths—more similar to the diatonic 7-note scale of classical than the pentatonic 5-note scale of rock-and-roll— you are hearing *Ah* and *Om* in their hyperspace blues and astral reds."

Thomas caught her reference to *hyperspace*.

Ander explained that they had psychedelics to thank for revealing the nature of sound to them.

Psychedelics also went with the advanced audio technology of Grateful Dead concerts, thanks to the acid-audio genius Augustus "Bear" Owsley Stanley III who made the first PA system specific to music.

Ray tried to articulate what he was grokking. "I thought it was the acid that made Grateful Dead concerts different from other concerts, but what you just said about 'hyperspace' sound makes so much sense. Their concerts are more like levels of consciousness than concerts, with each set being different."

Seven added, "And like tribal ritual with everyone stoned and at the same vibration, tripping to the music."

"Yes," Ander said, "we've listened carefully to several Grateful Dead concerts through our own sound equipment and definitely hear something multilevel, but we're not yet sure what it is." He looked at Lotke. "Sound research is why we are going to California. In particular, we are curious about all of the concert deaths and wondering if they have to do with *military* sound experiments."

"Like the Stones concert at Altamont?" Seven asked.

"Altamont and many others," Lotke said. "The Who concert in 1979 in the Cincinnati Riverfront Coliseum, Ozzy Osbourne in 1986 in Long Beach Arena, Public Enemy in 1987 in Nashville, AC/

DC in Salt Lake City and Heavy D in New York, both in 1991—"

The pilgrims glanced at each other. *The future.*

Ander continued. "Note the different geographic regions: California, Ohio, Tennessee, Utah, and New York. A friend of ours at Palomar studios told us that Hollywood produces 85 percent of all the world's rock videos, and that music executives come all the time into the editing bay with frequency codes to embed. And they're digitally re-mastering the old favorites with such codes. Meanwhile, people are being trampled at concerts. Is music being weaponized?"

Lotke counted on her fingers. "1994, Golden Life in Poland; 1996, Smashing Pumpkins in Dublin and Taegu in South Korea; 1997, *die* Toten Hosen in Germany and the Raimundos in Brazil—"

Ander shrugged. "Again, Poland, Ireland, Germany, South Korea, Brazil— seemingly a planned regional spread."

"Then 28 years after Altamont," Lotke said, "at a Stones concert in Pontiac, Michigan, a man dies just as before, only this time not from a fall."

"One Saturn return," Seven murmured.

"After the Michigan Stones concert," Lotke went on, "the deaths returned to Europe in 1999 and 2000: Mango Mango in Minsk, Hole in Sweden, Pearl Jam in Denmark. At the Pearl Jam concert, we took sound detection equipment and were far enough from the stage that the equipment registered a sound event just seconds before the crowd surged toward the stage and nine people were trampled to death."

Sadly, Ander added, "Our hypothesis is that some rock concerts are being used as laboratories for sound-brain experiments."

"Resonance causing mass stampedes," Thomas surmised.

Seven recalled being swept down Telegraph Avenue during a Berkeley street riot, like a switch was thrown somewhere to make everyone stampede. Had she fallen, she would have been trampled.

"What about strobes and drugs?" Ray asked.

Ander shook his head. "In the case of mass stampedes, a

broad resonance is being triggered and locked into phase, as Thomas says—probably by an external signal generator."

Lotke explained. "Brainwaves are electrical and must obey the laws of resonance which say that a strong vibration in one system can be induced in another system. A sound vibration could go out to an audience in a resonance chamber like a concert hall or stadium—"

Seven thought of the boxed-in Telegraph Avenue.

"—and suddenly brains are entrained to a frequency that triggers fear between 1 and 23 Hertz or cycles per second. We estimate the fear frequency to be in the *theta* range of 4 to 7 Hertz because *theta* can cause high emotion, frustration, or violence."

"Like soldiers marching in step over a bridge can buckle and collapse the bridge?" Mannie asked.

Ander nodded. "Exactly. Now imagine such a resonance entering the brain through the eyes, ears, or skin, and you are induced to follow a certain frequency. Strobes induce at 10 Hertz and bring on seizures. The audio spectrum is 15 Hertz for bass to 20,000 Hertz for treble. Of course, we can't hear this full range. For example, infrasonic is 10-15 Hertz, around 110-130 decibels, too low to detect. And below infrasound is ELF or extremely low frequency."

"A few years ago," Lotke said quietly, "during a subliminal music lawsuit in which the band Judas Priest was the defendant, the judge cited instances of the CIA using subliminal mind control to control the outcomes of national elections."

Silence gripped them, broken only by Ander's sigh.

"Your country and Europe are under this same silent compulsion technology. Our only hope is to comprehend how it works and why and when it is used. This is why we have come. We could have a comfortable life in Europe, but what does a personal life mean when so much is at stake?"

Thomas said, "At Yale, Dr. José Delgado experimented with

electrical stimulation of the brain, ESB, setting off mood changes, memories, even motor actions when the subject tried to resist. How does ESB tie in?"

Lotke responded. "In technologies targeting individuals like at Altamont and the other Stones concert in Michigan in 1997, a command that only the targeted individual would recognize could have been embedded below the melody line, or his brain could have been plugged into a plasma V2K or voice-to-skull computer commanding, *Dance on the rail! Now, fall!* This technology is highly sophisticated, and you are right—it all began back in the 1950s with Dr. Delgado."

Ander put his *dvojnice* away. "The new spy chief in Britain, the head of the Joint Intelligence Committee, is a Deadhead. He started out in Customs & Excise in '73 and rose through the ranks. Even the previous prime minister was lead singer at Oxford in a rock group called Ugly Rumors, taken straight from the cover of a Grateful Dead album." He looked at Thomas. "Is sound also being used to program and control our leaders?"

Thinking of the cook in Ash Fork and the press lying to cover up Paul McCartney's fatal car accident or murder on Wednesday, November 9, 1966, Mannie said, "What about feedback, layering, and backmasking, like in Lennon's *Turn me on, dead man* and all the rest? A friend in high school told me that John found a test tape in the EMI library entitled 'Number Nine Test Tape' and decided to leave clues throughout *Revolution No. 9* like *Paul is dead, I buried Paul.* He'd turn it around on the machine and memorize it backwards so he could record it in the studio and it wouldn't be discovered during engineering. In between 'I'm So Tired' and 'Blackbird,' he mumbled *Bleseg bleseg bleseg habadziliben* followed by the sound of a baby. *Paul is a dead man, miss him, miss him, miss him.* Reverse *Ride, ride, ride* and it's *Get me out, get me out* with horns blaring and a bell. Paul's *Uh, what, what* in reverse says, *Help, help* while flames crackle." A fine line of sweat had formed above Mannie's top lip.

"You are close to the truth," Ander confirmed. "We've listened front and back to the multilayered tracks on *Revolution No. 9*. Many Europeans believe that Billy Campbell or Shears had multiple plastic surgeries to replace the dead Paul, but Lotke and I may have proof: Before 1966, Beatles music was all diatonic, but from *Sergeant Pepper* on it's all pentatonic, like the Rolling Stones. Diatonic, 7 notes of 5 major centers and 2 minor—completion for the complete human soul. Pentatonic, incomplete, luciferic."

"What do you mean by 'Luciferic'?" Seven asked.

"In this context, Ander means eternal childhood," Lotke explained. "Diatonic enlivens the adult centers of the body, pentatonic is perfect for the pre-seven year old child. Keeping people as children may be the goal."

Ander shifted tracks. "The years 1966 to 1971, the synthesizer revolution years, began with the Beach Boys' 'Good Vibrations,' though Brian Wilson actually played a theremin, not a synthesizer, named after Leo Théremin, who also invented color television. Basically, the theremin coils around two high-frequency rods or oscillators that, vacuum tube-like, create a magnetic field. As practiced hands move delicately between the rods, they pluck invisible strings, *ether harmonies* with a range of 4.5 octaves. After demonstrating the theremin for Lenin in 1922, Théremin was kidnapped from his apartment at 37 West 54th Street in New York City where Einstein used to visit him. Forced to work for the Russian Academy of Sciences and KGB, Théremin didn't return to the United States until after the Soviet Union finally collapsed, when he spoke at the Stanford University Centennial of Music on October 1, 1991. He died at 97 on November 3, 1993—9/3/93 by the Julian calendar."

Mannie appreciated all the 9's.

Thomas was shocked. "The Soviet Union—collapsed?"

Lotke nodded rapidly. "In 1991."

"Since the 1960s," Ander continued, "music and weapons

have become kissing cousins, as you Americans say. Not only did Owsley create the best street acid going—1.25 million doses beween 1965 and 1967—but don't forget his Air Force electronics, radar, and jet propulsion background. Jerry Garcia was in the U.S. Army, too, just before creating the Warlocks that became the Grateful Dead in 1965," Ander said. "Together, Owsley and Garcia made fundamental advances in concert audio tech while doing the original sound mixing for the Grateful Dead. Owsley filed for patents and simulcast live on AM/FM, television, and quadraphonic for concerts. His wall-of-sound PA system tuned *each seat* for optimum acoustic accuracy. Thanks to the Air Force, he had advanced microprocessors before anyone else. Basically, Dead concerts were audio research labs with futuristic military state-of-the-art sound equipment. During the first Gulf War, a tour band lost its sound equipment and the military loaned them theirs on the proviso that they not photograph it. Timothy Leary said the Dead were a 20-year extension of Ken Kesey's Acid Test, and he was right, but they were primarily *sound* experiments."

Ander looked intently at the pilgrims. "Military technology is everywhere. Most electric guitarists, bassists, and vocalists choose vacuum tube amps over transistor amps because of how the vacuum tube substantially strengthens emotional sound. Add subliminals and emotion turns into *drive*. Even Japanese *karaoke*, which means "empty orchestra," utilizes CIA psychological operations technology—from 'California Dreamin'' with Zen Buddhist temple visuals to 'Love Me Tender' with military jet visuals."

Had Baby Rose been able to speak, she would have contributed much to the discussion, given that she had been an experimental subject of quantum waveform research under Project Montauk, quantum waves being neither in the audio nor the electromagnetic wave spectrum but transmitted by means of vacuum tubes to levels of consciousness that cannot otherwise be accessed.

Ander drove onward. "Then there are the obvious weapons

like Ultrasonic Acoustic Heterodyning hypersonic sound developed by the U.S. Navy and American Technology Corporation (ATC) to deliver audio bullets that exceed the human threshold for pain by 20 decibels. The FBI targeted the individuals inside the Branch Davidian compound in Waco, Texas in 1993 with this technology. Harmonic generators codenamed *ether-wave* can embed commands in harmonics and sound waves to manipulate the RNA sheaths in the neuron pathways to the subconscious. Even at the cinema, Loews Cineplex Theatre audiences are in thrall to Sony Dynamic Digital Sound (SDDS) with Theatre Vision. The SDDS tetrahedral pyramid logo being implanted in the American psyche is like the pyramid purportedly on Mars."

Seven thought of the Stargazer narrator saying, *Wars can only be waged by embodied beings bound to the soil, like Mars men.*

Ander went on. "ATC's 45-pound Long-Range Acoustic Device (LRAD) is capable of directing Metallica's 'Hells' Bells' and 'Shoot to Thrill' through a hardened MP3 player not just to disorient but to *thrash* the limbic brain while priming the rest of the brain with negative computer-enhanced EEG emotion signature clusters running under the music—Silent Sounds' S-quad technology (Silent Sound Spread Spectrum). The 33-inch dish-shaped LRAD can lay a strip of sound 15 to 30 inches wide with 120 to 170 decibels (dB) up to 1,000 meters. Compare 150 dB to an 80 dB smoke detector. Nose and ears bleed, and more than a few seconds of a 3,100 Hertz frequency can mean hearing loss.

"You should know how the LRAD works: Sound of Force Protection 'narrowcasts' a high-pitched tight 30° beam that acts like a sound tunnel at a 100-yard ground zero. Then LRAD sonic bullets tightly focus beams of infrasound—a directional sonic fire hose that can generate a supersonic vortex of air slower than 100 vibrations per second to knock down, disable, or kill just *one* target in the middle of a busy street without others even knowing what hit him. LRAD can deliver the Voice of God so it sounds like it's coming from inside your head. Maxwell Technologies' Hyper Sonic Sound System and Primex Physics International's Acoustic Blaster and Sequential Arc Discharge Acoustic Generator all focus sound waves. Your military loves it for placing distance between them and threat, but then it is not *their* mothers and daughters in the target cone—not yet, anyway."

From rock music to weapons in seconds flat. The pilgrims were speechless.

Lotke looked at their faces. "Leave off, Ander. You're overwhelming them."

He shook his head and fixed the pilgrims with a laser stare. "They need to know.—You realize what this means for prisoners and citizens alike, don't you? No-touch torture. For prisoners, it's Camp Nama. Abu Ghraib. Guantánamo. Deafening decibels of music playing 24 hours a day, like Metallica's 'Enter Sandman,' Barney the Purple Dinosaur's 'I Love You,' Eminem, Christina Aguilera, Dr. Dre, all loaded with silent-sound subliminals piped into Black Rooms or shipping containers where each isolated prisoner is chained to the floor after days and nights of no sleep, sensory deprivation, extreme heat or cold, etc. Scientific Applications & Research has a multi-sensory grenade that combines sound, light, and odor to completely isolate and disorient the target. Best of all, though, is the grenade's subliminal acoustic manipulation of the nervous system, more 'hearing voices' technology that makes targets feel, and go, mad. Ultrasound can be used to make bothersome neighbors move, while infrasound can turn internal organs to jelly or bring out the Beast—like the feraliminal lycanthropizer or low frequency thanato-auric wave generator."

Ander took a deep breath. "Directional frequency. On March 23, 1991, ITV News Bureau wire service in London reported that a silent sound technology known as MAD—the magnetic acoustic device nicknamed 'The Scream'—was successfully utilized in Kuwait against Iraqi troops during Operation Desert Storm. First, military command-and-control communications were knocked out so they had to use commercial FM stations to carry their encoded commands at 100MHz. U.S. Psychological Operations then set up a portable FM transmitter and overpowered the local station with The Scream, broadcasting a beam of sound for more than a mile at 100,000 watts, 20,000 Hz. At a low setting, the Scream delivers screams, shouts, gunfire, sirens, or heavy metal music, such as was used in Waco. But at a *high* setting, its sum kinetic force-generating shockwaves produce dizziness, nausea, bleeding from the nose, eyes, and ears. In Kuwait, they inserted vague, confusing military orders under patriotic and religious music while a subliminal Scream layer spoke directly to soldiers' brainwaves, penetrating and entraining them with negative emotional patterns. Psychoacoustic frequencies engaged their neural networks and made them surrender. The Voice of God (Allah) was tuned to a specific frequency range and reduced in size and power to sound like an individual voice in each soldier's head, while the range was increased to encompass the entire platoon.

"Like the French robotics researcher Gavreau's pipe organ that made him and his staff ill for days, infrasound can mean involuntary defecation, rupture of internal organs, nausea, disorientation, epileptic fits, and death. It can cause earthquakes and volcanoes. At 19 Hz, the frequency of your eyeball resonance, infrasound can drop temperature so you see phantoms or the dead. Lower the frequency enough and it can produce profound religious experiences."

Which led to a discussion of *AUM* and *Amen*. Lotke said the *Ah* and *m* were from *senzar*, the language of Atlantis predating Sanskrit, but she and Ander would have to think about the N. Vince said that ancient Mayans prayed *AUM*, the *Ah* being the fecundating power of the father, U the generative power of the mother, and M, *mehen*, the engendered son. Mannie said he thought that *YHWH* was actually just the vowel *Ah* in two variations pitched an octave apart, like *AhhhhhAAAAAYYYYY*. Lotke agreed, adding that the Y set the palate in a position to affect magnetic lines of force in the cerebellum across the corpus callosum. As for G-d, Mannie said it was pronounced with a small case *ah* and therefore was a holy word. Vince then blew their minds by saying that Jesus' last words *Eli, Eli, lamah sabachthani* in Mayan were *Hele, hele, lamah zabac ta ni* for *Now, now, I am fainting, darkness covers my face.*

As the embers finally died, Ander and Lotke set up their tent and everyone went to sleep. Snuggled beside Seven, Thomas dreamed he was a point of consciousness moving through a spacetime filled with real thoughts and thought-forms, Whittaker structures hiding in electromagnetic channels of the biopotential, teeming in the Time dimension. Physics and metaphysics share Time intimately, Time being the fundamental unit and not atoms. Jubilant that he hadn't contributed too many ugly, reprehensible, destructive thoughts to the ubiquitous Ocean of Memory, Thomas briefly grasped that *grace* was behind the KRMA broadcasts.

When he rolled away from Seven in his sleep, he encountered a phantom of an unknown man sitting beside him, looking about as if examining the weather. "The Threshold is growing porous, did you notice, Thomas?" the phantom said, hugging his legs. "Black adepts have forced it open prematurely to preempt the gods' plans and take advantage of Second Coming effects in the æther. They're tearing the Veil from below with drugs, sex, torture, voyeurism, mind control, ritual murder, and those blood sacrifices they call wars. Thousands of souls are being claimed by materialism and devoured by the beings that dwell between the Earth and Moon." He scanned the heavens as if reading a script Thomas couldn't see. "Yes, it is finally dissolving. Like birth, the beginnings of cosmic self-consciousness will be painful and bloody, your only joy being to finally be able to feel another's pain and know it first-hand."

The phantom smiled down at a gaping Thomas. "How is your sleep? Dreams spilling toward nightmares? Learn to live under the open heavens of the Apocalypse whose Veil has been rent. Intellectual speculation will be powerless against it. Retain authority over the subnature creatures you encounter so they do not consume you with their boundless appetite for what is human. And do not abuse them as the black adepts do." He glanced over his shoulder. "Ah, the JASON Group meeting is beginning. Come."

Thomas saw only desert, but some part of him obediently got up and followed the phantom man. Suddenly, they were in MITRE Corporation headquarters in McLean, Virginia where a discussion was already underway.

". . . billions were supposedly poured into the 12-ton Hubble Space Telescope launched in 1990, but all the public saw were 'double-star' pictures, and after October 1995, nothing. NASA's story was a warped-scratched-cracked mirror and security not allowing for clean procedures, but who would believe that?" The speaker shook his head. "Badly done. There should have been a better way to make sure the public didn't see what the Hubble was photographing."

Thomas' phantom protégé leaned over and whispered, "He's Yellow Lodge."

"Yellow Lodge?" Thomas whispered back.

"NSA initiates aware of EBEs, extraterrestrial biological entities visible in the atmosphere and even specialized chambers. A Vannevar Bush term for entities like the Venusian Jack Parsons encountered in the New Mexico desert."

So Gollum was an EBE. Whole new classifications.

The phantom whispered on as the JASON dispute heated up. "Under Project Grudge, I saw what they call the Yellow Book—photographs and films of EBEs, the thousand points of light." He leaned closer. "*Conscious*, bobbing and zooming points of consciousness. I've seen the NASA footage. They're all over the place up there." He smiled. "Oppenheimer quoted *Ramayana* and *Mahabharata* descriptions of airships like egg-shaped bluish clouds and luminous globes propelled by ether, pushing against Earth's magnetic field in order to rise, following a long, undulating trajectory with sweet, melodious sounds, light as bright as fire . . ."

Another JASON was talking. "To the best of our knowledge, these organic, psycho-physical ships are projections of intelligent entities—imaginal creations, not mechanical, powerful concentrations of energy that take on electromagnetic traits due to passing through our magnetic grid with ease, like freeway interchanges. And by manipulating our energy fields, they are able to extract our plasma bodies. Dr. Gottlieb thinks that the old limbic, reptilian brain is the portal for the extraction."

Gottlieb was there. Thomas had vague recollections of Gottlieb and Greenbaum peering down at him. He shook off the anxiety that arose with the memory with a line from Eliot's "Hollow Men": *Between the idea and the reality, between the motion and the act, falls the Shadow.*

Gottlieb stood. "The reptilian brain is the oldest brain. Long before the neocortex, we could *see* into the realms these EBEs inhabit. Like gods, they can create experiences for us that mime our 3D world. Sometimes they do it to make us feel more comfortable, sometimes to exert power over us."

"So Hugh Everett III's many-worlds interpretation was right," Thomas whispered to his phantom protégé.

He nodded. "For better or worse."

For good or evil, Thomas translated.

Another JASON spoke up. "Dr. Pugh has withdrawn from the research."

No one spoke, many silently contemplating how they wished they could do the same, due to a gnawing intuition that a *Satanic* element was engulfing the military and multiplying technology of such sophistication that things were getting out of control—the discs, the abductions with telling thermal effects and burn marks, car ignitions going dead, people disappearing, what happened at Livermore Labs . . .

Thomas' protégé whispered, "Up at Pilot Peak in Northern California at K-2 in the Plumas National Forest between La Porte and Quincy, southeast of Mt. Shasta, it's silent—no animals, even the clouds are behaving oddly. The manmade pond there is for underwater entry and egress to and from the large metallic underground chamber with tunnels and passages. When I was there, a bright white globe flew over me, hovered, turned bright blue, returned to white, then flew on with eight Air Force F-4s in hot pursuit."

"Was the base . . . ?" Thomas began.

"Ours, but the globe was theirs," the scientist affirmed. "Ever since the Van Allen Belt fiasco, they've been acutely interested in what our military has on the front burner." He winked at Thomas and recited, "*There be three kindes of fairies, the black, the white, and the green, of which the black be the worst.*" He smiled. "*The Examination of John Walsh*, 1556."

Suddenly, the meeting vanished and they were standing in a rural area where panel trucks marked *Smithsonian Institute* were parked. Men in coveralls were working on telephone and power lines.

Thomas' protégé leaned toward him. "An abduction is in the works."

"Smithsonian?" Thomas was incredulous.

The phantom nodded. "For confusion, if nothing else. The workmen are from the Air Force Office of Special Investigations (AFOSI) at Kirtland Air Force Base or the Defense Investigative Service (DIS). Piles of silver duct tape are used as markers for aerial craft, including twin-rotor Chinooks on patrol. Get close to one of our vector craft and you may see Tedlar strips made out of the same heat-resistant polyvinyl fluoride material that NASA uses on its rockets. Eye in the Triangle uniforms usually mean human, and they usually keep abductees in the family, meaning from military, intelligence, or defense contractors like McDonnell-Douglas." He scanned the studded sky. "Even world leaders are being subjected to sightings. Two years before he was slaughtering Christians and

297

eating them to acquire Western power, Uganda's Idi Amin witnessed a UFO splashing into Lake Victoria, then lifting back out. The prime minister of Grenada saw UFOs over the Caribbean and claimed God had appointed him to carry out a divine plan, but when he asked the UN to investigate them, a CIA *coup d'état* got rid of him."

He looked meaningfully at Thomas. "*Time* magazine may have called him a warlock, but the real warlocks are the JASONs and Yellow Lodge Brothers simulating sightings with parallel computing. By connecting computational fluid dynamics (CFD) and computational electromagnetics (CEM), Lockheed can create radar reflections of huge discs that aren't really there—physical optics approximation, making even radar believe that the scattered wave field must originate from the 'disc'—computers creating phantom bodies by means of flat facets, each with its own processor, illuminated by radar-induced electric current.

"But remember: *not all* is simulated.

"Then there's NASA's Landsat and Seasat, the U.S. Navy's Geosat—all bouncing radar pulses at the speed of light against earth and sea and calibrating the distances via Doppler radio signals to determine gravity magnitude and plate tectonics, where deep chasms called fracture zones meet the mantle. NOAA (the National Oceanic and Atmospheric Administration) was tasked with mapping the Caribbean and northwest Hawaiian Islands. Of course, 3D satellite mapping of the oceans comprising 70 percent of the Earth's surface makes sense, but Reef Relief in Key West was little more than a cover story, along with the private money gambit to resurrect Atlantis."

He guided Thomas along the country road past the Smithsonian truck. "An old Freemason friend—Yellow Lodge, though he'd never admit it—said they're scouting for undersea bases and portals in use for thousands of years. Brawdy Royal Air Force Base in West Wales is far more than a training center for jet aircraft pilots; it's an oceanographic base with hydrophonic sounding wire arrays leading into the Atlantic for remote listening." He chuckled. "The cover story is whale migration and song patterns for determining nuclear submarine movement and communication. Sure, we studied whales' ability to stun prey with 'gunshot' infrasound tonal projection, and the infrasound distress calls beached whales send out that can thrust veterinarians several feet back. Such studies led to anti-submarine Low-Frequency Active sonar (LFA) loudspeakers that emit 240 dB and cause whales to hemorrhage and beach. Most whales learn how to avoid the huge swaths of aboriginal routes in the northern Azores that we've wired, where acoustic readings are 120 dB and above. As you probably know, the Navy set 140 dB as the maximum level for human exposure, but these acoustic waves are *powerful*, and the lower the frequency, the farther they penetrate ocean depths.

"But these acoustic weapons aren't about whales or nuclear submarines; they're for the infrared discs zipping in and out of the ocean. Of course, we have our own on Stack Rock, the tiny island off the coast of Brawdy, but the real targets are the plasma discs little more than impersonal psychotronic devices or points of consciousness capable of distorting our perceptual reality—like the points of light you saw, Thomas. Some project images or fabricate scenes in order to throw our beliefs into disorder—subliminal seduction, Jacques Vallee called it. Ten meters of intense energy, pulsed light, vivid colors—electromagnetic radiation and microwaves distorting reality. Then there's the psychotronic aspect: an image causes psycho-physiological changes, perception distortions, loss of memory, time distortion, post-hypnotic effects, visions, voices, hallucinations, personality changes." He shook his head. "In the Forties and Fifties, *none* of them were ours. Vallee says it's a control system linked to our consciousness. Now, of course, the military's retro-engineering it all."

"Disc holographs that fool radar?"

His protégé shrugged. "That, too, but not just discs—other

bodies beyond virtual reality. Project Blue Beam with a phantom DNA twist." He dropped his voice. "What the military wants is the same psychic pilot-craft interface that these EEBs have. That's a big part of why from MK-ULTRA on, remote electromagnetic programming has gotten so *aggressive*."

"So Yellow Lodge NASA types know the 'extraterrestrial' hype is not about beings from other planets so much as about something outside our matrix of spacetime in alternate folds of reality?" Thomas asked.

The phantom nodded. "Our spacetime order is simply one vibrational frequency range in hyperspace. Next door are other vibrational frequency ranges that other conscious beings call reality. The military has spent *billions* on this—you can imagine. Besides the weapons build-up for planetary control, it's what the so-called Cold War was really about."

Thomas got it. Men like his uncle weren't content with the magnetic nodes that had been around for thousands of years; they were detonating and detonating to open more hyperspatial portals at similar latitudes. First, they'd locate the nodes, then study astronomy for the exact times the nodes would be optimal, Einstein having made it clear that hyperspatial portals meant contiguous spacetime. Star time and planetary time like the Sun Dagger once measured, but harmonically *exact*, like acupuncture points. Instead of delicate needles opening the Earth's energetic pathways so *ki* could rebalance, nuclear bombs were ripping open nodes and zapping Gaia's electromagnetic pathways deep in her magnetosphere, disturbing all sorts of levels from the visible to the ultraviolet and infrared, not to mention the molecular.

Anti-matter, Thomas thought, *what has splitting the atom done to us?*

"Are you dreaming now?" he asked his protégé.

The phantom stared for a moment, then said, "No, Thomas, I'm dead. They killed me."

And he was gone.

Thoughts tumbled over each other in their eagerness to inform dreaming Thomas of what he was normally too distracted and body-burdened to comprehend. Instantaneously, he intuited that the Schrödinger equation was being manipulated to produce a different physical reality. The laws of nature were to be bypassed, the temple of the human mind and soul assaulted, personalities split, altered, removed, transferred. Education would one day be little more than downloading software into the brain. Remote control, brain-computer interface, immune systems debilitated by satellite. Welcome to the machine.

Hydrocephalics with only five percent brain matter were able to live normal lives because the brain is not the origin of thought, only the mechanism. Did thought, memory, mind, and personality originate in the infolded Whittaker bi-directional electromagnetic wave structure of scalar potential? In order to build the specialized chamber for his Gollum, he'd applied Whittaker's infolded wave structure. But seeing it in human terms bumped it from physics to metaphysics.

Other thoughts ran through his own infolded Whittaker electromagnetic wave structure: action-at-a-distance, quantum potential correlation, nonlinear phenomena, time-reversed waves, negentropy . . .

Negentropy?

Thomas opened his eyes. The country road of the dream slate was gone. The Colonel was sitting at the picnic table smoking a morning pipe, a sleepy Seven was getting the oatmeal on, and Sirius was licking his face. Night consciousness was gone.

"Oh no," Thomas groaned, "I've lost the words . . ."

Seven smiled, stirring. "You mean, 'action-at-a-distance' and 'quantum potential correlation' and—" She scrunched her eyes and looked up to the right where her short-term memory was filed.

The Colonel picked up the thread. "—'nonlinear phenomena,' 'time-reversed waves,' and that difficult word . . ." He drew on his pipe.

"Negentropy!" Thomas cried victoriously. "Negentropy. But how——?"

"You listed them in your sleep as if your life depended upon them." The Colonel tapped his pipe on the bench. "What do they mean?"

Naked, Thomas leaped up and frantically dug in his pack. "I'm not sure, but they have something to do with the scalar part of Maxwell's quaternions and Bohm's hidden variables, not random." He paused to savor a sudden connection. "Not random, *variable*—a hidden order, like this inversion of Time we're experiencing. Chaos." Grinning, he held up his notebook and flipped it open, rambling on as if Seven and the Colonel could understand a word he was saying. "Back in the 19th century, Heaviside and Gibbs . . ."

And on he went as Baby Rose, Ray, Mannie, Vince, and their European guests awoke to morning oatmeal, toast, and tea. Once Ander and Lotke headed west, the pilgrims packed up and got back on 66 east. The first bumper sticker they saw proved that synchronicity was still at work—*Grateful Dead*

—and KRMA popped on with a bit of news.

"On the border between Arizona and Mexico, Fort Huachuca is home to the U.S. Army Military Intelligence Center and a legion of private intelligence corporations like General Dynamics in Scottsdale, Lockheed Martin and L-3 Communications in Mesa, Castillo Technologies in Phoenix, CACI International, ManTech International, AllSource Global Management, and Integrated Systems Improvement Services adjacent to the base in Sierra Vista. Telecommunications, interrogation techniques, synthetic telepathy, voice synthesis, satellite remote neural monitoring (RNM), data collection, and covert operations all need a multigenerational stream of experimental subjects. Intelligence personnel trained and programmed at Huachuca are sent to hot spot war zones like Iraq,

Afghanistan, and interrogation centers throughout the world . . ."

Confederate sympathizers had settled in southern Arizona during the Civil War—Knights of the Golden Circle with their German, Austrian, French, and Italian miners and tradesmen watching over gold bullion and coin at 1866 valuation buried all the way to California.

At Fort Huachuca, a female intelligence officer who'd been transferred from Fort Monroe Army Training and Doctrine Command on Old Point Comfort was as usual having trouble sleeping because beneath the soothing tape the base psychiatrist had given her, the Magician's voice was drilling into her subconscious.

"True spiritual evil can choose its orientation quite freely because it is not limited to the functional restraints and cognitive masks that force people to obey the fragmentary left-brain fixation on dualistic materialism. All evil needs is emotional damage in childhood or young adulthood or an otherwise fearful, angry, or lustful mental life, and soon a symbiotic relationship with unconscious spiritual evil will produce a preference for negativity. This is our objective. Souls like yours can consciously choose to collude with military-like hierarchies of negative beings that feed off of a constant current of emotional pain, fear, sadness, anger, violence, and of course blood . . ."

The intelligence officer rolled over, agitated. At a briefing the previous evening, she'd been trotted out with her severed womb to say that war would always be terrible but a world power deserving its reputation for humane action should pioneer the principles of non-lethal defense. Saying what she was told to say made her Army career soar and her sleep suffer, as if the vortex of buzzwords she was forced to swallow held her sleep prisoner: *life-serving, white paper, adventurism, insurgency, ethnic violence, terrorism, narco-trafficking, domestic crime* . . .

Groaning at the prospect of another day with no sleep, she got up and took a pill. *Anti-materiel. Chemical. Laser-blinding to incapacitate electronic sensors or optics. ARDEC. LCDM. HPM. Supercaustics millions of times more caustic than hydrofluoric acid* . . . Exhausted, she stepped into the shower. She knew what happened to people who couldn't take the pressure. At a briefing in Washington, DC, General Schwartzkopf had told the Joint Chiefs that one weapon stationed in space with a wide-area pulse capacity could fry enemy electronics. She'd waited for him to finish the sentence with *and enemy personnel as well*, but he didn't need to: everyone in the room had mentally finished it for him. Her vagina had spasmed at *low collateral damage munitions*. Drying off, the intelligence officer wondered how Dr. Herta Oberheuser slept. She had experimented on women at Ravensbrück.

About the time Thomas was remembering *negentropy*, the intelligence officer was outside the PX buying two warm tortillas with butter from a little brown girl with black eyes in a Brownies uniform. Touching the small believing hand had filled her bloodshot eyes with tears, and the warm tortillas reminded her of souls. Her stomach churning, she raced back to her car, desperate to go and do whatever she had to.

Baby Rose had had a fitful night, too, awakening off and on to the call of military UFOs overhead with their thousands of tiny LED lights of the future on them, their electrochromatics spitting out visions of religious superstars like Jesus, Mohammed, and Nuestra Señora de Guadalupe. She had watched holographic sky shows like the one at the Stargazer, then snuggling up to Seven or Sirius, trying to retreat into a world of dreams not unlike those Dr. Greenbaum had created in her in the Nazi underground of University of Rochester, Kodak, and Bausch and Lomb. She had awakened in many underground bases in her brief years: Camp David in northern Maryland near Thurmont; Raven Rock, Site R; under Cheyenne Mountain outside Colorado Springs where she had seen both American and Canadian military personnel; FEMA's National Warning Center inside Mount Weather near Bluemont,

Virginia. She wasn't sure if it was military or not, but she'd even been in a bunker under the posh Greenbriar Hotel in White Sulphur Springs, West Virginia, 250 miles southwest of the District of Columbia. And Mount Pony near Culpeper, off Route 3, the Federal Reserve Center where financial transactions were monitored via the Fed Wire. Dr. Gottlieb—his real name was Joseph Scheider—would own a farm ten miles northwest of Culpeper.

During the Reagan administration, $8 billion and eleven years would be poured into the Continuity of Government Program (COG), Project 908, a network of bunkers filled with high-tech communications equipment. Known as the Project, COG's construction was determined by expert advisors called the Wise Men. Ninety-six underground bunkers for Federal Relocation Centers in the Federal Arc, the 300-mile radius of Washington—FRCs in Pennsylvania, Maryland, West Virginia, Virginia, and North Carolina. They were in Santa Rosa, California, too—Denver, Thomasville, Georgia; Maynard, Massachusetts; Battle Creek, Michigan; Denton, Texas; Bothell, Washington. What were they for? The fifty fallout-resistant command post bunkers throughout FEMA's ten regions were linked by satellite, GWEN towers, and high-frequency transmissions, each equipped to function as an emergency White House if it had to. Baby Rose had serviced COG shadow government members whose terms weren't limited by elections. Black budget drugs, weapons, and child slavery funded FEMA. So expensive were the accommodations in these underground facilities that lies had to be leaked so the few honest Congressmen left would not snoop into the double ledgers. Strangely, Project 908 was overseen by Information Systems Command at Fort Huachuca, Arizona in a sole-source contract with Betac Corporation in Arlington, Virginia. Betac was code for former Pentagon intelligence and communications specialists.

Sometime between Seven and Sirius, Baby Rose had dreamed she was walking down one of those barren COG hallways and peering into rooms where doctors in white coats were bending over unconscious military personnel and children. The usual alarms must have been off because no one detected her subtle body. One room was like a grotto, moist and green. Entranced, she entered and made her way down a trail redolent with orchids and vines. From the undergrowth, a brown round face and gentle leaf-like hands waved her on to a clearing where Indian women in colorful skirts encircled a Michelangelo *Pieta*. Seven was the Madonna waiting for her. As she climbed into Mother Seven's lap, she awoke.

Everything was all right: Seven, Thomas, Sirius, the star jewels in the velvety heavens. She placed her hand on the Earth, closed her eyes, and again went in search of sleep but ended up staring south with fear growing in her belly. Something in her body was remembering the terror of a full moon night alone in tunnels below United Verde Hospital on Cleopatra Hill in Jerome where the low barometric pressure brought out miner and prostitute ghosts who'd died violent deaths from murder and the influenza that struck in 1917. At Barry M. Goldwater Air Force Range and Fort Huachuca, she'd been taken apart and put back together like Humpty Dumpty, then was forced to lick bufotenine from Sonoran Desert toads to see how close to death she could get. Outside Tucson, they'd made her smoke DMT so she would lock onto an electronic buzz and sing harmony with it. DMT had plummeted her into a supernatural carnival of demons over which a sky Viking ship with a dragon's head was cruising. People with bird heads had been on deck waving to her. She'd waved back, wishing she could go with them and get away from the men and women who hurt children for a living.

45

Firewalk With Me

"To think that a century of positivism and atheism has been able to overthrow everything but Satanism, and it cannot make Satanism yield an inch."
"Easily explained!" cried Carhaix. "Satan is forgotten by the great majority. Now it was Father Ravignan, I believe, who proved that the wiliest thing the Devil can do is to get people to deny his existence."

–J.K. Huysmans, *Là-Bas*, 1928

For a Tear is an Intellectual Thing,
And a Sigh is the Sword of an Angel King,
And the bitter groan of the Martyr's woe
Is an Arrow from the Almightie's Bow.

–William Blake (1757-1827)

It is also said that the ancients sacrificed human victims to Cronus, as was done at Carthage while that city stood and as is still done among the Gauls [keltoi] and certain other western nations.

–Dionysius of Halicarnassus, *Roman Antiquities* (60-67 BCE)

. . . an entanglement of interests extending back to the Middle Ages . . . has developed a monster-like existence through the course of the centuries . . . and it remains a well-concealed, well organized conspiracy with all its ramifications – a conspiracy aiming at world conquest and

subordinating all moral considerations to its aim . . . We must yield to
the evidence that it is not possible to explain a series of contemporary
phenomena without going back to their distant sources, some six or seven
centuries back. So much the worse for those who do not consider this a
serious method of investigation.

–Paul Winkler, *The Thousand-Year Conspiracy*, 1943

It was evening in the District of Columbia and Dr. Greenbaum was at home savoring the book *Là-Bas*, especially the words "Progress is the hypocrisy that refines the vices. When materialism is rotten-ripe, magic takes root." The two doctrines of the Anti-Christ were materialism and magic. He chuckled, thinking of how wrong the Austrian initiate had been—

The innate healing forces of the human organism, transformed
into knowledge, result in occult knowledge. This hygienic occult
capability is developing in a good way, and will be present in a
relatively short time.

His mind being tutored to invert whatever was good and true and then devise a practical use for the inversion, Greenbaum thus missed the import of the initiate's thought and extracted only what might serve his scientific art of mind control via the acquisition of forces derived from occult knowledge. In fact, in 1961 he had sought the opinion of a Jesuit friend in Rome, a member of the San Anselmo monastery assigned by the Curia to make a close study of all the Austrian initiate's works so as to school the Curia in what to expect regarding the Second Coming. The Jesuit had agreed with Greenbaum that "innate healing forces" referred to etheric forces, and "be present in a relatively short time" to *The deepest secret of the time in which we live is the etheric coming again of Christ*, announced in a 1920 lecture. The Jesuit cautioned him that the initiate had also indicated that the generations born during the first half of the first Jupiter cycle after the war, from 1945 to 1951, would have "very special capabilities as natural attributes." In other words, relatively high incarnations. Turn them, weaken them, destroy them, and the generations after would be easy pickings.

Greenbaum had then called the Magician who'd then called his corporate sponsors who'd called Lockheed colleagues at Defense Industrial Security Command (DISC), after which a Standard Oil of New Jersey CEO called Rand and proposed a two-tier meeting at the posh bunker 300 feet under the Iron Mountain Atomic Storage up in Livingston, New York. One phone call had led to what came to be known as the Iron Mountain meeting.

Rand in those years had been rogue, a place where anything that could be imagined could be discussed and done. For the Iron Mountain meetings, the Special Study Group (SSG) pursued solid institutional analysis on the one hand and esoteric analysis of the present *etheric* situation on the other. Other groups were scheduled to meet as decoys, like the Council of Economic Advisers then organized as the Committee on the Economic Impact of Defense and Disarmament (Nazis always think in terms of mirroring, doubles, twins, etc.) and the Ackley Study. Rand, Hudson Institute, and Institute for Defense Analysis were involved; natural and social scientists, humanities, economists, law. No women, just Brothers accustomed to absolute secrecy. Personal and medical dossiers were read aloud so secrecy in the group would remain absolute.

The SSG had traveled to the old iron mine that descended 22 stories outside Hudson and the Burned-over District. Throughout the meetings, they harped on the superiority of a permanent war economy for stability and culling populations while maintaining and increasing poverty to stock a social-welfare standing army and delaying medical advances. (After Vietnam, the draft would be eliminated, university fees raised, and security forces privatized.)

Expanding Schedule I drugs and prison sentences would continue to contain the minority races; air and water pollution would maintain profits for the pharmaceutical and medical industries, and cloning was all but a reality. Thus what Gottlieb and Greenbaum cared most about—cyborg research—was praised and assured a big future.

The Report From Iron Mountain was leaked to the press. (Due to the 99-year rule, none of the esoteric discussions were included.) The *Report* was discredited as a hoax, but Council of Foreign Relations member John Kenneth Galbraith under the pseudonym "Professor Herschel McLandress" wrote in *The Washington Post* (November 26, 1967), "As I put my personal repute behind the authenticity of this document, so would I testify to the validity of its conclusions. My reservations relate only to the wisdom of releasing it to an obviously unconditioned public." People hearing the truth and not believing it acts as an inoculation against the truth.

Envisioning the men sitting around the table under Iron Mountain reminded Greenbaum of how *addictive* power is, and how stupid it makes men. The addiction was due to the *auric mobius coil* invisibly producing a substance as addictive as heroin or endorphins. Little did such foolish men realize that the sycophants gathered around them were simply vampiring what they could from each man's spinning mobius coil.

Jesus engaged his auric mobius coil before commanding demons to offer up their name's sound or frequency so he could drive the demon back to its "address." That's how powerful the coils are. All energies, creative or destructive, have their own sound and shape and can be commanded by that which is able to exercise power over words and images. Australian aborigines translate sounds and shapes into drawings or songs in order to heal or destroy. Grasp the invisible shape of disorder, the frequency of its substance, its point of reference or dissonance point, and one can, as Jesus taught, move mountains.

Then there is the dreaming mind of the *etheric double* moving around at night while the physical body lies inert. Whereas the etheric double perceives the inaudible, the etheric body perceives invisible shapes. Intentions lie with the dreaming mind, actions with the waking mind. It was with the dreaming mind that MK-ULTRA is concerned, and it is the split from not acting according to intention that gives subnature entry through the subconscious. Command the dreaming mind and the soul has to follow, it is as simple as that.

Thoughts and emotions are *substantial* "subjective" impressions because souls are composed of a *substance* called "virtue" or "grace" that can be lost or vampired. Even hate composed of thought and desire is a willed creation of real shape and color frequency, an elemental that was previously not but now is. Hate opens demonic doors. Open your mental frequency and waveforms to the wrong thoughts and you open your body to "viruses" of corresponding frequency and waveform. The Bible alludes to this when it says that man is created in the image of God, meaing man is either a creator or a destroyer. As Crowley said, *Do what thou wilt shall be the whole of the law.*

Only grasp the principles of pattern, pitch, and point of reference and one can access the keys to the kingdoms of Heaven or Hell, white or black magick, as per one's desire, will, and intention. But if these principles are not constantly purified, they become subject to the mobius, the key tool of power requiring that one's point of reference be ever in the present tense, neither fearing nor longing, which is why true leaders, good or evil, can bring out the best (sometimes meaning the worst) in their followers, depending upon their intention.

Greenbaum's thought stream was interrupted by the word *Krishna* in a news broadcast coming from the kitchen. The Krishna cult had been one of his creations. He got up to investigate.

". . . The International Society for Krishna Consciousness, founded by Swami Srila Prabhupada in 1965, is awash in sexual abuse cases. Children are molested once their parents are sent to

311

other ashrams around the world to proselytize and beg for money. Most of the children are not properly clothed or fed, and are awakened at 2 a.m. for three hours of prayer. If they fall asleep during the day's long labors in field and house, they are doused with cold water or smacked. If they wet the bed, they must wear their soiled underwear on their head for the day. Some are scrubbed with steel wool until their skin bleeds. At the New Vrindaban commune in West Virginia, new mothers have a saying, 'Dump the load and hit the road' . . ." The broadcast faded.

Greenbaum pondered the radio, which was off. The housekeeper had left hours before. How had the radio gone on and off? And such a bad press leak.

In Philadelphia, the Qabalist was poring over his charts. The last solar eclipse of the second millennium would be on August 11, 1999, forming a grand cross with the Sun in the Crab, the Moon and Uranus in the Goat, Mars in the Scales, and Saturn in the Ram. In the midst of the tension, Venus would be conjunct Regulus, the heart of the Lion. During the eclipse, the Moon's shadow would swing across the Atlantic over Cornwall, then France, Germany, Austria, Hungary, Roumania, Turkey, Iraq, Iran, Pakistan, India, and the Bay of Bengal. The very first solar eclipse of the *third* millennium on June 21, 2001 would cross Africa.

He looked up from his computations. The *goy* Brothers had had their Grail Fitzgeralds, *fils de Gérald*, sons of Grail Spear rule. Had this Kennedy Fitzgerald been Arab, he might have been called *Caliph*; had he been Khazar, it would have been *Kagan*. The 10th century scholar Saadiah Gaon might even have called him *Hiram of Tyre*, to the chagrin of the Brothers who chose murder most foul for America's Arthur and Camelot. There would surely be hell to pay.

The Great Kagan of the Imperial Race had appeared in public only once every four months and would never have tempted fate by riding in a convertible with the top down. After 40 years of rule, not three, the Great Kagan too had been ritually killed; Alexander the Great had been allowed one Jupiter cycle before purportedly dying of malaria and being embalmed by Eastern masters in India in 324 BC. Like Lincoln's casket, his golden casket had traveled for months from Babylon through Mesopotamia, over Syria to Damascus, Aegae Macedonia, and on to Alexandria.

Then there was the Druid prince slain with the Triple Death at Cadbury Castle, the Iron Age citadel—sacrificed and folded in a fetal position, crammed into a tiny space at the base of the rampart constructed against the Romans. Another Druid prince had been ferried from *insula sacra* Ireland up the Mersey to Lindow Moss and sacrificed beside the Black Lake during Britannia's darkest hour.

Yes, there would be hell to pay for this Kennedy Fitzgerald sacrifice because it lacked *honor*. He had been given the Triple Death as triple shots at the Triple Underpass, the sacred three times three. The first bullet caught him full in the throat like the old garroting and slitting of the jugular for Esus, and he had drowned in blood in the throat for Teutates, and a bullet like an ax had taken the crown off his head for Taranis, but the rite had been tainted with deceit and spite and had not been for the health of the people at all. The Celtic headhunting aristocracy had acted in a muddled, petty, and savage way for their own gain. Sacred violence was dead and the Kennedy Fitzgerald murder proved it.

It had been more like the ritual murder of Prince Coh of the Mayas. Instead of three bullets, Prince Coh's brother Prince Aac had inflicted three spear wounds. The vital organs of sensation had then been removed, charred, and preserved in cinnabar, his brain in its own urn, his body consigned to the all-purifying fire. Like Isis and her sister Nephthys, Prince Coh's sister-wife Queen Móo and second sister Niké lamented his death. His coat of arms had been a headless winged serpent, like his Mayach land without him. His stone image atop his mausoleum in Chichén Itzá was a leopard with a human head staring south, awaiting the return of his spirit. *A headless winged serpent*, the Qabalist thought. Amaruca with its occult District of Columbia was now such a headless land whose future Presidents would be run by brain banks, committees, corporations, networks, and "teams" filled with hive minds and belonging to Egregores. *The king is the land and the land is the King* was no more. What would take its place?

Television had turned the disreputable Killing of the King into a spectacle of sound and fury. Re-runs of Guinevere crawling over the limo trunk to retrieve his brains evoked the myth of the sacrifice of the King again and again in the people's minds, opening the wound over and over again until the people felt nothing, certainly not renewal. In Britannia, Arthur would return to rule again, and peace and plenty would flow again once one who loved the people returned. In the United States, the assassins' hatred of Kennedy served to crush all hope. The public murder of the last kingly President announced the end of an era and dream. Guinevere would be married off to one of the conspirators, as in the Prince Coh version, and the re-run of Isis crawling over the trunk to retrieve what was lost would be all that was left of Camelot.

The Qabalist, a student of eternal things, knew that justice must one day prevail, but until then the people would be made to suffer, not the conspirators. Sleeping dogs might lie, but lies do not sleep. The United States would be subsumed in an unnatural technocracy that would rip the Veil of the Threshold and suck America down into a new brutal world order. It would take two Metonic cycles to anchor the Third Reich in America. The Nazi chapter in Europe had been but a prologue.

The Qabalist despised the smug Yale and Stanford "technicians of persuasion" he had to work with. He'd achieved his art the real way and could make mincemeat of them all. On the rare occasions that he had to attend a board meeting at AT&T or one of the networks, the merchant mentalities scarcely dared to look at him. *Goy* Americans were empty; even American Jews seemed dried

314

up and hollow. At least the Nazis had passion and ideals. He and Greenbaum and the Magician may have been ridiculed as "Nazi science" throwbacks, but in reality they were feared for what they might conjure, were they so inclined.

Even for the ritual slaying of the Fitzgerald, the Joint Chiefs had sought his expertise. Adding the public slaying of the other two lesser "kings" by precisioned and heartless Assassins had served to announce to the world the Working of the magickal number three. The geomagnetism that implanted crass materialism in Americans was truly Ahrimanic.

The Qabalist grimaced: he had another meeting to attend. How Americans loved their meetings, their bland avaricious faces and mechanistic minds posing around big tables, congratulating themselves on their power and wealth. He longed for Bavaria, the mountains, the good cognac, conversation about Goethe and *Götterdammerüng.* Was this America what the men of his generation had had in mind? These cruel, cretin Americans with vacuous brains who only knew how to be "team players," with no great past to contemplate? Could he endure the future he had helped to promote? Had he known . . .

He rose from his chair like the old man he was becoming and sighed. Later, he would have a cognac and listen to Liszt, perhaps read about Kaspar Hauser, the Child of Europe, and contemplate what might have been, had he been allowed to live.

East across the great drink, Laurence was in a London pub, waiting for his old college roommate Grant who now worked in the City of London Mayor's office. Grant had always been more accessible than many of the English public school boys Laurence had encountered, so when Grant entered, Laurence was surprised by the pinched look on his face. They shook hands, ordered pints, and spent a few minutes reminiscing and catching up.

At last, taking a long draw on his pint, Laurence took the

plunge. "What is it, Grant? Something is bothering you." Prosaically, he guessed it was either a woman or his job.

Grant stared at his ale. "Oh God, Larry," he said, pressing his fist against his forehead, "where to begin?"

Laurence had never seen him so upset. Quietly, he waited for his old friend to collect himself. The eyes meeting his registered *fear*.

Grant half-smiled. "You know, I once had dreams not of wealth or position, but of meaning, depth, relevance . . ."

The very thoughts Laurence had been wrestling with.

Un-English-like, Grant grabbed his friend's hands and squeezed. "Did you know, Larry, that Tolkien once mentioned a mysterious Celtic spiritual center or university here in the islands in 500 BC, called Numinor? Numinor, *noumen*, spirit . . ." He drifted, then continued dreamily. "Some believe that Joseph of Arimathea once visited these islands—even Jesus' mother. 'And did those feet in ancient time walk upon England's mountains green?'" He looked up. "Blake."

Laurence could scarcely believe the synchronicity.

Grant raised his glass and voice. "'Bring me my bow of burning gold! Bring me my arrows of desire!'" His voice dropped. Laurence swore his proud English friend was close to tears. Gathering himself again, Grant continued, "'I will not cease from mental fight, nor shall my sword . . .'—Excuse me, Larry." He got up and rushed away through the crowded, smoky pub.

Laurence glanced around, sipping, disturbed. Grant, so strong inside and out—unlike himself. What could be frightening him so? Until the last few days, his own danger had been to succumb to being a desert that never bloomed, toiling in the shadow of Blake's dark Satanic mills, making and moving millions at unredeemable cost to his soul.

Grant was back, smiling but not really. Putting a good face on it, the British called it. "Right-o," he began again, taking his chair and a long drink of ale. "Seriously, Larry, what I am about to say, you never heard. Agreed?"

Laurence nodded solemnly. "Agreed."

Grant searched his American friend's eyes. "I'm deadly serious, Larry. My life, and perhaps yours, could depend upon your silence." He glanced around.

The hair on the back of Laurence's neck twitched. Briefly, he wondered what could be so dangerous in this well-paid clerk's life.

Grant settled back in his chair. "You never became a Mason like your brother, did you?"

Masonry!

"No," Laurence said, "can't you tell by my career?" He was surprised by how bitter he sounded.

Grant smiled wanly. "Right." He glanced about again. Laurence suddenly realized why he'd chosen this mixed, lower-end pub. "Well, I did join, Holy Royal Arch and all, the full noose around my neck. Prince Charles' father Philip was initiated December 5, 1952 at Navy Lodge 2612, but grudgingly so. Six months later, Elizabeth was crowned. The story is that Philip never finished the three degrees. The Hanover dynasty has survived only because it has embraced, or at least smiled upon, Freemasonry.

"In the West Midlands, four out of five police are Freemasons. Scotland Yard has its own Manor St. James Lodge." He leaned closer and lowered his voice. "All who seek high position in criminal justice must register as Freemasons or as members of other Brotherhoods requiring similar blood oaths. Freemasonry is the *politboro* in London, Larry, not Moscow. Five hundred thousand Freemasons in these islands alone, and God only knows how many are in your nation where they habitually lie instead of bite their tongues. Lloyds Bank has its Black Horse Lodge of Lombard Street, the Bank of England its. The Church of England has been a stronghold of Freemasonry for over two hundred years, despite the best efforts of the clergyman from Sussex who wrote *Darkness Visible* in 1951, which only now have I been able to find and read." Grant pulled a copy of the small book out of thin air and slid it toward Laurence. "Put it away for now.—God, I feel like we're back at school and it's Lawrence's *Lady Chatterly's Lover* we're passing. But do look it over, Larry. I'm certain the States and Canada are in the same predicament."

He narrowed his eyes, whispering, "So who *is* The Great Architect of the Universe, GAOTU? Not Jahweh, not Allah, not the Triune God, not even a deist's deity. The Royal Arch has cleared this up for me." His voice was heavy with sarcasm. "GAOTU is Jaobulon, a composite triune being of *Jao* or *Jah*, perhaps for Jahweh, perhaps *Tao*; *Bul* for Baal of Tyre; and *On* for Osiris, Egyptian god of the dead. 1 Kings 18:21, *How long halt ye between two opinions? If the Lord be God, follow him; but if Baal, then follow him.*"

He paused to rub his eyes as though he were not sleeping well. He looked up. "Larry, I realize all of this may sound like nonsense, words middle-aged men utter to make their lives seem dramatic. But there is something utterly—Larry, I am involved in an un-Christian Mystery cult as far from what my heart longs for as the Moon. It may even be Satanic, I don't know." He was so wrought up he was practically breathless. "'Dark Satanic mills,' Larry. My God, what is going on today?"

Given the Freemason status of his brother, Laurence did not underestimate his friend's dilemma. "I'd say quit, Grant, but I know the Grand Lodge would view it as betrayal." No use quibbling over terms.

"Is your brother content?"

Laurence laughed. "Content? Hiram's riding the rocket to the stars, or thinks he is. He's risen in the ranks, belongs to a variety of Lodges, and has been duly rewarded. Truthfully, I don't think he's material for the 33rd and above degrees, he's not really clever enough, nor does he believe in half the jargon of Jah-Bu-Lon or Lucifer or whatever. But he's definitely their tool, and he certainly knows that the blood vows are not just words." He gripped his friend's forearm. "Grant—be careful."

The two friends looked at each other and raised their glasses for a somber toast. Grant recited one last quote among the many he had committed to memory in his youth. "'Do not swear at all, simply let your Yes be Yes, and your No be No. Anything beyond this comes from the evil one.' Matthew 5:34, 37.— God, Larry, why didn't they teach me what those verses were really referring to? Why don't they teach us what is really *out there* in the name of polite society?"

They parted when the pub closed. Laurence watched Grant disappear into the tube station and felt helpless, unimaginative. He was loath to leave London the next morning, sensing the danger his friend was in. This feeling business hurt. He could see why so many men chose not to feel.

It would be the last time he would see Grant on this Earth.

Returning to the hotel room he'd booked under yet another alias, he made a cup of strong tea and set out *Darkness Visible: A Revelation & Interpretation of Freemasonry* by Walton Hannah, published by Augustine Press. Over the years, he had picked up odd phrases and facts about Freemasonry: how Henry Ford was initiated in Detroit at Palestine Lodge No. 357 in 1894; that the Lodge St. George in Bermuda was the oldest Scottish Rite lodge outside of Scotland; that a Lodge of the Nine Sisters, one of Ben Franklin's several lodges, met in St.-Sulpice church in Paris; that Hitler had belonged to Lodge 99 in Dresden, *Der Freimaurerischer Orden der Goldenen Centurie*—99 lodges with 99 members each. Two quotes for him summed up the Freemasons and other secret societies: *Alchemists conceal in order to baffle the vulgar*, by the French occultist Emile Grillot DeGivry; and *They do not know because we lie to them*, by Grand Sovereign Commander of Scottish Rite General Albert Pike.

In *The Republic*, Plato defined the "noble" lie as a myth or untruth knowingly told to the people in order to maintain social harmony and power. Lying, then, was individually wrong but politically expedient—black and white so the grey could take over. How much do you tell? Who do you tell and not tell? What do you color and not color? *The first stage in the corruption of morals is the banishing of truth*, Montaigne said, and it was still true four centuries later.

Lying as policy was repugnant to Laurence.

The first phrase to meet his eyes was from the Ceremony of Raising to the Third Degree: . . . *the light of a Master Mason is darkness visible.*

He thought back to an El Greco portrait of Vincentio Anastagi painted in 1576. Anastagi had been Governor of Malta, dying ten years after sitting for the portrait while defending Malta against the Turks. In the original portrait, the Maltese Cross had been on his chest, the *croix-patte* of the Knights Templar, proving for all time that he was a Knight of Malta. The Spaniard Vasco Nuñez de Balboa had been a Knight of Malta, Prince Henry the Navigator in Portugal, and Cristóbal Colón married the daughter of a Knight. Recently, however (the museum brochure had delicately indicated), the *croix-patte* had been painstakingly removed from the Anastagi portrait. Had other crosses been removed from other portraits? And why remove them now? Laurence's mind leaped to the Reichstag fire. Was a historical purge underway? *The light of a Master Mason is darkness visible.*

The Knights of Malta were basically late Knights Hospitaller, Order of the Hospital of St. John the Baptist—the Knights who fought the Saracens and Ottoman Turks with the Templars, then inherited Templar holdings when the Templars were wiped from the map. The Hospitallers had fled to Cyprus and finally established themselves on the isle of Rhodes in 1310, just as their Templar Brothers were going under. They were evicted from Rhodes by the Turks in 1522 and the new Holy Roman Emperor Charles V gave them Malta for the rent price of one falcon per year. Their vow was distinctly Freemason—

I, -----, of my own free will and accord, and in the presence of Almighty God and this worshipful lodge of Free and Accepted

Masons, dedicated to God, and held forth to the holy order of St. John, do hereby and hereon most solemnly sincerely promise and swear that I will always hail, ever conceal and never reveal any part or parts, or any art or arts, point or points of the secret arts and mysteries of ancient Freemasonry which I have received, am about to receive, or may hereafter be instructed in, to any person or persons of the known world . . .

To all of which I do most solemnly and sincerely promise and swear, without the least equivocation, mental reservation, or evasion of mind in me whatever; binding myself under no less penalty than to have my throat cut across, my tongue torn out by the roots, and my body buried in the rough sands of the sea at low water-mark, where the tide ebbs and flows twice in twenty-four hours; so help me God, and keep me steadfast in the due performance of the same.

Since the Templars, all Catholic and post-Reformation Knight and Brotherhood vows had been based on Freemasonry. Had the Catholics and Freemasons buried the hatchet? Was that what Vatican II was about?

Laurence yawned. It was late and he was due in Paris tomorrow for dinner with Jean, another old school friend, then on to the south of France. He considered calling Caroline, but guessed Hiram's AT&T friends might be tapping his phone. Besides, Caroline was used to doing without him.

Sometime before dawn, he dreamed of Thomas' old nanny with eyes black as night and that coffee-and-cream skin Laurence liked—the Jamaican woman Hiram had gotten rid of. They were on an old European street and she was beckoning to him to follow her into a cemetery. She stopped at a gravestone and Laurence's dream self read—

December 17, 1833

Hic jacet Casparus Hauser [Here lies Kaspar Hauser]
Aenigma sui temporis [Riddle of our Time]
ignota nativitas [his Birth unknown]
occula mors [his Death mysterious].

He looked up at the old Jamaican who was speaking, pointing
to her mouth. He couldn't hear what she was saying but lip-read one
word: *Ansbach*.

46

First International Dark Sky City

There's a time when the operation of the machine becomes so odious, makes one so sick at heart that you can't take part, you can't even tacitly take part, and you have to put your body upon the gears and the wheels, upon all the apparatus, and you've got to stop it. You've got to indicate to the people who run it, the people who own it, that unless you're free the machine will be prevented from working.

      −Mario Salvo, Free Speech Movement, 1964

I seem to be a verb.

      −Buckminster Fuller

"But my mind is dying," Joe protests, shuddering.
Simon holds up an ear of corn and tells him urgently, "Osiris is a black god!"

      −Robert Shea and Robert Anton Wilson,
      Illuminatus! 1975

And we shall have a table round
So that no one of us
Shall be above another.

      −King Arthur, 680 CE

It was *fantapolitica* as usual in America, a typical network news day with scrambling to pad the news events being given top priority with video news releases (VNRs) and other news events being jettisoned for closed-door reasons.

Wannabe Lemurians at Mount Shasta were still calling America *Guatama*. Firestarters were starting fires with a glance, with 66-year-old Jack Angel about to awake in Savannah with a hole burned in his chest. A Los Angeles police officer was voyeuring his way through media files on the murders of Black Dahlia, Johnny Stompanado and Lana Turner, and Thelma Todd the Ice Cream Blonde. In Colorado, Ishtar the Lady of the *mei* data banks was spitting out information for NORAD (then known as North American Air Defense Command), and meth heads everywhere were picking up decongestant pseudoephedrine, 2-liter soda bottles, and household chemicals.

Rumor had it that the Soviets (who said it was the Americans) had sent a human cryogenically frozen at -474°F (-270°C) into space on cruise control at 18,000 miles per hour as early as the late 1950s. Thus when the Italian brothers Achille and Gian Judica-Cordiglia, 16 and 10 years old respectively, tuned their receiver to the Bochum Radio Observatory in West Germany and recognized an *S–O–S* signal they from a single point nine billion miles from Earth, people wondered if the cryogenically frozen person had awakened to his condition.

Thirty American research institutions serving Tavistock Institute grant monies were studying the Lewin-SS Heydrich-ONI *induced trauma long-range penetration warfare* model and line-graphing the three phases of inducing mass stress and trauma: (1) inundation with superficiality; (2) fragmentation; and (3) collective determinism that eschews the induced crisis and develops a maladaptive response of active synoptic idealism coupled with disassociation.

Three million animals were being injected between the shoulder blades with Destron-Fearing transponders, microchips covered in biomedical grade glass imprinted with a maximum of 34 billion codes that electronic wands could scan. Soldiers, intelligence agents, sleepers, MILABs, foster children, mental patients, the homeless, prisoners—in a word, the disenfranchised—were being chipped, as well. Transponders were just more of the global positioning system (GPS), beginning with Dr. Delgado's military-funded stimoceiver (1950s) and transnasal implants (1960s), and Dr. Daniel Man's behind-the-ear biochip (1970s) triangulating with satellites, GWEN towers, and helicopters. *Humans can be controlled like robots by push buttons*, Herr Doktor Delgado wrote—emotions, sensory impressions, hallucinations, brain transmissions. The brave new world of biomedical telemetry was in motion.

In Europe, the rock group Gong was to Tavistock Octave Doctors as Ander and Lotke said the Grateful Dead were to Stanford Research Institute, Bear Owsley, and military state-of-the-art sound equipment. Low-vibrational music was pulsing everywhere in America over radio and television waves, and alcohol-free teen club Raves were delivering subliminal resonant induction messages. Oooh-baby Classic Rock was massaging corporate stations and lulling people into political apathy while GodSmack, Marilyn Manson, and Nine Inch Nails thrashed young psyches with high-tech NSA Operation Clean Sweep infrasound in the name of peer bonding and Mafia ecstasy (MDMA) ego-melt, blasting open the lower three chakras for the invisible vampiric beings lining up for energy transfusions. Once the invisibles began feeding, feelings of paranoia, moods, and anxiety infused the young disconnected pumping bodies in the name of an American techno good time.

The pilgrims were chugging up the mountain toward Flagstaff, Arizona, all the while chewing over the awareness of sound that Ander and Lotke had infused them with and applying critical listening to songs spilling out of KRMA like the Grateful Dead's "Ballad of Casey Jones"—

Casey said just before he died
Two more roads that I want to ride
People said, what roads, Casey, can they be
Gold Colorado and the Santa Fe?

Thomas wanted to stop in Flagstaff to see if he could find some red filter lenses so they could practice looking through them at ordinary daylight to make the eyes briefly recalibrate their visual range into the infrared so they could see auras and maybe even ether UFOs. Charlie Manson had been directed to read Bulwer-Lytton's *Vril*, vril being the semi-material ether that "Vril conductors" used to influence weather, mesmerize, and transmit thoughts from one brain to another—what SS initiations had been about, thanks to the Green Dragon Society in Japan and Haushofer. *Vril*'s publication occurred when John Worrell Keely was harnessing water ether in Philadelphia and powering calibrated machines with it, and when Sir Oliver Lodge was telling the London Institute that æther was *an undivided substance that fills all space, that can vibrate as light, that can be divided in positive and negative electricity that in vortex movement creates matter and all that through composition and not pressure transmits all actions and reactions that the substance may yield.*

How could 19th century scientists have known that space was a plenum of æther, only to be followed by a century of scientists believing that space was empty? In the Fifties, a scientist had assured Thomas that the JASONs knew space held a dark matter or energy but not *quite* what it was. It had been a lie. The JASONs knew all along about the soniferous ether of all-pervasive space, the soul of the cosmos through which divine thought manifests in matter, Faraday's one common origin to all matter, including Nature's magnetic operations (leylines, sex, aggression, etc.).

Next, Whittaker had been suppressed. In his 1910 *A History of the Theories of Æther and Electricity*, he had credited not Einstein but Poincaré and Lorentz with the special relativity theory and $E=mc^2$.

Einstein was the JASONs' boy for keeping control over what science was to be allowed and what wasn't. Covert militarized science via DARPA, big defense corporations, and JASONs knew that æther was dark matter and dark energy, and an elite echelon was bent on engaging, manipulating, and controlling it, all the while funneling money into a secondary level of science to obscure what was really going on. It made Thomas feel crazy, but he of all people knew it was true.

Cosmic Coincidence Control interfered in the form of an old man standing beside a blue and white '57 Bel Air Classic Chevy and flagging down the little caravan.

"Hallelujah!" he cried when Thomas and Vince hopped out of the bus. "We're out of gas."

Inside the Bel Air, his wife was calmly knitting in the front seat while in the back sat a young woman and a far older, leather-faced version of her.

Once enough gas had been siphoned from the voluminous Caddy tank for the Bel Air to make it to Flagstaff, the pilgrims were invited to a picnic lunch at a windswept roadside lean-to a couple of miles ahead. Once they'd all pulled over, the old man and his wife heaved a giant picnic basket and cooler onto the bright tablecloth they'd thrown over a desert-dried picnic table.

"My wife likes to make sure we eat well wherever we go," he winked, pulling out potato salad, fried chicken, homemade pickles, radishes, lettuce, canned pears and peaches. From the cooler, they produced several bottles of a Bolivian soda called Coca Colla. "Clever," the old man said, holding up a bottle, "made from coca leaves used for thousands of years in cooking, medicine, and religious rites." He nodded appreciatively toward his wife. "Thanks to her, I've never been to a doctor. Her mother there is over a hundred."

It turned out to be a feast beyond gastronomic. "We're pure Santa Fe Trail stock," the man winked again, then louder, added, "right, mama?"

"Been here all my life," the leathery centenarian answered just as loud.

Conversation turned to desert sights.

"We lay out three or four nights a week and watch the show," the old man said, picking his teeth with a little metal toothpick he carried in his shirt pocket. "With an infrared sight, you can see discs, critters, you name it, *and* the military shootin' 'em down like prairie dogs with what I guess to be lasers. First time I saw it was in 1977 at Ellsworth Air Force Base in South Dakota while we were visiting our son. It's not right. No, I'm with the Muslims that recognize *jinns* havin' rights, too. Aggression breeds aggression, any fool knows that. Hell, they've lived in this atmosphere a lot longer than we have. Ever since the Robertson Panel, the Air Force has been debunking and lying, especially to kids in those Disney cartoons. And that damned Advanced Theoretical Physics Working Group settin' all the secret UFO policies like they were God Almighty. Why, I remember Ken Arnold sayin' he had entities in his home, phantom pilots from the discs that made the rugs and furniture sink under their weight like the Invisible Man." He spit. "Excuse me, ladies."

His granddaughter took a long draw on her Coca Colla, then said, "Grandpa, I read that in the former Yugoslavia 1,500 people were waiting in an airfield for spaceships, and when they didn't show up were told warplanes had scared them off."

"One born every minute," her grandfather muttered.

His wife had an insight or two. "Makes me think of that *Star Trek* episode 'Return of the Archons'—remember that one, Loretta? A puritanical group under mind control triggered at night for debauchery and violence, and in the morning for puritanical propriety, rememberin' nothin' from the previous night. Maybe these things are archons, alien intruders."

"Demons!" her mother barked. "Settin' themselves up as humanity's saviors. I don't like it."

"But mama," her son-in-law yelled, "maybe that's the

military lyin' to us, like when they messed with Ken Arnold. Maybe these *jinns* are here to take whatever we're willing to give 'em from our human experience. If we give 'em fear, they take advantage of us; if we leave the back door open with drugs, alcohol, violence, or sex, they take what's human in us. But if we give 'em respect and are firm about keepin' our *authority* as human beings . . ." He raised his eyebrows and shrugged.

"But Grandpa," Loretta said, "they're light years ahead of us in psychic skill. What if they're here to suck our energy by telling us whatever we want to hear in order to get it?"

"Well, I know one thing," her grandfather said, "I'm more scared of our military than I am of those *jinns*. American military's out of control."

The Colonel nodded. "Amen to that. While I was in the Air Force, I got interested in ancient Asian and South Asian sacred texts—the *Rig Veda, Mahabharata, Ramayana, Puranas*. They talked about *vimana* flying machines. I couldn't decide if they were just myths or historical references—like the one by Srimad Bhagasvatam that said, *Arrows released by Lord Siva appeared like fiery beams emanating from the sun globe and covered the three [ships] which could no longer be seen.*" He shook his head. "Life's themes play over and over, and only the variations change. The *vimana* and *jinns* seem related."

"*Vimana* running on ether or plasma?" Thomas asked.

The Colonel shrugged. "*I* think so. The texts describe them as double-decker, circular with portholes and a dome, flying with a melodious sound. But maybe the *jinn* take any shape they want—or you want, like Loretta says about their psychic skill—saucer, cigar-shape, animal. The Mahavira of Bhavabhuti described an aerial chariot like a dirigible that conveyed many people, a *Pushpaka*, the sky full of flying machines dark as night but capable of being seen with lights."

Vince was intrigued. "Like Quetzalcoatl, the Chinese *xian* were feathered and flew under their own divine power. *Yu ke,* feathered guest, may refer to ether conduction. The *Rig Veda* even described it—

> *Now Vata's chariot's greatness! Breaking goes it,*
> *And thunderous its noise,*
> *To heaven it touches,*
> *Makes light lurid, and whirls dust upon the earth."*

"*Fei tian* were flying immortals," the Colonel added, "and *fei che* flying vehicles, chariots drawn by 'flying dragons'."

Mannie finally got a word in edgewise. "What if the 'pillar of cloud' Moses followed was a *vimana*? Moses being a techno-magician, and the Reed Sea over a grid point, maybe Moses knew how to set up a force field of some kind."

"Far out, Mannie!" Thomas said. "Longitude and latitude are reciprocals to the speed of light, mass and gravity, so what if he directed the 'pillar of cloud' to create a wedge-shaped force field over the Reed Sea along its latitude, and forced the waters to part? And once the Israelites had crossed onto dry land, he withdrew the force field so the waters returned to inundate Pharaoh's army. I think Exodus even mentions an east wind displacing masses of air—"

"—and *vimana* quickened the east wind," the Colonel added.

The old man was fascinated. "Ever see *The Fire Officer's Guide to Disaster Control*, the national guide for firemen approved by FEMA? Chapter 13, 'Enemy Attack and UFO Potential,' begins with an account of the Los Angeles air raid on February 26, 1942 at 2:25 a.m. Firefighters saw fifteen to twenty 'things' in the sky. Sirens whined, searchlights, Army gun crews pumping 1,433 *ack-ack* rounds into the moonlight, volunteer air raid wardens doin' their best to contain public panic . . ."

"I remember that," the Colonel said, though he hadn't caught the futuristic reference to FEMA. "The 14 CFR 1211 Extra-Terrestrial Exposure Law passed by Congress in 1969 granted the

NASA administrator arbitrary discretion to quarantine all objects, persons, or other forms of life that are 'extraterrestrially exposed.' Supposedly, Project Blue Book ended in January and the Air Force passed its UFO concerns on to NICAP, the National Investigation Committee on Aerial Phenomena, headed up by Major Donald Kehoe. Beyond NICAP, there's MUFON, Ground Saucer Watch, Aerial Phenomena Research Organization . . ."

". . . CAUS (Citizens Against UFO Secrecy), CUFOS (Center for UFO Studies), and on and on," the old man added, "a dime a dozen, most if not all military or infiltrated, and yet who's shuttin' up UFO witnesses and doin' everything it can to make Air Force pilots and radar techs look foolish?"

His wife was even more irate. "Well, I've never seen Men in Black, but we've seen plenty of compressed and dehydrated vegetation, thick red-grey mist, flames, imprints in the ground, radiation burns and soil samples. One rancher had eye inflammation and temporary blindness." She shook her head in disgust. "All those MIBs are nothing more than professional terrorists subjecting folks to some kind of microwave brainwashing that causes nausea, mental confusion, and amnesia. That local police refuse to investigate is just their usual kowtowing to the feds."

"And don't forget the black unmarked helicopters," her husband added.

"And why did UN Secretary General U Thant say, 'I consider UFOs to be the most important problem facing the United Nations next to the war in Vietnam'?" the Colonel asked. "Senator Barry Goldwater is a retired Air Force Brigadier General and pilot but was refused permission to check Air Force files on UFOs. Back when he was a representative in 1966, the now-Vice President called for a House hearing on UFOs. Then there were the 1968 hearings before the Congressional Committee on Science and Astronomics, published as Symposium on Unidentified Flying Objects. Were they *all* on a publicly funded wild goose chase?"

The old man didn't know what the Colonel meant by "now-Vice President" reference, but let it pass. Once the repast for body and soul wound to a close, the two groups packed up and said goodbyes with the promise of perhaps seeing each other in Flagstaff, first International Dark Sky City and site of the Lowell Observatory.

"The Observatory's closed to the public today—" Thomas suddenly looked a little deflated over the news—"but there's a street dance," the sage old man winked as he got behind the wheel of the Bel Air.

As Thomas and Seven fired up the vehicles, Vince began talking about the Hopi belief in saucers bringing divine information. "They call them *Nan-ga-Sohu*, the Chasing Star Kachina. In Sumerian, *Nin-gir-Su* means Master of Starships. Hopi say their prayers go to the planets inhabited by spirits who, when they come here, put on phantom bodies so we can see them. Plains Indians still enact the Sun Dance to restore the dissipating energy of the universe and re-order the delicate balance between the creative and destructive forces of chaos."

Thomas understood. "Like entropy. Heat death. And their phantom bodies must be made of plasma, the fourth state of matter."

Vince nodded. "Wakan Tanka, the Great Mystery, has through history sent agents like White Buffalo Calf Woman to tell people how to renew universal energy. But if my grandfather is right about Aztec and Toltec priests having come again to harness nuclear and electromagnetic energy today not for renewal but for war, a Purification Day may be inevitable. Before it happens, though, Chief Dan Katchongva said that *Bahána*, the True White Brother, will come from the south."

Listening over the two-way, Seven thought of Raven's story about White Buffalo Calf Woman. Was Raven now in Hopiland? Was White Bull still in the Fort Defiance jail? Was Hermano *Bahána*?

Vince kept talking. "The Austrian initiate said that a time would come when humanity would be split and a new race of human beings would undergo black magick initiations that would tear them from the natural course of evolution, thus recapitulating what happened on old Atlantis. Bound up with electromagnetism, it is the doubles or *Doppelgängers* of the new breed that will eventually achieve dominance and develop instincts for evil to inhuman degrees."

Thomas thought of his uncle. "Has this split already begun?"

"Oh yes," Vince said quietly, "subtle influences bankrolled by large foundations are taking Americans by storm and they don't even know it."

Pulsed signals were traveling to and fro across America at lightning speed. Houses were being pulsed, power lines glowing, toasters and electric lights and hair and clothes dryers emanating, exuding, and leaking. Soon, cell phones, laptops, and wireless technologies would be glowing at frequencies millions to tens of millions times higher while pulsing at lower power. Military/ intelligence Intelink satellites, television, and telephone were catapulting data everywhere. Cable TV and PBS would be the first to use satellite signal to deliver multipoint distribution instead of coaxial video lines leased from telephone companies. TVRO dishes would capture signals in backyards via Home Box Office's Videocipher DES algorithm (MAACOM), and the rest would be entertainment history.

Flagstaff was packed, cars parked along the sides of 66, the main street closed off as Cuban-style *salsa* beckoned. The pilgrims parked and made their way toward the plaza, Vince mentioning that the Department of Forestry had dug up an old manmade lake somewhere nearby while looking for the buried treasure mentioned in an old papal bull. The glyphs they'd found on the bottom of the lake were only visible from the air, like the Nazca Desert lines in Peru.

"During the Conquest," he explained, "European royalty was interested in capturing New World minerals to fill their war-depleted coffers, but with every mining outfit the Vatican sent two priests with papal bulls detailing 200 symbols to look for about what had been hidden years before. Later, the Freemason Smithsonian took the place of the Vatican."

"But glyphs visible only from the air?" Mannie queried.

Vince smiled into the two-way. "In ancient times, Mannie, priests, *brujos,* shamans, magi, and some priests had amazing out-of-body powers. Some still do. Add that to a monopoly on ancient manuscripts…"

Thomas and Vince went back over Thomas' dream state of the man with dead eyes. Vince was sure it had been a *brujo* of great power looking for them.

In the Flagstaff plaza, music was lifting hearts. Young and old Mexicans, Indians, and *anglos* were dancing, children were running about, friends and relatives were smiling from the sidelines, everyone forgetting their issues with each other for the sake of a little joy. The pilgrims gorged themselves on burritos, tacos, and Navajo fry bread, drank glasses of foaming keg beer they bought at a stand, and strolled around. Then Thomas maneuvered Seven out onto the street.

The Colonel settled in his chair with a beer and gazed at Thomas and Seven as the band struck up a rumba flamenco, then the Who rock song "Won't Get Fooled Again." Mannie and Baby Rose danced the Sixties freestyle.

> *We'll be fighting in the streets*
> *With our children at our feet*
> *And the morals that they worship will be gone*
> *And the men who spurred us on*
> *Sit in judgment of all wrong*
> *They decide and the shotgun sings the song . . .*

Vince asked a Native girl in tight jeans to dance as Ray sighted a dark-skinned 17- or 18-year-old girl swaying to the rhythm with her girlfriends. Catching her eye, he twirled his finger. She giggled and took his hand.

I'll move myself and my family aside
If we happen to be left half alive
I'll get all my papers and smile at the sky
Though I know that the hypnotized never lie,
Do ya?

When the song ended, Thomas and Seven moved off the dance floor to wander. "This trip will keep me warm the rest of my life," Thomas whispered, kissing her. "Come with me and Sirius to look for the lenses?"

Leaving the plaza, they passed a hippie couple lying on a patch of scratchy buffalo grass and grama, talking.

"Remember Kennedy's proposal to the UN, 'Freedom from War: The U.S. Program for General and Complete Disarmament in a Peaceful World'?" The young woman sounded wistful.

"You mean handing over military power to the UN Peace Force?" her longhaired companion asked.

"Kennedy was trying to find a way out of the Cold War, but the military-industrial complex was already in power." She picked a blade of buffalo grass. "Ike left him and Bobby a real mess."

"And the Nazi thing . . ." Her partner was distracted by his hand on the nape of her neck. "I love this part of you," he said huskily.

She giggled. "Uh huh. What did you say at the meeting about the UN?"

He sighed and removed his hand. "That if the big corporations aren't dealt with first, the UN will work for them."

Thoughtfully, she stared at the blade of buffalo grass. "When they finally set the new world order in place as their beloved capstone, they'll dredge up Kennedy's Freedom From War speech and demand world disarmament in honor of 'peace,' then send UN Peace Forces to enforce it."

He looked appreciatively at her. "You're right. From April 1962 to May 25, 1982—when that Congressman dredged up the Blueprint for the Peace Race and entered it into the Congressional Record—was one Metonic cycle after Kennedy's elimination. By 1989, it had been amended 20 times.—Hey, let's dance. Vacation is supposed to be carefree. Besides, we're getting up early to catch sunrise at the Grand Canyon."

They got up and skipped hand in hand, laughing.

During the walk to the pharmacy, Sirius drew all the looks and Seven talked about Kennedy's fall equinox 1963 speech to the UN, two months before he was killed, regarding cooperating with Russia for an international "space race." Talks between the NASA Deputy Administrator and Anatoli Blagonravov of the Soviet Academy of Sciences had begun in March 1962 and they'd already agreed to work together on meteorological and communications satellites beginning with Echo II, and mapping the Earth's magnetic field. NSAM 271 specifically instructed the NASA Administrator to cooperate with the Russians.

"Which didn't make the Enterprise cold warriors happy," Thomas recalled.

"No," Seven agreed. "Kennedy was breaching their schedule and plans. The Cold War was just one Metonic cycle old and they needed more years of fear. Rightist Fascists, Trotskyists, internationalist Synarchists all. I wonder if they were aware of how capitalists had bankrolled the Soviet Revolution to split the world in half."

Thomas said, "Divide and conquer. Ander blew my mind when he said the Soviet Union collapses in 1991. Imagine: no Cold War."

Seven shrugged. "They'll drum up some other enemy."

Thomas nodded. "Remember the last report Kennedy read

before leaving for Dallas? The memo from his prep school friend about unofficial talks with the UN Cuban Ambassador Carlos Lechuga? Kennedy was set on détente."

"Then after his assassination, Lyndon Johnson committed us to fighting the Communist bogeyman in Southeast Asia, and the CIA-run NASA to a U.S.-only space effort, scuttling all talk of détente with Cuba…"

". . . and the Enterprise was back on track again," Thomas finished as they arrived at the pharmacy.

A cheer went up from the bandstand for a Cuban number honoring the marble bust of Ché Guevara orbiting in Soyuz 38. Thomas and Seven shared a smile, then Thomas instructed Sirius to wait outside. An ad in the pharmacy window read—

WANTED by ASRC Aerospace Corporation
Full-Time Human Intelligence Collector
Req'd Education: High School
Description: Excellent Employment opportunities for prior military
personnel who held the MOS 97E, Human Intelligence Collector.
Positions include instructors and managers at Fort Huachuca, AZ.
Excellent Pay/Benefits/Chance for Advancement.

Near the bandstand stood the dark-skinned men who had been passed over for day labor but were content to tap their feet to the music before going home empty-handed. Two of the men, one younger and one older, were discussing in Spanish and K'iché how Mexicans and Indians should make peace since they shared at least an ounce of blood and the common enemy of hunger. The older half-Guatemalan Mam Mayan in striped pants compared their situation to that of the Todos Santos crosses, one of ancient wood, the other of stone, one in front of the church at Todos Santos and one in the ruins above the pueblo at Cumanchúm. He explained how a *ladino* Intendente had pulled down the wooden cross in favor of a modern stone cross. Immediately, the wind rose, the weather became cold, no rain fell, the sheep and crops died. The Chimán Nam sagely knew what the problem was and put the ancient cross back up next to the new stone cross. Rain and abundance returned. "Santo Mundo is in charge, not *ladinos*," the Mam Mayan stressed. "We must all learn our station in life and get along."

His younger listener nodded, shifting into K'iché pure and simple peppered with Spanglish. "I came north to get away from the *federales* and paramilitaries and cartels." Both men shook their heads sadly. The younger continued. "When I first encountered Mexicans who look *indio*—their skin like ours, cheekbones, noses like hawks—I thought, *Ah, brothers*. But they had been too long away from their ancestors and land. They were like branches cut from the tree and cast on the terrible *el norte* fire, staring at me and asking who are you and what do you want, their words just sounds."

The older sighed. "But what can you expect when one degenerate supplants another? I do not mean Indians or Mexicans or *narcotrafficantes*. The Catholic Church brought the *Azteca* to their knees, but *both* were from dying civilizations. The Catholic Church no longer understands the Nine Worlds below. Europe over many centuries made a truce with what lived beneath its feet, but here things are not so easy as a *Hail, Mary* and sending the Virgin of Guadalupe to Tepeyac Hill to take the place of Tonantzin, our Earth Corn Mother, or spilling roses from an Indian's *tilpa* to justify building a big rich Basilica."

Both men chuckled, having joked many times about the simple-minded Catholics.

The younger spoke. "I have nothing against the Virgin or Jesus Christ who are much more pleasant than the Aztec gods. But does the Church not realize that these other beings, whether from beneath the Earth or hidden in the minds of Indians and Mexicans, will not be ignored? The Europeans should know where their nightmares and sleepless nights come from."

The older man smiled. "Nuestra Señora for the poor and La Conquistadora for themselves—as if the gods were theirs to do with as they wish. They are fools. The spirits will bite them in the ass."

Now the younger K'iché Mayan smiled. "It is a shame because they are not all bad, just foolish."

"To be a fool may be worse," the older said wisely.

"And what of La Gachupina? Her shrine is now outside Mexico City. After *la noche triste*, when Cuitlahuac defeated Cortés only to be killed by his own men, it is said that she hid herself for 20 years in a maguey on La Calle de Tacuba just west of the *zócalo* in the Centro Histórico district."

The older pondered. "Cortés brought her from Spain, probably to celebrate the treachery against Cuitlahuac. On the other hand, *Tacuba* may refer to Tlacopán on the west shore of Lake Tetzcoco."

The younger was still puzzled. "And after she was placed on the throne of Hummingbird, a church was built for her in Cholula on top of the Toltec pyramid."

"Ah, yes. The Europeans always do thus when they conquer a people—to take the powers for themselves. They are not all fools."

"And the maguey?" the younger queried.

"*Pulque*, of course. The divine liquor."

"The priests used the maguey spines for piercing their penises." The younger man shivered at the thought.

The older shrugged. "Mayahuel is goddess of the maguey plant and protector of wombs."

"And yet the Tzitzimime star demons tore her to pieces."

"From which the maguey sprang. From death comes birth."

The younger nodded. He enjoyed talking the fine points of gods with his wise friend. "So this is what awaits La Gachupina?"

"And her Church," the older man stressed. "Time is preparing to turn over."

The two men ceased their discussion as a truck pulled up.

Inwardly, however, a part of them continued contemplating the mysteries hidden like seeds within events, even seeds five hundred years old. While *el norte* merchant hordes in skyscrapers contemplated how to screw others out of a buck, Indians waiting for work carried on the essential business of deciphering treasures that neither moth nor rust can corrupt.

After Thomas and Seven came out of the pharmacy and turned back toward the bandstand, having achieved only an Albuquerque address of a lens maker the pharmacist who might stock such a speciality item.

Back at the bandstand, Vince and Mannie were still grooving while Baby Rose and the Colonel watched and Ray rapped with an older Black brother who'd taught Black history at UCLA.

". . . the purest of them all," the brother was saying, "when Mario Salvo, that Sonoma State University mathematics and critical thinking instructor, stood on the roof of that car and started the Free Speech Movement (FSM) of '64. It was *heavy*, man. From right to left, all the political booths had been banned around UC Berkeley, from Youths for Goldwater to Youths for Socialist Alliance, all united behind the First Amendment. *Free speech.* At the sit-in on December 2 and 3, even faculty were protesting." He looked at Ray. "The Free Speech Movement was all about consensus and community. Mario wanted to merge it with the antiwar movement, like King did with civil rights.

"May 1965, Vietnam Day. Fall 1965, antiwar march. Then in '66, Reagan ran for governor and *Life* and *Time* basically invited every kid in America to UC Berkeley and everything got hazy crazy, man. At that '68 Chicago Democratic National Convention, stupid ass Yippies were eggin' on 12,000 of Daley's thugs and 6,000 National Guard, and it turned the so-called Festival of Life into the same kind of bloodbath going on in Prague at the exact same time to radicalize all of America to one side or the other. Nixon won in Chicago, thanks to television, back when no one believed TV news would lie." He shook his head, chuckled, and continued.

"All downhill from then on. Scum DAs like Meese and Jensen began prosecuting FSM members. Jensen was Army Signal Corps, predecessor of the National Security Agency—you know, the spy agency that doesn't exist. In '73, Jensen was in on prosecuting SLA members like DeFreeze in the Vacaville Medical prison's MK-ULTRA program. Then Black Panther Huey Newton and the whole Jonestown thing—all CIA. That cat Jensen was their man. In '76, he prosecuted for that Chowchilla school bus carjacking with 26 kids buried in a moving van in Livermore Valley. Jensen had the kids hypnotized, man. He played Meese's terrorist for more fascist law and order in California, showing America how it's done." He drank some beer. "Then it was *Judge* Jensen. In '81, Reagan appointed him chief of the Criminal Division of the DOJ so he could cover up the October Surprise election theft, the INSLAW theft, Iran Contra guns-for-drugs, even file a false CIA affidavit in the Edwin Wilson trial. A real scumbag."

Ray was pondering the reference to 1981 while the brother paused to listen to the Patty Griffin song about Martin Luther King, Jr. coming from the bandstand—

I went up to the mountain
Because you asked me to
Up over the clouds
To where the sky was blue
I could see all around me
Everywhere
I could see all around me
Everywhere

Sometimes I feel like
I've never been nothing but tired
And I'll be walking

Till the day I expire
Sometimes I lay down
No more can I do . . .

The brother sang along with *But then I go on again because you ask me to*, then spoke again. "The People's Park almost united us—counterculture and political activists, hipsters and New Left. Then the National Guard was called in for four months, James Rector killed, helicopters, tear gas, then the Memorial Day march . . ."

Ray had admired political theorist Murray Bookchin until he'd missed what was going down in the Sixties with phrases like "traditional radical myths and political styles," "the sense of urgency," and "destructive heightened metabolism that loosened the very roots of the movement." Yeah, LSD and grass and a free flow of bread and cheap gasoline for staying on the move and great music might contribute to "destructive heightened metabolisms," but Bookchin should have taken a good long look at the FBI and CIA working together via COINTELPRO to put bad drugs on the streets and those Vietnam body bags filled with horse, and the two-way mirrors in the Village and Haight houses . . .

The brother was talking about it all as if it was in the ancient past. "We did our best, man. We were young and untried and honest, and they were big and organized and dishonest. It got violent on both sides, COINTELPRO and CHAOS infiltrating everything under IPS schemes and orders."

"IPS?" Ray asked.

"Institute for Policy Studies. Disinformation and discord, informants and provocateurs. Honky America believed it was all Communist-inspired and that George McGovern was KGB, GRU, Cuban DGI rolled into one, until the CIA Report in '69 finally admitted everything had been domestic." The brother shook his head. "'68, what a year. After the assassinations, resistance began leaning toward revolution, activists gave up on reform and wanted to dismantle the whole thing. Revolution was the revelation. FBI, CIA, IRS, NSA,

342

FCC, LEAA, HEW, MIT, Boeing, Bank of America—all grounded in violence and lies, so what was the chance of reform? White Americans sitting in their living rooms applauding Chicago police brutality, not realizing they were next. One in six of the Chicago demonstrators was an undercover provocateur. *Sub rosa,* man. Even the Yippies. G-men trained at 'Hoover University' Quantico in Virginia. I know—an Army buddy helped train Prince Crazy Demmerle to infiltrate the Yippies."

Ray thought about Mannie meeting Jerry Rubin's third cousin at a party in the East Village and how he'd rapped about Jerry organizing the first Berkeley teach-in on Vietnam in the spring of '65 with an attendance of 30,000. That summer, hundreds had sat on the railroad tracks to stop troop trains from entering the Oakland Naval Embarcation Station. When summoned before the House Un-American Activities Committee (HUAC), Jerry had worn an American Revolution uniform—a child of the first media generation, he knew the power of theater. The third cousin had then gone to New York in '67 to meet Abbie Hoffman and found the Youth International Party that Paul Krassner quipped into *Yippies,* an organic coalition of stoned hippie dropouts and New Left activists. On October 21, 1967 at the antiwar demonstration in DC directed by David Dellinger and the Mobe or National Mobilization to End the War in Vietnam, the Yippies had exorcised the Pentagon with Ginsberg—

> *Who represents my body in Pentagon? Who spends*
> *My spirit's billions for war manufacture? Who*
> *Levies the majority to exult unwilling in*
> *Bomb roar? Brainwash! Mind-fear! Governor's language!*
> *Military-Industrial-Complex President's language?*

After Mannie's third cousin story, Seven had spooked them with an Imbolc exorcism story from 1620 at the Quimper-Corentin cathedral in France. A bolt of lightning had exploded the lead-covered pyramid on top of the cathedral and caused it to fall to earth with a bone-jarring noise. People watched as out of the smoke and fire rose a phantom with a long green tail. Seven explained that people could still *see* then. They threw hundreds of buckets of water and cartloads of manure onto the fire, but the demon kept it burning until the priest put a consecrated host inside a loaf of bread and threw it on the flames, followed by blessed water mixed with milk from a wet nurse above reproach. That did it. With a piercing whistle, the green demon fled back to its home dimension. Mannie wondered if the Pentagon exorcism failed because neither the Yippies nor Ginsberg believed in blessed hosts and breast milk above reproach. The pilgrims laughed about the green demon but secretly wondered. Sacred substances and fluids were not unheard of.

Ray's attention returned to the brother saying he'd always been suspicious of the Yippies. Abbie had done an interview with Midwest Audiovisual News, an Army front, and Yippie planning meetings had never been busted for marijuana. Were Jerry and Abbie *agents provocateurs*?

Mannie said Jerry's third cousin had mentioned how whacked out Jerry's early years were, his parents dying within ten months of each other, him taking his kid brother to Israel and stopping in Cuba on his way back. True, he was a talented and competent organizer, as the first Human Be-In in '67 proved—and when he ran for mayor of Berkeley, he gleaned between 20 and 40 percent of the popular vote. But more than anything, everyone agreed he was an ego-tripper with his guerrilla theater, slogans, and confrontational tactics. *Rise up and abandon the creeping meatball! Run naked through the halls of Congress!* Was exploiting capitalism's contradictions with outrageous antics really politically effective? Most of the New Left didn't think so. And yet the American Revolution uniform had worked with HUAC, and from time to time Jerry said deep things like reality doesn't set limits but offers infinite possibilities if you have the *chutzpah* to pursue them. *Carpe diem!* The third cousin said Jerry changed after '68, maybe due to fame or being over thirty or that the Revolution had failed. Whatever it was, he decided to use his fame to broker a career.

Abbie had always been more thoughtful. He said democracy

wasn't something to believe in, it's something to *do*. Stop doing it and it crumbles like a house of cards. He'd worked as a psychologist at Worcester State Hospital under Abraham "Hierarchy of Needs" Maslow just before his overnight plunge into politics and being arrested in Mississippi during Freedom Summer. Maslow was part of the Esalen Mafia of Fritz Perls and Gestalt, Stanislav Grof, Carl Rogers, B.F. Skinner, Virginia Satir, Michael Harner, Richard Alpert, and Timothy Leary. Counterculture heaven with a long MK-ULTRA shadow. Abbie opened Liberty House in New York City and sold crafts from Mississippi co-ops, then took acid in '65 and fell under the influence of the Diggers who saw more value in feelings than political analysis—media stunts, havoc, and street theater instead of mass mobilization. Just after the summer of '68, Abbie was busted for coke and went underground. He wouldn't re-surface for an entire Jupiter cycle.

"I always wondered about that coke bust," the brother said. "After just four months of jail time in 1980, he hit the road with Jerry in that 'Yippie versus Yuppie' act, Jerry exhorting youths to change things from the inside while Abbie laments Jerry's cop out, ranting that working from within was bullshit, that justice and equality have to be wrested from the elite by force—like those stupid-ass vaudeville acts of G. Gordon Liddy and the Pope of Dope, and Eldridge and Bobby." He sneered. "Shee-it, you suppose the CIA financed Rennie Davis and the Chicago 7?"

Tweedledee and Tweedledum, Ray thought. *The Hegel thing.*

"Cleaver ended up a born-again, a Moonie, a Mormon, and voting for Reagan. And what's up with Seale recruiting for Temple University's African American studies program?" The brother shrugged. "Sounds like MK-ULTRA, Lodge Brothers, and betrayal. Power to the people Sixties-style is over."

He turned to scrutinize Ray and chuckled. "But man, where'd you get them threads?—Some believe that from the 1970s on, a new, cooler form of post-modern capitalism emerged once the hierarchic Ford model was abandoned. Networking, employee initiative, autonomy.

345

In comparison, socialism looks conservative, hierarchic, bureaucratic, and unimaginative. But were the anti-hierarchy and sexual freedom celebrated by student and worker demonstrations in major cities for real?" He scoffed. "It was just about a *feeling*, like a social orgasm, all orchestrated. Only one institution I know of with that kind of universality and ability to organize internationally, *and* reason to do it."

His eyes twinkled as he shook Ray's hand in a particular way.

Ray stared at their interlocked black hands. "Prince Hall?" *No way*.

"You bet, brother. Just like in 1776 and 1789, only this time we're puttin' the fear of God into populations, not 'liberating' them from the divine right of kings. Making things look like they just happen—*hoodwinking*." He grinned and Ray finally saw the gold in his teeth. "'68 was a hoodwink. Made you *feel* free, didn't it? That's all it was, brother, a feeling. Count on it: when the white man makes you feel free, new chains are on the way. Drop the idealism and change the threads, man. Get practical like I did." With that, he gave Ray a real brother's handshake and strode off whistling.

Ray thought long and hard about the handshake and what the brother had said. He was right about new chains on the way and *hoodwink* operations manipulating the *profane*, but Ray also knew that the cutting-edge few would go on experimenting with decentralization, voluntary association, mutual help, networking, horizontal decision-making, and rejection of the end justifying the means. *That* revolution of consciousness would continue, just more humbly than he'd envisioned. Seven was right: it had to begin with the commons, community, communal, collectives, new small societies arising as the overgrown, corrupt capitalist one crumbled. It wasn't about seizing state power and setting up another paternalistic fraternity, like in Cuba. *Form and content*. More free form, autonomous, participatory—a long, anarchistic process. Structural violence out, direct action in.

Seven and Thomas were gesturing to him. Time to rally and go. Walking back to the bus, Ray stared at his hand. Who would have known about the brother? Black or white was obviously not the only measure of a man or a philosophy.

47

The Sorting Hat

...At the same time, that capability at any time could be turned around on the American people and no American would have any privacy left, such [is] the capability to monitor everything: telephone conversations, telegrams, it doesn't matter. There would be no place to hide. If this government ever became a tyranny, if a dictator ever took charge in this country, the technological capacity that the intelligence community has given the government could enable it to impose total tyranny, and there would be no way to fight back, because the most careful effort to combine together in resistance to the government, no matter how privately it was done, is within the reach of the government to know. Such is the capability of this technology...

—Senator Frank Church, 1975

"Underneath Disneyland; that's where you'll find the real thing, my friend . . . Mickey's shadow side."

—Steven Weber as "Jeff," *Late Last Night* (1999)

Dusk was approaching and St. Elmo's blue glow enveloping the long twine of high-voltage power lines. The great *devas* across America—those inhabiting mountains, magnetizing sacred portals in lakes, rivers, islands, springs, trees and groves, standing and natural stones and their observatories, megalithic mounds, labyrinths, landscape carvings, geysers, volcanoes, caves where sages and saints sought silence and dipped their torches in pitch or resin, dragons and salamanders watching over their holy bones as *l'etoile flamboyante* makes its sacred rounds—were unsettled by the phased array radar emanating peak to peak, and it was bringing out the worst in them. Deity was no longer an object of worship but a nexus of energies and war a psychosis, a destructive irrationalism Reich christened the emotional plague as Oranur crept across the American landscape, assaulting people in their weakest organs and psychological wounds.

America America melding together in the cauldron, the witch's brew, the melding pot. On the Eastern shore, the Statue of Liberty on Bedloe Island was beckoning but not necessarily to liberty. Sculpted by Frederic Bartholdi, a Freemason Brother of the Alsace-Lorraine Lodge in Paris, she was Athena, the Illuminist Goddess of Reason springing from Zeus' brow to join human consciousness with the Omniscient.

In 1776, 99 percent of the Europeans coming to the New Atlantis were still Christian. Fifty of the 55 members of the Constitutional Convention were Masons, 53 of the 56 signers of the Declaration of Independence. The Boston Tea Party all American children were taught about was actually a recessed St. Andrews Lodge meeting led by Junior Warden Paul Revere. Freemasons and other secret Brotherhoods created new degrees and lodges for giving lip service to Christ the Grand Master, and steeples on churches (disguised obelisks of Nimrod the Builder) were added to announce that Masons had infiltrated them.

Now it was the 20th century and the mightiest religion was no longer Christianity but the State, a *Mystery Ship with its anchor in the sky* (Ravenol). Navigating this Mystery Ship were the Argonauts, the argot naughts, ancient Orders whose rites and vows and secrets were strapped to the neo-Atlantean Ship of State like Captain Ahab to the White Whale. *Are you on the Square? Are you on the Level?* Brothers ask with an Oddfellow handshake, attempting to find out what position the other serves on the Ship of State.

As the pilgrims settled themselves into the vehicles, a brown boy walked by, grooving to Michael Jackson's "Tabloid Junkie" from the future on his boom box—

> *Speculate to break the one you hate*
> *Circulate the lie you confiscate*
> *Assassinate and mutilate*
> *As the hounding media hysteria*
> *Who's the next for you to resurrect*
> *JFK exposed the CIA*
> *Truth be told the grassy knoll*
> *As the blackmail story in all your glory . . .*

While passing a laundromat at the edge of town, they decided to pitstop and see if Cosmic Coincidence Control had left anything for them. As Thomas reached for *The Shopkeeper's Notebook* and Mannie the 1988 *Report on Enhancing Human Performance* and the Colonel a July 17, 1957 issue of *Astronautics and Aeronautics*, the television in the corner burst into life and the pilgrims stood spellbound.

"[*Newscaster:*] August 3, 1977. I am here in room 1202 of the Dirksen Senate Office Building in Washington, DC. Presiding over this Joint Hearing on Project MKULTRA, the CIA's Program of Research in Behavioral Modification, is Senator Daniel K. Inouye, chair of the U.S. Senate Select Committee on Intelligence. The Senator is speaking."

> [*SENATOR INOUYE in a Groucho Marx eyebrows, nose, and cigar mask:*] We are focusing on events that happened twelve or as long as 25 years ago. It should be emphasized that the programs that are of greatest concern have stopped.
> [*CANNED AUDIENCE LAUGHTER*]
> [*SEN. INOUYE:*] We also need to know and understand the CIA is doing in the field of behavioral research to be certain that no current abuses are occurring.

[CANNED AUDIENCE LAUGHTER]

[SENATOR EDWARD KENNEDY:] While the Deputy Director of the CIA revealed that over thirty universities and institutions were involved in "extensive testing and experimentation," including covert drugs on unwitting citizens "at all social levels, high and low, Native Americans and foreign," a Freedom of Information Act release indicates that 86 universities and institutions were involved. The records of all these activities were destroyed in January 1973 at the instruction of then CIA Director Richard Helms. No one— no single individual—could be found who remembered the details, not the Director of the CIA who ordered the documents destroyed, not the official responsible for the program, nor any of his associates.

[CANNED AUDIENCE LAUGHTER]

[ADMIRAL STANSFIELD TURNER, DIRECTOR OF THE CIA in a Harpo mask and holding a Harpo horn:] It was CIA policy to maintain no records of the planning and approval of MKULTRA test programs.

[CANNED AUDIENCE LAUGHTER]

At the appearance of Admiral Turner in his Harpo mask, Baby Rose stood frozen.

[ADM. TURNER:] There were subprojects in such areas as electroshock, harassment techniques, extrasensory perception, 39 on the effects of drugs— MKSEARCH, OFTEN-CHICKWIT, all at Edgewood Arsenal Research Laboratories in June 1973.

[SEN. INOUYE:] Were the men running subproject 3, under which Dr. Frank Olson died, ever punished or fired?

[ADM. TURNER:] No, senator. They continued running subproject 3 for a number of years after Olson died.

[CANNED AUDIENCE LAUGHTER]

[SENATOR SCHWEIKER:] Under subproject 35 is an authorization to contribute CIA funds toward construction of the Gorman Annex at Georgetown University Hospital, where Dr. Geschickter continued researching sleep- and amnesia-producing

drugs under MKSEARCH through July 1967. The purpose of
the Gorman Annex appears to be "controlled experimentation under
safe clinical conditions using materials with which any Agency
connection must be completely deniable . . ." What "materials"
would those be, admiral?
(ADM. TURNER beeps his Harpo horn.)
[CANNED AUDIENCE LAUGHTER]
[SEN. SCHWEIKER:] Did the experiments at Gorman Annex
involve terminally ill cancer patients as subjects?
(ADM. TURNER in Harpo mask beeps his horn again.)

The channel blipped to video footage from space.

"NBC HardCopy here, June 6, 1992," the voiceover
began. "High above the Earth, as this video footage will reveal, the
'ice crystals' from space shuttle *Discovery* wastewater are actually
pulsating UFOs being shot at from Earth. This footage taken from
the *Discovery* is of only one of six Events during the STS-48 mission.
On board are active duty military personnel.

"Here is the infrared image sent back to Earth just before
Phobos II disappeared a year ago, a photograph released by retired
Soviet Colonel Marina Popovich. The image from the Center for
Unmanned Space Flight revealed something approximately *25
kilometers* long; this photograph reveals the same object's shadow
reflecting off Mars.

"UFOs are not new. What *is* new is our technology and
astronauts physically entering the ocean of space and transmitting
eyewitness reports of what is living and moving in and above our
atmosphere. When Major Gordon Cooper, one of the original
Mercury astronauts, left the atmosphere and entered space on
May 15, 1963, he reported seeing a greenish glowing object that
the tracking station near Perth, Australia was picking up on radar.
A Jupiter cycle earlier, Cooper had seen *metallic* saucers in fighter
formation flying east to west over Europe. In other words, the form

and composition of these objects vary. Their ability to disappear indicates that they may be *semi*-physical and made of plasma, which may account for the military's increased interest in the paranormal under Operation Stargate and a host of other projects.

"Since the National Security Act of 1947, the military has cast a shroud of disinformation over the issue of UFOs, making it difficult to tell if astronauts are seeing human-engineered vectored crafts or another order of being. Here is a partial list of early sightings—

1951: Donald Slayton; 2 miles up, April 1962.
May 11, 1962: NASA Pilot Joseph A. Walker; 50 miles up
July 17, 1962: Major Robert White; 58 miles up
June 1965: Ed White, James McDivitt; over Hawaii
December 1965: James Lovell, Frank Borman
July 21, 1969: Neil Armstrong, Edwin "Buzz" Aldrin; on the moon

"Two Metonic cycles after entering space, then-Senator John Glenn stood in a sound booth on the television sit-com *Fraser* on Tuesday, March 6, 2001 and said the following—"

[John Glenn:] Back in those glory days, I was very uncomfortable when they asked us to say things we didn't want to say and deny other things. Some people asked, you know, were you alone out there? We never gave the real answer, and yet we see things out there, strange things, but we know what we saw out there. And we couldn't really say anything. The bosses were afraid of this, they were afraid of the War of the Worlds type stuff, and about panic in the streets. So we had to keep quiet. And now we only see these things in our nightmares or maybe in the movies, and some of them are pretty close to being the truth.

"Five years later on 58-square-mile Orcas Island in Puget Sound, 56-year-old astronaut Charles E. Brady, who had orbited the Earth 271 times as a specialist in the Life and Microgravity Spacelab, died under unusual circumstances. The deputy who found him was named Clever . . ."

The television clicked off.

The pilgrims began talking all at once on their way out of the laundromat about how the broadcast fit with Flight of Apollo 11: The Eagle Has Landed they'd seen in tiny Ash Fork. In their vehicles, they passed the café with the big lumberjack that had been in the film Easy Rider and found themselves once again among the desert hills. Mannie read aloud from the Report on Enhancing Human Performance put out by the National Research Council of the National Academy of Science under the U.S. Army Research Institute for the Behavioral Sciences. They all agreed that the purpose of the report was to keep military psychological operations from public scrutiny. The Colonel then read aloud from Astronautics and Aeronautics about a sighting

> An Air Force RB-47, equipped with electronic countermeasure (ECM) gear and manned by six officers, was followed by an unidentified object for a distance of well over 700 miles and for a time period of 1.5 hours, as it flew from Mississippi, through Louisiana and Texas and into Oklahoma. The object was, at various times, seen visually by the cockpit crew as an intensely luminous light, followed by ground-radar and detected on ECM monitoring gear aboard the RB-47. Of special interest in this case are several instances of simultaneous appearances and disappearances on all three of these physically distinct 'channels,' and rapidity of maneuvers beyond the prior experience of the aircrew.

which inspired yet more conversation about UFOs and vectored crafts.

"Look!" Mannie cried, pointing up to the dimming azure sky.

A moving point of light was growing bigger fast. Quickly, Thomas and Seven pulled the vehicles over and they all got out. Thomas sighted the object through the binoculars.

"It's pulsating at the center," he said excitedly, passing the binoculars to Vince. The others watched it with the naked eye, including Sirius who whined and wagged his tail.

"It's like a living probe," Vince murmured.

Soon, it was the size of a dime over them, rotating in a blue-red gyre, the systole-diastole pulse still beating at its center. They held their breath as they beheld it and it seemed to behold them.

"Greetings," Mannie whispered into the binoculars.

How long the encounter lasted, no one could later say. It was as though Time stopped. It was definitely a *Dr. Livingstone, I presume?* moment. The pulsating globe or probe had apparently grokked enough and so ascended, growing smaller and smaller, then shot west and disappeared.

With night fast descending, they drove into the Meteor Crater RV Park to see if tents were allowed. Two women outside an RV with a giant satellite dish on top immediately hailed them like old friends.

"Just in time for dinner!" the heavier of the two shouted. "Camp by us and let's eat!"

Accustomed by now to Cosmic Coincidence Control, the pilgrims parked and got out, only to be assailed by a delicious aroma. On the large picnic table outside the RV was a big pot of stew, a big pot of brown rice, a big pot of *frijoles*, salad, bowls, utensils, and cold *cervezas* with lime wedges.

Thelma and Lou introduced themselves, the Colonel set up his lawn chair at the end of the table, and everyone else squeezed onto the benches. It was almost too good to be true, which was why Ray wondered if he'd still be hungry after another ghostly meal. They all shared where they were from and where they were headed while loading up their bowls. Thelma and Lou had a house and land near Gallup and were going to LA to see friends before all-consuming gardening began in May.

Digging in, Ray crowed, "This stew is out of sight! Is it chicken?"

Lou and Thelma laughed.

"*Cascabel?*" Vince asked knowingly.

"*Sí,*" Lou said impishly. "Two big rattlers just wouldn't leave, so the least we could do was honor them by making them into stew." She laughed again. "They're sacred messengers from the underworld, but they simply would not leave."

Ray stared at the stew, then shrugged, now hoping it was a ghostly meal, and took another bite.

The conversation turned to the satellite dish and the computers Thelma and Lou needed for their freelance jobs. After dinner, the pilgrims trooped into the compact RV to experience the magic of the Internet—connectivity, search engines, videos, news, "blogs," networks, advertisements . . .

Thelma puzzled over how little their guests knew about wireless computers.

Thomas was first to sit at the keyboard and move the mouse while Lou talked about how computers had transformed society, especially less privacy, thanks to telecommunications corporations being in league with the NSA; implants in people monitoring, recording, and transmitting to distant computers via the "wireless" air, hand-held computer phones and microwave towers, email and texting, Trojan horses implanted by email virus, van Eck phreaking, TEMPEST monitoring of keyboard strokes, wireless cameras and microphones, stray radio-frequency emissions, online snoopers—

Ray stared disbelieving at the monitor. "It's like a spy. Not cool."

Thelma went on. "eWatch Cybersleuth can make five thousand a pop for tracking your ISP—your Internet service provider signature—and finding your real name behind your screen name. Then your file goes to some CEO or intel operative and you're on a watch list. 'Safeguarding shareholder value,' they call it—more like Soviet-style surveillance for 're-education.'"

The Internet had gone public in the 1990s. The Kennedy look-alike President convinced 33 nations to sign the Wassenaar Arrangement to ban exportation of strong cryptographic software so each nation could read its citizens' emails with ease. Cyberwarfare is the name of the game in the 21st century, Thelma grimaced.

"Sell someone caliber encryption and you're basically selling arms. The President even has a Special Envoy for Cryptology, under the Department of Commerce in the back pocket of global corporations. And all in the name of a level playing field for freedom—freedom for corporations, not us."

From the little RV couch, the Colonel said, "But what would the 33° boys do without their encryption?"

Lou snorted. "You are so right, Colonel. 'Information superhighway,' my ass. All that happened in '98, 666 times 3, same year they shot John Kennedy's boy out of the sky and snuck in FIDNET, Federal Intrusion Detection Network—the NSA—to eavesdrop on nonmilitary networks, track banking, telecommunications, and transportation. In the name of fighting terrorists, the FBI snoops for 'offensive information warfare' when it's really about power consolidation. Big Brother Ministry of Truth and electronic Mind Control Central . . . "

Holding a lantern, Mannie stepped out of the RV. At the campground toilet, he found a glowing coverless copy of *Illuminatus!* beginning on page 333. The back cover said the authors had worked for *Playboy* magazine. *The whole key to liberation is magic.* He flicked through the pages: a lot of immanentizing of the Eschaton, dope-smoking and cunnilingus for the sake of the Great Mother Kallisti and Eris the goddess of discord, and something about the Knights Templar joining the Hashishim. Well, it *was* a novel. The character

356

Hagbard thought spatial metaphors like *right-wing* and *left-wing* had been inadequate for discussing politics ever since the House of Rothschild had begun dominating world finances in 1815. One world government was imminent, national sovereignty and private property old hat. Pentagon, pentacle, Lloigor, fascism, the Ancient Illuminated Seers of Bavaria . . . put-on language from the supra-conscious, contamination from the unconscious . . . Eater of Souls Yog Sothoth, Iok-Sotot, Federal Reserve notes . . .

Mannie stared. Adam Weishaupt was George Washington's clone? For how the Illuminati work today, the author said to study the founding of Israel and the National Security Act of 1947.

Then he hit St. Anthony paydirt: *Powers live in spaces between our words, our acts, and between the coming of night and the arrival of day.* From the gray matter between his ears down into the cecum of his gut and the marrow of his bones, Mannie knew this to be true. So why did the rest of the book—in fact, the entire trilogy—rotate around making fun of this one Gnostic fact? Illuminati conspiracies filled with midgets, Captain Nemo submarines and giant squids, Atlantis, Nazi zombies, and Erisians cast as the Sixties generation in a cloud of marijuana smoke and dewy mist of vaginal juices in pursuit of *guerrilla ontology* under Operation Mindfuck. Uncle Eli wouldn't approve of this smirky book bent on obscuring the truth and making people laugh when they should think. Did the Illuminati sponsor the authors?

When he returned to the trailer, everyone was outside setting up tents and Thelma's and Thomas' telescope. Mercury had been transiting the Sun earlier in the month when the Moon was new and now was pouring out into Gemini ruled by Mercury.

Adjusting her lens, Thelma said, "Long ago during the Golden Age, the vernal equinox was in Gemini and the autumnal equinox in Sagittarius, making the great *chi* X, the *skamba* of a perfectly balanced ecliptic-equator. Back then, the three worlds— the gods, the living, the dead— the Tropic of Cancer, between the Tropics, and the Tropic of Capricorn—were united in perfect harmony. Anu, Enlil, and Ea. Then it all shifted. Now, only the Seven Rishi in the north"—she pointed to the Big Dipper—"and the Seven Sleepers of Ephesus on board the Argo in the south keep us afloat in the imbalance I call 'ignorant armies clash by night."

Backing away from the lens to make room for novices, she added, "There she is in all her glory: Venus, handmaiden of the Sun with her thick sulfuric acid cloud cover, her year of 224.7 Earth days, her size our size but rotating clockwise with the Sun rising in her west, not our east. Hottest of all the planets: 850°F. Only Mercury is closer to the Sun."

Mannie peered through the lens. "She's beautiful. What was it like seeing Mercury transit the Sun?"

"Tiny," Lou laughed. "Colonel, remember the 1968 scare about the asteroid belt Icarus between the orbits of Mars and Jupiter? One Metonic cycle later on August 24, 2006, the International Astronomical Union redefined 'planet' and demoted Pluto to a *dwarf* planet smaller than Xena, the so-called 10th planet. Dr. Clyde Tombaugh, who worked at the Lowell Observatory in Flagstaff from 1929 to 1945, discovered Pluto in 1930. When he went public about a UFO he saw, his discovery was demoted. Go figure."

2006. Seven smiled at Thelma's assumption that only the Colonel might remember 1968.

Thomas wasn't surprised that even the IAU was stooping to rewrite history. Like the Smithsonian, it was no doubt packed with obedient Freemasons who served *Scientia est potentia*. He peered through his telescope at Venus, a morning star in the east for 236 days, invisible for 90 days, then an evening star in the west for 250 days, then gone another eight days before resuming her morning rounds. So elusive . . .

"Jupiter should be up in the east in the early hours, and the dwarf galaxy Sagittarius, center of our galaxy with the most intense wavelengths," Lou said excitedly. "Later this year, Jupiter will be as close to the Earth as it was in '63, and Uranus."

Vince leaned in for a look through Thomas' telescope. "In 2012, the Earth and Sun will align with the center of our Milky Way galaxy, and Sagittarius will release a thick stream of dark matter that will go straight through the Earth."

"And it's all coming out in politics, isn't it?" Lou said. "Jupiter entering sidereal Virgo like it did in '45 is like another birth." She rolled an American Spirit cigarette. "The Jupiter pulses since '45—'45 to '57, '57 to '69, '69 to '81, '81 to '93, '93 to 2005—and now we're in the 2005 to 2017 cycle. '81 was when the evil Reagan-Bush-Cheney *troika* took power—from the fixed election of '80 to now, we've been prisoners of the same cabal." She lit up and inhaled.

"Reagan President," Ray muttered as he looked through Thelma's telescope.

"And from 1980 to 2008 is a Saturn cycle—one generation," Seven computed.

"One generation," Thelma repeated, noting how disappointingly dim Mars was. In 2003, Mars had come the closest it had been to the Earth in 60,000 years and its opposition had been spectacular.

Lou exhaled. "In fact, Kali's Comet zoomed around the Sun perihelion in '86, passing close to the Earth conjunct with Alpha Lupi at 23° Scorpio. Not since 1485, the height of the European Renaissance, has such stellar influence been gathered in one quadrant of the Zodiac."

Vince contemplated that. The Renaissance had meant the resurgence of magick, and 500 years later when Kali's Comet brought bad news, the Reagan *troika* had been in power.

Thomas was thinking along the same lines. "Didn't the bookend conjunctions of Neptune-Pluto in 1400 and 1892 mark the degeneration of the Trans-Himalayan adepts known as the Great White Brotherhood in favor of a Grey Brotherhood degenerating over the centuries into magicians who forged alliances with old

Satanic family lineages?"

Thelma and Lou glanced at each other, amazed by the young man's insights.

Later, when they were all tucked into their sleeping bags, Seven slept but Thomas used a flashlight to peruse *The Shopkeeper's Notebook*, finding Bell Lab design notes for a *photonitron*, a device capable of projecting an image into pure space. Was the photonitron actually a scalar wave interferometer that could trigger light *from the object itself* to emerge from the vacuum in the target zone?

In the VW bus, the Colonel was envisioning the Argo sailing in the Southern Hemisphere sky and reflecting on lines from "Aratos" by Nathaniel Langdon Frothingham—

Against the tail of the Great Dog is dragged
Sternward the Argo, with no usual course
But motion contrary.

When he slept, the few lines sent some part of him to a celestial seminar that Sheikh Rahman was also attending. The Air Force uniform of the woman at the blackboard shone like a star.

". . . elected officials caught in the revolving door have to submit to bigger and bigger corporate crime syndicates, the military-industrial complex with its middle finger in every pie, whose black ops magick runs the gamut from graft and greed to bombs, zombie drugs, false flag events, and *in flagrante delicto* pedophile blackmail."

The Colonel thought of the Pearl Harbor and Gulf of Tonkin false flag events.

She continued. "Consider direct assaults on public buildings to be *Workings* against the order of law: the World Trade Center in New York City on February 26, 1993; the Murrah Federal Building in Oklahoma City on April 19, 1995; and the World Trade Center *again* in New York City on September 11, 2001. Two years between 1993 and 1995, six years between 1995 and 2001—a two and a six,

26—13, the magic cardinal number associated with the star Sirius, arrow of the gods shot from the bow of the distant stars of Canis Major and the Argo Navis sailing the Southern Hemisphere— Noah's Ark that bore Osiris and Isis away from Atlantis. *Argonaut, Argot naught.* In China, Sirius is T'ien-lang, the celestial jackal. Venus and Sirius share the ancient name of Ishtar or Isis—all part of the argot shadow cast by the Freemason veil, public events cast as spells . . ."

The Colonel's mind continued to descend. The America he had fought three, four, wars for, was slipping away . . .

Out among the stars, the dream body of Baby Rose was touring Magic Kingdom base programming sites at Disneyland— the Magic Castle, Mr. Toad's Wild Ride, Alice in Wonderland, Snow White, Matterhorn, Swiss Family Robinson Treehouse, It's a Small World, Jungleboat, Tinkerbell, The Parent Trap . . . The first Matterhorn victim of a Matterhorn car (one of the 10,000 Long Beach Elks visiting that day) had Mickey Mouse initials. Two Sikorsky S-61 helicopter crashes in 1968 and killed 44, the number of death and completion.

Baby Rose cruised over to Rue Royale and drifted down into the crypts below the Pirates of the Caribbean to see if Uncle Walt was still there. He was. His remains had been cremated at Forest Lawn on December 17, 1966, but one of his spirit bodies was in residence. He was a 33° Mason, like the Club 33 at Rue Royale in New Orlean Square near the Pirates of the Caribbean. Nine generations before, his forebear the warlock Reverend George Burroughs had been executed in Salem in 1692. But the real mystery was why Walt's Mickey Mouse was identical to the 700-year-old Mouse etched on the wall next to St. Christopher in the Community Church of Malta, Carinthia. No copyright laws back then?

Walt wasn't interested in her esoteric questions. He was bent on visiting Disney World in Orlando where it was warm. Baby Rose could tag along if she wanted. He climbed onto the back of his

Lion King and cracked the maze with Baby Rose flying alongside, listening to his boasts about acquiring ABC, a chunk of Times Square in New York City, a Civil War theme park in Virginia, and a town outside Orlando called Celebration. His theme park concept was spreading across the world! In Poland, Wolf's Lair staff wore Wehrmacht uniforms and people danced in Hitler's Bunker Disco. In Grutas Park, Lithuania, KGB agents chased visitors through a labyrinth of corridors, snapping their belts and threatening interrogations. In the U.S., Army Experience Centers were popping up everywhere—15,000 square feet of brushed steel and glass with UH-60 Black Hawks, AH-64 Apaches, Humvees, networked Xbox 360 pods and gaming stations with M-16s blowing virtual enemies to kingdom come.

Did Walt know what Mickey's Shadow Side was doing at night in his theme parks? Disney World day employees playing Cinderella and Mickey were finding smelly stained underwear with lice in them in their lockers. Neverland Disneyland Mickey Mouse Club child stars, some with anagram names like Britney Spears/ Presbyterians, were undergoing years of trauma-based mind control. Baby Rose had been there; she knew. Was Uncle Walt proud of that?

Uncle Walt decelerated when they hit the Interstate 4 thread to descend for a peek at the Holy Land Experience just down the road from Disney World. There was the Garden Tomb, Herod's Temple, the Scriptorium, the Goliath Burger at the Oasis Palms Café, Dead Sea Qumran Caves. Walt's chest swelled—so *American*, and he had paved the way. The Via Dolorosa Passion Drama was about to begin, but Disney World beckoned.

"Donald Duck and Jesus in resonance, mediated by corporate forces!" Uncle Walt cried as he zeroed in on Tomorrowland. "Walt Disney Imagineering! Lightstorm Entertainment! Industrial Light and Magic! DreamWorks! Digital Domain!"

At Bob Hope's ranch, Baby Rose had heard how Disney Imagineering, DreamWorks, and Digital Domain were plugged into intelligence agencies plugged into MK-ULTRA optics and acoustics. *Imagineers* like Spielberg, Coppola, Lukas, and Cameron had been handpicked to re-engineer the motion picture into a *psychic driving* vehicle *à la* subliminal imagery and sound. Giving Baby Rose a lascivious look, Bob Hope had snarked, "The sheeple will be socially engineered."

After Kubrick's *2001: A Space Odyssey* (1968), technology had catapulted ahead, thanks to MK-ULTRA. *Star Wars* (1977), *Close Encounters of the Third Kind* (1977), *Alien* (1979), and *E.T.* (1982) would get the alien thing going until Cameron's *Terminator* (1984) and *The Abyss* (1989) introduced spellbinding realism with the *morphing technique* of photo-realistic computer animation. Superconducting quantum interference device (SQUID) readers in Loews Cineplex theaters would heighten the subconscious experience of the audience, like in the aptly named 1995 sci-fi film *Strange Days* feedback process that reads tiny magnetic fields of quarks. Harry Potter's Sorting Hat preprogrammed audiences for SQUID sensors that read the human brain, as the book *Harry Potter and the Philosopher's Stone* by J.K. Rowling forewarned—

> *And now the Sorting Hat is here*
> *And you know the score:*
> *I sort you into Houses*
> *Because that is what I'm for.*
> *But this year I'll go further,*
> *Listen closely to my song:*
> *Though condemned I am to split you*
> *Still I worry that it's wrong,*
> *Though I must fulfill my duty*
> *And must quarter every year,*
> *Still I wonder whether sorting*
> *May not bring the end I fear . . .*

Walt taxied into the Tomorrowland Interplanetary Convention Center in the Magic Kingdom. A UFO documentary was being beamed to Connecticut, Tennessee, Alabama, Florida, and California, each theater an *Extra TERRORestrial Alien Encounter* with ghosts and dreamers and light-blob creatures with eyes and aureoles. Thanks to hidden tachistoscopes, Project Spectrux low light LTVR images flashed at 1/25 of a second and a hexidecimal color code blipped out one layer of subliminals for the public and another for the programmed in attendance.

Walt shook his head. "They've gone too far, but I like that Scanning SQUID Susceptometer, and the AI Dark Matter Search has obviously paid off." A slow smile spread over his phantom features, making him look less like an uncle and more like a ghoul. He flashed Baby Rose a laser look and shouted, "Tell SRI to keep up the good work."

Baby Rose scanned the dead, the sleeping, and the alien blobs of light in the audience to see if she recognized anyone. Suddenly, she remembered her friends in the desert, at which the Magical Kingdom began telescoping down to a nanodot on the end of a quark's nose. The last thing she heard was Walt calling, "Take *Captain EO* with you! Directed by Coppola with 3D special effects by Lukas, Michael Jackson plays Captain of the Light with fire coming out his finger tips!"

Catapulting earthward, the desert scalar potentials still busy altering the local rate of Time, Baby Rose thought, *The Internet is like cold fire...*

48

Maharishi and Meteor Crater

"Isn't Walt Disney's head supposed to be on the fifty-cent piece?"
Sammy said.
"Either Disney's," Al said, "or if it's an older one, then Fidel
Castro's. Let's see it."

–Philip K. Dick, *Ubik*, 1969

. . . an end run around national sovereignty, eroding it piece by piece,
will accomplish more than the old fashioned frontal assault.

–Richard Gardner, "The Hard Road to World Order."
Foreign Affairs, 1974

Hitler and his troupe of amateur magicians and hypnotists in
the 1930s and 1940s were able to reconstruct a technologically
advanced nation such as Germany into a vast theatre of illusion.
They were also able to induce educated and intellectual men into
becoming barbarians and oppressors of their fellow men. What,
then, is to become of the 1990s men once the Brotherhood is in
complete control of our destinies? What will happen to men in this
great operatic production of the Secret Brotherhood when we all
reach Act 3, the final, concluding segment of this ages old drama?

–Texe Marrs, *Dark Majesty*, 1992

After a rousing breakfast of potatoes, *frijoles*, eggs, fresh tortillas, *pico de gallo*, and strong coffee, the pilgrims bid adieu to Thelma and Lou whose last words were to hesitantly ask if Sirius wouldn't like to stay. Thomas remembered then how at breakfast, they had given Sirius double rations and spoke of having lost their dog of many years the previous winter. As if considering their invitation, Sirius stood a while, then (to Thomas' relief) jumped in the bus and they were off, deeper into Indian Country.

Time was unfolding and fanning out as the pilgrims ate up the Arizona high desert miles toward Four Corners south of Oraibi, Black Mesa, and Monument Valley.

As usual, the Colonel was riding shotgun in his Caddy and contemplating his past, particularly the Cold War conniving he'd loaned his forces to, which of course was what the Air Force was worried about, now that they didn't know where he was. Driving into Time future, the Colonel relished the fact that his old eyes were finally seeing UFOs, whether ours or "theirs." An intelligence cohort had talked about Blue Book being for public consumption and Project Aquarius being for occultists buried a level or two above the birdbrains called the Aviary. The DIA and ONI together, bound up with the Air Force Office of Special Investigation (AFOSI), all reported to Defense Intelligence's Directorate for Management and Operations, the officer said, all shrouded in half-truths and claims of aliens. "The rule of thumb is," he'd grinned, "the more outrageous or extensive the disinformation, the deeper black the project. When they import aliens being behind Jesus Christ, then you know you're in deep black."

The Colonel was privy to a little of the fact that the Air Force and NSA-CIA-DIA had been on a steep learning curve in the 1950s and 1960s. Phantom ships, discs, globes, and rods had shown up on radar and infrared detection equipment, and pilots and astronauts had seen more the higher they went, indicating that the visual of the EM spectrum was different *up there*.

Slowly, it had dawned on the brass that Earth was surrounded by an ocean of 4th dimension depths, just as the old Vedic texts said—an aerial ocean neither metaphoric nor vacuous but filled with ethereal traffic whose substance existed just outside or at the edge of human perception. To the military mind, this discovery was more uncanny and terrifying than anything found in the ocean depths making up 70 percent of the Earth's surface. Blobs and globes and discs of pulsating plasma light had extraordinary maneuverability and were surfacing at incredible speeds from seas, rivers, and volcanoes. What were they? What propellant and medium gave them such speed? How did they go visible and invisible at will?

"Everything amped up," the officer had said *sotto voce*. "The Paperclip Nazis were given the green light on cosmic physics—what we call quantum physics—with a Tibetan *magick* spin." He'd stared at the Colonel. "*Satanic*, and the brass don't care where it comes from. Nazism's not an acronym for the National Socialist Party; it's a religion with alien gods, if you know what I mean by 'alien.' The JCS don't get what those twelve years of Germany being virtually cut off from the rest of the world really meant."

The atomic bomb had never been the Nazi objective; they were after electromagnetic propulsion. So *everything* was poured into infrared detection of the aerial ocean so as to decipher and communicate with the plasma beings speeding with ease inter-dimensionally. For this alone, they developed the new organic chemistry based on an 8-ring carbon chain.

The officer had looked around, then back to the Colonel. "Ever notice how Paperclip SS Nazis always speak in reverent tones about Tibet? When they invaded the Caucasus, they planted the *swastika* flag blessed by the Black Order on the summit of Mount Elbruz, the sacred seat of the ancient Aryan race. The brass just think Nazis are being quaint, like hymns on Sunday, but a fire burns in them that's going to consume us, mark my words."

Soon after their conversation, he was transferred.

On the radio, Tim Buckley sang—

And though you have forgotten
All of our rubbish dreams,
I find myself searching
Through the ashes of our ruins
For the days when we smiled . . .

They stopped for gas in little Two Guns and Mannie headed to the outhouse out back, perhaps due to the *chilis* from that morning. Over the fetid entry to the underworld, he flipped through a beat-up *Com-12 Briefing: Mind Control Operations/Aquarius Group Activities*, curious as to why someone had relegated it to wiping posteriors over glory holes.

> *Mind Control procedures in their infancy involved rather crude and blatant processes using hypnotic-programming, thereby allowing the unconscious mind to be aware of at least the original process of programming through hypnosis. While greatly successful in some cases, these early methods had a high failure ratio when done in large population bases. The original studies and subsequent operations did allow for the US Army, Navy, Air Force, and related intelligence departments to field-test and observe those methods which obtained the highest success . . .*

"Hey! Mannie, you in there?" Ray's eyeball appeared through a hole in the door. "Contemplating your asshole? Come on, man, we're heading for Meteor Crater."

Mannie swiped, pulled up his Dockers, and grabbed a handful of unread pages, leaving the rest for the next seeker to ponder.

Back on the road, the Beatles was singing "Sexy Sadie"—

Maharishi, Maharishi

What have you done?
You made a fool of everyone.

A female voice with an Indian accent faded in. ". . . typically, negative mysticism seeks liberation from the Earth, pantheistic mysticism seeks the human as god, and theistic mysticism seeks relationship with the divine. Whichever you choose, the history of mysticism in the West is subject to the vise grip of elite Anglo-American Brotherhoods.

"At their World Parliament of Religions in Chicago on September 11, 1893, Swami Vivekananda, disciple of Sri Ramakrishna and founder of the Vedanta Society, greeted America by her occult name: *Hail Columbia! Motherland of liberty!* One Metonic cycle before, Helena Blavatsky founded the Theosophical Society in New York City, after which the Anglo-American Brotherhoods subjected her to the ancient mind control tactic known as *occult imprisonment*. Once she was out of the way, the British Fabian Society placed Annie Besant—the purported reincarnation of magister Giordano Bruno burned at the stake on February 17, 1600 in Camp Dei Fiori, Rome—in charge of the Theosophical Society.

"Eventually, Theosophists Besant and C.W. Leadbeater proclaimed the Indian boy Jiddu Krishnamurti, born in 1895, as the Second Coming of Christ and future Maitreya Buddha. He underwent three initiations—the first at fourteen in India, the second on Walpurgisnacht in the Sicilian Mystery center at Caltabellotta, and the third at Ojai, California on August 17, 1922 while sitting under a pepper tree. Krishnamurti could not break free of Besant and Leadbeater until he was 34. All those years, he suffered headaches, weakness, and tortuous pain in his spine and throat every evening between six and seven. Such was "Ascended Masters" access. In Madras in 1986, 91-year-old Krishnamurti warned—

[Krishnamurti:] *When genetic engineering and the computer*

369

meet, what are you? Your brains are going to be altered. Your way
of behavior is going to be changed. They may remove your fear
altogether, remove sorrow, remove all your gods. They are going to;
don't fool yourself. It all ends up either in war or in death. This is
what is happening in the world actually.

"Krishnamurti died in Pine Cottage, Ojai, California 386 years to the day since Giordano Bruno was burned at the stake. (The square root of 386 years is the moon node 19.646.) His final words were, 'My only concern is to set men unconditionally free.'"

Now, Ravi Shankar was playing sitar.

"West and East," the female narrator continued, "Zeus as Indra, Dionysus as Shiva. The *occult* has always been the consort of politics. In 1905, Fabians *cum* Theosophists established the Socialist Society of America (SSA) to finance the Lenin Revolutions of 1905 and 1917. Once Bolshevist Communism was on its way, the Fabians renamed the SSA the League of Industrial Democracies from which the Council on Foreign Relations (CFR) sprang in 1922. Fabians *cum* Theosophists midwifed the London School of Economics, the Royal Institute of International Affairs, and the Round Table, all of which, with their American counterparts across the Atlantic, contributes to founding the United Nations.

"Annie Besant was eventually replaced by Alice Bailey, née Alice La Trobe Bateman. In 1915, Alice came to California to join the Pacific Grove Lodge of the Theosophical Society where she edited *The Messenger*, then married Foster Bailey, a 33° Scottish Rite Mason. In 1920, the Baileys founded the Lucifer Publishing Company aka Lucis Publishing Company aka Lucis Trust, an umbrella organization for NGOs such as the Arcane School (1923), World Goodwill (1932), Triangle World Servers (1937), and for-profit corporations like Lucis Publishing, Lucis Productions, Lucis Trust Libraries, and the New Group of World Servers. Lucis Trust enjoys Consultative Status at the United Nations via the Economic and

Social Council (ECOSOC), oversees the UN meditation room, and hosts a weekly radio show from UN headquarters in both New York and Geneva. Both World Goodwill and Lucis Trust are engaged in Earth Charter advocacy.

"It was through the Baileys that the American Palladian Brotherhood—shaped by the 19th century Charleston medium and Mason General Albert Pike—set American Theosophy in a *Tibetan* mold separate from the British India Theosophy of Annie Besant. India for England, Tibet for America. Under the aegis of Lucis Trust, the Tibetan Lodge soared to 200,000. In the 1960s, both Dilgo Khyetse Rinpoche of the ancient Nyingma School of Tibetan Buddhism and the 16th Karmapa incarnation Gyalwa Karmapa of the Kagyudpa Order of Tibetan Mahayana Buddhism took up residence in America. Then came Tenzin Gyatso, the 14th Dalai Lama. Throughout the 1960s, the CIA poured $1.7 million a year into Tibetan resistance against the People's Republic of China, including training Tibetan troops in Colorado."

Tibetan throat singers accompanied an American voice saying, *May all spiritual leaders enjoy long lives and prosperity. May the Sangha multiply and fulfill their duties. May the blessings of the Dharma liberate all departed souls. In the world may sickness, poverty, wars and all evil influences be cut at the root and destroyed. May all things of the Kali Yuga be dispersed.*

"By 1954, the Arcane School had graduated 20,000 and given birth to enterprises like Elizabeth Clare Prophet's Church Universal and Triumphant (CUT), the Tara Center, the Robert Muller School, and the Temple of Understanding, an Externalized Hierarchy of Ascended Masters for the sake of Sanat Kumara, Lord of the World. Robert Muller's World Core Curriculum won the UNESCO Prize for Peace Education in 1989, the same year he addressed the U.S. Governors Conference on Education and administered a $12.9 million grant from the U.S. Department of Education for Denver-based Mid-Continent Regional Educational Laboratory, whose acronym McREL sounds suspiciously like McReligion, the endless

Happy Meal of World Teacher Kuthumi."

[Beatles:] Maharishi, Maharishi
You broke all the rules
You laid it down for all to see

"Founders of the Temple of Understanding in 1963 were Dame Margaret Mead (Order of St. John), Canon Edward West (Order of St. John), UN deputy secretary general Robert Muellar (Muller), Winifred McCulloch of the Teilhard de Chardin Society, and of course the ever-watchful Lucis Trust. The present Temple of Understanding board overlaps that of the Trilateral Commission. After a critical exposé in the April 1, 1962 *New Hampshire Sunday Times News* by Edith Kermit Roosevelt, granddaughter of Theodore Roosevelt, the Temple languished until it was revived in 1984 at a Cathedral of St. John the Divine ceremony presided over by the Dalai Lama and American blueblood Bishop Paul Moore. Bishop Moore, along with along with Bishop James Armstrong and Rabbi Maurice Davis supported CIA agent-sleeper Jim Jones and his People's Temple.

"The Temple of Understanding embraces everything but Christianity: Tibetan Buddhists, Sufi Freemasons, Mother Goddess worshippers and Wicca witches, disciples of Masters Djwhal Khul and Kuthumi, and of course the British Venerable Order of Malta that performs solemn ceremonies and invokes entities in the Crypt below the Episco-pagan Church of St. John the Divine. Illuminized Freemasons who've achieved the Knights Templar degree worship there, the Very Reverend Dean of the Cathedral being President of the Temple of Understanding.

"Under the ECOSOC umbrella, World Goodwill encompasses a Hydra of NGOs: the World Health Organization (WHO), World Wildlife Fund, UNICEF, Peace Corps, Habitat for Humanity, Physicians for Social Responsibility, Amnesty

International, Emerson College, the North American Interfaith Network, the Wichita North American Assisi Conference, Wainwright House Institute for Spiritual Development, the Soviet-American Council for Joint Projects, Win-Win World, Foundation for Co-Creation, Institute of Noetic Sciences, Independent Commission for a Viable Future, and on and on and on. Juggernauts by association and conference attendees read like a Who's Who of global elites. Former chancellors, prime ministers, presidents, and World Bank officials signed its Universal Declaration of Human Responsibilities.

"Lucis Trust is the nexus between the UN and world occultists. The board of trustees governing Lucis Trust—many connected with the Council on Foreign Relations, Trilateral Commission, and Bilderbergs—has included John D. Rockefeller (Standard Oil), Henry Kissinger (Secretary of State, 1973-77; National Security Adviser, 1969-75), Norman Cousins (World Federalist Movement), Robert McNamara (Secretary of Defense, 1961-68; President of the World Bank, 1968-81), IBM's Thomas Watson, Jr. (former Ambassador to Moscow), and Henry Clausen, Grand Commander of the Supreme Council, 33°, Southern District Scottish Rite (Palladian)."

> *[Beatles:] Maharishi, how did you know*
> *The world was waiting just for you?*
> *Maharishi, oooh, how did you know?*

"So who is this Ascended Tibetan Master Djwhal Khul who gives Lucis Trust its marching orders, whose master plan for the Age of Aquarius prophesies the appearance of a *mahatma* or Great One served by the old Mystery religions preserved through the ages by Freemasonry?

"UNESCO, the United Nations Educational, Scientific and Cultural Organization, is affiliated with Lucis Trust's Triangles in Education and World Youth Service and Enterprise (WYSE), both headquartered in London. Triangle World Servers obey Djwhal

Khul. In April 1999, a Triangles World Server was superintendent of Littleton, Colorado schools when two drugged youths opened fire in Columbine High School. In September 2003, another Triangles World Server was superintendent of District 81 in Spokane, Washington when another youth opened fire in Lewis and Clark High School. Coincidence?"

[Beatles:] Maharishi, you'll get yours yet
However big you think you are
Maharishi oooh you'll get yours yet

"*This Ascended Masters nonsense is not nonsense.* Whether Djwhal Khul broadcasts from London or Lhasa, Langley or the astral plane, his followers have friends in very high places and high-stakes politics lurk behind Djwhal Khul occult rituals and sigils."

[Beatles:] We gave him everything we owned just to sit at his table
Just a smile would lighten everything
Maharishi, he's the latest and the greatest of them all

To another infusion of Ravi Shankar, the Indian voice said, "Remember when Eastern religion inundated the Sixties? Timothy Leary's fellow Harvard psilocybin psychonaut Richard Alpert morphed into Baba Ram Dass under the guru Neem Karoli Baba. Alan Watts, a former Church of England minister, became deeply involved in the American Academy of Asian Studies, later renamed the California Institute of Integral Studies. Sri Swami Satchidananda founded the Integral Yoga Institute, Shunryu D.T. Suzuki introduced Zen Buddhism to America. The Devi Mandir or Temple of the Divine Mother Goddess is in the hills of Napa Valley just off of the Shree Maa Way intersection with Highway 128. Tibetan Buddhist Chogyam Trungpa founded the Naropa Institute in Boulder, Colorado in 1974, the same year Allen Ginsberg and

Anne Waldman founded the Jack Kerouac School of Disembodied Poetics there. East meeting West at Esalen Institute, in est, Baha'i, etc.

"Politics and the occult have also merged at the Center for Advanced Military Science that now graces the Institute of Science, Technology and Public Policy of the Maharishi University of Management in Fairfield, Iowa. The Maharishi's empire broadcasts over its own private satellite channel from a converted monastery in Vlodrop, Holland.

"But Maharishi is a latecomer. Sufi author Idries Shah, born in India in 1924 to a Scottish Stuart line mother and a Hashemite father said to be related to the prophet Muhammed, is one of the founders of the Club of Rome created in 1968 as a 'foreign policy' bridge between the Jesuits (whose own has at last been enthroned as Pope) and the Atlantic Alliance, known also as the Olympians, the Magicians, the Family, etc. 'Foreign policy' for the Club of Rome is a cold equation of population and resources—in a word, eugenics. In 1957 and 1968, two studies on world population growth included the feasibility of developing a microbe to attack the autoimmune system of various 'populations' via a vaccination delivery system. [Cf. *The Limits to Growth, a Report for the Club of Rome's Project on the Predicament of Mankind.*]

"That was 1968. By 1972, the National Ordinance Laboratory in Chicago had come up with Acquired Immunodeficiency Syndrome (AIDS); by 1974, it was ready for delivery through the Expanded Program on Immunization (EPI) of the World Health Organization (WHO). In 1977, WHO launched a smallpox vaccination program in Africa. In 1978, the Center for Disease Control (CDC) in Atlanta—a mobile reincarnation of Fort Detrick's chemical and biological warfare division—launched a Hepatitis B vaccination program in poor Black districts and Native American reservations. By the time WHO's EPI ended in 1990, a lucrative delivery system for future population control agents was in place with the world believing that childhood vaccinations against polio, measles, whooping cough, tetanus, tuberculosis, and diphtheria were essential. Any of these vaccinations could now be piggybacked with other agents. By 1999, AIDS had claimed 16.3 million lives.

"Disease as a eugenic solution, the atomic bomb as a manifestation of Luciferian light. For them, nuclear technology means the Externalization of the Hierarchy of Illumined Minds that will usher in the Age of Maitreya as Age of Pisces nation states drop away and a "hive mind" civilization comes online."

[Beatles:] He made a fool of everyone
Maharishi . . .

"Even Vladimir Lenin was a pagan member of an Astarte cult. He participated in ecstatic dances and sexual rites on Monte Verita in Ascona, Switzerland not far from the neo-Marxist Frankfurt School meeting place for the Soviet GRU and the Philby-Burgess-Maclean British spy networks."

[Beatles:] However big you think you are
Maharishi . . .

"The Russian Academy of Sciences has always had its nose buried in everything New Age. In 1988, the year before the Berlin Wall fell, the Academy threw big money at the Global Conference of Spiritual and Parliamentary Leaders on Human Survival in Oxford, England. The *glasnost* man from Russia with the port-wine birthmark on his forehead subsequently lived high on the American hog at the Presidium in San Francisco while his 'liberated' nation starved. As one of the hidden Externalized Hierarchy, he is revered as the Pathfinder for the New Consciousness foretold by Edgar Cayce, 'new consciousness' meaning to twist *narodniki* (the people's will) and *mir* (the village community) into the hive mind. A balance between the New and Old Beliefs (*Raskolniki*) may look unchristian for a while, but not for long . . ."

White noise ended the transmission as the pilgrims pulled into the Meteor Crater parking lot. They decided to walk the rim at the Colonel's three-legged pace and at first talked about the broadcast they'd just heard. Then the crater began to blow their minds. Over 4,000 feet across and 550 feet deep—as deep as the Washington Monument was tall—it was like being on another planet. The brochure said that 50,000 years ago a meteor had smashed into the Earth there. However, no large meteor fragments had ever been discovered.

Thomas had another theory. "What if it was a huge atomic-type explosion below the surface, perhaps due to geometric instability of the magnetic grid? Ancient scientists messing around like they are today, or a war that distorted the force fields of the grid and set up stresses? Too bad I don't have my Geiger counter."

Ray pointed at Sirius sniffing ahead and not liking what he was smelling. "There's your Geiger counter."

The Colonel stared into the crater, ensnared in thoughts about Mithraism. Lenin, Anatoly Lunacharsky, Maxim Gorky, Hitler, and Goering were all devotees of the Mithra cult to which the Roman emperor Tiberius belonged, whose rites are still enacted in the emperor's villa grotto on the Isle of Capri. The cult of Mithra had made its way from Iran to the Roman Empire in the century before Christ, beginning in Tarsus of Cilicia where Saul/Paul was born in the geographic trine of the Black Sea, the Hebrides, and the Sahara. Initially, most Mithra believers were slaves and soldiers, but gradually the secret cult would claim the highest in the land. Like most Middle Eastern religions, Mithraism foresaw the birth of a god and beginning of a new age. The local god in Tarsus was Perseus who stands in the heavens above Taurus with his *harpe* poised—*Kosmokrator*, the force controlling the Earth's magnetic poles and therefore Earth's relationship to the cosmic scaffold. *Kosmokrator*,

Meteor Crater. Did Lenin go mad like Caligula when his initiation took a wrong turn? The Colonel had met high-level NSA-CIA-DIA officers who bathed in the focused light of the Dog Star at Palomar, and apparently Robert Strange McNamara bathed in the Potomac under the full Moon's light. In fact, many heads of state bathe in moonlight and engage in ecstatic dances.

As they wound around the rim, Stargazer Drive-In tidbits arose, then Kennedy's hope for a shared space race, then how the Pelly Amendment—passed by the House a month before the assassination—required that no part of any NASA appropriations be used for any manned lunar landing with a Communist country.

"Sputnik means companion or fellow traveler," the Colonel contributed. Sputnik was sent up in the International Geophysical Year of 1957, shot across the steppes of Kazakhstan from the big SS-6 ICBM Sapwood. National boundaries extending beyond the atmosphere into space still sounded laughable then, so Sputnik may have been Russian but by God it was *up*. A new era had begun, and the gap between science fiction and science was closing like Scylla and Charybdis. God may still have been in His heaven, but now so was man. First Sputnik, then Luniks and Vostoks; then in 1959, the UN Committee on Peaceful Uses of Outer Space wrote the first international space law. Then came the Mercury, Gemini, and Apollo programs, Surveyor missions to the Moon, Mariner flybys to Mars and Venus, and next it'll be unmanned voyages and surveilling people from space."

He pushed his cane forward as Baby Rose guided his other arm. "A lot to be proud of, and a lot *not*. The National Reconnaissance Office (NRO)—by budget, the largest U.S. intelligence agency—was secretly established in 1960 to run national security space projects. Its 1961 budget for building and operating space satellites was $7 billion. (Four of those billions would remain absolutely unaccounted for.) Eisenhower's military-industrial complex—the profits and power in weaponizing everything possible."

The NRO's existence would be kept secret from the American people until September 1992.

"You should see the classified photos snapped by the CIA's U-2 and SR-71 Blackbird—Vietnam, Soviet intercontinental ballistic missile (ICBM) launch sites and surface-to-air missile (SAM) launches in Cuba, nuclear silos and plutonium plants in Israel, the detonation of the first Chinese atomic weapon, the first Soviet nuclear accident in Kyshtym in 1957, the Six-Day War in the Middle East. Everything seen by the eyes in the sky. Above top-secret, its argot full of words and acronyms with double meanings for military and intelligence Brotherhoods. *MAGIK, ULTRA, PEARL, THUMB.* Compartmentalized—"

He shut up. He'd already said too much. Operations Corona (CIA) and Samos (U.S. Air Force) had revolutionized aerial spying with cameras that could take images in 200 spectral bands for analysis of surface composition. The first Corona went up in January 1958—94 performing elliptical orbits 500 miles above the Earth, including all the Keyhole generations that were pure spying. Each orbit took an hour and a half, with dual cameras snapping thousands of stereoscopic images. They lied to the public about retrorockets firing film capsules earthward to be snatched up by Air Force planes. The truth was that military computers were relaying photographic images to listening posts and sophisticated computers and analysts with SI (Special Intelligence) and TK (Talent-Keyhole) clearance at the NSA, National Photographic Interpretation Center, and CIA. Postage-stamp detail. The Colonel kept his old eyes on the ground.

Seven began sing-songing a verse she'd learned in 5th grade Special Progress in New York—

Oh little Sputnik, flying high
With made-in-Moscow beep,
You tell the world it's a Commie sky
And Uncle Sam's asleep.

Their laughter eased the Colonel's guilty conscience. "Uncle Sam is definitely awake now," he said, pausing to lean on his cane and breathe, "as Sir Halford Mackinder defined wakefulness in 1919—

Who controls reconnaissance watches the enemy;
Who watches the enemy perceives the threat;
Who perceives the threat shapes the alternatives;
Who shapes the alternatives determines the response."

Mackinder had been right. Soon, high above the Earth the increasingly sophisticated children and grandchildren of Corona and Rhyolite—Jumpseat, Argos, Aquacade, Chalet/Vortex, Magnum, Indigo / Lacrosse, IKONOS, Quickbird, Orbimage, SPOT (Systéme Probatoire d'Observation de la Terre)—would be patrolling and surveilling humanity. Radio, telegraph, telephones, television, and the airplane had begun it all, and now other technologies, he was sorry to admit, would probably end it after he was gone.

Rounding the last arc of the crater, the Colonel spilled the beans. "The Cold War was always about providing the cover and money to get the satellites up. You may think of low-orbit television relay satellites like Earlybird, or electro-optical medium orbiters playing radar ferrets for ocean surveillance, or even high orbiters like Telstar in 22,300-mile geosynchronous orbits concentrating on early warning, navigation, communications relay, missile telemetry, and ABM radar ferreting. But I think of eavesdropping, signals intelligence or SIGINT. Rhyolites monitor phone calls and walkie-talkies and intercept telemetry signals. High-orbiters intercept microwave transmissions and radio traffic. Keyholes read our license plates and soon the Indigo will beam microwaves from 275 miles up and measure reflected energy day and night, cloudy or clear. And they'll sell the images to the highest bidders. The EOSAT (Earth Observation Satellite) owned by RCA and Hughes Aircraft will be multi-sensor and polar-orbiting—The brave new world's on its way, and that's not even including the armed satellites, which of course I can't discuss."

When they pulled out of the Meteor Crater parking lot, two white government E-350 vans with G-14 plates whizzed west.. The bumper sticker on the front read 'Special Access,' and the one on the back read 'Once you've gone black, you never come back.'

Over the two-way, Mannie added, "Here comes another one with 'NEVADA IS NOT A WASTELAND' on the front—"

"—and 'Earth in Upheaval' on the back!" Ray hooted. "Billy Joad, where are you, man?"

CONTINUE TO BOOK 3

"INDIAN COUNTRY"

Made in the USA
Coppell, TX
21 October 2020

40075441R00223